Curse of the Ninth

Curse of the Ninth

Ruthie Marlenée

E. L. Marker
Salt Lake City

E. L. Marker, an imprint of WiDo Publishing
Salt Lake City, Utah
widopublishing.com

Curse of the Ninth is a work of fiction inspired by real people, places, and events. Some names and identifying details have been changed to protect the privacy of individuals.

Cover design by Steven Novak
Book design by Marny K. Parkin

ISBN 978-1-947966-23-9

For Captain Jeff Gunn, my anchor

. . . And whoever was never able to, must creep tearfully away from this band!

Symphony No. 9, Beethoven

Optometrist Falls from Ladder and May Die

GLENDALE, Sept. 29, 1930—Falling ten feet from a ladder on which he was working, Dr. W.C. Marnier, optometrist, today received injuries that may cause his death. Dr. Marnier struck a work-bench as he fell, landing heavily on the cement floor of the workroom at the rear of his offices at 114 East Broadway.

Dr. James Belyea, who attended Dr. Marnier stated that his skull was fractured and that three vertebrae were broken, and that the fall had cut a bad gash in the victim's scalp.

Dr. Marnier was taken to the Emergency Hospital and later transferred to the Glendale Research Hospital.

LOS ANGELES TIMES (1886–Current File): September 29, 1930, Pro-Quest Historical Newspapers, *Los Angeles Times*

1

The Crash

**September 1930: Los Angeles, California—
Dr. Wesley Charles Marnier**

The coroners would rule it an accident.

Almost a year after the "Crash" of '29 and the headlines read "Optometrist Falls from Ladder and May Die." The newspaper reported that I, Dr. Wesley Charles Marnier, "received injuries that may cause his death." Accordingly, I struck a workbench as I fell, landing heavily on the cement of the workroom at the rear of my offices on East Broadway, Glendale, California. In Glendale, I'd also been given a second shot at love but as things turned out, it would also be where the road ended for me. Dr. Belyea, who attended me, stated my "skull was fractured, three vertebrae were broken and the fall had cut a bad gash in the victim's scalp."

Well, I certainly was the victim, but this was no accident. I must admit, dying wasn't that painful, but it wasn't quick either. Most agonizing were the memories I'd relive before exhaling my last breath.

I'm not proud of what I'd have to do. While exacting revenge had not been the goal, and it wouldn't be sweet, staying connected to the love of my life, my darling, would be close to divine.

**1949: US Naval Hospital, Oakland, California—
19-Year-Old Charley**

Beads of sweat drip into my eyes, the salt stinging like crazy as I try to open them. Short of breath, my head is killing me. Across the room, the vertical shadows of the venetian blinds slice the wall. *Oh, hell no! Am I back in a Tijuana jail cell?* Blinking like a toad in a hailstorm, I look around and then lift my arm to scratch an itch, but stop when I feel something raw and crusty—a fresh tattoo! Rubbing my eyes, I strain to make out the upside-down purple lettering *Viva Mexico. Damn! I am in Mexico. I've gotta be tripping.* But then I notice some diplomas on the wall and an award certificate issued to a Dr. Ewen Savage, United States Naval Hospital. It's signed by President Harry S. Truman. I sort of remember. Peering a little closer down my arm, I see a paper bracelet manacled to my wrist. The band reads: Charles Lee Marnier, DOB 9/30/30. US Naval Hospital, Oakland, California. *Shit, this can't be good.*

I feel pretty crumby, as if my heart's being whipped around inside a giant blender. There's definitely some crazy shit brewing. But crazy's nothing new. You see, I came into this world full of bad juju—full of some damn curse. Even the air I breathe is flooded with poison.

September 1930: Los Angeles—
Doc

The day before the "accident" and my ultimate demise, the Santa Ana winds—devil winds—were kicking up something fierce, jangling my nerves worse than the wheels on the train I'd just stepped off. We were still in the midst of a drought and the forgotten dog days of summer were revived; the sun shining brightly and licking at my sweaty face.

But the hot air wasn't the only thing waiting to greet me at the Glendale Railway Station. Dead, dusty autumn leaves eddied around me as I stood on the platform. A whoosh of air plucked off my hat, sending it skidding across the parking lot. I chased it down, wincing until I retrieved it; I was too tired for this and, at fifty-five, definitely too old. Plastered to the windshield of my Buick were more dead leaves, dirt, and debris I cleared off before climbing into what felt like an oven set on broil. I should have left a window rolled down a bit, I thought, reaching up to adjust the blistering rear view mirror. And then, I gasped when I saw my optometry assistant staring at me from the back seat.

"Welcome back, Dr. Marnier," Jack Warrington said, face flushed pink as Spam. He hid his eyes behind sunshades and his damp toffee-colored hair stuck flat to his head.

I grabbed my chest as my heart hammered inside. "What the hell! Is everything all right?"

"Just waiting for you, Doc." He slithered out of the back of the car, slipped his suspenders up over his shoulders and then climbed into the front seat where he pulled out a cigarette. Jack, a young father with another child on the way, lately seemed rife with misery, but these were desperate times after all, and doomed only to get worse. This was just the beginning of what would be called the 'Great Depression.' Jack, however, showed promise as a fine optometrist and there would always be a need for his services. I also felt confident someday he'd be able to take over for me. In the meanwhile, to show my appreciation and my faith in him, I'd given him a raise.

"I thought I left my car locked." My heart really ticked now.

The corner of his lip curled as he held up a key. "You keep a spare in the right-side drawer of your desk."

"What are you doing here?"

He exhaled, clouding the space between us. "I knew you were headed back this morning and most likely wouldn't be coming into the office what with Mrs. Marnier's concert tonight and all."

Indeed, I'd traveled all night from a business trip to Sacramento in a hurry to get home to Phoebe. My wife, the love of my life, would be performing from Beethoven's Ninth Symphony in our home this evening and I dared not miss it for the world.

"And I'll be seeing you tonight, so why the urgency?"

"I didn't think you'd appreciate business talk during Mrs. Marnier's performance."

"Absolutely not."

The inside of the car was stuffy and teeming now with the smell of smoke and sweat, leather and liquor; Jack squirmed in the passenger seat. His hand trembled as he pinched the cigarette between his fingers. Pursing his lips, his gaunt cheeks were even more pronounced, his pallor the color of the ashes drifting down onto his crumpled gray flannels. Jerkily, he rolled down the window and flicked out the cinders, simply leaving his elbow resting on the frame.

"Jack, what is it?" I asked, gripping the bottom of the steering wheel.

He took off his shades, combed his left hand through his sticky, sweat-soaked hair and turned to look at me with puffy red eyes. He blasted me with a gauzy blanket of smoke. "That's what I'd like to know. What's with the goons visiting the office?"

I choked, fanning the space in front of me. "What the hell are you talking about?"

"They said they'd come to check out their new business?"

"That's insane. What goons?"

"George brought them."

Anxiety slipped in like a frightened field mouse, but I smelled a big fat rat and his name was George Gimble. *Now what's he up to? Another case of when the cat's away.* I pounded the steering wheel. *Damn it, George.* It had been twenty long years since he first came into my life when he moseyed into the Hollywood Masonic Lodge up on Highland. George was a bad cold I couldn't seem to shake.

"So, you're selling the business out from under me?" Jack asked.

I heard my molars click. "Don't be ridiculous. You're my right-hand man."

"Doc, when was the last time you were in the office? You're so busy with all of your other land deals. Do you even know how hard I work? And, by the way, where are my shares of stock?"

"Stock? Calm down. There is no stock, for God's sake. I signed that assignment you wanted. Patience, my boy. You'll be taken care of."

"I think I've been patient enough," Jack said, reaching into his vest pocket.

I gasped, suddenly unsure of Jack, as I reached for the door handle.

"Besides," he said, "my attorney says it isn't worth the paper it was printed on and that if something were to happen to you, I'd get zip, and now you're selling the business."

"I'm not selling the business." Spit sprayed through my clenched teeth.

"I need you to sign this one instead," he said, pulling a document from his pocket, "in front of a notary—and Phoebe, too."

"Phoebe?" Incensed, I let go of the handle.

"Yes, she's your wife," he said, as if I needed reminding. "Community property."

"Ludicrous. It can wait. Nothing will happen to me before Monday."

Tiny beads of worry formed across his brow. "Without Phoebe's signature and without the notary's jurat, the document is no good," Jack said, swiping his forehead.

"Listen, I heard you but I've been traveling all night just to make sure I don't miss Phoebe's concert. This will just have to wait. Rest assured, I'm not selling the business and there are no shares of stock to transfer to anyone. I'll get to the bottom of this, but right now I need to get home. So, unless you need a lift somewhere, please exit my vehicle immediately."

Jack climbed out of my car, but not until I agreed to meet him at the office the next day.

1949: US Naval Hospital, Oakland, California—
19-Year-Old Charley

"Can you hear me?"

Sure, I can hear you, Savage. I just can't see you. I struggle to pry my eyes open again, but my eyelids are like paint-stuck doors. My hands tingle and the blood in my head pounds. I reach up to hold my heavy skull. *Oh God, please make it stop!*

"Charley, are you awake?" he asks, sounding bored.

My eyes quiver as the lighting from the overhead fluorescent tubing blinds me. I wipe them with the back of the sleeve from my white hospital-issue patient pajamas.

I must've crashed, but I sort of remember walking into this place. *Hell, was that today?* It stinks of some mixture of sweet tobacco, a smell I've grown to detest, and sauerkraut, the color of which also happens to be slapped onto the diploma-infested east wall. Except for the occasional "zap" of the desk lamp barely illuminating a room starved for light, all is quiet.

"Charley, do you know where you are?"

In a corner droops an umbrella plant same as the one Mother had in the foyer back home—Shirley, she'd named the schefflera. All of her things had names; her china, her silverware, her cars, her plants and her piano. As for me, sometimes she ended up a little confused and simply called me "Darling." The word pretty much covered the bases.

As I turn my head, I catch my reflection in the window. I'm shocked when I see the distorted familiar blue eyes swimming in a sea of red. The crew cut is still a sandy blond, but the face, skeletal, something out of a horror show, is me. Damn!

September 1930: Los Angeles—
Doc

My first glass of champagne girded me against feelings of unease. Jack had rattled me worse than the wind. Goons? What were they doing at the office? George and I were definitely due for a long talk. But for now, I'd made up my mind to leave my anxiety at the threshold of our Woodside Manor home, a replica of the French chateau in Normandy where Phoebe and I had a second honeymoon almost twelve years ago. She'd fallen in love with the castle during our stay, in particular its acoustics, and so I'd built her this home, especially for an occasion such as this evening, and filled it with antiques purchased at Christie's in London. After the completion of the home, I arranged for the delivery of the nine-foot Steinway—Cleopatra she'd named the piano, her constant companion until the end.

2

Woodside Pastoral

September 1930: Los Angeles—
Doc

Before entering the chamber room, I walked into my library where Melody, my ever-faithful, three-legged chocolate lab, rushed over to greet me. She'd been waiting for me in her spot under my desk. I set my glass down and took a seat to scratch behind her withers. "Did you scare off the bad guys while Papa was away?"

She barked, wagging her tail like a metronome. Poor brave dear. Years ago, she'd gone to battle with a coyote and while the coyote lost his life, Mel only lost her front leg. Since then, she was an inside dog, unless I was with her. "That's a good girl."

In this room, truly a man's refuge—what with all of the bronze Remington statues, the African masks, the stuffed bear and a moose head hanging over the door—I was surrounded by shelves filled with treasured books. I stuffed my pipe with Velvet tobacco, lit it and glanced out the window framed by the heavy blue-velvet drapery hanging from iron spears. Just outside, a thirsty lawn stretched all the way down to the brook, now only barely trickling through the property. Next to the window in the corner stood my gun case filled with two rifles—one a Winchester. Lost in thought about why I hadn't gotten rid of the shotgun after the fatal accident years ago, I heard a bang, causing me to nearly jump out of my tuxedo.

Mel yapped, scurrying to the window, and I scrambled to unlock my top right drawer. As I reached for my revolver, I heard another loud boom. My heart thumped so hard I thought I might have a heart attack. I peeked out the window and breathed a sigh of relief.

Down the way, an auto backfired as it struggled to make its way up the drive. As the guests rolled in, I felt about as excited as a kid at Christmas.

"Stay here," I said to Mel and then hurried into the foyer, sliding across the polished parquet floors where I almost tripped over the schefflera plant.

The air tingled with electricity. A ray of sunlight bounced off the chandelier under which stood a tuxedoed waiter at the ready, balancing a tray of crystal-etched flutes bubbling to the brim with imported champagne.

"Don't mind if I do," I said to the waiter, setting down my empty. Munitions in hand, I waltzed across the Oriental-carpeted living room replete with the movers and shakers of Los Angeles. Not too shabby for a poor, skinny kid from Panora. I caught a glimpse of myself in the gilded mirror hanging over the marble fireplace and stopped to adjust my bow tie before pushing my shoulders back. Sadly, I once stood six feet tall, and while the weight of the world might have flattened me down a bit, at that moment I felt no pain. As I dusted a piece of lint off my shoulder, I noticed my hair, full of static, standing out like the quills on a porcupine. Not quite as thick or wheat-colored as it had been back in the day, I tried to smooth it down. Next, I balanced my glasses needed for hyperopia (the inability to see things right under your nose). Surprisingly, after little sleep in the train car, my eyes were bright—as my future, I dared to hope—and clear as a drop of morning dew.

"Very dapper," said a woman in the mirror. Marie Hotchener, an older, yet striking bejeweled woman, stood behind me, her hair a polished silver. She was Phoebe's friend and mentor from Mills College of Arts for Women.

I turned to kiss her tiny plump pillow of a cheek, but received a tiny shock and rubbed my prickled lip. And then I sneezed. The woman and her perfume overpowered me.

"Bless you, my dear. You're not getting sick?" She pointed a finger. "I see you haven't slowed down."

"I'll slow down when I'm dead, thank you very much." I tried to be gracious as I excused myself and headed into the music room. A busy body with an air about her, Marie unnerved me worse than the Santa Ana winds.

She laughed, following me into the music room. "Doc, by the way, on behalf of the orphanage, I wanted to thank you. The donation was quite generous."

"Yes, well, my pleasure," I said. "Children are the future after all."

"You must be proud." Her voice resonated like the echo inside an airport hangar.

I turned toward her. "Indeed, I am. Phoebe has worked very hard for this."

"Yes, I'm sure, but I was speaking about all of this," she said, sweeping wide her flesh-shaded valance of an arm. Her mouth yawned wider. "Ahhh!" she said, hitting a single high note. "A perfect marriage of music and architecture; as pleasing to the eye as Phoebe's music is to the ear," said the multifaceted diva. Having been an opera star, she now dabbled a bit in architecture. "During rehearsals, I ran the diatonic scale and found your home's keynote. Now, it is alive."

"Alive, you say?" I chuckled. "Thank you, for giving it life. So now Marie," I said, peering into her eyes, "whose spirit inhabits my home?"

Marie hooted, slapping my arm. She'd always spouted a lot of theosophical gibberish and whenever she and Phoebe were found together, I never knew what the subject matter might be. I remember one afternoon I'd walked into the living room to find Marie, Phoebe and several other past members of the Order of the Rosy Cross holding a meeting. Phoebe had been seated on the ivory-colored damask davenport holding open a book. They were discussing the differences between reincarnation and the transference of consciousness.

"There is existential proof the physical body is merely a temporarily occupied vehicle for the incarnated, eternal spirit-entity," Marie had said loud enough for the china teacups to rattle. She then licked off some yellow salad from her upper lip, chasing it down with a gulp of tea. "It's quite evident."

Phoebe dabbed her lips with a linen napkin. "Yes, but let's just be clear," she added in her feathery soft voice, as she picked up the book. "It's talking about the transference of consciousness, not ordinary reincarnation."

"They are two different phenomena," Marie said, pointing a mayonnaisey finger.

"Indeed, *Phowa* is the practice of conscious dying," Phoebe replied, raising her head. "We must always be prepared in order to—"

"Oh, here we go again," I said, walking into the room and interrupting their cryptic chitchat. This wasn't the first time Phoebe had brought up this subject of the undying spirit. I pivoted on my heel, making an about face.

"Doc, please join us," Marie called out to me.

I turned back around, flourishing my arms out dramatically. "Well, I could leave my fine specimen of a body here, but I think," I said, tapping my forehead and then hooking a thumb toward the window, "I'll transfer my consciousness out into the orchard to check on the crops."

Everyone had laughed. I'd learned to take what these people discussed with a grain of salt, but somehow when the time came, I would remember about *Phowa*.

In the music room now, Marie had found my home's voice.

"The two of you have finally got it all," Marie said. "You must—"

"Not quite," I replied, knowing I'd come a long way since leaving Panora, Iowa.

For a tall, skinny kid from the sticks, I'd had my fill of culture, both social and artistic. The Twenties had caught up with everyone and politics had normalized in the wake of extreme patriotism during the War. The economy boomed. And then last year the stock market crashed and things turned pretty shaky. The atmosphere was toxic.

But now, because of Phoebe, I'd become a glass half full sort of fellow and for tonight, the champagne would pour freely. For the next couple of hours, we could unburden ourselves and be carried away by the music. I took my fluted glass and moseyed on into the chamber room. Two waiters strolled by, one with a silver tray packed with puffed pastries stuffed with liver pâté and steak tartare; the other with the champagne. I exchanged my empty, grabbed a meat tart and took a seat in the Bergere where the open french doors cooled things a bit.

"Dr. Marnier," the Mayor said, and I stood. "You made it back. How was your trip?" he asked, pumping my hand heartily.

"Couldn't have gone better. I'll stop by the office Monday to tell you all about it," I said, remembering my promise to Phoebe to drop the politics tonight.

Outside, high-top tables bloomed with colorful flower arrangements mesmerizing me as they glistened under the light of the ivory paper lanterns. The winds had died. Relaxed finally, I closed my eyes for only a moment when all of a sudden I felt a weight in my lap.

"Milty," I shouted and opened my eyes to see my four-year-old, sandy-haired nephew suited up in a miniature-sized tuxedo. I wrapped my arms around him, giving him a little squeeze. I loved this boy as if he were my own. During childbirth, there'd been irreparable damage when the umbilical cord wrapped around his larynx. Little Milton Earl Armstrong was a special child, smart as a whip—if only people could understand him. He could hear all right, but he couldn't speak. "Where's your father?"

He pointed and skipped off to sit with Earl and Ann who sat next to Phoebe's turban-wearing sister Dorothy "Dodo" and her journalist husband, Arthur Weiderholz.

"Good evening, ladies and gentlemen. Welcome," announced a cello-shaped musician holding his own violoncello. "The performance will be starting shortly. Would everyone please take a seat?"

The sound of chairs scraping and quiet coughs filled the room as the audience settled down to take their seats. Ebullient as champagne bubbles, legs stretched out in front of me, I took another sip, feeling quite comfortable in my own home; in the world I'd created.

I felt the heat from the fireplace enter the room and tugged at my shirt collar as Jack Warrington strolled in looking a little fresher than he had this morning. His wife Elizabeth, a petite, piqued-looking young woman, accompanied him. Years ago, I'd been delighted when I learned he'd found someone to settle him down, someone to love after I'd taken Phoebe off the market. He wasn't seated long before his foot tapped on the polished hardwood floor. This morning's encounter with him at the train station had certainly left me quite unsettled. I drained my glass. And now, directly behind him, sat Congressman Evans, with whom Newport and I had just negotiated the land deal in Sacramento. *Everything will be all right just as soon as I'm elected city planner next month. But for now, everyone will be taken care of on Monday.*

The lights dimmed and, looking like a pack of tuxedo-sporting penguins, in waddled the musicians.

Beethoven had his Beloved and I had mine. Phoebe, a luminescent creature, appeared out of the darkness and set the room abuzz with life. We were all her honeybees sitting in a field as she cast a charmed net around more than just me. In her presence, the world seemed a better place, a joyful sweet kingdom. People had learned to feel joy because of her. Others, such as George, Jack, and even my ex-wife Stella, had loved her in spite of themselves.

And she was beautiful, too. I found myself beguiled the moment I first set eyes upon her nearly twenty years ago when she first crossed my path. Tonight, she fastened a gardenia above her left ear. Her cinnamon-hued hair had been curled and styled; pinned up to expose a long, graceful neck from where a long strand of iridescent pearls hung, swaying hypnotically as she floated across the stage, and, as the sewn-on glass beads from her gown twinkled all around her under the light of the crystal chandelier, she was a star. She'd chosen the Chanel chemise from Paris for its drop waist designed for ease of movement when doing the Charleston, but Phoebe hadn't been dancing lately. After twelve years of wedded bliss, and at thirty-nine years of age, Phoebe, glowing now, carried our first child. She would have our baby, but not for another few weeks.

She searched the audience, found me and winked. Her sparkling emerald eyes were framed in wispy, long lashes—plumes of exotic feathers. I'd forgotten to breathe until I saw the crowd turn to smile at me. I could feel myself blushing to the roots of my hair. I winked back and she nodded, taking her seat behind the piano.

She closed her eyes, taking in a deep breath. Except for the distant sound of a wind chime outside, all was quiet until she exhaled softly, slowly raising her delicate hands. Her slender, tapered fingers with pearly white nails nimbly struck the keys to Richard Wagner's piano arrangement of Beethoven's Ninth Symphony and I wanted to weep.

And then, *what the hell!* My back went rigid. *What is he doing up there?*

There, standing next to Phoebe, stood George dressed in a black tuxedo, accessorized with a bright green bow tie—his stab at *panache.* My little boat started taking on water.

A chair scratched the floor and I turned to see Jack get up when he saw George. He exited before George belted out the first notes of the operatic rendition of *Ode to Joy.*

O Freunde, nicht diese Töne!
Sondern laßt uns angenehmere
anstimmen und freudenvollere.
Freude! Freude!

Taller than average height and packed with brawn, George couldn't enter a room without going unnoticed. He wasn't really a bad-looking sort of fellow if a grizzly bear was what a woman fancied. Except for Phoebe, the ladies seemed to swoon in his presence, and there he'd be to catch them, not because of any chivalry, but because he wanted to carry them into his bed.

George was a two-sided coin, on the one side managing to piss me off and then, on the other side, surprising me all at once. I found his singing to be quite adequate.

And when it came to George, also a heavy gambler, I thought I held all of the cards. Unfortunately, he took bigger risks than I. While I might have been an optometrist, blind when it came to some of my friend's shenanigans, George was a salesman chockfull of blind luck. The time had come to sever our relationship; I could no longer afford to be associated with him. But, I reasoned, he'd been there for me when times were rough. And, I'd more than rewarded him, I'd justified. I'd deal with him tomorrow.

I wondered what the devil he'd been up to this time. Poor Jack. I'd get my answers, but again, not tonight. I settled into my seat, nothing could be done now except to wait until tomorrow. This night belonged to my Phoebe.

At last, the magical river ride ended. The audience stood cheering, "Bravo!"

George took his bow, dark slicked-back hair still in place, and then reached for Phoebe's hand. I'd never been jealous of him until that instance, for it should have been me holding her hand up there.

As she stood, I swore she'd grown even larger since she first took her seat.

My emotions rippled along the surface of my being. I'd waited all of my life for this exquisite evening and despite George making a splash, I'd never been happier than at that very moment. The baby would only be the icing on the cake.

1949: US Naval Hospital, Oakland, California— 19-Year-Old Charley

I crack my right eye open and look down to see I'm seated on an olive-colored Naugahyde couch a few feet across from his desk. Lifting my head, both peepers are open now and I can see his face through the haze of tobacco smoke. And then I can't help it. I crack up. I swear I'm eyeballing a monster straight out of that flick we just watched on the Fireside Theater Show back at the ward with the other *Looney Tunes*. You see, I grew up on movies and everyone I meet is straight out of a motion picture film. My whole life has been one goddamn epic dramatic saga, except I do especially love cartoons and the Three Stooges.

As a matter of fact, Dr. Savage, with his light-bulb shaped head, sort of reminds me of that Curly character and if he were an animal, he'd be a turtle. When he puts on his government-issued reading glasses, his eyes grow to the size of coconuts as he proceeds to flip through the voluminous amount of paperwork attached to his clipboard. He nods and then, slowly, his slit of a mouth moves and he seems to be speaking except no words come out as he reads on. And then when he finally does talk in his quiet voice, he practically lulls me back to sleep. Plus, the calculated way he moves, reminds me of a turtle. He actually comes across as very shy; the complete opposite of the man I think he ought to be which is why I don't trust him one iota. You can never trust anyone who's only playing a part in a cartoon feature I call *Life in the Looney Bin.*

"Charley, I'd like you to talk," he says, reaching for the tape recorder I've just noticed on his desktop. "What's going on with you?"

There's no way in hell I'm telling this cat I've been having my father's thoughts again. Sharing this crap has only landed me in these sorta joints. You see, this ain't my first rodeo.

But now, worse than ever, I'm having trouble connecting the dots; something I've been trying to do my whole life. As a kid, the memories would roll up in the morning like an empty Good Humor ice cream truck, and then again in my teens like a dark, smoke-filled limousine stocked with booze and reefers.

By age seven, I finally figured out the baritone noise in my head belonged to my father, Wesley. "Doc," as everyone called him, saw it all, knew it all, and seemed to dominate their world, even in death. I'm so tired of him holding up a dogged lens of his life and trying to control mine with a leash and a collar. I need to stop him. But, apparently, this is the end of the road up here in the naval hospital where I find myself sitting in front of Dr. Ewen Savage. Too bad I'm not willing to share any of this with Savage.

With balled fists, I cover my eyes, trying to drown the stentorian voice in my head. Doc, my old man, wants to speak and I don't have the strength anymore to stop him. Drained and numb, the ear-splitting tone causes me to pitch backward.

His voice, a dust devil, swirls inside my skull until everything turns white and my own thoughts are swiped away and I begin to remember it all as if it had happened to me. *Oh, but it had happened to me.*

I close my eyes and breathe in the tobacco smell, taking me back. The smell, plus Savage told me they'd upped the dose to fifty micrograms—a new drug he called LSD, short for Lysergic Acid Diethyl Amide. Said it would help open me up, make me remember, some sort of truth serum. Cure my depression. More likely, they're killing me.

3
There Is No Tenth

September 1930: Los Angeles—
Doc

We were in bed after midnight. I dimmed the lamp and rolled over to kiss Phoebe. "You were brilliant, Darling. I can't wait to hear you perform Beethoven's Tenth," I whispered with a knowing chuckle.

"There is no tenth, silly." Her face scrunched as she placed her hands beneath her, straining to push herself up. "That's the 'curse of the ninth.'"

Musicians had their superstitions as did their theater friends, who considered it unlucky to put their shoes on the dressing table, but, at the same time, it was considered a fluke if they tripped during a performance. Long ago, Phoebe had shared another anecdote connected with the history of classical music. "A composer who produces a ninth symphony," she'd said, "has reached a decisive landmark—to embark on the tenth is to challenge fate."

"Well, my love, I don't believe this will be the end of your music," I said, plumping the pillows to stuff behind her back. "You'll have plenty of help, including me. I've arranged to cut back on my work."

She smiled, but her eyes said, *If only what you said was true* and her lips said, "I'm glad to hear you're finally ready to hand the reins over to Jack."

A puff of wind fluttered the window sheers. Crickets chirped as Phoebe stared out toward the empty sky, her smile waning, her pink-rimmed nostrils flaring subtly. The day had been electric, hot and dry, but the temperature had dropped significantly and I smelled the rain coming. It would be a damp and chilly fall. I felt it to the marrow.

She pulled the covers up around her neck as I climbed out of bed and walked toward the window. "I promise to be more involved this time around," I said, turning to look at her.

She stared out into the dark space.

"Darling?" I asked.

She blinked and turned to me. "Do you think he's ready for you to transfer over?"

"Transfer over?" I took a deep breath, thinking of Jack, George, and other business partners. I wasn't quite ready to turn things over—give up complete control to any of them—but I was also aware that not everyone gets a second chance. "Who?"

Phoebe remained quiet, as if straining to hear some warning whispered on the wind. I shut the window.

Slowly, she turned to face me. "Darling—" Her eyes filled. She pursed her lips to prevent the tears from slipping out, but they rolled down her cheeks anyway.

"What is it?"

"You need to be careful."

I climbed back into bed. "Oh, my Beloved, of course. Don't you worry about anything," I said, trying to soothe her, cradling her heart-shaped face, soft as a newborn kitten, swiping away her tears with my thumb. I kissed her on the forehead. "I won't let anything happen to you. You are the love of my life."

"I'm talking about you," Phoebe said. "There will be consequences, if you're not prepared."

The same way my bones might announce the rain, Phoebe had a special gift—she also called it a curse—for knowing things, but I also knew expectant women developed an acute sensitivity, a sixth sense as it were. As a husband though, I had a duty to be understanding during this special time.

"I'm ready. Now, you've had a very long day. The baby is coming soon and you need your rest," I said. "I still can't believe you were able to pull off tonight's concert."

"I promised you the 'Ninth' in our own home," Phoebe said as she laid her head on my chest, draping an arm around me. "I never break a promise."

"You've made me a happy man," I said, cupping her silky, swollen breast.

She removed my hand, kissed it and then replaced it onto her stomach.

"Even though this was not planned, I see it as a blessing," I said, rubbing her very round belly, a globe containing my whole world.

"So, a blessing, and not a curse?" She giggled, seemingly having hung her worry away in some back closet of her mind.

"I don't think I can last another three weeks," she said, rolling away from me onto her side, stuffing a pillow between her knees. "My back is killing me."

Curling around her body like a question mark, I tried to transfer some of my body heat, and suddenly there was no question how much I wanted her, as my penis, a divining rod with a mind of its own, searched its way.

"Poor dear. You've been patient," she said, reaching around to pat my flustered friend.

"I don't think I can wait until we make love again." My heart beat at a tempo *allegro*. "I ache for you." I kissed that special place on the back of her neck.

"I feel the same, Darling," she said, her voice smooth as fluttering silk. "I can't even remember how long it's been."

"Well, I can," I said, reaching across for my pocket watch on the nightstand. I snapped it open and held it up. "It's been two hundred thirty-three days, thirteen hours and seven minutes."

Phoebe laughed. "I'm sorry, but I do have a feeling he'll be here a lot sooner."

"*He?*" I chuckled. "Well, I suppose there's always a chance he'll arrive early, just as there's a chance he could be a *she*." Phoebe shook her head assured, as she was about most things, that our baby was a boy.

"He'll carry on your name, Wesley Charles Marnier." I wrinkled my nose and she giggled. "But we'll call him Charley."

And then, as if on cue, I felt our baby kick and Phoebe's smile quickly returned.

I snuggled up even closer to recite our nighttime ritual: "I love you more today than yesterday."

"But not as much as tomorrow." She squeezed my arm.

"Goodnight, Sweetheart."

"We have quite the life, wouldn't you agree?"

"And it's only just the beginning," I said, cradling her tighter into my body.

"Doc, you know I've loved you since the first moment I saw you."

"And I will love you until the last."

I pulled the cover off and stepped out of bed.

"Now, where are you going?" she asked.

"To take a cold shower."

1949: US Naval Hospital—
Charley

I'm experiencing something so deep and, on the surface, my skin and my face are burning hot; it's embarrassing. My heart hurts, and with the back of my hand I wipe the tear sizzling down my cheek.

"Charley, you've been here fourteen days," Dr. Savage squeaks.

I swipe my nose. *Holy shit, a whole fortnight, and I thought I'd only been here maybe two days—three max.* I open my eyes to see a tin of Prince Albert tobacco on his desk and Dr. Savage holding out a tissue as he clenches a mahogany pipe in his mouth. He then crosses his arms across his chest and, after an eternity, he sets down the pipe and opens his mouth. This time I'm actually able to hear his words as they dribble out.

To try and stay alert, I move from the couch to a hard metal chair, but it's like sitting on a damn block of ice. Since I've lost my appetite, there's even less padding on my butt. At six foot one, I've always been pretty lean and any muscles I'd developed since joining the Navy have turned to mush. I adjust my tailbone, crossing one leg over the other to try and get comfy. I'm shivering, and without lifting or turning my bulky head, I eyeball the room. Whatever they've given me is obviously still floating around in my system making everything seem a little fuzzy. I do feel a little better though, sort of like you do after puking your guts out after a peyote trip down in the Sonora Desert.

"You seem a little disoriented," Savage says. "First of all, do you remember why you're here?"

A little disoriented? There's just a little smog in the noggin. I shrug my shoulders and slowly shake my heavy, aching head. Truth be told, I do remember my side of the story, but I don't have the strength to answer. Anyway, I flex my brain muscles to try and recall the exact details leading up to now.

Rubbing the fresh tattoo on my upper arm, it comes to me, but I don't open my mouth. I'm here because some asshole down in San Diego has it in for me. I'm not the first sailor who ever needed to get bailed out of a Tijuana jail cell. Of course this all happened only a couple of weeks after I'd gotten drunk while babysitting my commanding officer's kid. Admittedly, I fucked up. But drinking is the only way I know to drown out Doc's voice— booze and loud music.

"Charley," Savage says, looking up from his clipboard. "What happened to Phoebe?"

I look at Savage and the memories scatter down into the bunker of my mind.

4
The *Phowa* Overture

September 1930: Glendale—
Doc

The morning after the concert, I sat at the kitchen table sipping my coffee. I smelled the cloying cologne before I ever saw him, and set down the paper as George took a seat across from me. The concert had been a late night affair and it wasn't unusual for him to spend the night in the guest room, especially during the week of rehearsals. It had been a comfort knowing Phoebe wasn't alone while I worked up north, but now I feared he'd been up to his old tricks. We needed to talk.

"George, what's going on over at my office?" I'd asked. "Jack seemed more than just a little agitated over some *goons* that came through."

Without setting down his paper, he answered. "Ah, Doc, it's nothing, trust me. Jack doesn't know what he's talking about. Joe and Tony dropped by just to look around."

"Why?" I reached across the table and grabbed his newspaper, startling him. "The place is not for sale. Besides, last time I checked, it's still my business."

Hidden in the shadows beneath brambly black eyebrows lurked his pistol-gray eyes, but George wasn't looking at me. Instead, he stared down to his left, a sure sign he lied about something.

"Why are they snooping around? What's going on?"

"It's the way I negotiate. You know. Trust me. All I did was buy some time. I don't happen to have anything in my name."

Trust me? Something becoming harder to do. "And it's the way you want it, George. Nothing in your name, remember? That's how you lost everything you owned." I stood, repressing an urge to punch him in the face. "So, you used the business . . . my business!"

"Got myself in a bit of a jam."

I knew his foibles. I always believed people could change.

"How much do you owe this time?" I asked, setting some documents onto the table.

"Oh, it's not much. You know there's nothing I wouldn't do for you. I'd even take a bullet for you."

"Now, that's a little extreme," I said, remembering all the times he had been there for me. Especially, the time he brought Phoebe back into my life.

"What's that, boss?" George asked as he looked over at the papers.

I couldn't stay mad. "It's a copy of the deed to the Valley View property and the check."

"You sold the property above Brand Avenue?" George asked, the furrows in his brow smoothing out.

"Indeed, I did," I said, and a wave of relief washed over me. "Deal's done, my boy, and I will retain water rights through Woodside. My trip to Sacramento wasn't a total waste of time, after all. You know the old saying, 'if you can't beat them, join them.' Not only is my election to city planner a guarantee, but just as soon as I'm elected, I'll be able to put a stop to the road construction through Woodside as well."

"Excellent news!" George said.

"Yes, and the deed records Monday. After that, I can cash the check," I said, waving a check for twenty-five thousand dollars, and then slid the documents back into my inside coat pocket. "With your share, there should be enough to make those goons go away." I stood. "George, especially with the election coming up, there can be no hiccups."

George stood also and patted me on the back. "No worries, boss."

I stiffened. "One more thing, George—"

He looked at me, waiting. "Never mind," I said, wishing to tell him we were finished and the time had come to part ways, but I couldn't, at least not yet. I still needed him.

I wouldn't let anything bother me that morning. Everything seemed to be going my way. "Right now, I need to find a way to sneak over to meet Jack and put this copy into the safe," I said, as I patted my breast pocket. "But Phoebe insists there be no more business this week."

"Meet Jack. But why?" George asked, arching a bushy eyebrow.

"He wants me to re-sign an assignment to the business assuring him that just in case something happens to me he'll be protected."

"Nothing will happen to you," George said, inspecting his newly manicured nails.

"With the baby on the way, it's time to put things in order." I placed my hand on my forehead. "By God, Phoebe knows nothing about my businesses. You're the only one, and if anything were to happen to me," I said, pointing a finger, "she needs to see how she and the baby will always be taken care of."

"Don't worry," George said, bringing the side of his thumb to his lips and nipping off a hangnail. "You're as strong as an ox and as stubborn as a mule." He removed the nail from his tongue and flicked it to the floor.

"Hee haw," I said, "an older farm animal that Phoebe and the baby will most likely outlive, but for now, I'm not ready to be put out to pasture."

George's smile didn't match his pupil-dilated eyes, a sure sign something frightened him.

"Sure, Doc. I mean. Can't it wait until Monday? I'm sure—"

"And after this land deal closes, there should be no need for anyone to worry about money or water rights. Hell, by Monday, I'll be worth more dead than alive."

Just then, the back door swung open and with his bulging biceps rippling out from underneath his rolled-up shirtsleeves, in bowled my brother-in-law Earl with little Milty in tow.

I could hardly imagine how Phoebe, refined as sugar, could possibly be related to someone as one-dimensional as her brother. Except for the scar running through his eyebrow—and his slurred speech—it was even harder to imagine Earl had once been a formidable middle-weight boxing champ. But when Earl got Ann pregnant, well, I made sure to end his boxing career, and gave him no choice except to marry her. Phoebe gave me no choice but to invite him into our circle.

"Who's dead?" Earl asked.

"Whoa there. Law's not chasing you again is it, brother?" I said as Earl reached out to shake my hand so tight, our Mason rings clinked. "I don't think Congressman Evans will be so quick to help you out this time," I said, almost regretting having made the statement, but pulling favors especially for the likes of my sorry ass brother-in-law wasn't something I was fond of doing.

"Yes, gambling is one thing," George said, crossing his arms over his chest, "but bootlegging is a whole different can of worms." George broke into laughter.

I narrowed my eyes at George and then Earl. I suspected something was up again down at the store involving the two of them. Just last year, Comalt, one of our competitors, got busted during a raid for bootlegging. With my name on the lease for the store Earl managed, I couldn't afford to be a part of any such trouble, especially with elections coming up. So, no, the Congressman wasn't about to turn a blind eye when it came to the sale of alcohol.

"And, did you have to bring up the dam break to Mulholland last night?" I asked Earl.

It had been a couple of years since the deadly collapse of the St. Francisquito Dam. Mulholland, the head of the Los Angeles Department of Water and Power, had taken full responsibility for what would be the worst engineering disaster in the twentieth century. Times were tough, but last night my guests had been invited over to enjoy themselves in the intimate setting of my home.

And then, with a smirk, Earl added his unsolicited two cents. "I believe this is what you call karma. You keep going like that and somethin's gonna give."

Milty walked up quietly, tugged at my shirt and pointed to the cookie jar on the counter. I nodded. Anything for Milty. Everything I'd done in the past for Earl had been because of Phoebe, and now I did it for Milty. He smiled at me sweetly as I handed him a cookie.

"Sorry, Doc. I gotta get back down to the store," Earl said. "Phoebe said she'd watch the boy."

"Perfect, I planned on stopping in later this afternoon. See how things are going." I'd planted some fear.

Earl's face shifted into a smirk. "Then, I'll see you later, old man."

"Watch it, pal. I'm still young enough for your sister," I said.

"And virile enough, too. Aye?" George said with a smirk.

"Barrymore's got nothing on me," I responded.

Phoebe waddled into the kitchen. "Ah, it's little Milty," she said.

"And big Earl and George are just leaving," I added.

"Bravo again, George," she said, as he headed out of the room.

"Darling, how are you feeling?" I asked, as she lowered herself into a chair.

She held my hand, whispering, "I'm just a little run down, probably from all last night's stimulation."

I looked at her and laughed. "Indeed, you should have read the flattering write-up in the *Los Angeles Times*. The guest list reads like a *Who's Who*. It was nice to see your composer friend Cadman again." I crossed my arms over my chest and huffed. "And George was certainly in his element what with that bright green bow tie of his."

Phoebe giggled, patting my leg. "Sounds like someone's just a little green with envy."

I was no longer jealous of the composer Phoebe had spent time with in Europe right after our honeymoon. And, envy wasn't the word I'd use to describe how I felt about George; the word was more like exasperation.

"Oh!" Phoebe screamed suddenly, reaching for her back.

1949: US Naval Hospital— Charley

I don't want to talk about my mother. Besides, I'm sure Savage already knows why I'm here. My CO told me he wouldn't report me if I'd come up and "volunteer" for some observation. I'm not stupid and I'm not here of my own accord. Really, I don't care anymore if I get kicked out of the Navy. It wasn't my idea to join at seventeen in the first place. My life had been so out of control and with the way things were going, the choice was either the military or a future in prison. I never imagined I'd be stuck on the 2nd floor of the US Naval Hospital. So, I didn't have too many options. And hell, yes, I'm scared shitless. But the real truth is, I'm not sure who else Doc wants me crossing off his check list.

So, yeah, I volunteered for this, too. Now, in addition to Papa Doc, Uncle Sam has let me down. "Join the Navy and see the world." *Yeah, sure.*

At the end, except for a couple of liberty trips south of the border, I never even left the shipyard out of San Diego. I rub my arm. It still smarts. And now the trip to this shithole. Nothing is making sense right now.

Stationed as a corpsman down in San Diego, how could I do my job with hands so jittery; how was I supposed to hold onto my own dick to take a piss? I hadn't been sleeping. It wasn't my fault I slept through my watch. They'd probably been slipping bennies and shit in my coffee for weeks. Probably putting radioactive crap in my oatmeal, too, while they were at it.

By the time I entered the Navy, my nerves were already so fried and we weren't even at war. Hell, I'd experienced my own personal war at home. Goddamn World War III if you ask me.

But now, this place is driving me crazy. There's just something so disturbing about the dismembered, crazy-eyed, shell-shocked World War II vets they keep doped up in the ward. I'm a good listener, a Navajo Tracker with my ears to the ground, whose code can't be broken. The old vets fill my head, already jammed to capacity with stuff about Nazi concentration camps, Jews, Russians and communism.

"I'd just poured a cup of coffee when the first wave of dive bombers hit Pearl Harbor," said one old sailor. "Yellow bastards! Blew the ship out from right underneath us."

And suddenly I remembered where I was on December 7th, the day the Japs bombed Pearl Harbor. Mother and I were all alone in the big dark house huddled together next to the radio. I needed to be brave; after all, with George gone, I became the man of the house, at least figuratively. We kept the place dark and the windows covered, living in fear for quite some time.

"We were sitting ducks," the old guy shouted. "Never saw the Japs coming."

After a while, he had me singing the same song. The next morning my mates found me huddled under my bunk taking cover. I'd heard the planes buzzing overhead again. "The Japs are coming! The Japs are coming!" I shouted as the orderlies reached in to pull me out from under my bunk.

5

Calando—Falling

September 1930: Glendale—
Doc

It would be a while before the doctor could see Phoebe, who assured me the pain had gone by now. But, in less than an hour, I'd dropped Phoebe off at her doctor's office and brought Milty with me across the street to my optometry office.

The door was unlocked and the little bell tinkled to announce my arrival. I set down my umbrella, removed my hat and hung it on the hat rack as I called out, "Just me, Jack."

No answer. Everything was dark. I turned on a lamp in the reception area. On one wall hung an eye chart and on the other stood an old grandfather's clock I'd had with me since the turn of the century. The time read two-fourteen.

Milty settled himself quietly on a Persian rug in my reception area to play with the Lionel train set I kept around for visiting children. He munched contentedly on the Baby Ruth candy bar I'd purchased from one of my markets along our way to my office.

I walked down the hall to see if Jack might be in his office. He hadn't arrived, so I headed across to my office and gasped when I found it in shambles. Except for my thumping heart, my body stopped in place. Slowly, I willed my legs to move in as I scanned the area. What were they looking for? And then I remembered the cash and looked up toward the top shelf, realizing there was hardly enough for anyone to go to all of this trouble.

I kept the safe hidden up behind some books on the highest shelf of the floor-to-ceiling bookcase. From the looks of it, the crook hadn't found the safe because only the books on the top shelf had been left undisturbed. I raised my head and saw that thankfully the glass case stuffed with my rare medical books had been undisturbed, the same for the case filled with my tinctures, potions and medicines. I looked closer, relieved to see that the box with the ninety-seven hand- ground glass lenses separated by a soft leather divider all seemed to be in place and unbroken. It had taken hours just to categorize the lenses all according to the shape and type of lens and the prescription or magnification.

"Jack!" I shouted, proceeding to pick up the papers.

The skeleton propped in the corner still stood wearing a pair of glasses. What might you have seen? All at once, I remembered how Jack had mentioned "goons" coming through the office claiming to be shareholders. Was this some sort of message? My initial shock had now been replaced by anger. No one would mess with me or my family.

My stomach lurched and I walked out into the hallway to check on Milty. He looked up and smiled at me. I saw his little chocolate-smudged face and it warmed my heart.

I returned to my office and righted my desk lamp and then, in the midst of a jumble of papers, I saw a colorfully wrapped gift with a note card. I picked up the heavy package and peeled back some of the wrapping—a bottle of whiskey with the Dragna label.

Thank you, Dr. Marnier, from all of us, the note read, *Sincerely, Giuseppa.* Giuseppa was the older sister of Tom Dragna, infamous for more than just bootlegging. I'd treated the whole family.

So, they're the ones, I thought, setting down the bottle. Was this some sort of warning?

I considered calling the police, but knew better and had to trust that what George had told me was true; this would all go away come Monday.

Controlling the anger brewing in my gut, I proceeded to do what I'd come here to do in order to hurry back to Phoebe. Quickly, I ascended the ladder leaning against the bookshelves. I climbed to the very top, and before I moved some books, I looked around to make absolutely sure I was alone. Normally, I would have closed my door, but I needed to keep an ear open for Milty.

With the coast clear, I reached for the safe hidden behind some books I would never read again, one entitled *Phowa: A Guided Meditation for Time of Death.* I moved the books and was just about to turn the tumblers on the vault, when I heard the tinkle of the little bell from out front.

Holding my breath, I listened to the staccato of a woman's heels as they punctuated the tiled hallway. I couldn't imagine Phoebe's examination was over already.

"Darling, I told you to wait for me," I shouted, but heard no response.

I proceeded to descend the ladder again calling out, "Darling?"

"You never called *me* Darling."

The short hairs on the back of my neck stood at attention and I turned to see Stella, my ex-wife, draped in the now-matted fur coat I bought her when we first moved to Hollywood. The fur, which seemed to swallow her up, seemed no worse for wear; it was Stella who appeared to be time worn. If it hadn't been for the familiar crooked smile, first intriguing me about her nearly thirty years ago, and her puffy face capped in one of the shorter, darker hairstyles of the times, she would be unrecognizable. Her face looked as if part of it had died.

"And how is the little interloper?" she asked with a lopsided jeer. "Nice write-up in the *Times*. I'm surprised you allowed George to take the lime-light." She barely stood straight.

"It wasn't up to me," I said, descending the ladder and then standing to face her.

"I suppose it wasn't. Sometimes, you're just so blind." She sounded like she sucked on pebbles. "But then it does run on your side of the family."

"That's a low blow. You don't know what you're talking about."

"Don't I though? Anyway, I phoned your home. George took the call. Good old George," she said with more than a hint of mockery. "Don't you worry about leaving him alone with your little *Darling?* You know he always did take a shine to her."

"Enough. What do you want? Not more money. I just had George send you your check. The kids are grown, the house is paid for. You have property. If anything, I should be cutting back. How much more could you possibly need, Stella?"

"Need?" she asked, swaying like a drunken sailor. She reached for the ladder to steady herself.

"Did you drive yourself here all the way from Hollywood?" I asked, incredulous.

"Do you really care?" she asked, reaching out to touch my arm. I recoiled and she pulled her hand away.

"Wesley, you know times are tough," she whined, slurring her words.

I knew better than to engage with her, but I couldn't resist. "Which is exactly why you should be cutting back on the booze and pills."

"Easy for the man holding the purse strings." Stella pouted and then whimpered, a manipulation that used to work.

"What do you know? My doctor says it's what's keeping me going what with everything I've been through. Everything just comes easy to you. You don't know what it's like."

"My God, Stella, let's not start this all over again. It's been fourteen years. You weren't the only one affected."

My insides churned. I'd only had coffee that day. If ever I saw myself murdering anyone, it would have been Stella.

"You never even cried." She wiped her eyes with the back of her hand, and it was a wonder she didn't give herself a black eye with her latest piece of gaudy jewelry, a ring with a piece of glass the size of a golf ball. While it was hers to do with what she pleased, I learned she'd hocked her wedding ring years ago to spend it on the booze.

"You keep things bottled up." She used her sleeve to swipe her runny nose.

"And you, you should put a cork in it. You don't know anything," I yelled.

Once again, like she had been so good at during the marriage, she had aroused an ill wind in me.

"You don't want me to be happy? The mother of your children or have you forgotten?"

I bit my tongue. Of course, I hadn't forgotten. How could I possibly forget? Not a day went by when I didn't think about our children; our son. Unfortunately, any of the compassion I ever had for this woman had waned.

"Are you having this child to replace Leland? The same way you replaced me—"

"Stop!"

"That is, if you're even the father? You know, Phoebe and George have always been rather—"

"Shut up! Stella, get out of my office!" I said, grabbing my chest. I had to stop her or she'd finally succeed in causing me a heart attack. I turned away, climbing up a step to show her I was finished.

As the pounding in my ears increased, it's a wonder I heard the sound of the other set of footsteps coming down the hall.

"Jack, I'm back here," I called out.

Ruffled, Stella craned toward the sound and quickly darted out the back door, but not before she snatched the colorfully wrapped box of whiskey sitting on my desk.

I walked out into the hallway but didn't see anyone. Again, I checked Jack's office and found it empty. I checked on Milty still playing in the reception area with the train. I tapped his shoulder and asked, "Was somebody here?"

He pointed to my office. "The lady," he signed back.

This is peculiar. I returned to my own office. I picked up the book and climbed back up the ladder. In the process of moving the books to get to the vault, I heard someone call out my name. I swung around to see Jack standing in the doorway. His hair was disheveled and the suit he'd worn last night looked rumpled. His eyes were glassy. He appeared not to have slept for days. He then walked toward me pointing a gun. I panicked and reached out to grab a rung, but still I hung onto the book *Phowa*. And then I felt the ladder rip away from the shelf. I lost my grip and fell ten feet striking the back of my head on the cement floor.

Dazed, and yet still conscious, I saw stars. I rolled over to push myself up onto my knees—panting, chest heaving—and then I was struck in the back of my head.

1949: US Naval Hospital— Charley

Dr. Savage turns off the tape recorder and proceeds to read from his clipboard.

"Says here, your commanding officer wanted you out. Didn't want you inciting the crew anymore with talks about Russians and Cold War."

Someone's gotta warn them.

"Charley, how can I help you if you won't talk to me?"

The chair beneath me creaks.

Dr. Savage sets the clipboard down on the edge of the desk and as he crosses his legs, he knocks the board to the floor. I rush over to pick it up for him and now I can see clearly the words scrawled across the top of the page in his handwriting: "Candidate Charley Marnier. Schizophrenic. Project Chatter." Before I can make out the chicken scratch beneath, Savage scoops up the clipboard and then catches me staring at him.

So, now I'm tempted to answer his earlier question. Of course I know why I'm here; the real certifiable reason they stuck me here. I thought it was because I hear a voice, but now I know it's because Savage thinks I'm schizophrenic and something else to do with whatever it says in the document attached to that clipboard. I'm curious to ask, but instead I make a mental note to find out more about this "Project Chatter." And then finally, I manage a silly goofball smile. "I'd walk a mile for a Camel."

Savage returns a civil smile, offering me a cigarette. He lights it for me.

I inhale deeply as he waits for me, patiently. Finally, I decide I owe him something, so I open up just a little. Give him just a little taste.

"That's some good shit you're giving me, but I'm confused. You see, I'm having these thoughts that aren't my own." I figure I can use this opportunity to reveal a little bit about myself.

Savage flips a page on his clipboard and leans in. "If you're having trouble, perhaps, I can help you remember," he says, adjusting his glasses as he reads from some documents. "It also says you were sent here because you talk to yourself." Savage cocks his head. "Who is Doc?"

My mouth snaps open just a bit but no words leak out. Except for "uh," I remain silent. Savage looks back down at his file.

"You're acutely depressed. Not sleeping. You're irritable. You're drinking too much."

Who can blame me? I'm silent. I know better than to argue.

With an index finger he pushes back his glasses. "Also says you suffer from nervousness; that you worry about your mother and need to get home to help her. That it's because of you she's losing the house. You are useless to her here. You feel depraved and you feel life is not worth living." He looks up at me. "That about right, Charley?"

I sit up straight. "I wouldn't put it like *that*, exactly."

"How then would you put it—" he asks, crossing his short legs and sitting taller in his chair, "—exactly? How do you feel about your mother? How would you describe your relationship with her?"

"I'd rather not talk about her."

Savage passes a chewed-up pencil over his notes and then, without looking up, he points his pencil at me. "Very well. At least you're talking. This is an excellent start," he says, without even asking me about the confusing thoughts I'd been having. It's as if now, since he knows I'm not a mute, he's going to shoot from the hip.

But I figure I'm a faster Quick Draw McGraw, until he says, "Earlier, you were humming Beethoven. I recognized parts from the *Pastoral* and *Eroica* Symphonies. He happens to be a favorite composer of mine."

Bang! He's got me. I pull a hand over my heart. "It's calming," I answer.

"Interesting, the two symphonies are so diametrically divergent . . . polar opposites, in fact. While one celebrates the greatness of man, the other celebrates the love of nature," he says.

Ain't that swell, Savage has a hard-on for old Ludwig. My cigarette is stuck to my mouth as I jut my lower lip out like a monkey and play with the Camel.

"Beethoven—"

The cornball's lost me. Not hard to do since I have the attention span of a gnat. I'm cross-eyed as I look down to watch my cigarette bob up and down. Savage stops talking. All of a sudden I'm a kindergartner sitting in the principal's office again. I turn my focus to Savage and notice he's staring up at the ceiling, quite pleased with himself, no doubt. He raises an index finger as if he might go on. *Oh, please, for the love of God, my ears are going to explode.* He must be reading my mind because he stops his dissertation, bringing his finger to his lips. He smiles as he jots something down on his clipboard.

"Charley." He clears his throat and peers over his reading glasses. "I want to ask you about some things you've shared earlier."

I chuckle, but really I'm scared. I don't remember sharing anything earlier. "You mean I did more than just hum a few bars. I actually shared some shit?"

"You said you may die?"

Inhaling, I choke. *Oh damn!*

"That you fell off the ladder after which you were struck on the back of your head. Can you please tell me some more about the experience? Search your memory."

I feel my brows squeezing together and try to compose myself as I sit up stiffly in my chair.

"Who is Jack?"

Double damn! I pull deeply on my cigarette.

"Try to get a picture in your mind. Maybe by remembering, we can help you."

But my memory is a mummy covered in gauze; slowly, I'm unraveling. I exhale and have the sensation of falling through space and then I'm there—I'm the one being transported to the hospital—Phoebe, my mother, is holding my hand telling me to hang on. Hell, I'd always hoped I'd only been dreaming.

I collapse in my chair, terrified of my past and even more petrified about the future. I'm not ready to open up. I have an uncomfortable feeling that whatever I've said, I've talked myself into a corner.

"Doctor Savage, I'm really tired. Everything seems very hazy. Can I please go back and lie down for a while?"

"I don't think we're progressing fast enough," he answers. "By now, I would have expected you to open up a little more. I'm increasing your dosage."

Oh, hell, no! I didn't know this was a race. I'm trying to cooperate. I'll try harder.

I struggle to sit upright in the chair but my elbows only make it to the tops of my knees, where I've been resting my chin in the palms of my hands. I make an effort to look up but my eyes really feel bruised, like I've been hit over the head with a fuckin' frying pan. Licking my dry, cracked lips to speak, again I forget what I want to say.

I swallow on the sad, hard truth and nod. "Oh, yes, Jack, I remember now. Jack was my father's optometry partner. Yes. He killed my father."

Dr. Savage bends forward, eyebrows lifted. "You don't say. What happened to him?"

I scratch my head. "Oh, he got his," I say and all of a sudden, out of the corner of my left eye, in the midst of a cloud of cigarette smoke, the image of George appears—clearer and more defined than ever. I can see him in Doc's optometry office standing over me beneath an oscillating ceiling fan, blood gushing from my head. But just as soon as he appears, he disappears in a whir. *What is George doing here?*

"I'm really not feeling so hot. Can we please just continue this tomorrow?"

Savage reaches for the phone, and shortly an intern enters to take me back to my room where I'm watched closely as I take my medication. My head is still throbbing and I fall to the floor.

6
Opus 21—Beethoven's Musical Joke

September 1930: Glendale—
Doc

I'd come to twisted sideways on the floor of my optometry office, still holding onto the *Phowa* book. I strained to open my eyes and looked across the room to check on Milty and saw his fuzzy image underneath the desk where he'd taken cover in the reception area. His O-shaped mouth emitted no sound, and his wide eyes had welled with tears as he clutched his Lionel train. I could not speak and made an effort to summon him with my eyes, batting them repeatedly, tapping a Morse code, and slowly, he entered the room to kneel by my side. With the back of his small hand, he touched my cheek.

For a moment, I closed my eyes and imagined myself back in my mother's kitchen, where the warmth and the damp smell of chocolate comforted me. I opened my eyes to see Milty lying with his chocolate-stained face on the floor next to mine. Breathing heavily, his sweet breath warmed me. He reached out for my shattered glasses and replaced them on my face. He then left the room and scurried down the hallway and out onto the street. Milty had been my witness, but with no form of communication, the secret would chase me to the grave.

As I drifted in and out of consciousness, someone touched me and I thought Milty had returned to stay with me. I strained to open my eyes and when I looked through my shattered glasses, I thought I saw George. Oh, thank God. George, help me! And then I lost consciousness once more.

He was gone when I awoke to the sound of Phoebe screaming. She'd rushed to my side, where she dropped to her knees and caressed my face. Phoebe, the love of my life—my angel, my all, my very self.

Looking into her eyes, I took in my reflection, horrified by the vision. As she stroked my blood-mottled hair, she slipped off my glasses and peered into my soul, something only she'd ever been able to do. And in the twinkling of an eye, I saw the other side, a place where I didn't want to be without her. I hoped she might keep the reflection of me, a part of me, forever, as I would keep hers.

She took my hand, gripping as if she'd never let it go. She kissed me, and knowing I was in good hands I surrendered to the quiet and to the darkness I'd fought from overtaking me.

While the ten-foot drop off the ladder and the bash to the head were shocking, I must admit, dying wasn't so painful, but it wasn't quick either. I drifted in and out of consciousness for the next several hours.

I'd made some mistakes in my life, things for which I can't be forgiven. If only I could go back and change things; do things differently, make things right. If only I had more time. It isn't only your life you see flashing before your eyes as you die—I can tell you the truth of that—but foremost are the regrets haunting you during your final brief period of time. I can capture tintypes of memories; strung together like a movie scene or freeze framed for another day.

I can see how, in a lifetime, not everyone gets a second chance at love. My heart spilled over with so many things to say to her, but death is Cupid's poisoned arrow. I also worried my endeavors, like my words, would be forgotten; trapped like the important papers in the vault I had intended to open only a short while ago.

As a man who had always fought for control, had I this time left destiny to chance only to lose dominion over it?

Musical memories slowly filled the spaces where blood vacated my body; where cracks and fissures had broken away. And then a silly superstition floated across the forefront of my mind and I struggled to connect the meaning. Was this a musical joke or was this my *Curse of the Ninth*? While I wasn't a composer of music and had always discounted this concept of the curse, I wondered if somehow I'd struck a wrong chord with fate. Was it wrong to have wanted more? Was it wrong to attempt a tenth? Was our baby to be the tenth symphony of my life, and therefore a mistake—? No!

Phoebe's kiss rested on my lips, infusing my being with a warmth so powerful that once again I found myself back in Panora, Iowa, nestled along the banks of the Middle Raccoon River, the place where I was born; the land of my youth. And then from this perspective, I saw all the beauty of the land, the lights of the city beyond—a city full of hopes and promises for a better life than I could ever have on a barren Iowa farm. The birds sang even louder and the rush of the river sounded so grave until the tornado came and ripped away the farm, my world.

I stumbled upon the cemetery where my mother and father were buried so many years ago. There was a place for me, but this was no longer my home.

Along the river, I heard the birds in harmony and in the midst, I heard the piano. Phoebe! The sounds of flutes, cellos and violins filled my ears with a fortissimo in A major, then touches of D, G, and C minor. Autumn had arrived and like the palette of the Beethoven's First, a brilliance of color engulfed me. I looked west to my destiny and witnessed a most dazzling citrus-colored sunset. My feet again touched the ground and I discovered myself in California.

California, where I'd come on my search for something more, as if things might show me the deeper meaning of happiness? What could be greater than love? I had a world overflowing with love, and instead of being satisfied—happy—I had forsaken it all for more: just one more deal, just one more property, more business. Happiness was a simple thing; a *thing* that couldn't be laid away, bought, traded, bartered for or used as collateral. Finally, I came to understand all of this, but much too late, for I'd created this tragic, reckless end by wanting to take control of everyone, everything in my life. Finally, I saw it all so clearly. On the floor of my office, my eyes flickered open for an instant to see a seagull perched upon my chest to take me home. I looked into the eyes of the bird, whose pupils dilated until all at once I saw the image of my earthly angel. Phoebe leaned over me, and beyond her shoulder were men in white coats who had come to transport me to the hospital. They scrambled about and finally lifted me onto a gurney. Phoebe held my hand and leaned over me, and I felt the warmth of her breath on my cheek and heard her sweet voice as she begged me to stay with her just a little longer, and to please hang on for our son's sake for she knew he would be a boy and all at once, so did I.

"Live! My darling beloved. Not just because I love you, but because our son needs you."

Just a few more breaths and I'd be dead. My valiant struggle for justice—my insurrection against mediocrity—and just look where this defiant know-it-all would end up. Dead.

1949: US Naval Hospital—
Charley

It's raining today. I was born in the middle of the devil winds during a nine-year California drought so I'm more familiar with chapped skin, bloody noses and fires. Rain's bad news for a person who stumbles around with his head in a dark cloud even on a dry, sunny day. I try to be optimistic, if only for a nanosecond, for rain can wash things clean. But not everything—not a blood stain. I'm not in a hurry to reveille. I'm an outdoors sort of cat and since there are no outside activities today, I'm stuck here inside germsville. Except for the dream where I was flying over Iowa, then riding in the back of an ambulance with my mother, the sound of the pelting rain on the rooftop kept me awake most of the night.

I roll onto my side and watch as the rain drips down the window, casting eerie shadows on the wall. I squeeze my eyes shut and turn over to prop myself up on my pillow. Lately, I've been having more than just snippets of memory and thoughts. I'm watching a goddamn movie on the backs of my eyelids. Since birth, I've been nothing but a movie house for Doc's viewing pleasure, but now it's different.

Now I stare out the streaked glass and fall into a sort of dreamy underwater mood as I watch the clouds pass. Seagulls sail and swoop in the sky and all at once, I'm one of them, swirling into an image of me as a child. The image where I'm with my stepfather George and we're driving my seagull to the beach. I close my eyes and cast them back. I remember the windy, rainy night Sammy, the bird, had crashed into my bedroom window. Mother wouldn't let me keep him. My heart hurts.

In the distance, a foghorn blasts. I roll out of my bunk and step to the window where a reflection of George appears again. I try to shake his image out of my head but then I'm looking up at him from the floor of Doc's office as I lie dying—as Doc lies dying—as we lie dying. Everything hurts. I can feel the pain. We can feel the pain. I wipe the window with my hand and smear blood. Holding up my hands, I see the blood on George's hands as he walks away from us.

I squeeze my eyes shut and struggle to put the pieces together. I wonder if—I wonder how George might have had a part in his death?

"Find him," Doc booms suddenly, his voice echoing in the tiny space.

7

Roll Out the Barrel

1949: US Naval Hospital—
Charley

In the mess hall, I take a seat at the piano. I'd gotten a gig playing piano tunes where everyone sings along to songs like "Don't Sit Under the Apple Tree with Anyone Else but Me" and "GI Jive." But with the mood and all, I pound out the "Beer Barrel Polka," instead.

I turn to see the troops, some in wheelchairs, some in beds, some just standing around singing at the top of their lungs:

> . . . *Roll out the barrel, we'll have a barrel of fun*
> *Roll out the barrel, we've got the blues on the run.*

Man, I thought we were having a good time so when their cheers turn into boos, I get peeved. I turn and see the reason for their discontent. A skinny, pimply-faced corpsman in a wrinkled white uniform has come to rattle the cage.

"Charley," he says. "It's time for your session with Dr. Savage."

"Sorry, boys. Time for an intermission," I say, standing. "Hit the head, grab some popcorn and a soda pop and I'll be right back."

I really don't feel up to having a little chitchat with Dr. Savage this morning, but unless I want to get more doped up, I have no choice. I'm really not digging the side effects. Last night, I hid the pill under my lip and when no one looked, I spit it into a planter.

I don't want to be moved again to a different room, so I shuffle down the hall behind the orderly with the funny-looking ears. One slipper at a time I follow, determined to cooperate fully today.

When I walk in, Savage is already seated behind the steel government-issue desk. On the corner rests a chipped ivory-colored cup with remnants of yesterday's coffee, cold as a corpse, and an ashtray that hasn't been emptied since the war. Outside, the leaves are plastered to the wet, weeping window as a cold wind blasts across the San Francisco Bay. A disoriented, drenched seagull lands, taking shelter on the sill, covering the spot where the paint is peeling. Savage's eyes are closed as he waves a pencil to the music playing on the phonograph on a small table near his desk.

"Beethoven—" he says when he opens his eyes, motioning for me to take a seat.

What a cube. Like listening to Beethoven makes you hip.

"It's what calms you, right, Charley?"

"Used to," I answer, sorry for thinking badly of him. He's just trying to be helpful.

"So, how'd you sleep?"

"Not that great," I answer. "May I have a smoke?"

He slides his cigarette case toward me. "Must be the new surroundings. I find it always takes time to adjust to a new place. You are taking your medication?"

I nod, bringing the match to the tip of my cigarette. When I look up, he's peering at me. I'm some sort of lab specimen staring up through the microscope into a magnified eyeball. I inhale.

"Well, then, perhaps tonight I can prescribe something to . . . to help you sleep."

I exhale and then chuckle. "What, electro shock therapy?" I shake the match. "A lobotomy? No thanks." I've seen plenty of vets just lying around here with vacant tombs for eyes. I don't want any of that. There's a reason I'm not sleeping, or at least if I do, it's with one eye open.

"You've got quite an imagination."

"Who's imagining? You think I don't know why I've been pulled out of the other ward? You think I don't know why I'm here?"

The needle scratches across the record that just keeps spinning. I hook a thumb toward the phonograph and Savage finally gets up to check it out.

"I understand you're our resident musician," he says, returning to his desk. "I must wander over to listen to you play sometime." He folds his hands on top of the desk. "Your mother was a musician."

I nod.

"Tell me a little about her?"

"Fine," I say. I see where this is going, but I don't let on. Classic Oedipus—little boy wants his mother; wants his father out of the way. Well, in my case, it ain't so simple, Daddy-O. My struggle's been about trying to figure out who I am and what I want. And I don't want my goddamn mother, I can tell you right now. Any impulses I might have had as a baby are normal. What isn't normal is Doc trying to impose his super-ego on me.

"Truth is, I can't give a shit about my mother," I say. "All she cares about is her music. I think she's pathetic, a pushover, too passive. I hate how she lets others control her, especially men. More especially, me." *How's that for an answer?*

"Interesting. And, your father?"

I glare at Savage. *Have you not been listening—taking good notes?*

"Oh yes, he died." Savage recovers quickly. "You told me yesterday. I'm so sorry."

"What I said was that he was murdered. Died—murdered. I don't think it's the same thing."

Dr. Savage continues to scribble, and as if murder was something to be glossed over, no big deal, he adds, "You were an only child. No father, great responsibility, man of the house. You let your mother down."

"I had a stepfather, George. He's the one who let her down." Now, I'm really getting frosted. I inhale and feel something catching in my throat. Doc's voice wants to rear its ugly self up. I struggle to stifle it, choking as I blow smoke. I stub out my cigarette in the ashtray on Savage's desk and then grab the water he's poured for me. Wiping my mouth with the back of my fist, I stand to escape to the other side of the room.

"So, you had a stepfather?"

As Doc fights to make himself heard, I pull my hand over my mouth. *Tell him he's the one who wanted everything I had. He's the one who wanted to be me. To have my life. To have Phoebe. He was jealous of me.* I take a seat. Crossing one leg over the other, I reach into my pocket and pull out a pipe.

"I hadn't noticed you smoked a pipe," Savage says.

"On occasion. I picked this one up over at the exchange." I reach for my throat. My voice has lowered an octave. "Not much of a selection and they don't have my brand of Velvet tobacco. I see you've got Prince Albert in a can. That should do. Do you mind if I let him out?" I slap my leg, hooting out loud, wondering now if I'm also thinking out loud.

Savage laughs, too, as he offers me his tobacco. "And where is George now?"

"What? Yes, well." I fan the match. "Heaven only knows."

Savage jots down some more notes as I suck on my pipe, making my own mental note to go and find George once I bust out of this joint. I haven't seen him since I was twelve.

"I have some questions and when I find him, he'd better have some answers." I clamp my mouth and eyes shut. I can see George's image again. I can see Doc dying on the floor. I shake my head again and then I can feel George wallop me with his belt.

Dr. Savage is scribbling like a mad scientist as I get up to rub a phantom pain on my caboose. I sit back in my seat, bury my head in my lap and remain silent. Strange, but I do miss George. It all starts to make a little more sense. From the moment I came into this world, I've had this love-hate relationship with him. I've wanted to love him as a son should love a father, but the other part of me hates him for stepping in and taking my father's place. Just as I hate Doc for trying to take over my life, Doc must hate George for ending up with his life, with his wife, his house, and his kid.

I'm playing this all out in my head when I hear Dr. Savage. "I just want to help you. If you don't want to talk, I understand. You're frightened, but you need to trust me, Charley."

I set down the pipe and lift my head. *Oh, yeah? I can trust you like I trust every other adult in my life, like every other authority figure telling me what to do. I know the game I need to play with you—the same one I played with other doctors like you, teachers, truant officers, my commanding officer and Phoebe.* I turn to stare into Dr. Savage's beady eyes so that he might study my pupils to see they are neither dilated nor constricted; to see there is nothing wrong with me; to see I'm not crazy. But soon, I'm distracted by the seagull out on the windowsill.

"Depression is simply anger turned inside," Dr. Savage says.

And so, what is anger? Some innocuous fleeting emotion without merit?

"Says here you assaulted a shipmate. You are suicidal."

The bird cocks its head and looks at me. I smile. *What kind of bullshit have they told him? What else is in my file?*

"We'll take it slow," Dr. Savage says. "Perhaps tomorrow, you'll want to open up a little more. I'll have the orderly take you back to the ward."

And with that I turn to speak. I'm in no hurry to get back to the ward with the other infirmed guinea pigs. I definitely don't want to be given more medication.

"Suicide sounded like a good option," I blurt out, remembering how I thought everyone would be better off had I jumped off the Coronado Bay Bridge.

Dr. Savage perks up.

"But I couldn't go through with it. I'm not so fond of heights and the Bay Bridge is pretty damn high." I chuckle.

"Was that the only time you ever thought about it?"

"What? Jumping off a bridge?" I laugh nervously.

"Killing yourself?" Behind his glasses, Savage has narrowed his eyes.

I'm silent for a few moments as I remember just how many times I used to think about it—killing myself. Another time, I even thought about jumping off a bridge, the Colorado Street Bridge, but I got too dizzy and turned to see the blue lights of a cop car.

"Son, climb back over," the cop had said, before clamping on the handcuffs. I got hauled in not because I was suicidal, but because the car I parked on the side had been stolen. It had looked like Mother's Buick when I hotwired it.

Dr. Savage rests an elbow in one hand, placing his fist under his chin.

"You ever read that book 'Johnny Got His Gun'?" I ask.

He nods.

"Well, I'm like the character Joe who tries to suffocate himself but realizes he doesn't have control. I keep banging out a Morse code on my pillow with my head, but I'm cursed to live out my life in this condition."

"And what condition do you mean?" Savage asks.

"The one I'm in," I answer, knowing I'm being vague, but I'm not ready to tell him who controls my life.

"I see," Savage says, bowed down, jotting notes like crazy. He lifts his head and pushes back his glasses. "What about the assault?"

"I was only defending myself."

My legs are jittery as I stand and pace. I'm my own defense attorney. "I had to defend my mother's honor. You see, I'm not a son of a bitch. I'm not a bastard. I did have a father."

"So, words hurt you, Charley?"

"Not so much, but they can be heavy, man. They carry a lot of weight. They're strong enough to convey love and hate—two of the strongest emotions."

"Interesting. And speaking of love and hate, you mentioned you were defending your mother's honor, and yet you hate her?"

"Love has nothing to do with that," I say. "Words can move mountains, take down a nation. Make a person want to kill."

"I see," he says, scrambling to write it all down.

"Like mind control." I grin, staring at the top of his white head, waiting for him to look up, but he doesn't seem to get the obvious connection. "You see, I know what's going on here. I know where this is all leading. I've heard the others talk. We're all just lab rats for the government's big mind control experiment. The Russians are coming and you'd better get ready."

Savage looks up from his notes, obviously ignoring what I've just said, and smiles. "A love-hate relationship has been linked to the occurrence of emotional ambivalence in childhood. Were you close with your mother growing up?"

So, he's going to go fucking Freud on me after all. He peers back at me over the top of his glasses. *Too bad he can't see so well.*

"For God's sake, no. I told you. She was never there." Now I'm pissed. *What difference does it make about my relationship with my mother?*

"Hmm," he mumbles and I allow him all the time he needs to take more notes. Besides, I've already said too much. I walk to the window as he lifts the receiver to make a phone call. A seagull lands, frightening off the pigeons flapping outside on the ledge.

"Love-hate is also the result of poor self-esteem," he says.

Well, I'm not loving my time with Savage, that's for damn sure; as a matter of fact, I'm hating the grating sound of his voice. I hear the march of footsteps on the linoleum in the hallway. Thank God.

An orderly enters, and as the door slams behind him, the seagull takes off to fly across the bay to some subterranean world crowded with smoky bars, hip jazz clubs, and enlightened finger-snapping hepcats. *Oh, take me with you, Sammy.*

"For some reason, it keeps skipping," Dr. Savage says to the orderly, who adjusts the knobs before dropping to his knees to check the outlet.

He's still on his knees crawling around when I notice the pink bubble-gum stuck to the bottom of his shoe. I'm staring at the sole when all of a sudden the image of a man appears.

Jack Warrington, Doc's business partner, is marching toward me down a sidewalk in Glendale. I don't know whether to laugh or to cry when, in the middle of his stride, he turns to see the pink ligaments stretching from the bottom of his shoe. His face is red and seems burdened by the weight of his corrugated brow.

I shake the image of those angry eyes, but I can't shatter the vision of what happens afterward. I see a man's shoe where it's ended up near the gutter. The image of the pink bubblegum stuck to the heel sticks to me.

"Plug's loose, Sir," the orderly says.

Savage rubs the top of the machine as he dismisses the corpsman and turns to me. "You're laughing, Charley," he says with an encouraging smile. "What's so funny?"

"Just an old memory."

"Oh?"

"Yeah, I noticed the gum stuck on the bottom of the orderly's shoe and it reminded me of something. It's actually not very funny."

"So, would you mind sharing with me?" Dr. Savage asks as he proceeds to turn up the dial on the machine.

"Not really," I say. I'm not ready to tell him about the whole Jack Warrington fiasco. I'd speak up if not limited by events beyond my control.

And then slowly the space fills with the sounds of violins, cellos and violas from Opus 125, Beethoven's Ninth. My body tingles as the music washes over me and through me, sedating me, and by the time I hear the drums and cymbals crashing, the tears have come tumbling down.

Go on. Tell him! Doc screams inside my head. I put my hand over my mouth and clench my teeth together so his words can't come out, but over the flutes I can still hear his voice loud and clear.

About to go ape shit, I continue to clamp my jaw shut as I reach up to grab my head and bury it into my lap.

"Charley, what is it? What's wrong?" Dr. Savage asks, his voice even higher now.

"Just leave me alone, for chrissakes."

"Shall I have the orderly take you back?"

I can feel the voice rumble up in my throat, but I'm too weak to stuff it down. And then, Doc, the puppet master, pulls a string, lifting my head and opening my mouth. He speaks out in a voice so loud, I don't know what to do. "No. I'll talk. I know you don't want to hear this, Charley, but I need you to know all I've ever wanted to do was help."

I'm staring helplessly into Dr. Savage's eyes. "I'll speak, Savage," Doc says again, a little softer now, "but we'll start with when it was I first met Phoebe."

"Your mother?" Dr. Savage asks.

"No, my wife," Doc says, and I see my hand reaching for the pipe.

8
Phoebe Mae Comes to Town

1910: Hollywood—
Doc

Before Phoebe, I suppose the whole trouble began with my first-born, Leland. For months I'd been obsessed with finding a cure for him. My head spun with thoughts from the day. I'd let myself be so consumed I hadn't noticed my surroundings until the minute I heard the piano music pouring from our home.

Suddenly, my body no longer felt numb. The music lifted my spirits and when I looked up, I noticed the shades of pastel splashed across the sky. The buttery sun melted into the fragrant pepper trees that had once blocked my horizon. I could smell the fresh cut grass and the fragrance of the orange blossoms in bloom. I heard the starlings serenading each other in the citrus trees surrounding me. And, as I neared our home, the music grew louder and somewhere back in the cobwebs of my childhood, I remembered hearing the same tune.

The melody grew stronger as I crossed onto our property, a little Victorian house on a dusty acre of land. I left my shadow at the threshold where the wooden gate slammed after me, forcing me to leave the day behind. Carrying my leather case, I ambled up the walkway like a man twice my age and, as I neared the first step, the music grew louder. At that moment, I recalled we'd recently purchased a piano, but until then, I'd never heard it played.

Helen, our eight-year-old daughter, had shown an interest. A sweet, blonde girl, with a turned-up nose and a slight overbite, she was my princess. On nights I arrived home early, she would greet me with a strong hug and announce, "Daddy's home!" She would then curtsy, dance and swirl around me. So when she asked for a piano, how could I not get her one? Sadly, I never heard a single note played on this piano until that particular evening. I wondered what I might have missed. Helen has quite some talent, by golly.

Peeking in through the front window, the unforgettable spring evening would forever be suspended in time, like a hummingbird hovering over a flower.

There on the bench sat not Helen, but Leland, my bespectacled son, looking never so relaxed and sure of anything in his life until then. As a lanky boy, Leland stood taller than the boys in his class. With ears protruding slightly out of a shock of unruly, thick blond hair, his glasses had no trouble staying upon his head. Next to him, with perfect posture and her back to me, sat a young auburn-haired woman holding a magnifying glass over the music. Smiling, she turned in my direction, igniting a flame inside me. Certain neither had seen me through the window, I took a seat on the porch slider to listen further.

My heart weakened the more I heard; taking time to sit back and listen to music had become a luxury I had not afforded myself in quite some time. And now, to hear this very raw, simple piece, it soothed me in a way I'd not experienced in a very long time. Clean, unpolluted, solitary notes of music lifted me out of the cares of tomorrow and the pains of the past. Nothing else mattered except for the joy I felt. In that instant, the music connected me to my son in a way we had never been.

I loved my son the only way I knew how; the way I imagined my own father would love me had he not died of consumption before my first birthday. Leland and I used to hunt and fish; I'd passed on my Winchester '86 I had as a boy. I used to help him with math and science projects in school; granted, I did most of the work. Still, those were only some of the things we used to do together. He and I used to have a bond.

As Leland's vision grew worse, I'd spent more time away from home and at work looking for an answer. As an optometrist after all, how could I not help my son? I didn't know Stella had allowed him to stay home with her from time to time. Had I known, I wouldn't have permitted it. Leland should have been at school doing his best to learn reading, writing and arithmetic. Even though he was whip smart, how else would he survive this world without that knowledge? I rejected any notion that Leland was not like other young children.

Together, he and Stella would listen to the Victrola. Eventually, Leland spent more time inside with his mother, isolated from his peers and playmates.

Before I stood from the porch slider to go inside, I removed my glasses and wiped my eyes. Stella met me when I entered the foyer and relieved me of my briefcase as I replaced my glasses.

"Softy," she said, poking my midsection. She appeared riveted, more alive—not the same stoic woman I had grown used to. She practically jumped out of her shoes.

"It doesn't appear he's going to be following in your footsteps after all, now does it, Doc? Seems he's got my ear for music." Stella loved music but never had an ear for it except to be entertained. She could not carry a tune in a basket much less on a piano. The only thing she could play was the Victrola.

Leland saw me standing in the foyer and stopped playing. I wanted to tell him to continue, to go on forever and never stop, but then Phoebe stood and I lost my voice. I inhaled for some sort of reinforcement.

"Doc, this is Miss Armstrong," Stella said. "She is Charlotte's grand-daughter. You know, Frank Milspaugh's folk from back home."

I smelled gardenias before she even shook my hand. Phoebe stood perhaps six inches shorter than I. Without raising her head, she looked up at me to make my acquaintance. Her eyes were green as clover. Her handshake, firm and sure; soft as cool rose petals.

"Good to meet you, Dr. Marnier," she said, in her fluttery, silky voice. Immediately confounded, I attributed it to the music that seemed to have left me vulnerable and exposed. I looked out the window to avoid the eyes that already seemed to know more about me than I did. I could swear all of the planets had aligned and sparks had rained down from the stars crossing over me. I immediately lost control of my faculties. My heart began to beat so loudly, I thought surely everyone heard it. This sensation unnerved me. Never in my life had another human being affected me in this way. I prided myself as a man of great restraint. My hand was so damp, hers slipped from mine.

"My p-pleasure," I stuttered finally, clearing my throat, taking a moment to regain control. "The Milspaughs were good friends back in Iowa," I said, turning to Leland. "Son, I am impressed."

"He's actually quite a natural, Dr. Marnier." Phoebe placed her hands on Leland's shoulders. "He wanted to surprise you."

Indeed surprised, I gasped and then coughed uncontrollably.

"Can I get you some water?" she offered.

I shook my head, but Stella scurried out to get me a glass anyway.

I met Stella back in the foyer and after I stopped choking, she whispered, "Helen is also doing quite well, but Miss Armstrong seems to believe Leland is quite gifted. She says she has never had a pupil take to music as quickly as he has, especially at this age. She says we should have gotten him started much sooner, but assures me he will be up to speed in no time."

Stella handed me an etched crystal glass. "What is this?"

"This calls for a celebration."

Except for when she'd been high on her medications, I'd not seen Stella this giddy in quite a long time, and accepted the drink she poured for me. As evidenced by her rapid, squeaky way of talking, she'd already helped herself. Stella always found occasion to take a drink; no matter Hollywood was a dry town with a nation entering a period of alcohol prohibition. But this one particular spring evening was a joyous one, truly filled with cause for celebration. I would not let her drinking bother me this one night.

I looked back into the parlor where Leland had resumed his playing. *When? How did this happen?* It seemed as if he'd been born to play the piano. I listened to the beautiful music my son made and stifled the tears threatening to flow once more. Something else welled up inside of me though, not just tears. The man I used to be had become a stranger to me and the stranger seated next to Leland appeared to be quite a vision indeed.

To think we had waited all these years to make this discovery about Leland. The piano had been delivered for Helen, who now sat on the davenport awaiting her turn. Usually bouncing around, she sat as mesmerized as I, quietly twirling her blonde pony tails which she had plaited herself that morning with red ribbons to match her dress. She'd just learned to braid her own hair and was quite proud. Her long bangs cascaded over her blue eyes, but this didn't seem to bother her. How she could see anything, much less read music, baffled me. But, apparently, Leland had been the one to rush home from school to seat himself at the piano. Again, I wouldn't know because I rarely came home early enough. I certainly didn't mind the separation from Stella, whose mood swings had me coming and going. Her melancholia was an albatross hanging around my neck, threatening to pull me further into the depths of despair. I needed to stay away just to keep strong, just to stay afloat, just to survive.

But today she seemed buoyant and high-spirited, as ebullient as champagne bubbles. She topped off her glass. "Oh, Doc, this makes me so happy. I think this will make all the difference with Leland. And Phoebe is a dear. She is the sweetest thing. Leland seems to have taken to her like nothing I've ever seen. I hope you don't mind, I've asked her to stay for supper."

Except for the new space added next to Helen, we took our usual places at the dinner table. Stella had sliced tomatoes and cucumbers she and Helen had brought in from the garden. Tonight was Helen's turn to say grace, but Leland volunteered and Helen yielded. I looked at Stella dumbfounded. This was a first for Leland and one of the first times Helen did not raise Cain. Stella clapped her hands together to say grace. I bowed my head until Leland had finished the blessing. When I looked up, my glasses slipped, and as I pushed them back I saw, over folded hands, Phoebe gazing my way. I nearly dropped the dish Stella had passed me.

"Leland, you seem to enjoy the p-p-piano." I sounded like a ridiculous schoolboy.

Leland did not respond. Clearly smitten, he stared at Phoebe.

"Leland, your father is speaking to you," Stella said.

"Yes, Father," he said, but couldn't take his eyes off his new piano teacher.

"And Miss Armstrong, what piece was he playing as I entered the room?" I stood to carve the roast Stella had reheated from Sunday's dinner and continued, "I know it."

"Why, that was Beethoven's *Jesu Mans Desire* or *Ode to Joy,*" Phoebe replied sweetly. I noticed the way her lips parted, pursed and perked when she pronounced the word *'Jesu.'*

"I don't know if it was because Leland played it or if it was just the composition, but it was so moving," Stella said.

"Indeed, it nearly moved me to tears," I added.

"Music is a constant and the reason humans have such a strong visceral connection to it. *Jesu*—" Phoebe said the word again, practically hypnotizing me, "is one of those songs that can take one back instantly to a moment, a place, or even a person. I'll bet you can remember where you were, what you were doing the time you first heard the song. No matter what else has changed in you or the world, that one song remains the same, just like that moment."

I thought about how I'd always remember this brief period, but instead, I said, "My mother used to play it."

"Someday, I will play the entire Ninth Symphony," Leland said, gazing toward Phoebe. He scrunched his nose up like a miniature accordion in an effort to push his glasses up in place, before using his index finger to get the job done.

Phoebe smiled. "Not everyone realizes Beethoven was deaf when he composed this last symphony," Phoebe said, picking up her knife and proceeding to cut her roast into small portions. She took tiny delicate bites, chewing slowly, closing her eyes, savoring every morsel.

"Stella, the vegetables are quite flavorful this year," I said, and Stella glowered at me as if I'd grown a third eye. I didn't usually eat vegetables.

"I grew those in the garden, Daddy!" Helen squealed and then blew the bangs out of her face, leaving her hands free to use her utensils properly.

Not that Stella or I ever raised our voices in front of the children, nor were they unruly, but there'd be no friction tonight at the table, no undercurrent of discontent, and the children had rediscovered their manners. What we were having was a conversation. Everyone seemed cheerful. Phoebe had become the salt and spice adding flavor to our meal.

"Miss Armstrong, you said 'last'? Beethoven's last?" I asked.

Phoebe set down her fork and looked me straight on. "Why, yes. He died before completing his tenth. You see, there is this notion—the curse of the ninth—"

"Yes, I have heard of that," Stella said.

"Well, it's only a superstition connected with the history of classical music," Phoebe said. I could only focus on the sound of her sweet voice and her quiet humble laugh—all just part of her musical charm, the low lilting minors, natural, melodic and harmonic, having to do with dusk and gardens and starlight.

Then, sounding like a dissonant note from an out-of-tune piano, Stella spoke up. "Oh, yes. We just read a story about how Mahler had hoped to escape the *curse of the ninth* and avoided numbering *The Song of the Earth*. Leland and I love his music."

"Mother told me he died," Leland said, as if he was proud to be able to participate in such an adult conversation.

"What? Who died?" I asked, shaking my head. As a Mason and a person with certain moral integrity, I found myself struggling to push back any impure thoughts about the new piano teacher. But I was also a man, for God's sake, and the purest thought a man can have is to make love to a woman and to propagate the world. Conquer the weak. Just like an animal, a man has certain primal urges. What could be more natural?

Phoebe smiled at me and then winked at Leland, who seemed to be sitting a little taller in his chair.

"To those who give credence to the notion, a composer who produces a ninth symphony has reached a decisive landmark and to then embark on a tenth is a challenge to 'fate'. I know it may very well be a silly superstition—"

"And there are those who believe in Santa Claus and the Easter Bunny," I added, immediately sorry I'd interrupted Phoebe.

"I believe in Santa Claus, Daddy," Helen shouted. "And the Easter Bunny. And this Christmas I'm asking for new skates, like Skinny Suzy's."

"Her skates must be pretty special," Phoebe said.

"They are. You can go to places that are only in your dreams."

"Like a magic carpet ride," Phoebe added, and Helen beamed.

"Well, this *Curse of the Ninth Symphony* sounds a little outlandish," I said.

"Some people believe it to be true, not only for the composer," Phoebe said, picking up her fork and piercing into a tomato slice, "but for those with whom he becomes romantically involved."

"I suppose the safest thing would be not to become involved with a musician," I said.

"Curses only have power if you believe in them," she said, smiling, and I knew I'd fall if I let go of the reins of my emotions.

9
Orange-Tinted Cheaters

1910: Hollywood—
Doc

The following week, the glow of the setting sun streamed in through the window, lighting up the parlor room. I found myself seated on the porch swing half an hour earlier listening to Leland play the piano, but also sneaking a peek at Phoebe.

When the lesson ended, I entered the room. "Oh, Dr. Marnier," Phoebe said, "May I have a moment of your time?" I was prepared to give her all the time she needed, and if I needed to borrow some, I'd go out and purchase more. I hadn't stopped thinking about her the whole week.

"Excellent job, son. Now run along to help your mother."

Leland scrunched his nose, taking his time shuffling out of the room as I took a seat in my leather-upholstered chair and crossed my legs. Phoebe sat on the davenport across from me, folding her dainty porcelain hands. I noticed the pearly white curvature of her nails. Twilight had arrived and everything in the room had darkened except for Phoebe, who stood out like an afterglow—like a green flash after sunset. In one's lifetime, not everyone is privileged enough to witness one, but suddenly I had.

Basking in her glow, I lost myself in her eyes when she spoke. "I've asked Leland to remove his dark glasses when he's playing, but he says the light bothers him and that's why he wears them, even in the house."

"True. He has a dis . . ." I wasn't ready to admit my son had a disease. "I fitted Leland with the orange-tinted lenses to block out the light's harmful rays."

"The design is remarkable."

"Thank you. It was Leland's idea. I fashioned the temples to look like twin Winchester rifles. He used to go hunting with me."

Phoebe laughed, nodding her head. "Yes, I see. I think that's quite clever."

"I commissioned one of my brothers from the lodge to help me," I said. "Henry Eastman owns an injection molding company out in Commerce and together we were able to create a mold into which was melted a celluloid material that hardened into an almost glass-like substance. The advantage being, it's more durable than glass."

"Extraordinary!"

"Forgive me for boring you."

"No, no. Please go on."

"Soon even some of Leland's playmates asked how they might get a pair," I said.

"That is so impressive," she said. "Pardon me for asking, Dr. Marnier, and stop me if I'm getting too personal, but what is wrong with Leland's vision?"

I hesitated. I hadn't been prepared to open up about this, but cleared my throat. "Leland has Stargardt's disease," I said, trusting I could tell her more.

"Stella and I tried everything with Leland. Even took him up to Krotona to see some snake oil quack. Dr. Horatio Bates promised to restore eyesight naturally, without surgery or glasses. Of course it didn't work, but at least she had some short-term hope. Unlike most boys his age, he could always be found on the run. He was a wind up toy just spinning all over the place, expending enough energy to light up a whole city. But sometimes his movements were slow and calculated. Like moving a rook or a pawn on a chessboard, he needed to contemplate his next move before he budged. He was never good in sports or, shall I say interested in sports—something at which I was quite gifted—so I wasn't overly concerned about Leland's poor hand-eye coordination. I reckoned this was something carried over from Stella's side of the family," I said with a chuckle, and Phoebe smiled, too. "But by the time he turned seven, the problems he caused in school had become intolerable—unable to focus on things he enjoyed such as marbles and hoops, even hunting with me up in the canyons. When he ventured outside, Leland strained as he adjusted to the light. Inside, he also found it difficult to read, complaining of gray, black or hazy spots in the center of his eyes. I grew increasingly alarmed, for I'd recognized this condition only in my older patients. The disease, we in the medical world termed 'senile degeneration.'"

Phoebe's eyes were fixed upon me, her breathing slow, her hands folded daintily upon her lap. The way she listened was more eloquent than speech. Phoebe seemed genuinely interested and I found myself quite comfortable talking to her, so I couldn't help but carry on. I'd long ago stopped talking this way to Stella, who had trouble keeping her eyes open when I tried to explain things to her.

"A couple of years ago, the worst of my fears manifested itself when a new report came out of Berlin by an ophthalmologist named Karl Stargardt. He had discovered a new type of juvenile macular degeneration causing progressive vision loss to the point of blindness, sometimes beginning around the age of six." I stood and walked to the window.

"You mean Leland is going blind?" she asked.

I turned away from the window and went to switch on the reading lamp on the end table. I needed to look into the face that seemed to comfort me and draw me out of the darkness.

"When I first heard the news, I prayed the illness wasn't what afflicted my own son, but when Leland was ultimately diagnosed with Stargardt's disease, I fell into a short-lived, deep melancholy and then ultimately refused to accept the truth. This could not happen to my son. As I did with most matters out of my control, I strove to take control. Part of the reason for my long hours at work is I've been poring through medical books and journals and different studies trying to find a solution for a disease without a cure. In the process, I stumbled upon a unique manner in which to block certain types of light waves. I found when light bounces off a surface, its waves tend to be strongest in a particular direction . . . usually horizontally, vertically, or diagonally," I paused. "I'm sorry. I must be boring you."

"No, please. I find it fascinating. I always wanted to be a nurse."

"Very well. You see, sunlight bouncing off a surface like water or high levels of ultra violet light from the cameras will usually reflect horizontally, striking the viewer's eyes intensely and creating glare. I laminated the material with tiny vertical stripes allowing vertically angled light to enter the wearer's eyes, thereby eliminating glare because the horizontal light waves cannot bypass the vertical filter. The new lenses will help Leland for now. I have vowed to devote the rest of my life to finding a cure. But, in the meanwhile, Leland will wear the orange-tinted sunglasses, even in the house."

"Absolutely, Dr. Marnier." She smiled and hesitated. "That lamp is pretty bright. Would it be possible for me to get a pair?"

10

The Worms Crawl In . . .

1949: US Naval Hospital—
Charley

Seated behind his desk, Dr. Savage has removed his glasses and rubs his eyes. Smoothing back imaginary hair, he focuses on me.

"So, Charley, this is an interesting story about your father, but so far, I don't see where this is going. He had another family before you?"

"Yes," I answer.

"Are you suggesting Phoebe tore the family apart?"

"Absolutely not," Doc says, imposing his voice and correcting Savage. He laughs. "She was just what you might say what the doctor ordered. Everyone loved her. Stella adored her. We couldn't wait to see her at the end of the day."

1910: Hollywood—
Doc

We were all seated in the parlor one evening after the children's piano lessons. I'd made it a point to get home to have dinner with the family especially on the days Phoebe came to give the children lessons. Stella insisted she stay for dinner. On some evenings, Stella had gone so far as to invite some of the ladies from church whose sons might be potential suitors. She enjoyed having company. Phoebe happened to be well-educated and well-traveled and one with whom anyone might easily have a conversation. We loved the stories of her journeys to Europe and India.

"Oh dear, I cannot imagine," Stella said. "Traveling alone with those Indian natives. I'd be frightened half to death of tomahawks and arrows flying!"

"India—the place next to China," I said to Stella as I walked over to the hutch to pour some sherry before dinner. Noticing Stella's glass already full of something, I turned instead to offer Phoebe a glass.

"Why India, Ms. Armstrong?" Stella asked.

"I went to deepen my study of esoterism," she replied as I handed her a glass.

I nodded skeptically, being somewhat familiar with the theosophical teachings in freemasonry. I knew it had something to do with promoting the unity of humanity by encouraging the study of religion, philosophy and science. As I mentioned before, I wasn't a religious man, and as far as my philosophy went, I viewed things as either black or white. I was however a man of science, so the idea of bringing all of these ideas together as one and the same would be a hard pill for me to swallow.

There was a knock at the door.

"Ah, that must be George," Stella said. "He phoned earlier looking for you, Wesley. He said he had some good news. I invited him over for dinner."

Stella tilted her head toward me and motioned with her eyes over to Phoebe, who watched as Helen ran to the front door. After a bit, Helen skipped in with a sucker in her mouth. George trailed behind carrying a bag and a bouquet of flowers he handed to Stella. He gave Leland a lollipop. Despite everything, George did have a few wonderful qualities, one of them being the way he interacted with my children, treating them as if they were his own. He froze when he saw Phoebe and then reached out to take her hand.

"Haven't we met before?"

"Oh dear, George, if that isn't the oldest line in the book," I said.

"I don't think so," Phoebe said.

"I'm almost certain we—" George swallowed. "I would never forget a face like yours."

"George, this is Miss Phoebe Mae Armstrong," Stella said, holding up her glass. "Pour yourself a drink, and freshen mine, if you will."

George pulled a bottle of wine out of the bag and set it down.

"So, George, Stella tells me you called earlier. You have something on your mind?"

"That's right," he said without taking his eyes off Phoebe. "Very important. Yes, very exciting news." He then turned to look at me. "I stopped into the office, but you'd already left for the day." He guzzled his drink and poured himself another.

Stella raised her glass. "Don't mind if I do. We are celebrating some good news, after all," she said. "Isn't that right, George?"

And then as if he saw something swimming at the bottom of his glass, George wagged a finger and nearly choked when he said, "That's it. Now, I know where I've seen you. Over at Blondeau's Tavern."

"You're right," Phoebe said.

"A couple of the fellows and I used to stop in after a lodge meeting. You remember, Doc. Anyway, that's where I saw you, but you were always too busy to even say hello."

"The last time I was at the tavern," I said, "was when I signed the deal for the property bordering Blondeau's."

"That's when you were going to be a citrus farmer," Stella said with a snide laugh. "You and your big ideas."

"A farmer?" Phoebe asked, perking up.

"Sure, everyone from Iowa comes out here wanting to be a farmer," George said. "Not me."

I was reminded of the time back in Iowa when I used to dream about the girl in the cartoon advertisement in the window on Main Street, a young Miss Southern California beauty giving an orange to a farmer. 'Oranges for health, California for wealth!' That was the propaganda that lured me here across the Rockies years ago.

"My dream of being a farmer was cut short for lack of water, among other things, beside the fact Hollywood was literally a dry town," I said.

George lifted his glass in a salute. "I, too, hail from Iowa. Left Des Moines a couple of years ago, and came west to buy up real estate."

"Trouble with that is one needs money to buy anything, right, George?" Stella said with a bit of sarcasm.

I remembered the day George walked into my office holding the newspaper ad I'd placed looking for an assistant. He told me he was the man I'd been looking for. He knew nothing about optometry. I, nevertheless, became immediately impressed by his confidence and thought I'd be able to use him in other business matters. I'd learn later George "Gamboni" was the man the authorities and others had been looking for back in Chicago. But in the meanwhile, he ended up working for me, not as my optometry assistant, but as my right-hand man. I gave him the room above the optometry office.

"So now George is helping him become a big real estate tycoon," Stella said, mockingly.

"But, you're already a successful eye doctor," Phoebe said, smiling.

"An eye doctor who can't help his own son," Stella added, pouring herself another drink. I wanted to explode. Her lower jaw jutted out when she spoke. And there we had it. She'd made it to the whining stage of her drinking where we no longer saw her upper teeth, as if they'd retired for the evening, and we hadn't even sat down to dinner. We were either in for a very long night or a short one, depending on how much Stella already had to drink during the day.

I tried to calm myself. "So, Phoebe, you worked at Blondeau's?" I asked, unable to picture someone so refined working in a tavern.

"Oh, yes, that's where I met Mrs.—"

Stella had slowed a bit but reacted quick enough to interrupt Phoebe. "Phoebe was telling us about her travels," she said, standing and then staggering into the dining room. "It's time for dinner. Everyone must be starved."

We took our places at the table.

"Tell us more about China, Phoebe, I might consider going there someday," Stella said, returning to the table.

"I've never been to China, Mrs. Marnier."

"Stella, she was talking about India," I said.

"Oh, I'd never go to India," Stella responded, slapping her hand down on the table. "Frightening place. Too many natives."

"I was in good company and never afraid. I stayed with a family friend, Marie Hotchener. She was my tutor up at Mills College. She mothered me, especially after my own mother passed away."

"Oh, you poor dear! When did your mother die?"

"Only a couple of years ago."

"How sad."

"Oh, she had a very good life on earth. She told me not to fret," Phoebe said, casually brushing Helen's bangs off her brow. "She told me she'd found happiness in the Higher World and not to sorrow, but instead to bring joy to my father and the rest of the world."

Stella's mouth gaped open, but then she took a swallow of her drink.

"Hold your horses," George said. "She spoke to you—after she died?"

Phoebe nodded, reaching for her glass and taking a sip.

"So, you speak to the dead?" Stella asked, eyes widening.

"Not anymore."

Stella nodded and turned to me, giving me a sloppy grin, and I knew what she thought. She'd been nattering lately about going to a fortuneteller. I told her it was against her religion.

"I'm sad. Floppy died," Helen said suddenly, her lower lip quivering over the top one. We'd told Helen her bunny had gotten lost up in the hills and that perhaps he'd find his way home one day. For the longest time, she'd leave a carrot on the back porch just in case he might return hungry. That was until Leland found the carcass out in the orchard. Floppy had died in the jaws of a coyote.

"I'm sorry, sweetie," Phoebe said.

"*The worms crawl in, the worms crawl out . . .*"

"Leland, you may be excused," I said.

"Oh, Doc. Leave him alone." Stella glared at me. "Leland, help Helen clear the table."

When both children had gone into the kitchen, Stella placed the edge of her index finger at the corner of her mouth. "Death isn't something Doc likes to discuss. As a matter of fact, he is uneasy in the presence of emotions. You'll find him laughing off the rough edges, smoothing out any friction, erasing the ugly, the abysmal—death. I, however, am quite fascinated with the subject."

"It's because you're morbid, Stella," George said, winking at her.

"And you're a shallow grave," Stella said with a wicked cackle, holding up her glass. George walked over to pour her some more wine. "My father died ten years ago, I shudder to think what I'd do if he ever talked to me now," Stella said.

I, too, quaked at the thought of how she would react. Stella had already found ways to cope with life's minor stirrings, none too gracefully.

I watched as the liquid dribbled down her chin. "Phoebe, you don't suppose you could contact my father for me?" Stella said, swiping her lips with a napkin. "I miss him so. He was the one who believed in me, told me I might have been a great musician. But then I went and married Wesley and my life was changed forever." She stared at me, prepared to lunge should something spill out of my lips.

"Stella," I said, reaching across to squeeze her hand. "That's enough. Phoebe doesn't need to hear about how I ruined your life." I chuckled, sliding her glass away.

Phoebe didn't need to listen to how I took Stella away from her home—from her daddy. She didn't need to hear how I should have been more like her father, the town's most successful man. She didn't need to hear how I worked so much, how tough I'd been on Leland. And worst of all, she didn't need to hear how as an optometrist I couldn't cure him of his eye affliction. Some days, I wish I'd never returned to Iowa after I'd gotten out of the Army. I should have just kept going forward with my life. But I'd made a promise to Stella and returned to marry her. And she would continue to blame me—the reason she drank.

"Yes," George added, as if trying to calm the seas of domesticity—never mind he'd never been in a relationship longer than the life of a mayfly. "And, I'm uneasy listening to your squabbles, to when things go kaput, and then your wars against each other."

Poppycock. George lied. He fed off stage productions. And Stella was right, I felt forever on edge around her, constantly trying to quell any possibility of a drama. Now, this scene simply mortified me. Phoebe stood and asked to take my plate.

"No, no. Miss Armstrong, you are our guest," Stella said. "Please stay seated. Helen made a rhubarb pie." Stella bolted up, nearly tripping as she wobbled into the kitchen.

"Pie-eyed again," George said, chuckling.

I noticed the concern in Phoebe's wide-eyed face. George cleared his throat and changed the subject. "So, Phoebe, how did you end up here? Everyone who ends up in Hollywood has a story."

Phoebe straightened up and smiled. "I find people are more open . . . more like-minded."

"Say, Phoebe," Stella said as she staggered across the dining room. "Why don't I arrange a séance? Oh, I'd love to hear from Daddy."

George encouraged Stella. "Yes, and maybe we could call forth Jesus and George Washington, and—"

"I'm sorry," Phoebe said. "That's not really something I do. It can be quite dangerous and there are consequences. Some say it's a gift. I say it's a curse."

Thankfully, George changed the subject, reeling us back. "So, Phoebe, finish your story about coming to Hollywood."

"I also wanted to make my own way, to earn my own money, so I took a job over at Blondeau's Tavern," she said, smiling as Stella returned from the kitchen holding a pie. "That's where I met Mrs. Marnier."

Stella dropped the pie onto the table.

"Too hot?" Phoebe said. "Are you sure I can't help you, Mrs. Marnier?"

"So, Blondeau's Tavern?" I asked. "Stella, you never told me you'd been into Blondeau's. Is that any place for a woman?"

"Oh, every once in a while . . . they have good coffee," she said, hiccupping.

Good coffee, my foot. They didn't call Blondeau's "Blind Eyes" for nothing.

The ban of liquor had eaten into the profits of many eating establishments, including Blondeau's, but Mrs. Blondeau had become good at looking the other way, and no doubt Stella had been a good customer.

"Miss Armstrong used to manage the nickelodeon in the back room," Stella replied, piercing the middle of the pie, sending a tendril of steam to the ceiling.

"And then before I knew it, I was hired to manage the nickelodeon down at their tavern afternoons and weekends," Phoebe continued. "But when it comes to business, I'm not very good. I'm adequate with numbers, but when it comes to dealing with people, I'm quite shy."

"You certainly could have fooled me," George said, slicing into his pie. "You don't give yourself enough credit, Miss Armstrong."

"So, finally, I gave it a try. In the late afternoons when all was quiet, I worked with the exhibitors to set up the chairs, the projector, and the screen. I worked as cashier, something I learned to enjoy actually, until the time came for me to take my place at the piano."

Phoebe looked nervous as Stella attacked the pie with the knife. "Are you sure I can't help you, Mrs. Marnier?"

Stella shook her head. "Go on with your story."

"I'd see the sad faces on some of the women whose husbands were at work and children were at school. It made me grateful I hadn't chosen the path my parents had hoped for me."

Stella turned and put down the knife. "You make marriage sound like a jail sentence, Miss Armstrong," she said, wiping her hands.

"No. Absolutely not. My parents were married twenty-three years. They were the happiest couple I've ever known. Who wouldn't want that? Please forgive me for speaking so insensitively."

"Sad women?" George said. "I'm sure I could have cheered them up."

"Either that or scared them off," Stella said, voice cackling.

"But then with the ban on alcohol, they had to shut the tavern down and I lost my job. I learned a lot. But now I teach piano to get by. Anyway, I think I'm better suited to teaching."

"Yes, you are, Phoebe. I was so sorry when they shut down the place," Stella said.

"Yes, it saddened me when they forced Mrs. Blondeau to close. It's a shame it has to sit there empty," Phoebe said.

"Or does it?" George said, standing suddenly and clapping his hands. "By golly, Doc. That's why I'm here. I have an excellent idea."

Oh, but of course. Leave it to George to be scheming and putting together the next deal. With his rather big, oval-shaped head, necessary, as he put it, to house his larger-than-average brain, he always had excellent ideas—hare-brained ideas were more like it.

"That's the reason I called you. This afternoon, a gentleman from New York stopped by the office looking to rent space to make motion pictures. I thought about your properties, but this might be the answer. We just need to talk to Mrs. Blondeau."

"All right, gentlemen," Stella said, "it's time to take your cigars and your business into the parlor. I'd like to spend some more time with Phoebe."

As George and I left the room, I heard a glass being filled as Stella said, "Now, Phoebe, do tell me more about this *curse* you possess."

11

Picture Worth a Thousand Words

Sometime later, a journalist from the *Los Angeles Times* came out to do a story on me and my special sunglass designs. The reporter also wanted a picture of me. George suggested it be taken in front of the optometry shop. "Let the folks back home see how far you've come, aye, Doc?" George said.

Indeed, things were progressing quite rapidly, especially in the movie industry. It would be said that Hollywood was a bear in hibernation, awakened with a roar, hungry and anxious to stretch its sinewy limbs to the limits. And, as my optometry practice also grew, I added an optical store to showcase some of my newest designs. Using my credentials, George posed as a real estate broker to negotiate a deal between the movie people and the Blondeaus. Now my patients, including movie stars who complained about their red eyes caused by the studio lighting, flocked toward me like blind moths toward bright porch lights. And, with his quicksand personality, George sucked people in. I let him keep the small finder's fee and the commission. He suggested I build bungalows, hotels and markets on my property adjacent the movie studios. He'd help me manage and take care of the financial dealings. He acted as my representative, standing in for me where I couldn't. I even trusted him enough to sign for me when necessary. He'd shown me his handiwork one day. "Pretty good, even I can't tell," I'd said.

"Come on, Pal. This wouldn't be happening without your marketing and business sense," I said. "Get in the picture with me. Let's have us a big smile."

George shied away, a contrary behavior for him. "Come on. This will get you discovered." Finally, he let his ego get the best of him and acquiesced.

The article came out the next day and news about my designs spread across the country. I received more design requests and more people made appointments for fittings. Business was good, but still I hadn't been able to find a cure for Leland and, because I'd never be able to cure my son, within a few years I would lose interest. I would drop the ball only to have Sam Foster run with the technology all the way to the copyright office where he would patent the first pair of polarized lenses. He would get credit for something I'd worked on so hard.

I arrived home one evening and noticed Phoebe wearing Leland's sunglasses. She turned to face me. "You'd think the bright lights would make all the difference," she said, tapping the frames softly, "but with these glasses, I can actually see the notes even more clearly. What a difference, and I tried them on outside as well. The clarity is astounding. Please, I must have a pair," she said, enthusiastically.

"Of course," I said, as Helen sprinted up to hug me.

"Daddy, listen to my new song," she said, and I took a seat in my leather chair. Helen's eyes sparkled when she looked over at Phoebe, as if Phoebe held some sort of magic fairy dust.

Indeed, Phoebe delighted us all and, in no time, everyone in the family had taken to her. She turned out to be a breath of fresh air in a home stale with melancholy. She brought in a new climate in a natural setting, much like the motif of Beethoven's Sixth Symphony, wherein we were shrouded in pleasure. I'd learn to find my equilibrium in the heart of nature, in the essence of this young woman, a songbird who floated lyrically into our lives.

And then I cringed as Helen played the first few notes. No magic potion could help my poor little princess play the piano.

"Bravo," I cheered with a clap, but wanted to cover my ears.

"But Daddy," Helen said, "it's not over."

"Oh, sorry," I said, crossing my legs and extracting my pipe from my vest pocket. Even as busy as I'd been at work, my mind toiled with thoughts of Phoebe. She'd been coming around our home more often, not just to give piano lessons. She and Stella had become good friends and Stella relished the company while I worked. It turned into a happy time. Life at home seemed a lot better, and at five o'clock, I'd grab my coat and hat, eager to head home. Undeniably, things were so much better after Phoebe came into our lives. She was the sun and we were the planets orbiting around her. Our world turned dark when she left to go home at night.

Helen had pushed away from the piano, finished finally.

"*Bravissimo!*" I shouted and stood. "Encore!"

"That's all there is, Daddy," she said with a bow.

Phoebe finished clapping and grabbed her coat.

"You're not staying for dinner?" I asked.

"Oh, no, thank you. I have a dinner engagement," she said.

I felt a slight stabbing near the heart. Was this jealousy, love's evil twin?

Anxiously, I awaited as the rising sun sent her back to us the next day.

In a town set on prohibition, Phoebe was just too intoxicating to turn away in my mind. I made love to Stella that night imagining her to be Phoebe; imagining Phoebe to be my possession. Nine months later, Stella delivered a healthy baby boy and was never the same.

Phoebe had been a great help to Stella during her time of need and had eventually moved in to help with the children. I'd never seen Stella so melancholy and yet I filled with joy just knowing Phoebe was around.

One evening, I walked in just as Leland and Phoebe were finishing with a lesson.

"Doc, can I speak to you for a moment?" she asked.

Leland left the room and I saw the tears in her eyes. "I'm really concerned about Stella. I hate to see her this way. Doc, I can't help her." I took a seat on the piano bench and wrapped my arms around her, close enough to feel her heartbeat. "The children need their mother."

"She was like this after the birth of Leland. It got so bad she needed to be hospitalized. I'm afraid that might be the only answer."

I heard a noise in the hallway. "Leland, is that you?" I stepped out to see Leland and Helen climbing the stairs. They'd been listening.

Phoebe pulled away and stood. "Just let me know what else I can do to help."

Just before eight a.m., I sat in my office between patients when I thought I heard someone climbing the back stairs to George's room. I hurried out to see the blood on the staircase leading to his room. I pounded on his door. "George, it's me."

He opened the door holding a bloodied washcloth to his face. He had a fat lip and a gash on the side of his eye.

"What happened?" Shocked, but not surprised, this wasn't the first time I'd seen George a little messed up. Blood puddled on the floor where he stood. This all looked more than just a little messed up.

"I've been discovered or rather uncovered."

"What are you talking about? What happened to your face?"

"You should see my ribs," he said, attempting to break a smile.

"George, what sort of debacle are you in the middle of now? Who did this?" My mind immediately went to a bad place filled with crooks, prostitutes and bootleggers.

He shook his head.

"George!" Not in the mood for guessing games, I wanted to slap him myself.

"Well, you see, Doc. If I might explain. I've kind of been on the run since I left home back in Chicago."

"I thought you were from Des Moines, full of prospects," I said, moving his hand away from his face to get a closer look at his injuries.

"I was there for a while, but my prospects added up to zero. I headed west," George said, wincing as I dabbed away some blood. "Unfortunately, I can't swim, so this is about as far west as I can go. Sorry, Doc. I'll get out of your hair, just as soon as I pull together enough cash to pay them back and then take a bus home."

"So, this is where they found you. Above my office?" My heart raced. I didn't need this element around my business or my home—or my family.

"I told you I didn't want my picture taken."

"What did you do, George?"

"There's a good explanation, really—all just a misunderstanding. The signer had made a mistake so I changed the number on the check."

"How much do you owe?"

"Five hundred," he said, covering his face with the washcloth.

"Dollars?" I asked, thinking the amount seemed astronomical, but somehow I felt responsible. More importantly, I needed to protect my family. "God damn it, George. I'll see what I can do to fix this. We can probably use some of the properties as collateral. I'll have the money for you by tomorrow. I hope that's all."

Ear-splitting wails assaulted my ears the instant I stepped off the streetcar in front of the house. The baby cried so loud, it drowned out Leland's piano playing in the parlor. I ascended the stairs, stepping over Helen's book bag, and walked into the bedroom to find Stella in bed passed out, still wearing her nightgown. My stomach lurched when I noticed the bottle of morphine on the nightstand.

She drooled spittle onto her pillow. Helen sat in the rocking chair holding baby Karl.

"Shh! Mama's sleeping," she said.

"Where's Phoebe?" I asked.

"She's gone."

Our world fell apart.

12

Look Who's Talking

1949: US Naval Hospital—
Charley

Savage peers at me, too sucked in to have the talking stop, chin resting on his fist, elbow on his desk. He's removed his glasses to listen to Doc's story that I, too, find quite riveting.

"So, George and Stella sound like bad news."

Doc speaks through me in his baritone voice. "Let's just say they enjoyed more than just a drink together every now and again, I'd come to find out. In the meanwhile, Phoebe would not be coming back. I was given no explanation."

"But you obviously saw her again?" Savage kneads his forehead. "She's your mother."

"My wife," Doc responds, correcting him.

"Oh. Yes, I'm sorry."

I cross my legs in front of me, interlacing my fingers behind my neck. *Oh, this is really getting good.*

"I phoned Phoebe's home the next day only to be told she'd left for France to join the Red Cross," Doc says. "The news devastated me. I didn't understand. I looked at Stella passed out in our bed and wondered how Phoebe could have left us.

"It had all been too much for Phoebe and she left. The music faded away. I would hold onto her sweet image like a child sucking on a candy," Doc says a little more quietly.

"But you were still married to Stella. And what about George, he was your friend—" Dr. Savage says, quickly correcting himself, "—your stepfather?"

"He was," I say, interrupting.

"Charley, I'm confused. Are you saying you're Doc and you married the piano teacher, your mother, Phoebe?"

"That's right," I say, sitting erect.

"So, who are you now?"

Doc jumps in. "Do you want to hear the rest of the story or not?"

1913: Hollywood—
Doc

The loss felt like a death to me.

She wasn't just a piano teacher. Phoebe had been part of the family. We found a new piano teacher for Leland, an austere skinny man in his thirties with a nose much too prominent for his miniature head. Mr. Fleming's long fingers, five-fingered arachnids, knew how to crawl around the keyboard. But with no Phoebe, we were lost. Without her around, the world she had given us a glimpse of, would never be the same.

Stella hit the bottle even more heavily; where she'd been getting her supply was beyond me, for by now most of the nearby pharmacists turned her away.

Soon, home turned into a place to be avoided and my only concentration seemed to be on helping my Leland. I saw myself in him. As a child, I'd learned something about being in isolation and I didn't care for it. I didn't want that for my son, so I put more and more hours in at my office. Ironically, while isolating myself from the family, I'd distanced myself from him. Other than the sunglasses, I hadn't made any breakthroughs for Leland.

As far as my other businesses were concerned, it wasn't even necessary to leave my office to expand my wealth. With all of the hustle and bustle of activity of Hollywood, it became too easy to accumulate riches. George had a keen eye for business and for putting deals together. He had me grabbing up land for development and property, both residential and commercial, faster than a player in *The Landlord's Game*. Without trying, I'd purchased gas stations, markets, hospitals, banks, churches. Opportunity abounded. George, my right-hand man, my confidant, and eventually my fixer, left me time to find an answer for Leland.

But I needed help. I couldn't do this on my own. I had to branch out and find an answer before time ran out. Turning to the Hollywood Masonic Temple, I sought refuge at least once a week—a sanctuary where I took comfort in the camaraderie of brotherhood, something I never found in my family, church, college or even in the Army. Not that I didn't love my family, but sometimes a man just needs to be surrounded by his peers. Stella, of course, would never be happy about it, but then again, she wasn't happy about anything it seemed except her booze and pharmaceuticals—and to think, people envied me. "Oh, what I wouldn't do to be you, Doc. You've got it all, old man," George told me time and again.

So, I immersed myself in Masonry, as well as business; anything to avoid looking at the situation at home. For if I didn't see the problem, there wasn't one. Stella wasn't a drunk if I didn't see her drinking. Leland wasn't going blind. And I believed pretty soon I'd find the cure for Leland; never mind there was no cure. I just needed to try a little harder; to look elsewhere and to leave no stone unturned. So, on nights I wasn't working, I'd be found at the lodge surrounded by intelligent, positive, goal-oriented, like-minded men; men who might have some answers for me.

Unfortunately, I found no answers, but many of my future business transactions would also involve my fellow Masons.

Another night and I couldn't make myself go home. Feeling empty inside, I passed a storefront window on my way to a meeting and nearly jumped out of my skin, as thin and stretched over my bones as it was. My heart nearly stopped when I saw the ghostly pallor of my face. I gasped *Dear Lord* when I noticed my suit hanging on me like it would if Leland were wearing it. *Dear Lord,* something from inside me echoed as I exhaled. I felt hollow. I'd turned into a rotting carcass of a man with neither a soul nor the fat and sinew to hold his bones together. I needed to fill the void and to find something to wrap me in comfort.

There were times I dared to imagine running away; every man for himself. Oh, to disappear. But I'd never do that. A responsible man would never abandon his family. But if something didn't change soon, I might just disappear into thin air.

On occasion, wives and families were included at the lodge. There were the annual or biannual dinners combined with educational speeches, celebration of new or existing marriages by Masonic ceremony, celebration of birthdays and wedding anniversaries within lodges; all kinds of occasions where I might have included Stella, but to her I never extended an invitation. The risk of her showing up inebriated would have been too great. I would have been suspended from all rights and privileges of Masonry with my jewel suspended pending a trial. Besides, no one ever asked about Stella anymore. As hard as I tried to cover up for her and make excuses, it was no secret something in our lives had been thrown terribly off balance.

Stella lay awake when I returned home from the lodge. I entered the foyer and before I could set down my "bricklayer's apron" and my hat, a force like a bullet struck me in the middle of my forehead. Stella stood in front of the fireplace mantel. She'd been waiting up for me and demanded to know whom I'd been with. Finally, my wedding ring came to rest near the bottom of the stairs. She'd thrown it at me with a ferocity and dead aim only Annie Oakley might have managed. Earlier, in my haste to leave our home, I'd failed to lock my wedding ring away.

"Who is she?"

To argue with this drunk woman was insane, and why I owed the person who had just hit me an explanation seemed beyond me, but there would be no sleep for me tonight unless I clarified this misunderstanding.

"It's tradition."

"To cheat on your wife!"

"Stella, I am not cheating on you." How could I explain that before taking his degree, a Mason had to remove not only his wedding ring, but anything of a mineral or metallic substance was to be removed, too. The tradition was part of the 'Rite of Destitution,' an experience Stella would fail to understand. She'd never understand how I'd embarked on a path I hoped would make me a better man in the days to come. How could I explain she should be happy for me—for us? For Stella, it seemed easier to believe I was having an affair, than to understand why a husband took off his wedding ring before entering the inner sanctum of the brotherhood of Masons.

"You think I don't know. You think I don't know about your tryst with Phoebe!"

"What? Oh, Stella, you're drunk!" I looked to make sure the children were not present.

"You're a sick, sick man! I don't know what she saw in you—what any woman would see in you. You're nothing but a lousy husband and adulterer. That's why I dismissed her."

"You what? You let Phoebe go?"

For someone who hated melodrama, I certainly lived in the wrong town. Stella's theatrics were difficult for me to handle. She made events bigger than life with her sweeping grand gestures, furrowed brows and constant pouting.

I climbed the stairs to our room.

"I saw how she looked at you," Stella said, following behind me. "I saw how you leered at her."

"What are you talking about?" I entered our bedroom. "Why did you let her go?"

Stella took a seat on her padded hope chest at the foot of the bed and removed a shoe. She shook the shoe at me as she rolled her eyes and heaved a sigh. "You're a beastly horrid pig! You think I don't know how you and Phoebe have been carrying on?" she said, standing there, hands perched on her hips. "It's obvious you and your little concubine were fucking underneath this roof the whole time."

I gasped. "Stella, you're crazy. Watch your mouth, you'll wake the children."

"Well, then you can explain to them that you're a cheater, Doc!" she screamed as she threw her shoe at me. I ducked and it smashed into the family picture we'd sat for during Karl's christening.

"Oh, my Lord! What did Phoebe say?" I asked.

Stella got up and hobbled over to me with one shoe still on, glaring at me. With a crimson face and lips pursed tighter than a granny knot, she filled with so much adrenaline her pupils dilated black, eclipsing her cold blue eyes. "She didn't have to say anything. She knew she was wrong," Stella said as she sneered at me, fist clenched. "No, she didn't say anything. Daddy did."

"Daddy? What the hell are you talking about?"

Had Phoebe held a séance, I wondered? Were these the consequences she'd mentioned? The curse?

"He told me to open my eyes and take care of my family. Not to let the devil in. Phoebe is the devil in sheep's clothing!"

"Stella, you're crazy."

"Fuck you, Wesley!"

The shock at hearing her use vulgarity surprised me less than when she next slugged me in the stomach. She left me doubled over and out of breath, and as she opened the door to leave the room, standing by the threshold were Leland and Helen. Stella pushed them out of the way and marched down to the kitchen. Helen held her hand over her mouth then ran back to her room, but Leland remained frozen in place, blinking at me. He removed his glasses to wipe the tears streaming down his face.

"Leland, go back to bed. Everything will be all right."

Everything had to be all right. Part of my stubbornness was refusing to let go, believing I could fix things that couldn't be fixed. Finding answers to hard questions was part of the challenge: *Why do I stay* and *How much longer can I take this?* I needed to keep my family together for the sake of the children. Certainly, family and wives were challenging and important, but at least once a week, I crossed the threshold where, together with my wedding ring, I felt happy to leave that world behind, if only for an hour or two.

But if only I'd spent more time at home, tragedy would not have struck my family.

13

Sweet Adelaide!

1915: Hollywood, California

Only home from the office for a short while, I would be leaving again for my lodge meeting. I walked into the parlor to say goodnight to the children, who were gathered around Leland as he practiced for his big recital the next day.

Wide-eyed and anxious, Leland swung around on the piano bench to face me. "Father, where are you going? I have a recital tomorrow."

Leland and his music selection had matured exponentially and, while it wasn't because he lacked skill or confidence, he seemed to be over-practicing.

"I'm sure you'll be fine." I knew, when it came to his music, he took it seriously and would never perform before anyone unless he knew the piece inside and out, backward and forward.

"But I wanted you to close your eyes and really listen this time," Leland said. "Make sure it's not just fine, but perfect. I'll be performing the Opus 46."

I stopped in my tracks and tried to push back the thoughts of yester-year. At that time, I wasn't prepared to travel down memory lane.

"Son, you know I have a lodge meeting," I said, quickly noting the disappointment in his face as he turned back toward the piano.

Helen had settled herself in a chair near the fireplace with her book *The Flying Girl*. She set it down. "Leland, I'm here."

Karl had taken his favorite place under the piano and tickled Leland's feet. I took in the scene with my adorably perfect children and wanted to cry—to think I'd wanted to escape so quickly. I heard Stella in the kitchen rummaging around and then heard her on her way into the parlor.

"I can stay for a few minutes," I said. "But most certainly, I'll be at the recital tomorrow."

Stella joined us and sat on the davenport with her drink.

I motioned for Karl to come out from underneath the piano. "Come, Karl, you behave now," I said with a chuckle.

"I will, Daddy," he said, crawling out and jumping into my lap.

Leland cheered up and I wrapped my arms around Karl, kissing the top of his head. Leland then stretched out his arms, wiggling his fingers before striking the first notes on the keyboard.

I closed my eyes. "Let's have a listen."

And then the first notes he played swept me away to the time I'd first heard Phoebe play Beethoven's Opus 46.

She'd explained how the composition was an ambitious undertaking of a German love poem set to a moderate tempo, where the modulations through the flat keys created a dreamy atmosphere, where the lover saw his beloved wherever he wandered. Enraptured, I'd tried to comprehend how the music correspondingly wandered through a great range of keys and rhythms. The way her fingers floated across the keyboard, the way her slender body swayed rhythmically on the piano bench, hypnotized me. As she played, the music lifted me out of my world and into what I only imagined heaven would be—with her in it. For quite a while after she went away, I found myself wandering through my lonely days looking forward to sleep, where I'd be with her at last in my dreams.

As I watched Leland sway now rhythmically on the piano bench, I remembered watching him during his lessons and sensing he had a crush on her. Who wouldn't? Who didn't? As for the music, I'm sure he never fully appreciated nor understood the amorous composition as Phoebe played. He simply gazed up at her. She could have been playing "Chopsticks" or "Mary Had a Little Lamb." I didn't care and I don't think he did either. Clearly, he had a crush on Phoebe. And I'm sure mine wasn't the only heart broken when she went away. Both he and I would suffer the aftermath of her departure. "Oh, Father, I was just a silly boy and that was years ago," he'd said later. "How silly it would have been for her to wait for me like I'd asked. Besides, I'm sure she had suitors more her age."

As he sang the simple opening to the Opus, I recalled that, while obscure, it was also a *cantata* for voice with keyboard accompaniment, but Leland didn't sing. Or at least that's what I thought as Karl nestled into my neck. And then as I inhaled the sweet, sweaty smell of my younger son's head, Leland sang the first note. I cleared my throat. My body felt as if it had ignited.

> *Your friend wanders alone in the garden of spring,*
> *Gently bathed in lovely magical light,*
> *Which shimmers through the swaying branches of flowers:*
> *Adelaide!*

I took off my glasses and turned to Stella. *When? How did I not know he sang?* She nodded to the beat with her eyes closed. Helen looked at me as if to say, "You see. Isn't my brother grand?" I wanted to get up and exclaim, "That's my boy!" or, applaud and run up and shake Leland and ask him to explain where he'd come from, but I refrained as the music became more intense, holding me in my seat.

> *In the reflection of the river, in the snows of the Alps,*
> *In the golden clouds of sinking day,*
> *In the fields of stars thy face beams forth,*
> *Adelaide!*

My fingers and toes tingled and my heart felt as if it had expanded to twice its size. My son could sing! I'd been squeezing Karl so tight, he finally squirmed out of my lap to dance around the room. I slipped my fingers up behind my glasses to wipe my eyes.

Except while he was in the shower, I'd never heard Leland sing.

> *Someday, o miracle! a flower will blossom,*
> *Upon my grave from the ashes of my heart;*
> *And clearly on every violet petal will shine:*
> *Adelaide!*

I stood, cheering. "Bravo, Leland!"

He swung his legs around the piano bench and stood to bow.

"Bravo, Leland!" Karl said.

"Son, it's perfect," I said. "I don't know what you're so worried about."

"She'll love it," Helen said, and Leland blushed to the roots of his hair.

"She?" I asked, not knowing there would be someone in the audience whom he wanted to impress. I knew Leland had been heartbroken after Phoebe left and I'd worried he'd never be the same.

"Who's going to love it?" I asked.

Helen looked at Leland and said as a matter of fact, a fact about which I had no idea, "Adelaide."

"Leland and Adelaide sitting in a tree, k-i-s-s-i-n-g," little Karl sang as he danced around the piano.

"Hold on. That's her name?" I asked and the children nodded.

All at once, the complicated composition he'd chosen, "Adelaide" Beethoven's Opus 46, made sense to me. He was in love for the first time since Phoebe and through the music he would be able to show his love for Adelaide.

Reclined now on the davenport in the parlor, Stella barely focused as Leland practiced. She'd stared at the metronome and nodded to the beat until she just about passed out. The sight of her both saddened and sickened me. I'd grown frustrated trying everything with Stella. I'd even moved the family to this town of temperance thinking it might stop Stella from drinking. Not that I'd minded a drink now and again. As a matter of fact, I did my share of imbibing over at the lodge, someplace Stella could not frequent. She found a way to get what she needed, however, and that night she would succeed once more.

"Good night, children," I said finally, as I swooped Karl up and kissed him good night.

I looked over at Stella, struggling to keep her eyes open. I hugged Helen and said, "You'll need to help Karl to bed, sweetheart."

I then turned to Leland and said, "Son, you make me so proud. I'll see you in the morning. You have nothing to worry about."

Leland had nothing over which to fret but I had a feeling I should have stayed home that night. I decided I'd simply make an appearance at the lodge and come home early. I grabbed my coat out of the closet in the foyer and my stomach constricted when I heard the clink of glass. Unfortunately, that sound had become all too familiar and I searched further until I felt the cold little bottle of whiskey in the pocket of Stella's mink coat. I thought twice about just leaving it there but decided to bring it with me to dump it somewhere along the road on my way to the lodge. I knew this act to be frivolous and futile, for I also knew with certainty Stella had other bottles hidden elsewhere. But it gave me a certain amount of pleasure to remove this vice from our home.

Five minutes after arriving at the lodge, where Marie was in the middle of her sermon about the science of happiness and the joyousness in suffering, I felt an earthquake force jolt me to my core. I stood, grabbed my hat and coat, headed out the door and sped home. My heart thumped so hard, my hands were so sweaty, I barely held onto the wheel.

♪♫

Helen ran out to my car as I rolled up the drive. "Oh, father!" A cry wrung out from her like the agony of a lost soul. "There's been a terrible accident." She stood red-faced, hugging herself as she sobbed, barely able to speak.

"What do you mean?" I shouted as I got out of my auto and ran past her into the house. "Where's Karl?"

"He's asleep," she shouted, clenching her fists to her sides.

Through her sobs, I couldn't get much more information. All Helen could say now was "Leland."

I turned and peered at her, her face streaked with tears. I begged God—if there was one—to keep my son safe.

"Mother was so drunk and only wanted more. She was in no condition to drive so Leland drove her. The police want you to call—"

"What do you mean, Leland drove her?" I didn't wait for her to answer. I shook my head and hurried back outside. I dashed toward my car when a sleepy-eyed, barefooted Karl came tumbling out onto the porch.

"Daddy!" he screamed.

"Take care of your little brother," I shouted.

"No, Daddy!" Karl ran toward the car. "Please don't leave us again!" He wrapped his arms around my legs and I came undone. I picked him up and helped him into the back seat.

I rushed out of the neighborhood headed directly to the hospital across town. My heart ached as I breathed in something suffocating, painful and dry. All the while, I blamed myself for not protecting Leland against his own mother. I glanced over at Helen, the streetlights bouncing off her anxious face. She held her hands to her lips.

"So, when did Leland start driving?"

She dropped her hands into her lap. "George has been giving him lessons," she said in a whisper.

I pressed my foot down on the accelerator even harder. "Is this an ongoing thing? Leland buying her booze?"

"No." I saw out of the corner of my eye how she wiped the tears from her face as she shook her head. I reached into my pocket and handed her my handkerchief.

"After you left, Mother got really sloppy like she gets. I was so relieved when she started dozing. I figured she was down for the count, but then when she snorted during the practice, Leland yelled at her. Then she jerked herself awake and picked up her glass and guzzled up what was left of her *medicine*," Helen said quietly, turning to check on little Karl, seated in the middle leaning forward on the backrest behind us, wide-eyed and frightened. "Then she stood and staggered over to the closet to search her mink, but she couldn't seem to find what she was looking for."

I remembered the bottle, immediately sorry I'd thrown it out earlier.

"She got really angry as she rummaged through the rest of the coats. And then finally, after all of the coats were strewn in a heap on the floor, she slipped into her mink and walked back into the parlor. She clapped and announced she was going out. Leland asked her if it could please wait and that maybe you'd pick something up for her on your way back. He went to the phone to ring you up at the lodge.

"She said, 'No, that's all right. We don't want to bother your father.' She told us she'd be back before you got home. She then told Leland to get ready for bed because he had a big day tomorrow. Oh, Leland—" Helen sobbed, and after a spell, she blew her nose and then tried to compose herself. "He was so excited for tomorrow."

"Princess, we don't know anything yet. There's—"

"They'd kissed during a game of Post Office, and he planned on stealing another one after the recital."

It warmed my heart to know Leland confided in his sister.

Helen wiped her tears. "Poor, kind Leland always coming to Mother's rescue. He ran into the kitchen yelling for her to wait and I knew where he was going. It's no secret that Mother hides bottles with the cleaning supplies in the broom closet. But Leland came back into the parlor empty-handed and, by now, Mother already stood out on the porch. Leland insisted he go with her. 'Let me at least drive you there, Mother,' he said. She told him he didn't know where she was going, but Leland said he did know. I knew.

We all know where she gets her *medicine*. He then grabbed the key out of her hands.

"And then she shouted. 'Leland, give me the key! I'm still your mother and I insist you go inside.' Leland told her it was late and that she was drunk and could hardly walk. He told her to go back inside. She argued for him to give her the goddam key. I was afraid the neighbors could hear and then Leland said 'Fine,' and headed toward the car. 'I'll drive,' he said and got into the car. He then took the wheel, turned on the ignition and disappeared down the street."

At the hospital, an officer intercepted me and tried to fill me in, but he also asked me questions about my wife's drinking. At the scene, she'd reeked of alcohol when the police arrived. Apparently, Leland had just left the parking lot of the Roscoe Pharmacy. The car barely made it onto Los Feliz Boulevard when a truck making a nighttime delivery slammed into the driver's side.

14

Dear Leland

1949: Oakland—
Charley

Curled up on Dr. Savage's sofa, I'm a sobbing kid. My heart hurts so badly and the pain of what I've just experienced is all too real. I feel a rivulet of tears trickling into my ears and, without opening my eyes, I recognize the sour smell of Dr. Savage's office.

"Did Leland die?" Dr. Savage asks.

The air from a fan is blowing into my face, drying out my eyeballs when I open them. Life is blurry. I turn to look at Savage and somehow know clearly Leland had not died.

"Not yet." I turn to look at the potted plant on Savage's desk in dire need of some water.

1915: Central Receiving Hospital, Los Angeles—
Doc

I arrived at Central Receiving Hospital and was greeted by Dr. Whitehead, who had just left Leland's room. He stood in front of me, and pulled down his mask to reveal a harsh medicinal face. "Dr. Marnier, Leland is unconscious and has lost a lot of blood."

Aghast, I lost myself in the furrows of his brow, trying to comprehend his words. He appeared irritated. "I'm sorry, Dr. Marnier," he said, "but we won't be able to reattach his arm."

I became unmoored, reeling through the dark skies of my reality and then being slammed to the ground. Stupefied, my whole body trembled from head to foot. Dr. Whitehead walked away muttering: "Alcohol, the devil's folly."

His arm? Oh, dear God, no! A cool sweat bathed over me. Again, the floor had dropped out from underneath me and I was falling. As the room spun a nurse took my arm and directed me to a chair.

"Can I please see my son?" I asked.

"Not yet, but you can see your wife. She's been asking for you," the nurse said in a hushed voice.

I dragged behind the nurse up the tiled hallway, until I felt the crush of reality weighing on me. I slumped into a chair in the hallway. Stella, this was all her fault. The anger bubbled to the surface. I'd need to control myself before facing her. What she'd caused would destroy the family. I buried my head in my hands.

♪♫

The nurse led me to the room where another nurse attended Stella.

"Oh, Wesley!" she sobbed as I approached her. She reached out to hug me around the waist. "I begged him to stay home, but he wouldn't listen."

I peeled her arms off me. "And did you listen when he asked you to stay home?" I said, knowing it was futile to argue with a drunk.

"They won't tell me anything. Please tell me everything will be all right."

The cloying smell of booze overwhelmed me. I couldn't look at Stella.

"He's still unconscious," I screamed, "and he lost his arm!"

"What do you mean?"

"Stella, you are pathetic."

"Wesley, oh please. Don't say that," she blubbered. "I am so sorry, I promise—"

"How could you? And then knowing he's even more blind at night!" I shouted.

"Oh, my dear, sweet boy. On Leland's life, I swear I'm going to stop drinking."

I turned to the nurse and asked, "Will she be okay?"

The nurse told me Stella was fine and had merely suffered a few minor cuts and bruises. She'd be free to go home as long as someone watched her for the next twenty-four hours.

"I'll be damned if I spend even the next twenty-four seconds with you," I said and stormed out of the room to go be with my son.

Two weeks after having suffered a concussion, two broken ribs, and the loss of his left arm, Leland came home from the hospital just in time for the break, for the Easter celebration, a time of renewal and rebirth. I was elated to have him home. Stella, beside herself, had just that morning renewed her vow to change. This time I really believed her. What normal person could come through such an ordeal and not be transformed? Surely Leland's suffering had not been in vain—had been the turning point for her?

I walked into the kitchen for a cup of coffee, where it smelled like a confectionary shop as Stella and Helen busied themselves baking for the next day.

"Good morning, everyone. Is Leland up yet?" I asked, surveying the kitchen strewn with utensils, bowls, mugs, construction paper, watercolors, flour and a plate of cold scrambled eggs abandoned by Karl, already so full of excitement and sugar.

"Not yet," Stella said. "Wesley, let's try to be civil today. I've invited some of our friends to come over after church services tomorrow," and I wondered which friends she might be talking about. She'd never been very social, but I appreciated how she seemed to be bending over backward to make everything seem perfect, as if she hadn't just caused our son to lose his arm. *Civil?* Therein lay the problem. Always civil, I was the one who walked away from her tantrums. She wanted everything to look normal, but the sad irony was most Saturdays she normally remained in bed with a hangover. She'd asked Helen to help her little brother decorate Easter eggs at the kitchen table.

"Like this?" Karl asked as he held up an egg. "Daddy, look!"

Before saying anything right or wrong and as if I wasn't in the room, Stella jumped in and said, "Oh, your father thinks it's simply perfect."

I set down my coffee cup and nodded my head to keep the peace. "Yes, Karl, that is what I think," I said, thinking instead about strangling Stella, but this was also to be a time for a change of attitude.

Stella frosted a chocolate cake as Leland walked into the kitchen. Hair matted, he was still in his striped pajamas with the sleeve folded up over his left arm, bandaged at the stump just above his elbow.

"Well, good morning, son. Can I get you some breakfast?" Stella asked, moving to push the hair out of his face. He jerked back motioning her away with his right arm, and then adjusted his glasses before he ran his fingers through his scalp. He perused the kitchen. "Water. Can I please just have some water?" he asked.

"Leland, I'm so glad you're home," Helen said, "all the kids at school have been asking about you. They can't wait for you to come back."

"Will your arm grow back?" Karl asked as he colored another egg.

"Karl, don't be rude," Stella said. Her hand trembled as she handed Leland a glass of water, sloshing onto his hand and then onto the floor. He accepted the glass and Stella quickly grabbed a towel to dry his hand that he pulled away as if protecting the only limb he had left. She dropped down onto her knees to wipe up the floor.

"Karl, that is a perfectly acceptable question," I said. "No, it will not grow—"

"Wesley," Stella screamed, looking up.

"But, Stella, I think it's time we started being honest."

Stella glared at me. "Now is not the time for that. Everyone, let's just let Leland be." She got up, smoothed her apron then returned to her task, asking, "Leland, would you care to lick the spoon?"

Leland didn't respond. He finished his glass of water and then walked out of the kitchen.

♪♫

Easter morning, Stella pulled back the drapery in our room eager to get a jump on the day. I looked out the window to an ominous-looking sky filled with low clouds, the kind that kept the sunshine hidden. Stella insisted I continue to act as if everything were fine and to help her hide eggs and candy out in the orchard for the children. She'd also invited children from Karl's school and from the neighborhood to attend after we returned from church services.

Leland sat in a chair in the back yard in his orange-tinted sunshades, still in his Sunday suit, looking dapper and serene as he soaked up the warm sun finally burning through. He watched the children frolic through the orchard. It warmed my heart to see an occasional smile spread across his face, a ray of sunshine through the dark clouds. At one point, he even rose up out of his chair to show Karl an egg hidden in a lower branch of an orange tree. He seemed to be cheering up until a young auburn-haired girl walked up to him. He then quickly dashed into the house without giving her a second glance.

"Please, Leland. What did I do? Please look at me. Everything will be all right," the girl said, following him into the house. "It's not the end of the world."

"Easy for you to say, Adelaide."

So, this was Adelaide.

"What good am I without my arm? I'm a circus freak!"

This was the first time I'd heard Leland utter more than a sentence since he'd been home. "Just leave me alone, Adelaide. I'm better off dead."

Hearing my son speak this way shocked and pained me. Even when faced with the possibility of losing his sight altogether, he never spoke with such hopelessness. He'd simply made adjustments. He'd compensated. He was so gifted at piano, able to play just about anything by ear. But now, without his arm, he'd have to find a new passion.

"Leland, don't say that," Adelaide said. "You can't mean that."

"Please go away. I don't ever want to see you again."

The fair creature burst into tears and I stepped in to try to smooth things over. "Adelaide, he doesn't mean what he's saying."

She ran out the back door in tears just as Helen came running in.

"Is everything all right?" Helen asked.

"Just fine," I said. "Please go back outside. Let me handle your brother."

"Oh, Father, what do you know?" Leland said, tears dripping down his stubbly cheeks. "You don't know anything about me much less about what I'm feeling. You and Mother want to hide the truth like it's a colored Easter egg. Well, I'm not Karl," he said and laughed. "I'm not completely blind yet. I can see what's going on."

"Son, you're just upset. Everything is going to be fine."

"Hell, yes, I'm upset and everything is not going to be *fine*," he said, raising a fist. "For the first time in my life, I had something—someone to call my own. I wouldn't have to compete with you anymore. I didn't have to be like you."

I sucked in a sharp breath of shock.

"I had something I was passionate about and someone who loved me. After the recital . . ." he said, struggling to hold back tears. "Silly me. After the recital, I imagined her standing in the crowd applauding. I'd take my bow and then I planned on asking her to be my girl. What a fool."

And what a fool I'd been. My son had fallen in love and it was no longer Phoebe for whom he pined. Adelaide seemed to truly care for him and she'd never break his heart. I reached out to try and comfort my son, but he backed away. "And now you just sent her away?" I said, clutching my chest.

"I don't need pity. Besides, isn't that what you always do? You sent Mother away."

"You know your mother was sick." I felt like I might be having a heart attack. We'd never discussed it, but Leland had to be old enough by now to understand why throughout his life Stella had been in and out of the sanatorium. "You know the rest only did her good."

He looked away from me. "Not everyone finds his passion," he said. "Don't you understand? I had a calling. You couldn't stand how she paid more attention to me. You couldn't stand that I could be better at something. Phoebe saw it, but you sent her away."

Phoebe? His words were daggers to my heart. Is this what he meant by 'compete'? "Son, what are you talking about?" I wasn't the one who sent Phoebe away. She was the best thing ever to happen to Leland. Seeing Leland happy made me happy. Leland had been my everything, but as the years went by, he and Stella grew closer and I felt like I had to compete, not for Stella's attention, but for his. And as for Phoebe, I never thought we were in competition. It wouldn't be until later that I'd find the poetry he'd written because of and for her.

"Even Mother saw it, but she's the sick one and you're the one who makes her sick. You're the reason she drinks."

"Is that what you think? Is that what she told you, Leland?"

"She didn't have to. I've spent my whole life trying to please you. Mother does the same. We all do. We're not good enough for you. That's why you're never home. Mother says you never wanted children in the first place."

Crushed, I said, "Oh, Leland, I hope that's not what you believe. That's simply not true."

Stella could be cruel, but this took the cake. Before I even married her, all I ever wanted was children. She knew I wanted a family. As a fatherless, only child, except for a stepsister old enough to be my mother, I always envied large families. And then, when we had Leland, more than my own desires, it became even more imperative to give him siblings—to give him everything. "You are the world to me . . . my first son. I love you and I will figure something out. Everything will be fine, I swear."

"Oh, sure, you always have the answers. You're always going to figure something out, like how you cured me of macular degeneration."

A slap in the face. A punch in the gut—as if all the sweetness had been amputated with his arm. I was speechless. I could hear Stella in his voice and I tried to reason with him, but that had never worked with his mother.

"Leland, I'm working on it. These things take time. I have hope."

"Father, there is no cure and you know it." His tone changed, softened. "Funny, I used to believe there was nothing you couldn't do. You were a god to me, but we all know there's no Easter Bunny, you're the one who said there's no god," he said, heading toward the staircase. He paused before climbing and, without turning to look at me, he said, "Just let it go, there is no hope for me. Everyone would have been better off had I never been born."

"Leland, don't talk that way."

He lowered his head. "Mother wouldn't need to drink—maybe the two of you could have tolerated being in the same room together. Really, I'm better off dead." He stormed up to his bedroom and slammed the door.

Like a heap of laundry, I crumpled onto the bottom step and buried my head in my hands. When I looked up, I saw a pair of laced-up brown leather booties. Helen stood in the hallway.

Close to midnight and the last thing I remember before falling into a deep sleep was talking, praying, begging to whoever might be listening. "Show me a way." My hands were still in a prayer position, leaving an impression on my cheek, when I woke to the sound of a shot echoing from the depths of the orchard. I bolted upright and looked over at a snoring Stella.

I dashed out of the room and down the hall, but before I descended the stairs, I checked on the children. Helen was fast asleep. I closed the door to her room and crossed the hall to check on little Karl, who was asleep curled up with a new picture book the Easter Bunny had brought him. And then

I peeked into Leland's room and panicked when I saw his bed, empty and still made up. Stifling a scream, I approached the bed to take a closer look. I then patted the mattress as if my tactile faculties were better than my visual. I felt nothing except for the needle-like pricks throughout my body. I ran a hand through my hair and tried to think. *Dear God, please let everything be all right.* I checked the bathroom. He wasn't in there. By now, all reason had escaped me. Had he run away? As I looked out the window, suddenly his words echoed in my head: *Maybe I'm better off dead!* I hurried down the stairs and out the back door into the orchard where I called out my son's name, "Leland! Leland! Where are you?"

The raven moon, with its sinister grin, spilled enough light onto the orange trees to cast twisted shadows dancing eerily along the path overgrown with weeds. And then I saw the bare feet sticking out of the striped pajamas. That is where I should have kept my eyes, for when I looked up I saw his body slumped on the tree trunk—his Winchester rifle off to one side, his head lolled to the other side. His spectacles dangled from one ear, for the other ear had been blasted away by the gunshot boring a dark tunnel through his brain.

♪♫

The California Certificate of Death described the cause of death as a "Gunshot wound through the brain inflicted accidentally by himself."

I would forever wonder what I might have done differently for my son. I'd failed him and now it was too late. I would never see him again. I'd never hold him. I'd never hear his music or his singing. I'd never hear him perform the Ninth Symphony. I was dying inside—inside, where I'd hold it all in for the sake of the children.

15
Act of God

Starting the fire was a crime, as was the death of my son. *The Los Angeles Times* would later report that lightning had struck the Roscoe Pharmacy causing the fire that burned down the whole block. In legal terms, the tragic fire, like an earthquake or flood, had been outside of human control and the tragedy therefore would be considered an act of God. I knew better.

The evening after the funeral, I pulled into the pharmacy's parking lot and turned off the headlamps, milky in the dusk. Thoughts swirled like debris in a tornado, all funneling down to the fact that George also had dealings with Roscoe and had planned some sort of retribution of his own. But this was my vengeance, and only the beginning. I would punish everyone who had anything to do with my son's death, starting with Stella's suppliers. I would take matters into my own hands and not wait for George. I'd wanted to kill him after Stella confessed that it was he who'd introduced her to the "pharmacy."

"But Doc, I had nothing to do with this," George had whined. "Stella was getting the stuff on her own. I swear. Doc, please. What can I do?"

"Just stay away from me and my family!"

"Doc, you gotta hear me out. I'll do anything you say. Let me take care of Roscoe for you."

"Just let me handle my own affairs." I finished arguing. I couldn't think anymore. It would take energy I didn't have to sort everything out.

"But Doc—"

"Get out! And, if I ever hear that you're involved in something like this again, I will hunt you down and kill you myself."

I stepped out of the car and walked to the trunk to retrieve a gas can. I then marched over to the building and proceeded to pour gasoline along the perimeter of the structure. I could smell the gasoline on my fingers.

I inhaled deeply as if the fuel could anesthetize me; kill the pain. I lit a match and watched the flames kiss an ebony sky. Facing the heavens, I waited for the rain to come and wash away my sorrow.

My son was dead and nothing would bring him back. His death had blackened my insides, leaving me barren and numb. The embers would smolder for a long time and I wondered if I could ever rise out of the fire; I wondered whether I even wanted to.

But I'd become as resilient as a pinecone after a fire. I'd take root, emerge stronger, and take control, vowing never to let God take from me again.

By the time I returned home after the incident, I felt energized. As the sun rose over the distant mountains, a seed of strength bloomed inside my gut. Inside, the house was dark and quiet. The children were still curled up in bed.

"Daddy, what are you doing in here?" Helen asked, rubbing her eyes.

I'd gone into her room to wake her up. "You're getting up."

Earlier in the week, neither Myrtle, our latest maid, nor I had been able to get Helen to come out of her room. Helen hadn't wanted to speak and I thought it best to allow her the time to mourn her big brother. For days, she'd locked herself in her room, missing school and refusing to come out to eat. We'd load trays with soups and sandwiches, apples, glasses of water and milk. At the end of the day, she'd leave the empty tray outside her door. Myrtle, frustrated by both Helen and Stella, eventually quit, leaving Karl and me to fend for ourselves.

"I don't want to get up," Helen said.

"I didn't ask you. I'm telling you. You're going back to school." I walked out.

Karl, flaxen hair standing up in cowlicks, already sat at the kitchen table pouring himself a bowl of cereal.

"Good morning, son."

"Morning, Daddy. Is Leland coming home today?"

I looked into his eyes, the color of wonder, a child always full of questions. "Will Mommy ever stop crying?" he'd asked, or "Did they sew on his new arm, yet?"

I'd never had the strength to explain anything to him, but this morning as I took a seat across from Karl, something took root in my belly. I reached out to pour some milk onto his cereal.

"He's not coming home, son. You know that," I said, assuming Karl already knew and that he merely needed to talk about it with someone; someone like his father. "Today or ever."

I folded my hands in front of me. "You remember Skipper?" Karl smiled, eyes wide as cereal bowls. "Remember, when he went to sleep and wouldn't wake up?"

Karl frowned, setting down his spoon. The previous year, he'd brought home a kitten he'd discovered mewing in the orchard. He'd found Skipper one morning walking in a circle, moaning until she finally dropped. I heard Karl screaming and when I ran into the room, I found him holding his dead kitten.

"She's buried in the back yard under a lemon tree," Karl said, pausing for a moment with his mouth open. His tiny face scrunched up as he looked toward the back yard. "Is Leland buried back there, too?"

"No, Leland is buried at a place called Mountain View Cemetery." A place where we all would be buried someday. At the time of the burial, Stella had insisted I purchase a family plot, so we'd all be together forever. "Leland's body was buried," I said, "but his spirit has gone to heaven."

"Oh." He nodded bravely, smiling as a tear slipped from his eye. "To be with God."

That had been enough of an answer for him. Perhaps, Sunday school hadn't been a waste of time after all.

Perhaps, church might be good for me as well, I'd thought before the funeral service. While I'd never been a religious man, having only attended church with Stella for the sake of the children, I agreed to the ceremony for our son. The church overflowed with Leland's friends, teachers and the administration from Hollywood High School. Adelaide was obviously missing. The members had taken up donations, looking the other way when it came to the sinner. There were those who believed self-murder to be a sin against God even though we'd insisted it was an accident. After the service, friends had come up to give their backhanded, insensitive condolences, saying things like: "He's better off. It would have been difficult for him to get by without an arm," or that we were "better off because now at least he wouldn't have to go off to war." No one could believe how this could have happened. "He was such a quiet, good boy." Those who suspected the scandalous truth said they'd pray for his soul so he wouldn't burn in hell.

Later, I'd catch people simply staring or walking past the house and pointing. Marie Hotchener had come to the home to visit. "The tragedy you've suffered will force you to understand certain things, things you might not comprehend right away," she said.

I thanked her for stopping by, escorted her to the front door and stopped myself from booting her in the ass. I didn't care what she said; there was no way I would ever understand why my son had to die.

No one would ever be the same after his death. Soon, we'd never speak of it. After a while, we'd never mention his name at all. It would be as if he'd never existed, as if he'd never been born, but the stigma associated with what he'd done would cling to me like a human stain.

I'd become a different man; a walking ghost, adhering to my routine so as not to feel the pain. I wouldn't be present in life. I'd pour myself into my business and yet it would suffer. My patients would stay away or find other doctors.

Helen walked in as I slapped some deli meat between some bread. "Daddy, what are you doing?"

"Getting the lunches ready."

"Let me help you," she said.

"Just help your brother, Princess," I said and kissed her on the forehead.

Almost noon and Stella finally decided to come downstairs. I sat in my library waiting for her when she walked by.

"Oh, good, you're up," I called out.

She looked around and then peered at me curiously. "Did the children get off to school all right?"

"Yes, we all managed."

She hugged herself. "Wesley, why aren't you at work?"

"We're going for a little ride," I said, standing.

She burst into tears and backed away. "Oh, Wesley, please no. I'm sorry. I'm really trying. You see," she said, spreading her arms then pointing to her face, "today I've showered, even put on some rouge and lipstick."

It all seemed so pathetic. I could only manage a sad smile as I stood and walked toward the front door.

"Don't I need to pack some things?" she asked somberly.

"Your bag is already in the car," I said, opening the door.

"How long this time?" she asked, crossing over the threshold.

I didn't want to come across as some sort of vindictive god, but she gave me no choice except to take action. "Until I decide you're ready."

16

Prodigal Son

I didn't know how much longer I'd survive. It had been a year since his death.

Because I could no longer bear the accusatory looks in the only place I'd ever found solace, I'd quit coming to the lodge. I missed my brothers. I missed the camaraderie of my lodge. But earlier tonight, there'd been a knock at the door and there on the porch stoop stood Marie Hotchener and her driver.

"Grab your coats. You're coming to a meeting. The Sisters of the Rosy Cross are putting on a concert and we don't want any empty seats. Besides, it'll help take your mind off things."

"But I'm not dressed," Stella protested.

Marie marched to the closet, extracted Stella's mink coat and handed it to her. "I know how you love music, Stella. Put on some lipstick and let's go. It will do you a world of good. I'm singing tonight." Marie winked at me. "Plus, tonight we have a special guest."

♪♫

Master Toberman in his plumed fez was the first to come up and shake my hand as I waited in the foyer of the Hollywood Masonic Lodge. "Welcome back, Doc," he said, his voice ricocheting off the marble floors.

We found our seats next to Brother Gilbert Stevenson. He stood to take my hand. "Good to see you, Doc." He nodded and looked at Stella. "Mrs. Marnier. Welcome back, you've both been missed."

Recently home from the sanatorium, Stella was getting through the day together with the aid of her medication and her gift of denial. For me, every minute of every day since his death seemed like a lifetime. By the time I'd been ready to check Stella out of the hospital, our marriage had disintegrated into ashes and there would be nothing to bring it back to life. As civil and constant as I'd tried to remain, my repulsion hadn't escaped her notice nor that of the children. Stella also did not help the strained and distant relationship with the children. Helen had always been my little princess, but now she would never again enter the magic kingdom to be with me. And, as soon as I arrived home from the office, Stella would send Karl to his room. She'd decided if she couldn't be in a room with me, then she would make sure the children couldn't either. "Your father needs some time alone," she would tell them. I would protest, but to no avail. I didn't have the strength to argue anymore and I didn't think the children would understand, so why upset them further? It was no secret I suffered. We all did. Helen and Karl both missed their brother tremendously.

♪♫

All my brothers were here at the lodge. A prodigal son, I'd missed being around my peers. I couldn't really blame them for the way they'd all reacted to my son's death, so it had been easier to stay away.

We took our seats as the lights went down. A single conical light danced on the stage and out walked the conductor, who took a bow before fading to the right. And then behind him, like a wide-eyed doe, appeared a most alluring vision—a striking young woman with auburn hair swooped up into a loose chignon. She had an easy smile, curling up gently at the corners.

I felt the quickening of my heart just as Stella reached over and squeezed my arm. "It's Phoebe," she whispered, smelling of liquor, and I remembered the pockets of her mink coat, but before I could say anything, Phoebe looked into the audience. I thought she'd recognized me as she nodded and then took her seat at the piano.

In the five years since I'd seen her, I'd lost at least twenty pounds and was more salt than pepper, especially at the temples. Of course, Phoebe, too, had changed, but she'd simply become even more stunning—no longer the waif who'd graced us with her presence in the parlor like dandelion snow drifting in and then out of our lives. Her facial features had sharpened as if life had chiseled away a part of her, and yet she'd developed into an even more refined woman.

Phoebe played a short introduction as Marie took her place on stage. The singing began. I sat through the concert with Stella clinging to me as if she feared I'd abandon her. Her mink coat absorbed the tears, streaming down her cheeks and neck as we stood to applaud. "That was beautiful," she said. "The music almost makes you forget everything and remember everything at the same time."

The lights went up and before I could exit my row, George stood there with Phoebe. My blood drained to my feet.

"Dr. and Mrs. Marnier, so nice to see you again," George said. He looked happy since the last time I'd seen him and had wanted to kill him. "You remember my girl?" My heart lost its rhythm. Phoebe opened her mouth to say something—to protest, I prayed—but before she could utter a sound, George had taken her by the waist, pulling her into him.

"Why, yes, George," Stella said, taking my hand, practically piercing my palm with her fingernails. "Hello, Miss Armstrong."

George did not deserve Phoebe. He'd always had lots of girls and not one of them had ever denied him, at least not according to him. At that moment, I'd hoped Phoebe wasn't another of his conquests.

Phoebe caught my eye and I hoped she couldn't tell how my smiling lips quivered. She then reached out to take our hands. "My sincerest condolences, Dr. and Mrs. Marnier. I am truly heartbroken over Leland."

Stella looked at me at a loss as to what to say next, for in the year since his death, no one had ever mentioned my son's name.

"He was such a dear boy. I loved Leland as if he were my own blood."

I cleared my throat. "We were so moved by your performance, Miss Armstrong."

"Thank you, Dr. Marnier. I hoped to see you again someday," she said, looking at Stella. "I would have come to the funeral, but I was in France working with the Red Cross."

George stepped in, taking possession of Phoebe's hand to kiss her fingers. I could see her blush. She looked uncomfortable as she pulled her hand away. "The doctor opened a new office over on Prospect," George said.

Stella slung an arm possessively through mine and then approached Phoebe to give her a kiss on the cheek before returning her grasp of me. Stella's civility astounded me. "Bravo, Phoebe. And I thought your *Für Elise* Sonata was the most brilliant piano composition I have ever heard," Stella said.

"Thank you." Phoebe smiled and asked, "And how are Helen and little Karl?"

I cut a glance at Stella who'd always been a good actress, but tonight she outdid Florence Lawrence right out of a scene from *The Pawns of Destiny*. "Just fine and not so little. Growing like weeds," Stella responded. "Why, just yesterday little Karl lost a molar, and Helen has her first beau."

"I've missed them so," Phoebe said.

Hearing her sweet, melodic voice, I realized just how much I'd missed Phoebe Mae Armstrong. I remembered her gentle ways with the children. When she'd been around, an aura of happiness and serenity filled the hours. Even Stella had more good days than bad until the day she didn't—until the day she sent Phoebe away.

Lodge members and the concert audience were being escorted out of the meeting hall as the lights went out.

"Helen must be close to fifteen by now," Phoebe said as the crowd pushed her into me.

I recognized her French perfume, the smell of citrus, jasmine and tal-cum, but also something earthy washed over me. In a flash, and with every cell in my body, I wanted her. More than any other endeavor I'd set my mind to, this one carried the most weight. I had to possess her. I didn't want this night to end.

My mouth seemed to step out in front of me as I said, "You must come out to the house." The words spilled out like a split-open sack of grain.

Stella grabbed my arm, digging her nails in. I could feel her eyes searing a hole through the side of my head.

"Tonight?" Stella asked. "Doc, it's late and I'm sure Phoebe and George have plans."

"Oh, but I'd love to," Phoebe said, without missing a beat.

George looked at me and shrugged his shoulders.

"Karl was just a baby the last time you saw him, so you won't remember each other, but Helen would be thrilled to see you again," I said.

"Doc, the children are asleep and—"

Before Stella could protest further, I came to my senses. "Oh, but of course. Well, then, George, you and Phoebe must come for dinner Saturday evening."

Nothing else mattered. In that instant, it didn't matter that I was a married man. George's presence didn't matter even though the last time I saw him, I wanted to kill him. I was prepared to give it all up, let it all go, only to have Phoebe. There had to be some way to be with her. It would be unbearable to lose her again. I had to find a way. And so, I would become obsessed. Thoughts of Phoebe would consume me until the day I died.

"Splendid idea," George said. "By the way, there are some ideas I wish to discuss with you."

I watched as he slipped his arm through Phoebe's. What a tearing to say goodbye, but at least I had hope for Saturday.

17
Hope

The scent of Phoebe lingered as I lay in bed next to Stella. I tossed and turned, my mind spinning so loudly I feared she might have been able to hear, but she'd already passed out. The encounter with Phoebe left Stella quite agitated—not that she needed an excuse to drink. She'd come home and drank to the point where I had to help her up to bed. Finally, I stood and headed out of the room.

"Where are you going?" Stella asked with a snort.

"Sorry, I thought you were asleep. I'm going downstairs. I didn't want to bother you."

She rolled over and went back to sleep.

I found myself staring out the streaked front window. The moon seemed so close I held out my hand, wanting to reach out and take it in my arms; hold onto it and let it wash me in its light. I craved its warmth to make me feel alive again. I felt so alone; I was separated from everyone and everything by the invisible glass shield through which the moon's rays were lighting up the keys of the very dusty piano. For the first time since his death, I looked around the parlor where tintypes lined the mantel; where dead flowers drooped in vases on tables covered with a thick patina of dust. Too afraid to enter this room, I'd done whatever it took to avoid it, to the point of entering and exiting our home through the back door, but now I felt dazed and not in control of my faculties. The encounter with Phoebe had left me undone as well.

Slowly, as the moon continued to illuminate the room, things were being revealed to me; things I had tried so hard to keep hidden—lies I told myself. For deep inside I knew the truth. I knew from the first moment I saw Phoebe Mae Armstrong sitting on the piano bench five years ago, I had fallen in love with her. For obvious reasons, it wasn't right and I pushed down any indecent thought of her and me. I was a married man and she was practically still a girl. And as miserable as my marriage had become, I remained strong. I remained true.

I padded over to the piano, took a seat and uncovered the lid. I brushed my fingers across the keys, tracing over where Leland had touched. I inhaled slowly and breathed in the scent of the gardenias that were always soaking in a shallow crystal dish on the piano. Drifting back to the time I first heard Leland playing, for a brief period I felt happy, almost euphoric. From where I sat, I saw myself peeking in through the window as I had that spring evening five years ago. I saw myself as perhaps Leland had seen me.

I saw Phoebe seated next to him on the piano bench as he played the music I'd been missing: the music I'd always miss.

And indeed as the *Ode to Joy* intensified, I fell back to those few precious days when Leland was alive with laughter and hope and the promise of another kiss from the girl he loved. I could see a happy Helen and a pregnant Stella growing with child as did my fondness for Phoebe. I closed the piano lid and left the room.

Through the window, the moon lured me outside onto the veranda where I could hear Leland playing *Moonlight Sonata*. I sank into the porch swing. I found myself with my son again, fishing off the shores of Santa Monica, hunting in the hills of Hollywood, designing his glasses—the ones with the miniature Winchester rifle replica on the arms and the orange-tinted shade. "Oh, Leland, my joy," I sang softly.

Tonight, as soon as Phoebe first walked out onto the stage, the music had returned to me again and it would stay with me until my death. Without a doubt, Phoebe connected me to Leland. A heavenly angel, she'd also come to lead me into the light.

♪♫

It seemed like an eternity before Saturday night would arrive, and the days following my last encounter with Phoebe had left me lost and bewildered. Shamefully, I ached for her. I struggled and wrestled with my conscience, but ultimately, I'd made up my mind to pursue her. I simply needed to find a way.

Saturday afternoon, I stepped into the kitchen where Stella, a Nervous Nellie, prepared for our guests. She gave orders to Hazel, the new maid, a light-skinned negress in her late twenties with a spray of freckles across a nose too small for her plump face. She had a nice demeanor. Helen and Karl adored her, and so far, she hadn't quit.

Hazel had just rinsed the last of our best china. The blue calico curtains above the sink had been washed and pressed. I noticed the new stove, and wanted to ask Stella where it came from and what happened to the old one, when I smelled the burning cigarette in an ashtray next to a small glass of whiskey. I didn't think they belonged to Hazel, but would address all of this later. Nothing would ruin my evening.

"Your hair looks nice," I told Stella. She'd had her hair done earlier down at the beauty shop, a sort of tight creation tugging at her temples and giving her eyes a stretched out foreign look—an attempt at looking exotic, I surmised. She'd even had her nails manicured, one of which she used to point at the help as she ignored my compliment, and, without looking at me, she asked, "What stinks? Is that a new cologne?" She then turned to the help. "We'll start with some champagne and *horse devores.*"

"*Hors d'oeuvres,*" I said, causing her to shoot me a spiteful look that could have sent me to my grave a lot sooner.

"Just make sure you don't bring them out too soon," she told Hazel. "Allow the guests to get comfortable. I'll let you know when we're ready."

"Yes, ma'am."

Useless in the kitchen as usual, I decided to go to the parlor to make sure everything was in order. Before I exited, Helen stepped in primly to say goodbye. Dressed in her tennis skirt and shoes, she headed off to tennis practice. Her scramble of freckles seemed more pronounced nowadays from her time spent running around in the sun.

"But you'll be back soon? We have company," I said.

She didn't seem as interested or enthusiastic as I thought she might be. Initially, she had been angry with Phoebe for going away, but I thought the anger had dissipated with time. Nowadays, she focused all of her attention on the Hollywood High School tennis team, where she had a crush on one of the boys who helped the tennis coach.

Helen sniffed contemptuously. "I'll try, Father," she said, peering at me. "Your hair looks different. Did you change your part?"

"I haven't combed it yet," I told her as I ran my fingers through my hair. Earlier I'd noticed a spot that seemed to be thinning and, instead of slicking it back, I parted it to one side.

"It looks nice that way—makes you look younger, more relaxed," Helen said with a giggle and grabbed a warm *hors d'oeuvre*—a toasted cracker with cheese—and ran out the back door.

"Helen, do try to be home by five," Stella called after her, "I'll need help with Karl and I want you both cleaned up and presentable."

♪♫

Promptly at seven, I heard a knock at the door. Karl, eager to have company, ran ahead of the help to see. "George," he screamed and jumped into his arms. I held my breath and there, next to George, stood Phoebe holding a bouquet of flowers. Her face was hidden under a blue felt hat, with a small bejeweled replica of the Eiffel Tower pinned to the side.

"Come in. Come in," Stella called out from behind me, and before they had taken two steps in, she said, "Who needs a drink? Doc, take Phoebe's coat."

The night was cool. The collar of Phoebe's coat came up to practically swallow her chin. When she finally looked up, I caught my breath and the same electric current I'd felt at the concert sparked once more. I lost myself in eyes that twinkled over the backdrop of a heavenly star-filled sky. George stepped in to remove the coat cinching her tiny waist and handed it to me. Oh, how I longed to take that waist in my arms and swoop her into me.

We were all seated in the parlor as Hazel brought in the drinks. Helen, all washed up since tennis, walked in wearing a simple white linen dress with a pink silk ribbon that framed her tanned face. Phoebe gasped and stood to greet her.

"Oh, Helen, you're just lovely." She reached out her hand and Helen gave her a limp wrist. But now Helen's eyes darted from Phoebe to me as if she imagined the possibility of Phoebe and me being together. Her face said she couldn't take any more changes. Her chilly reception did not warm up throughout the meal—a meal she left untouched.

Dinner seemed like old times except George now sat where Leland had, many years ago, next to Phoebe. Helen, not the same talkative little girl she was many years ago, sat across from me—all of us during that time competing for Phoebe's attention. But Helen had also been there the night Stella accused me of having an affair with Phoebe, and then again later, she'd said because of Phoebe, Leland was dead. So much had been said in anger. I hoped time had healed all of us. I hoped Helen didn't believe what her mother had said.

"May I be excused?" Helen said, scraping the legs of her chair. She'd merely scooted her food around, rearranging it on her plate.

"Yes, I suppose, and take your brother," Stella said.

"Oh, Mother. Can't I stay up just a little longer?" Karl asked.

"How about if I come up and read you a story after you're all tucked in?" George said. Karl nodded and pushed away from the table, dashing up the stairs ahead of Helen.

"Good night, Helen. It was so wonderful to see you again," Phoebe said, gazing at Helen as she left the room. She then turned to Stella. "She is so beautiful and seems so mature, Mrs. Marnier, what's your secret?"

Stella, about to take another sip, set down her glass. "Thank you. It's all about setting an example." She then turned to me. "Isn't that right, Doc?"

After a dinner I'd scarcely touched, George and I retired to my study. He wanted to discuss business matters. I only wanted to discuss the matter of Phoebe.

"Listen, Doc, there's some property I'd like to show you out in Glendale where there's a natural stream of water. There's also a business opportunity on Central Avenue. You can pick them up for peanuts."

"George, I'm not interested. My mind is just not into business matters anymore. Surely, you understand," I said, almost glaring at him.

"Right, right. Just hear me out. There's just so much opportunity. I'm telling you, Glendale is the fastest growing city in the nation. We could drive out next Saturday. Bring the girls."

"The girls?" I asked.

"Sure, Phoebe and Stella. Make a day of it."

"Well, let me think about it," I said, not needing to think about it. "Pour us some more brandy, George."

I found Stella weeping as I entered the other room. Now what?

"Leland talked to Phoebe," Stella said, dabbing her eyes with a handkerchief. "He says he's all right. Isn't that right, Phoebe?"

I turned to Phoebe and shook my head. "Pardon me?"

"What, what else does he say, Phoebe? Tell us," Stella insisted.

I noticed the curtains fluttering and then with an air of detachment, Phoebe turned and addressed Stella. "Leland wants you to know he forgives you."

Stella gasped, clasping her trembling hands to her heart and then reached for her drink.

"But, Stella, he also wants you to get help," Phoebe said, and Stella immediately set down her glass.

When Phoebe turned to me, I felt myself drowning in a pool of cool waters. "Doc, he wants you both to be happy."

Stella sobbed and hugged Phoebe. "Oh, thank you, Sweet Phoebe. Please, tell him I promise to quit drinking." Stella looked around the room and called out, "Leland, I promise." Finally, she pulled away.

Stifling a tear, I forced a smile and, as was typical for Stella who always wanted more, she asked, "Is that all? Is there anything else he wants to tell us, Phoebe?"

Phoebe paused, tilting her head as if she listened to the soft, orange-scented wind picking up outside and causing the drapery to billow. "He forgives me for going away long ago," she said, closing her eyes. I sat in silence afraid to disturb her, afraid of what else she might say. "He understands everything now," she said, opening her eyes, turning to me once more. "Doc, he's sorry you had to find him that way. He asks you not to blame yourself. He says, 'Learn to live. Go with your heart and be happy.'" She smiled, holding her gaze on me a little longer.

Stella sunk into the davenport and put her head in her hands just as George entered the room.

"Say, what did I miss? Did someone die while I was in the other room?" George had never been known for his diplomacy; I don't know what Phoebe ever saw in him.

We all made plans for an excursion out to the Glendale property and said goodnight, but in the meanwhile something uncharacteristic had been awakened in my wife.

18
'Til Death Do Us Part

Stella wanted a divorce. She announced it on a rainy morning while I sat in the kitchen warming my hands with a cup of hot coffee and the newspaper. I'd been reading about how the war in Europe had really heated up, and I wished I could have been commissioned. In our own battle-weary home, we'd reached a truce, but little did I know it was just the calm before the storm.

"I saw Phoebe last night," Stella said.

I was eager to hear more about Phoebe, but instead I said, "You didn't come to bed," my morning voice cracking. I could smell that old familiar stink.

"So, what of it?" she said. "I needed to think. I'm surprised you didn't come looking for me. You're always checking on me. I can't stand it anymore." She grabbed an empty cup from the cupboard and poured herself some coffee.

I'd been distancing myself from her, allowing her enough rope to hang herself.

She pulled a bottle of whiskey out from the pocket in her robe, set it onto the table and plopped into a chair. "There, I'm not going to hide it anymore. Divorce me if you want. I'm tired of living as your prisoner."

"You said you would quit."

"And you said you were going to leave me alone," she said, pouring a generous portion of whiskey into her cup. She was picking a fight, something she did when she needed an excuse to drink. "I'm tired of you trying to control me."

She poured some cream into her whiskey coffee and stirred, breaking the silence with the clinking of the cup. She took a long drink and seemed to settle down. I pulled the newspaper up and hid my face. A heavy rain pelted the windows. "I attended a lecture up at the Rosy Cross Temple,"

Stella said. "Marie gave a talk on the theosophical views on marriage and the church."

I turned the page and listened to see where this might be going. It was no secret how vocal Marie could be when it came to freedom of thought and secularism, the latter about which I couldn't disagree, but I always thought religion was good for people like Stella and, seemingly, the only thing to keep her in line.

"Pretty soon, women will be able to vote," Stella said.

I stopped reading. Was this an attempt at having a civil conversation? If so, I wasn't interested.

"You know, George was telling me about Nevada. It's now possible to obtain a divorce there. He said some of the men from the lodge have already obtained one. You might want to look into that," Stella said.

"And why on earth would I want to do that?" I said, and tried to change the subject. She was obviously already drunk and getting bolder by the minute.

"Stella, where is this coming from?" I said, standing to leave. "I'm not so sure you should be hanging around those people."

"Those people?" she said, pointing her spoon at me, her hands bony and dry. "You mean Phoebe and your pal, George, and Marie. Doc, you should be happy about that. Trouble is you're not happy at all. As a matter of fact, you haven't been for a very long time. I can't bring our son back. I can't make you happy." She peered at me with her sad, old familiar crooked grin. "But there's someone who can and she's showing me a different way."

"Stella, I'd advise you to take Marie with a grain of salt."

"Marie? I'm not talking about her," she said with a chortle. "It's no secret. I see how you are around Phoebe. It was obvious the moment she stepped into our home."

"Oh, here you go again. That's ridiculous," I said. "Besides, Phoebe is George's girl."

"People are not possessions. Doc, as smart as you are, you're not very evolved."

"What in tarna . . . what the hell are you talking about, woman?"

"I can't bring him back. I don't want his death to be in vain. You heard what Phoebe said. He wants us both to be happy." She cried. "I want you to be happy—really I do." She stood to face me, tears streaming down her face. "Wesley, I want a divorce."

"A what? Stella, I thought you said you were going to quit drinking. Tomorrow, you won't even remember we had this conversation."

"No, Wesley, quite the contrary. There's not a day I don't remember. It's on my mind constantly. I can't change what happened. I can't change who I am. I can't quit and I can't do this anymore. It's killing me. Let this be my amends to our son. I'm letting you go." She put her head down onto the table and sobbed.

And with that I picked up my umbrella and opened the back door. I wanted to run, before Stella came to her senses.

♪♫

Six months after establishing residency in Las Vegas, the marriage was over. I returned home so that Stella and I could talk to the children.

Helen slammed her bedroom door, refusing to come out. "Please, sweetie, we need to talk."

"There's nothing to talk about, besides, I don't want to hear what you have to say. Mother already told me. Just go and be happy."

Karl ran across the hallway and wrapped his spindly arms around my legs. "Don't you love us anymore?" He cried and my heart cracked. "Daddy, please don't leave."

I picked him up and held him in my arms.

"Oh, Karl, of course I do. More than you'll ever know. Daddy is just going away, but not far."

"Please take me with you."

"Son, it's just that I'll be spending more time at my new office and you have your school here and you've made some friends." I swiped away the tears on his cheek. "Mother tells me you already have a best friend?"

He smiled. "Henry. He's six like me." He held up five fingers and an index finger. "Can I come visit your new office?"

"Absolutely. As a matter of fact, this Friday after school, you'll pack a bag as if you're going on a trip. Perfect."

"What about Helen?"

"I don't think she's ready yet. This weekend, it's just you and me, pal."

And my spirits lifted knowing there would be a way to spend time with my son. "I have so much I want to show you."

19

Yes

I'd purchased a two-story Craftsman-style home on Central Avenue that sat right in the middle of the hustle and bustle of Glendale. The optometry business was operated downstairs; the living quarters were upstairs. Dr. Phillip Warrington, who'd run the business since 1905, had fallen ill and had hoped to leave the business to his son, Jack Warrington, but Jack didn't seem to have the same calling as his father nor was he ready to take over. George, a circling buzzard, had found out about this business opportunity for me, and had swooped in on the deal. Part of the terms of the sales agreement was that I would mentor Jack for as long as he remained interested, and when the time came I'd consider the possibility of making him a partner.

Karl and I walked into the office. To find Jack working on the project I'd assigned him, pleased me. I figured all he needed was some guidance he hadn't received from his own father.

"Jack, this is my son, Karl." Karl reached up to shake his hand. Jack, a thin dapper young fellow and a sharp dresser, gripped my son's hand.

"Hello there, Karl. Going to be an eye doctor like your pop?"

"Nope, I'm going to be a fighter pilot," Karl said, holding out his arms and tilting sideways as if he were gliding through the skies.

We then walked to the front of the office to a small reception area where immediately I heard her sweet voice. "Good morning, Dr. Marnier."

I almost lost my breath.

"Phoebe!" Karl shouted and ran into her arms.

George had hired Phoebe to run my new office. She'd been in need of a job and a distraction. After a long illness, her father had recently passed. You'd never be able to tell how much she suffered inside. She beamed when she saw Karl.

"Hi, sweetie, so good to see you. Are you here to help your papa?"

I offered my condolences and then tore myself away, leaving Karl with Phoebe so I could get back to help Jack with his project. I'd noticed some things needed correcting, but waited until we were alone.

"A little tightening here," I said, referring to an area where the lenses attached to the frames, "but otherwise, looking good, Jack."

"Doc, I think I've found my wife," he said, looking toward the front of the office where Phoebe was stationed. "I think I'm in love."

The following week, George dropped by the office. "Are you ready, Doll?" he asked as Phoebe grabbed her coat. My blood began to boil. If anyone were to have her, it couldn't be George. And it couldn't be Jack. I felt a bit possessive, but a tad even more competitive. She needed rescuing, I told myself.

"We're meeting up with Phoebe's brother Earl," George said to me as he helped Phoebe with her coat. "He's in from Vegas. You should come along."

"Maybe next time. I've got some work to finish up here."

"Doc, don't you ever go home?" Phoebe asked. I'd been the one to lock up after her and Jack every night.

"This is my home," I told her, and she raised her eyebrows.

The next evening, as I escorted the last patient into the waiting area, I found Phoebe tidying up the small room. The patient left and she turned off a table lamp. Except for a few pleasantries and discussion about the patients, we'd exchanged no words about my marital status. The days had become unbearable. My heart pounded constantly; every step I took felt unsteady, like a toddler learning to walk. As Phoebe made her way back to her desk, I gave her ample room so as not to get too close or brush up against her accidentally. We seemed to tiptoe around each other. Later, Phoebe would tell me it had been uncomfortable for her, yet thrilling and, quite frankly, she hadn't known how she would be able to work around me knowing I was a married man.

I handed her the patient's file. "Mrs. Phillips will need to be contacted again once her new lenses are in," I said, a little too business-like.

"Of course," Phoebe said, staring at me. "Anything else?" she asked just as Jack came out of the exam room.

"Can I give you a lift, Phoebe?" he asked, his eyebrows lifted in anticipation.

"Sure, just let me finish up this paperwork," she said, scribbling some notes.

Jack smiled, rubbing his hands and rocking back on his heels. I felt the ground slipping away.

Phoebe then looked up. "Oh, Doc, before I go. Mrs. Jones called to ask if there might be a possibility of squeezing her in tomorrow morning. I told her I'd call to confirm. Sorry, Jack, this might take a few minutes."

"Jack, run along," I said. "I'll take Miss Armstrong home." Jack's eyes narrowed and he finally left, but not without a look of reluctance.

I breathed a little easier as I looked over Phoebe's shoulder at my calendar, careful not to get too close, but she smelled of vanilla and jasmine. "I suppose we can move Mr. Cranston up, but then you'll have to call him, too."

We were alone and no more words were exchanged as Phoebe turned and stood to face me. She wrapped her arms around me and turned her face up to kiss me. Her lips were warm and soft. I could taste the residue of sweet coffee. I slumped onto the desk and pulled her in, holding tightly. Her heart beat as fast as mine. I was drowning. "Oh, God, I love you, Phoebe," I blurted out.

She gazed into my eyes, running her fingers through my hair. Tugging gently, she said, "I know," and kissed me with even more passion. I never wanted to let go.

Eventually, she opened her eyes and pushed away. "Oh, dear, I must call your patients," she said breathlessly, and then pulled me back for more.

1949: Oakland—
Charley

The steamy clouds outside Dr. Savage's office window are stretched out across the sky, escaping the large locomotive that is San Francisco beyond.

"I'm feeling restless. I could use some exercise right about now," I say to Savage as I tug at the collar of my shirt. I'd asked to be given something other to wear than pajamas. The shirt makes me feel more human, but it must have belonged to someone with a pencil neck.

"I think that's a great idea," Savage says, "and then perhaps tomorrow you can continue with your story. I'm assuming that until Doc and Stella divorced, Phoebe waited in the wings."

Like a train coming up the tracks of my throat, I feel the vibrations and unfasten the button on my collar just as Doc's voice tumbles out of my mouth.

"Not exactly."

Savage leans back in his seat.

1917: Glendale—
Doc

Phoebe had been working for me for only a few days. I wouldn't waste any more time. I asked her to marry me. I'd driven her out to the property in Woodside. We were creek side where she sat on a fallen sycamore trunk. As the sun set over the Verdugo Mountains, I knelt down on one knee.

"But why not. Why won't you marry me?" I asked her, rising back up on my feet. "I love you, my Darling. Is it because you're dating George?"

"No, I tell you, he's just a friend."

"But does he know that?"

"I think so. I've never led him on?"

"And what about Jack?"

She shook her head. "Jack? He's a silly school boy."

"Well, then, what is it? Don't you love me?"

Phoebe took my hands. "It's not that. It's because I love you that I won't marry you."

"I don't understand." I took a seat next to her.

"I am unable to give anyone a child."

"You poor dear. I am so sorry." I hadn't even thought far enough into the future to consider having children with her. With her, I always found myself in the moment. "We could find a specialist, if that's what you want. We could build our home here. As long as I'm with you, I'm happy. I'll do whatever it takes."

Phoebe shook her head. "It's just—I am devoted to my music. If I wasn't in need of money, I wouldn't be working for you now."

"But this is perfect. I already have children," I said, and as soon as the words came out of my mouth, I was sorry I spoke.

She stood rigid, hands curling into balls, and I could see her trying to be brave. "Yes, you have Helen and Karl," she said and wept. "Oh, Doc, you mustn't abandon your children. I couldn't bear it. I love Karl and Helen as if they were my own." She covered her face, lowering her head.

"Absolutely not, Darling. I could never do that." I took her in my arms and kissed the top of her head.

"And what about Leland? You can't just pretend he never existed." She pulled away.

"Darling, not a day goes by that I don't think about him." I took her hands and peered into her eyes. "You make me so happy and I know we could make this work. You could spend the rest of your days surrounded by music. Just say you'll marry me."

"I can't," she said, looking up. "What about Stella?"

"She says she only wants me to be happy. She wants to be happy."

"I'll need to speak with her," Phoebe said, turning her head away.

So, it wasn't exactly "no."

1949: Oakland—
Charley

Savage scratches his head and leans forward. "But when did she say yes?"

I light a cigarette and look up toward the ceiling, suddenly remembering the time I found a newspaper clipping amongst Mother's things.

"After Phoebe talked to Stella and determined there'd be no going back, they were married almost immediately."

"So were George and Jack invited to the wedding?"

I shake my head. "It was even reported that Stella had made the wedding garments for Phoebe," I say to Savage. "But only because she was under Phoebe's hypnotic influence," I laugh, holding up both hands, raising the middle and forefinger in the air to emphasize the quotation.

Dr. Savage's eyes widen.

"Unbelievable. Yeah, I know." I stand to stretch.

"But, so I'm curious," Savage says, standing also. "How did Doc handle George and Jack? They were both obviously smitten with Phoebe."

Hands on my butt, I arch my back. "The way he handled it was not to do anything. George and Jack found out about the nuptials after the fact."

Dr. Savage purses his lips, shaking his head. "Not very nice."

"I tell you," I'm bending sideways at the waist now, "Doc put Doc first."

"It's hard to imagine what Phoebe might have seen in him."

"Phoebe put Phoebe first, too," I say.

"Perhaps," Savage says. "Just one more thing. You said she was unable to have children and yet here you are."

"That's right," I say, walking toward the door. "I think I'll go for a swim now."

Dr. Savage smiles and opens the door for me as I head down the hall toward the pool.

"See you tomorrow."

In the afternoon, I'm melting from the humidity and as soon as I dive into the pool, I'm transformed. I hold my breath the entire length doing the breaststroke. After several laps, I rotate to a crawl, thrashing my arms and legs and puffing out my cheeks. I'm trying to empty my mind of any thoughts of my past—or Doc's. I flip over and continue with the backstroke. The clouds scud by and for a spell I'm on my back, creek side with my childhood sweetheart—a little girl named Teresa whose face I've never forgotten. A welcome memory.

We're looking up to the sky, trying to make out shapes in the clouds. *I see my papa,* I tell her. I have no idea that's not where he's dwelling—up in the heavens with all of the other angels and saints from Milty's church. I'd been so wrong. I flip back over.

Now, I see sand at the bottom of the pool and seaweed. I know I'm not dreaming because everything is in color. Kelp and red algae sway like hula dancers as a school of tiny yellow and grey fish swim by. Soon, I'm surrounded by bright orange garibaldi and blue-banded gobi. Euphoric, I don't ever want to surface, but I need to breathe. I pop my head out of the water to gulp in some air. And when I do, I choke back tears of sorrow.

Savage had asked about Mother's inability to have children. Why did they even have me? A question I've asked myself over and over. Was I just another mistake of Doc's? Would Doc have loved me as much as he did Leland? Would my sessions with Savage reveal the truth? Afraid to think about it anymore, I take a deep breath and dive back under.

20

Three's a Crowd

1917: Catalina—
Doc

After an invigorating swim in Descanso Bay, I returned to my room where I'd left my blushing new bride to rest following a night teeming with music and passion. Phoebe had shown me a different side of herself. She was a surprise—a progressive woman with no inhibitions about sexuality.

Later, when I returned to our cottage nestled only a short distance from Avalon on the island of Catalina, she was bathing and so I waited for her on the bed hoping for another go-round. Silhouetted, in the bathroom doorway, by the morning light, I took in the glorious vision. Like a halo around her head, she'd wrapped a white bath towel. Her luminescent skin shone almost as white except for the flushing after her hot bath. Viola-shaped, she was a little broader at the bottom with a narrower waist and breasts, round and firm; her areolas, the hue and feel of fresh rose petals. A tigress sneaking up on its prey, she approached me, the towel slipping from her hair as she slinked into bed. She slipped her hand under the sheet and onto my erection.

"I see the ocean swim did you no good." She leaned down to kiss me and I pulled her into my arms.

"My darling, I love you more today than yesterday," I said after we'd made love again. "I love you more than you will ever know. I live only because you love me."

"Oh, you mustn't say that," she said, rolling away and pulling up the covers. "That is quite a burden you put on me. I am not your reason for living." Her admonishment, a sharp chord in *fortissimo,* cut me. But then, as if she were speaking to a child, she switched to a *pianissimo,* softening her tone.

"And so, Darling, when was it you first knew you were smitten with me?" she asked, now hugging her knees to her chest.

"Smitten? I knew I was in love with you the night of the concert over at the lodge."

"Yes, but you were smitten with me when you first saw me through the window of your home giving lessons to Leland."

"You saw me?"

She nodded, twirling a loose damp tendril. "I sensed something that moment and turned to see you take a seat on the porch swing. I knew something was about to happen."

Until I met Phoebe, I'd never believed in the notion of love at first sight. The idea seemed ridiculous. But truth be told, she was the warm, ebullient sensation you get after a sip of champagne, the most intoxicating creature I'd ever set eyes upon.

"And so, when was it you knew you loved me?" I asked.

"Oh, I've always loved you, Darling. You are my moon, and my stars."

"But only *part* of the constellation?" I said, half joking. "I thought we were soul mates. Isn't that a reason for living?"

"Certainly, my darling, and indeed we sustain each other on this journey called life, but I am not your life and you are not mine." I felt deflated as she kissed me sweetly on the lips and jumped out of bed. "I'm famished. Shall we venture out for some breakfast?"

Her declarations crushed me. After the night of love making and the declarations of love exchanged, I felt demoralized. I'd let thoughts of her consume me for so many years. I'd dared to think she was the reason I couldn't stay in my marriage. But that wasn't true. She was merely the light in the dark. I had now committed the rest of my life to her. There was nothing I wouldn't do for her. I wondered if I'd misinterpreted things. The way she smiled at me; the way she loved me the night before, surely I meant more to her than merely a star-crossed lover?

1949: US Naval Hospital—
Charley

The next morning, Beethoven is spinning around again on the phonograph, as I sit in Savage's office eager to let Doc share with him all that had been revealed to me the day before about the trip to Catalina.

"Are you finished?" Savage asks, and I turn to see him staring at me.

"What, oh, I'm sorry," Doc says with a deep chortle. "I was just remembering more of the honeymoon. I'll spare you the titillating details. But the next part is where it really gets interesting. You see, I learned a little about Phoebe's lovers and you can't imagine who we ran into on our honeymoon—not just one ghost from the past."

1917: Catalina—
Doc

We'd taken a carriage into the small town of Avalon, and along the way I could see there'd been some progress made after the fire that had swept through the town a couple of years ago. Clearly, tourism had dropped off, and now the little beach lay empty except for a few lonely women and their children.

"Doc, promise me you'll make your children a priority. I'll not stand in the way nor should you allow your business to," Phoebe said.

"I promise. As soon as we get home, I'll speak to Stella about letting the children spend more time with us."

I helped her out of the carriage and we strolled along an empty promenade, my fingers threaded through hers. Small boats bobbed in the harbor as the fishermen unloaded their fish, hungry seagulls circling above. I could smell the bacon wafting out of a new restaurant that had just been re-opened. My stomach growled, and as we passed what used to be a dance pavilion, I heard a familiar voice.

"Doc!"

My whole body prickled. I turned to see George and two other men who had just stumbled out of the newly-rebuilt Pilgrim Club, a gambling casino for men only.

What the hell was George doing here? I didn't recognize the two other goons at first. George marched our way. He seemed angry, but with the way his bushy black eyebrows ran together, he could have been a squinting mole coming up from out of a hole.

"Well, well, well. Here you are?" he said, pointing his cigar at me. "What are you two doing here?"

"George, we're on our honeymoon," I said.

"How could you do this to me, Doc? And, I thought I was your best friend. You rotten scoundrel."

This caught me off guard. Phoebe had assured me there was never anything between the two of them besides their music and they had never shared anything romantic.

My stomach lurched as the other two goons came closer. I stepped in front of Phoebe when I recognized Tom Dragna and Joe Shaw, who managed one of my stores.

George laughed and wouldn't stop. "Oh, Doc, you're a riot. You steal my girl and you think I'm mad at you. You think I'm here because of that?" He turned to the others and slapped his thigh. "Isn't that hysterical?"

"I'm not your girl, George. You know I never was," Phoebe said.

George peered at Phoebe, who squeezed my hand a little tighter, and I wondered about the truth of this. Even if there had been something between the two of them, I didn't care. I loved her so much and wanted her bad enough I would be willing to overlook anything.

He looked as if he were about to say something to her, but instead asked, "Doc, you remember Tom Dragna?"

Of course I did. Since the time I'd first met Dragna at one of Earl's boxing matches, he'd come up in the mob world and I wasn't too pleased George had been spending so much time hanging around him. And then George had also changed. He'd become a little edgier and a little rougher around those edges. In only a few more years, Dragna would go on to make history as a bootlegger, mobster and become a member of the Los Angeles crime family.

"So, I was looking for you, Doc," George said. "Someone told me you'd gotten married and were honeymooning on Catalina Island." He looked from Phoebe back to me and said, "Why, you old son-of-a-gun. My invitation must have gotten lost in the mail."

"It was just a small civil wedding ceremony."

"What a coincidence, I thought," said George. "You see—"

"We're actually here on business," Dragna said, and as soon as he interrupted George, I noticed George become a little restless, teetering on his toes.

"Tom's part of a little shipping operation running between here and the Port of Los Angeles," George said, stuffing his hands into his pockets.

Shipping business indeed. I arched my left eyebrow.

"Doc, I'm just hurt. That's all. You're my best friend and you didn't let me give you a proper send off." He pulled a cigar out of his pocket and handed it to me.

"And so, George, why are you here?"

"For a little R and R. I figured I should check the place out for myself. You know how I love a good card game," he said, pulling his hands out of his pockets and hooking a finger over at the casino. "Say," George continued, "I might ask you the same thing, Doc. What exactly are you doing here?"

"I told you, we're on our honeymoon."

"We're on our way to breakfast," Phoebe said.

George shook his head and sneered. "What a coincidence."

"What's that supposed to mean?" Phoebe asked.

"Doc, I'm the one who told you this place was for sale, did I not?"

Perhaps he had, but like most of his ideas, I'd put it out of my mind.

Phoebe immediately let go of my hand. "I'll meet you at the restaurant," she said and proceeded to walk away.

"No, Darling. We're finished here." I glared at George and turned to follow her.

"Doc, we should talk soon," he said, pointing in the direction of the harbor. "We're staying over at the Hermosa Hotel."

"For God's sake, George, I'm on my honeymoon!" I said, loud enough for my new bride to hear.

♪♫

Through the window of a little seaside diner, I could see the steam billowing from a steamship as it chugged closer to the harbor. Inside, the restaurant smelled of coffee and fresh-cut lumber. I could smell the bacon as the eggs popped in its grease on the skillet.

Phoebe had barely touched her breakfast. Her face looked inscrutable. She knew every fiber of me and could very well hurt me if she had that sort of temperament. She could carve out my soul and wring it out like a beach towel to dry, again if that was her temperament. But it wasn't.

"Darling, is everything all right?" I asked.

Always smiling, it made it difficult to tell whether she was upset or not. But, I'd also learned by now she also had an amazing way of simply detaching when a situation became unpleasant. The encounter with George had certainly left me feeling quite unsettled. I never saw her get angry; she would just go away and disappear into her music.

"I'd like to go back and rest," she said, and then she winked. "Last night's activities seem to have left me a little fatigued."

"But this is our honeymoon," I said. "I should come with you?"

"No, Sweetheart." She patted my arm and smiled. "There wouldn't be much resting then, now would there?" She winked again. "I don't want to be your distraction. Nor do I want to stand in the way of you doing what it is you came here to do. I'll be fine. Now, go see the sights and I'll catch up with you later."

What I came here to do? We'd only been married a few hours, but this had been the beginning of a turning point for Phoebe. Left alone at the restaurant, I wondered what she meant. I came here for our honeymoon. I had nothing up my sleeve, but the temptation to investigate the real estate opportunity in Catalina was too great. And I worried about the rather second-rate shipping business George might be getting involved in. I headed over to the Hermosa to seek him out.

Later, the music spiraled up out of the Descanso Hotel as I ascended the steps. I'd just left a meeting with George in town and had marched straight through the afternoon sun. I removed my sunglasses and as my eyes adjusted, through the window, I saw three guests in the parlor, two men around my age. Phoebe sat at the piano but I didn't recognize the music, a bit livelier than anything I'd heard her play before. One man stood off to the side tapping an Indian drumbeat on the tambourine. When my wife saw me walk in, she beamed and I melted into a seat to listen.

When she finished, I went up to kiss her cheek, possessively. "That was quite interesting, Darling."

"It's from a new Opera *Shanewis*. Oh, Doc, may I introduce you to Mr. Charles Wakefield Cadman? And this is his conductor, Monsieur Pierre Monteux. Charles is famous for his American Indian music, songs like *Land of the Sky Blue Water and*—"

"You don't say," I said, reaching out to take her away. "Excuse us."

We walked to the shoreline. Phoebe stared out across the ocean. Beyond, spun the world we'd left behind.

I was ashamed of my behavior. "Please forgive me."

"There's no need," she said.

"So, tell me again. You met Cadman in France?"

"Yes, he and I shared our love of music and we still do."

First George and now this Cadman. I worried about what else they'd all shared.

"As a matter of fact, he's asked if I would consider touring with him again next spring."

"What? You did tell him no. That you're a married woman."

Her glance could have cut me, but then she smiled. "What I told him was it would be a dream come true and a chance of a lifetime. I respect his work and his vision."

I panicked. "But, we—"

"I told him I'd discuss it with my husband, but that I was ready to settle down to a simpler life." She took my hand in hers. "Doc, I thought you wanted a simpler life?"

"Of course I do, what are you talking about?"

"What was all that business talk with George? Didn't you see those poor lonely women on the beach, some of them widows; some whose sons and husbands are at still at war?" She peered at me. "What is it about the more man acquires, the more man takes away? When is enough, enough, Doc?"

Phoebe turned to stare out across the ocean. In the distance, I could see the mainland where for just this week I was to leave my old life behind.

"Doc, there's something I need to share with you," she said, turning to me.

It scared me to death to hear what she might say: that she'd made a mistake by marrying me; that she had some terminal disease; that she was in love with Cadman and that he'd come to take her away?

"Darling, now that we're married, I don't want there to be any more secrets," she said.

"Absolutely, nor do I." My heart beat fast as I wiped my damp hands on my trousers. "I'm listening, Darling."

"Silly of me but I'd been waiting for you to ask," she said.

"So, please. What is it you want to tell me? What am I to ask?"

"It's about the beau who left me in France."

Beau? Cadman? Had he come to take her back? I felt myself drowning. I gulped in some air, unaware I stood in water.

Her eyes glistened with tears and I pulled her into my arms. "How could he?" She brushed away a tear with the back of her hand. "I'm listening. It's all right, you can tell me anything. It won't change how I feel about you."

She looked into my eyes and spoke slowly, in clipped sentences but to the point. "His name was Guillaume." She sniffled. "He was a soldier, killed as he led a charge against the entrenched Germans."

I stepped out of the water and shook out my shoes. "I'm so sorry." It took a few seconds for me to wrap my head around the fact that first of all Guillaume was a hero. Was he also the one who'd been her soul mate? Would I forever be eclipsed by the one who'd been her sun, her moon, the stars and the whole god-damned constellation? Was he the one she'd given her heart to—a heart broken and still taking time to heal?

"I always felt so guilty," she said.

I looked at her and wanted to comfort her. "But why?"

"Because it was you. Doc, you were the one I thought of when I was with him. Yours was the face I saw every time we made love. Oh, Doc, since the first moment I saw you . . . I thought it was merely a young girl's crush. I knew it was wrong. I thought it wouldn't last. I've loved you from the first moment we met."

"Oh, my darling," I said, pulling her into me. "I will love you until my very last breath."

21

Castles in the Air

**1949: US Naval Hospital—
Charley**

Savage is smiling. "So, Charley," Savage says. "You are here. Obviously, your mother was able to have children."

"Yes," Doc says. "But that wasn't until twelve years into the marriage. So much took place before then."

"If you're going to continue, I'd like something to drink," I say, annoyed Doc is hogging all my time with Savage—yet, I'm intrigued to hear whether he'll talk about my anticipated birth. "This is all leaving me just a little parched."

Savage points to the water. "Help yourself."

I get up and walk over to the credenza, where a pitcher and two glasses are set out. I pour myself a glass and then return to the sofa, where I light the pipe, sit back and cross my long legs just as the sounds of the piano solo from Beethoven's Symphony No. 9 fill the room.

**1918: Glendale, California—
Doc**

The war ended and, nine months after the honeymoon, Phoebe left me to tour with Cadman who'd become a self-proclaimed expert on American Indian music. I'd accompanied her for a lot of the American concerts but was unable to get away from work to go to Europe. Beside myself, I did what I did best; I worked even harder.

After a month, I could no longer stand it so I arranged to surprise her while she performed in Paris.

"My darling," she'd shouted when she saw me standing at the end of the piano. She sprang up and ran into my arms.

Cadman would have to find a replacement if only for the summer. I swept her away for a second honeymoon to Normandy. She'd wanted to show me the land and had fallen in love with the architecture of the castle *Château d'Ételan*.

After over a year, the tour ended and Phoebe returned home to me. I drove her out to Woodside to surprise her. Except for the smaller-size chateau, the gargoyles and a few other flamboyant touches, you'd never know we weren't in Normandy. The emerald front lawn rolled gently all the way down to the creek trickling through the property. I'd built Phoebe this home; a palace she'd never want to leave—a peaceful home. There would be enough room for Phoebe to add her own personal touches, and she would eventually add items here and there, but her focus would always be on her music.

I had to catch her as her knees buckled after walking into the chamber room to see the nine-foot Steinway. There it stood, all shiny and black, above the rosewood parquet floor.

"Oh, Wesley. You are too good to me," Phoebe said, weeping.

"Go on, sit down. See how it sounds."

She took a seat and turned to look at me, puckering her lips to blow me a kiss. She closed her eyes and disappeared to some faraway place. The music took her places I hadn't traveled; places I'd never been where people spoke a different language. She opened her eyes and saw me staring like a child left behind at the train station. She smiled. "Come, sit next to me." She scooted over, her voice pitched low, almost a whisper. "Place your hand over mine and close your eyes, my darling."

I wanted nothing more than to take her in my arms and hold her as I wrapped my left arm around her waist. I took comfort in the warmth of her body and felt at home, but readied myself for the journey on which I was about to embark, placing my right hand over hers. I felt the firmness of her thigh and noticed her silk-stockinged foot already depressing the pedal. She spread her left hand into an octave as I closed my eyes.

Slowly and very quietly—*pianissimo*—a lamentation; she played the melody and then, her touch like a captive fluttering butterfly beneath my hand, seemed almost hypnotic.

And then I recognized the simple melody I hadn't heard since before my son passed. *Ode to Joy.* I pulled my hand away.

"It's all right," she whispered, luring me back. "Just clear your mind. Hear him calling." Before I could change my mind, the music swooped me away. And then it grew a little louder—*mezzo forte.*

"Feel," she whispered.

Her thigh slackened as she released her foot from the pedal and depressed it once more.

"Feel the joy," she said, entering into a new movement of relative calm. And then with a handful of staccatos, I felt each moment of my son's death like a painful detachment, but lasting only a short time until the next sharp pull.

"Remember the good times, my Darling," she said.

Every note stirred up a different emotion, until ultimately the movement brought me into a cheerful disposition. I could see the first house out in San Bernardino where I stood as Leland took his first steps. He called out to me in his baby sweet voice, "Papa!" I held out my arms and he ran to me and took my hand. Together we walked until he pulled away and let go. He wanted to do it himself. Proud as I felt, sadness also overcame me. He would no longer need my hand.

The stormy final movement filled me with a most unbridled form of emotion. Its ferocity astounded me.

"Feel the pain," Phoebe said, raising her voice.

The heavier use of staccatos, together with more very loud passages, created a powerful sound jolting me like an electric current, yet Phoebe played predominately softly throughout. I knew I was in good hands and would be all right, but I could also see Leland struggling.

Papa, my eyes hurt. Papa, I can't see the words anymore. What is happening to me, Papa? It distressed me not to have any answers for him. I felt helpless, but I needed to be strong for him. I had to find an answer. He looked at me with a trust only a child can have in his father; and then, within the seemingly turbulent *sonata-allegro* . . .

"Let go of the pain," she said.

At last, unable to hold onto the pain which I'd held with a clenched fist, it slipped through my fingers, through her fingers, transforming into something beautiful. My emotions exploded over the keyboard. My pain had turned into something artistically divine.

By the finish of the sonata, I sobbed uncontrollably, but I felt a weight lifted. Elated, I felt light as a music note. Phoebe took me in her arms and let me cry. I looked into her face and saw her also crying.

"I loved him, too," she said. "Whenever I play the piano, he will be with us. I promise someday I will perform the Ninth Symphony for you in its entirety just as Leland had hoped. In this house, we will always remember Leland."

September 1930: Los Angeles, California—
Doc

Phoebe's music had reminded me of everything I'd been taught in life, every experience, everything I'd searched for, but had failed to see or comprehend. Music was the balance I'd yearned for; it had always been around me, but I hadn't really heard it. And now, as I lay dying, it had become too late. Phoebe connected me to the music. Music also connected me to my son, Leland.

"Live! My darling beloved," she cried. "Not just because I love you but because your son needs you—our son needs you." She kissed my cheek.

I'd drifted in and out of consciousness and, as the blood dripped into my ears, I could hear her music, or might I have been remembering? My thoughts scattered like startled birds darting through a dark forest. Music would have set the scales, if only I'd opened my ears. If only I'd opened my eyes to the beauty all around me. If only.

Ah, so much left unsaid; so many loose ends. But now, the words would not come and I feared they would all be forgotten. I prayed my endeavors had proven my love and that she'd always remember I only wanted to give her the world. Music was her world. And then, the music seemed to push out the last ounce of blood until there was almost a void and, like the sentiment of Beethoven's Fifth, I knew the struggles and joys of victory. After twenty-four hours, the race, the journey, was over. She'd never left my side, but the time had come to go.

"Darling, are you comfortable?" And indeed I felt nothing as I lay in the hospital bed, except for her warm, soft hand caressing my face. I was floating. "Picture the sky, a golden light of the Holy Spirit—the wisdom and compassion of all the enlightened beings. Open your heart to their presence and trust they are there."

Like a dead weight, I sank, entering a dreamy state, and yet this process of death gave me a certain diaphanous clarity. A brilliant thought then came drifting across the stage of my brain. *Phowa. Phoebe is helping me transfer. But into what pure form?* At that moment, it didn't matter. *What better way to go—and then come back? And now since there is an opening at the crown of my head, what could be easier?*

"Through your guidance and blessing, and through the power of the light streaming from you," Phoebe prayed, "may all the negative karma, destructive emotions, obscurations, and blockages of my husband, Wesley Charles Marnier, be purified and removed . . ." A joy so intense, an inspiration so profound washed over me, filling my heart. ". . . May he know the time has come to let go into the process of taking a new rebirth. May he know this life is over and whatever mistakes he may have made have been forgiven and cleansed. May he know his family and friends love and appreciate him and want him to move on without regret, and with confidence and ease . . ." *I hope this is true.* ". . . May Wesley be guided towards a new and beneficial birth in a place where he can accomplish all of his virtuous aspirations."

A silence fell over me as I soaked it all in. I felt her warm breath on my face.

"Darling, can you see the rainbow light from the heart of all wisdom?" She took my hands. "The light is streaming into your heart. Pray with me, Wesley. Oh, Magnificent King of boundless light, I lay down before you. I take refuge in you."

As ridiculous as I thought *Phowa* had been when I'd first heard about it, it made perfect sense now to transfer my consciousness from the fontanel of my head into an innocent pure form. Why not? This could be my answer. This would be my last chance to have more time with Phoebe, to take care of my child, to change things myself and take back control. And so, without any time to spare, I continued the process of transferring my consciousness.

"Please bestow upon me your countless blessings."

Unfortunately, there would be a problem with the transfer. According to Eastern religion, one must prepare by letting go of earthly possessions; one must die with a pure, clean mind in order to die a happy, joyful death. In other words, I should have stayed on the farm, lived a better life, been a better person, spent more time with my children. But I'd made some mistakes along the way and pissed some people off. Bad karma, Phoebe called it. There were even more people, in addition to Warrington—George, a brother-in-law, and an ex-wife—who would have liked to see me dead. My dying thoughts should not have been about how angry I'd been with Jack Warrington. He had seen to it that my life and that of my family was ruined. What he couldn't see, however, was how he would pay for what he had done.

And, regrettably, things would spin out of control. What happened next was terribly and irreversibly wrong and I would bring other victims to the scene of the crime, specifically my unborn son and the woman I loved most—the woman who told me she was happy and didn't want anything else; that she already had everything she could possibly dream of. Worse than any last thoughts of revenge was the last idea of the purest form I could imagine: my unborn son.

Phoebe let go of my hands, before screaming out in pain. I felt the earth move as she collapsed to the floor.

A marionette master, I would direct my son to carry out my wishes, but eventually the threads binding us together would tangle and he'd look for his own justice, for his own solutions and a way to cut the cord forever.

22

My Last Chapter—Final Movement

1930: Queen of Angels Hospital—
It's a Boy!

Phoebe had gone into premature labor. I could only imagine what she might be feeling, and yet all the suffering she experienced and would continue to experience would be numbed by this incredible force rumbling inside her.

Do not suffer, my dearest creature.

From somewhere deep within a warm, dark underwater place, I strained to hear the low sounds of a man, and then he shouted at Phoebe. "Push, Phoebe, push!"

"The baby is breech," Dr. Larson shouted in a frequency so loud I shuddered. "We need to prepare her for a caesarean."

The bones in my soft skull vibrated and then, from somewhere even deeper, the warbled sounds of Beethoven's Ninth—his final, complete symphony—surfaced, becoming more acute. I knew she had to be hearing it, too.

Allegro. Things started tuning up. Queer, I thought I would have had more of a vacation, get to play the harp or something. At least I wouldn't come back like one of those reincarnated cows Marie saw in India, or a grasshopper. *But why must I come into this world the wrong way—breech? This can't be good.*

I know this creature that is me has been submerged in warm water for months where I'd felt safe and secure . . .

Molto Vivace. My surroundings in the middle of this human tornado livened, with a vast spectrum of sound overwhelming me. The pounding of her heart, like a summer thunderstorm, coursed blood through veins and arteries connecting me to her. The sloshing of fluids enveloped me. Lightning struck again and I could hear her skin stretching, and then more lightning and the piercing of metal through skin. The sound of slicing, then tearing, then voices, more metal and beeping and footsteps on linoleum; steel doors opening and closing, drawers slamming open and shut; the zapping of electricity somewhere out there jolting me, and lightning struck again . . .

Adagio. The pace quickened, so spirited and yet so lyrical. I was no longer afraid. And then . . .

The *Finale.* I heard a suctioning of fluids, and then a peal of thunder so fierce startled me out of my quiescence. Another crack of lightning jolted me from my serenity, and I heard the violins. Gradually more notes and more instruments were added, building and building, and then someone grabbed my foot and suddenly, I heard a chorus of voices and my world flashed so bright. I screamed in the key of D Minor.

Mother blinked repeatedly and then rubbed her eyes. One of the nurses attempted to hand me to her, but her limp arms dangled. *I'm all tucked down somewhere snuggly and warm when all at once I recognize the scent enveloping me. Confused, I sense things, but can't place anything at this time.*

Is the world not prepared for me? I couldn't open my eyes, but I could hear, "It's a boy. Phoebe, you have a son!"

"Oh, Wesley! We have a son!" Her voice sounded hoarse, but joyful. "Wesley, where are you?"

I squealed even louder. I wanted to shout out, "I'm here, my Darling!" But I only managed to let out a scream in the language of a frightened baby! Frustrated, scared and confused! *What is happening? Where am I?*

I couldn't make out the white masked creature lifting a knife toward me. I wailed and, once again, I had become disconnected.

23

Kiddos Need Nurturing, Too

1949: US Naval Hospital—
Charley

The ceiling in Dr. Savage's office has a rusty Africa-shaped water stain. As uncomfortable as the olive green Naugahyde sofa is, it's better than some of the places where I've crashed over the years—definitely better than Verdugo Park, where I spent many nights propped up against the trunk of a sycamore tree or curled up on newspapers on top of the hard-packed dirt creek side—and certainly better than the shitty floor of the city jail.

"That was a nice little trip down memory lane," I say. But, it really wasn't. I'd merely laid back, closed my eyes and let my father take stage as he spoke through me, like a caged bird squawking from a branch on my larynx. I'm intrigued not only by what I'd heard coming out of my mouth, but by what I'd experienced. It's all been quite a trip, but it's left me feeling uncomfortable, and yet I'm exhilarated to finally begin putting together some of the puzzle pieces of my life. For years I've been struggling with the part of my brain that's been beating itself to pieces trying to make sense of the mess. Savage is staring at me, his face awash in gravity.

"Interesting, you remember when you were born, Charley? You described your birth."

I nod. "My birth and Doc's death, a sorta musical changing of the guards, you might say."

Savage brings a hand up to cover his mouth, cradling one elbow with the other hand, and then takes a deep breath. It's obvious, he's having a hard time believing any of this, but at least I have an unbiased person finally listening to me. I'll need to take it slow.

"Of course I remember being born." I gurgle, wiping the drool from the side of my mouth as I swing my long legs off the couch onto the floor. "I was born an old soul . . . practically had to help the doctor remove the placenta." I chuckle, noticing Savage's old-geezer fingers trembling as he reaches over to turn the volume up on the recorder. "My mother took one look at me and cried, but she couldn't hold me right away," I say, dangling my arms by my sides. "Her arms were numb and limp, like wet noodles. Later, though, when she could, she was too afraid to touch me."

"Why?" Dr. Savage asks, adjusting himself in his chair, rolling onto one hip and then the other, trying to get comfortable.

I stare Savage square in the eyes. "Because, I reminded her of my father. I was actually a cute kid with all of those curly blond corkscrew curls," I say, running my fingers through phantom curls, "blue eyes and a little button nose. How could anyone resist?"

Savage smiles, nodding. "But you said she loved your father passionately."

"And therein lay the problem," I say, rubbing my thumb across my index finger. "My mother was psychic so it should have been obvious what was going on."

"Excuse me, Charley, but what do you mean *psychic*?"

"She was able to speak to the dead, or rather, they spoke to her."

Savage inclines toward me.

"It was a curse and the reason she focused so hard on her music."

"So that she couldn't speak to the dead?"

I nod. "Again, only the dead were able to contact her and since Doc wasn't dead—well, not exactly—"

Dr. Savage eases back in his chair. "Go on."

"It's obvious I stirred something in her. Something unnatural," I say, peering at him. "Don't you see, Doctor?"

Savage's face is blank. *Oh, do I really have to draw this head doctor a picture?* I feel a hangnail, look at it, and then bring my finger to my lips. "And I'm not talking your classic Oedipus complex here," I say, chewing off the dangling piece of dead skin, spitting it off to the side.

"Classic," Savage says, "would be you wanting to replace your father so you could be with your mother."

"Oh, no. That's just sick. Besides, George was the one who wanted Phoebe."

"Your stepfather?"

I nod.

"So, you never wanted George around."

"Not me. Doc was the one who didn't want him around."

"Your father?"

I stand, but before I can answer, Doc has latched himself onto my throat like a boat barnacle. He's just getting ready to speak in that arrogant, smug way of his. I wrap my arms behind my back and walk toward the window and then, in his stentorian voice, he speaks through me. I turn around.

"I couldn't bear to witness George hanging around Phoebe and Charley," Doc says. "He lived the life I should have had. I wanted him to keep his bloody hands off her."

Pointing a finger, I turn to face Dr. Savage who has opened his mouth to speak, but then his eyes narrow as he cocks his head. "Is he talking now?"

"Well, I wanted George," I say defensively, hands on hips, interrupting both Savage and Doc. "He was the only father I ever knew. He took me fishing and showed me how to ride a bike."

"I see," Dr. Savage says. But I'm not sure he did.

"I should have been the one to do those things with you," Doc booms.

"Cut the sentimental crap, Doc," I say.

Savage's eyes widened.

"Oh, no. Not you, Doctor Savage." I hold up a hand, chuckling as I point to my temple.

Savage merely shakes his head. I realize Doc won't let me have the stage anymore. "Say, this has all been swell," I sink into the sofa, "but really I'm beat. You know, it takes a lot out of you to be born. It's not just tough on the mother, but birth is hard work for the kiddo, too, after all."

I look at the withered potted plant, so lonely looking. "Doesn't anyone water it?" I ask. "You know plants need nurturing, Savage. Have you ever tried talking to it?"

A new orderly arrives to escort me back to my room where I might sit in solitude until dinnertime. That cat reminds me a lot of George, I think, as I slump onto my cot—especially with those brambly eyebrows and beady gray eyes. After he closes the door behind him, I try to sort things in my head; I've opened up the proverbial Pandora's Box today about Mother and Doc.

"Indeed, he bears an uncanny resemblance to George," Doc says out of nowhere. I cover my ears and roll over to face the wall.

"Go away."

There is a moment of silence. I can't shake the image of George from my mind. I put my arms behind my head and cross my legs as I recall the time George banished me to my room; this time for making a shocking announcement at one of Mother's concerts about my father. I couldn't help it. I knew stuff even at only seven years old. I knew Jack had killed my father. I didn't think my punishment had fit the crime.

"By the way, you never should have been sent to your room," Doc says.

This time I don't say anything.

"You were only speaking the truth about what Warrington had done to me. I never saw it coming. I was a damned trusting fool when it came to both him and George. I must admit, however, George and I certainly shared some good times together."

"And the same wife," I say, sitting up. It's obvious Doc still wants to blather on. He isn't going anywhere, so I pull out a cigarette from the pack on my nightstand and light up.

"I should have paid closer attention to him back then," Doc says. "Good old George; always there to lend a hand. Helping me with business, my finances. He's the one who helped me finally obtain my divorce so I could be free of Stella." Doc pauses. "And then he helped himself to my life."

"Doc, can you just give it a rest and leave me alone?" I shake out the match. "I don't really give two shakes about your life before me," I say, reaching over to turn the knob on the little radio on the nightstand next to my bed. Nothing but static.

"But you cared about George, I heard you tell the doctor how he took you fishing; my best friend who stole my life," Doc says. "You do know Phoebe was never in love with him?"

"This really isn't my business, Pops," I say, wondering now if Doc might have arranged to have me kill George, too, if I hadn't joined the Navy. I stand to leave the room. I need to get out and head down to the rec room to play some of the honkytonk that makes Doc's ears bleed.

Later, outside my window, the night rests under a nearly full moon. My eyes grow heavy and I set aside a book I've been reading. I turn out the light on my nightstand and stare out the window at the seagulls drifting around a cloudy sky. *Oh to be a bird and fly away.* My eyes are so heavy, it's hard to keep them open and I have the sensation I'm falling, falling. Down and down off a ladder. I hit the surface of the water and splash into an ocean of blood where I find myself floating, and then a single seagull flies in on a note from Beethoven's Ninth and sits heavily on my chest, peering into my eyes. I see Mother's loving, caring eyes. "Live, live for your son who loves you." And the next thing I know, I'm staring into George's watery gray eyes as he stands knee deep in blood, holding up a document.

"Help me, George!" I strain myself screaming. "Please don't let me die."

There's a knock on my door and George runs away. The same young George-look-a-like orderly walks into my room. "You skipping dinner tonight?" he asks, handing me a note and then leaving.

I open the note. Dr. Savage wants to see me again at eight o'clock the next morning.

24

Dr. Spock

Seven-fifty-five the next morning, muscles burning and I'm sitting across from Dr. Savage in his office, clutching a hot cup of Joe. Sitting behind his steel desk, hands clasped over his clipboard, Savage looks just as eager as I am to get this over with.

"So, how did you sleep?"

"Better, thank you. Before I hit the rack, I try to do some calisthenics. Did over two hundred push-ups last night—the kind where you clap in between," I say, setting down my cup to massage my arms, "then I fell asleep reading a book."

"Oh, which one?"

"George Orwell's latest, *Nineteen Eighty-Four*. It's about a place where there's perpetual war, omnipresent government surveillance and public manipulation. The protagonist's job is to rewrite history to support the party line. He secretly hates the Party and dreams of rebellion."

"Sounds like an interesting character."

"Yeah, I can relate to having to rewrite history, that's for sure," I say with a hoot.

"Are you rewriting it, Charley, or remembering it?"

"Good question, Savage. I'll have to get back to you on that one."

Savage nods and then asks, "So, you like to read?"

"Sure," I say. "As a boy, I used to spend quite a few lonely hours perched on a stool down at the library. Doc had a great library at the house, too. I read everything from Twain and Poe to stuff on science and medicine. Stuff by Edison, Albert Hofmann and even Freud. History books, geography, science books, you name it."

By now my muscles aren't as tight. I ease back in my seat. "You know, man's gonna be walkin' on the moon pretty soon."

Savage smiles. "You're quite an intelligent young man."

"Well, I ain't no Yale grad," I say, hooking my thumb toward his Yale diploma on the wall, next to the one from Pritzker Medical School. "I know enough to keep me outta trouble." I chuckle. "Well, let's just say I know a little bit about a lotta things."

"You're welcome to borrow any of my books," he says, motioning to his shelf.

"Thanks," I say, sheepishly. "As a matter of fact, I already borrowed a book from your shelf."

"Oh?" He turns to look at his shelf. "Which one?"

"The one about using us as lab rats for your little experiments."

The look on Savage's face is priceless.

"I'm pulling your leg," I say, but now I'm further convinced there's something to what I've just said.

"I borrowed Dr. Spock's book *Baby and Child Care*."

Dr. Savage laughs and brings a hand up to squeeze his mouth. He then nods, pulls his hand away and says, "Interesting choice; boring enough I suppose to help you sleep."

"Not really."

I'm excited to get started and share what I've learned. "You know a baby doesn't come into this world with too much comprehension of feelings like loneliness, fear, anger or hatred, sadness, happiness. He learns all that stuff later."

"That's true, Charley. All a baby cares about is having his basic needs met. Babies are only born with twenty-five percent brain development, so as long as his basic survival needs are met, he should be all right."

"And I *should* have been all right," I say, "but there was always something else pulling me in a direction I couldn't resist and earlier than on my baby timetable."

"Slow down, Charley," Savage says, reaching over to turn on the tape recorder. "I'm not quite following."

"You see, I had a caregiver. I'd come to know and trust my nanny, Geneva. But unfortunately, as attentive and nurturing as she was, I wanted more."

"I'm not following you. Every child wants his mother."

"But you just said as long as the basic needs were met, I should have been all right. Before I ever had a chance to experience real loneliness, nannies and other loved ones would surround me. But, still I experienced the loss of intimacy from Mother. So, if I felt that loss, then it became Doc's loss since he'd used me to stay connected to Phoebe."

"I don't understand. You're saying you felt what your father felt?"

"We're just two peas in a pod."

"You're like Doc?"

"We live under the same roof, you might say. The loss he feels is stronger. It makes sense; he had more to lose." I lean in and speak directly into the tape recorder. "Do you know anything about *Phowa*?"

"Can't say I do," Savage says. "Tell me about it."

I watch Savage's face cloud over as I explain the phenomenon of transferring one's consciousness into a pure form at the time of death. He curls and purses his lips, scratches his head. When he nods, I know he's skeptical.

"Interesting. And you believe this?" he asks, removing his glasses.

I'm a little tentative. "I . . . I do."

Wiping his glasses with a cloth from his pocket, he says, "Spell it for me, please." He then reaches for his clipboard, getting ready to scribble with his shaky girly hand.

"P-h-o-w-a."

Smiling now, he looks up to address me. "Charley, I'm glad to see your enthusiasm. You've undoubtedly done your research on baby development, but I'm not sure what you're getting at here. Help me understand where this is going."

"Don't you see? Doc, with one hundred percent brain development, knew nothing except for what he desperately wanted the day he died. In addition to Phoebe, he'd wanted to maintain control, make sure everyone would be all right. As for revenge on Jack, he'd have to wait a few years before I'd even come across Jack, and then I wasn't going to make it easy."

"Jack?"

"Sure, the man who killed Doc, my father."

"Wait a second."

I trace my thumb along the edge of the sofa as I waited for him to scribble some more.

"You see, it would take years after I was born for me to ever comprehend how my father had invaded my body with a plan he intended me to carry out, but I wouldn't be ready yet. And I don't think he knew what he'd gotten himself into. A baby is born very selfish, after all, and doesn't care about the needs of others. And so, for instance, if Father Doc had an agenda, it would have to wait until I had some sort of comprehension, until I'd learned the art of manipulation, negotiation, compromise, and more than just basic survival. Everyone knows how hard it is to put a baby on a schedule. I had an agenda of my own which was to be a little boy first. You know, baby development is not a race."

"True," Dr. Savage says, sitting quietly for a moment. We seem to be getting somewhere.

He narrows his eyes at me. "Can you describe for me what you mean when you say your father had a plan? Did something happen to Jack?"

I nod. "I'm ready to tell my story as long as Doc doesn't interrupt me. That okay with you, Doc?" I ask my father. "I'd like to begin with my beginning."

And then I hear his voice say, "I'm here when you need me."

"That's as good a place as any," Savage says, crossing his arms and leaning back in his chair. "I want to know what happened to Jack."

"Just Jack? You know, if you really want to know everything, you should ask Woodside." I chuckle. "That house has big ears and knows all the secrets and the whole god-damned get-out-while-you-can story."

"Just do your best, Charley."

25
My Chapter One—My Prelude

1930: Glendale—
Charley

Two weeks after I was born, Mother came home with me from the hospital. Flowers were crammed into her room like a funeral parlor. Her doctor had released her once she'd become ambulatory and had her stitches removed. A week later, we received our first visitors, well, that is, besides Marie Hotchener who hadn't left her side since my father's death.

Uncle Earl and Auntie Ann were her first real visitors. They brought along my four-year-old cousin.

"Milty?" Dr. Savage asks, before taking a sip of his coffee.

"Yes. Later Milty filled me in on a bunch of stuff, too," I say. "He and my wet nurse Geneva, that is." I chuckle, holding my hands out as if I'm holding melons. "She was a stout woman with big bosoms."

Savage, seated now on the couch, laughs as he crosses his legs.

"But wasn't Milty mute?"

I nod. "Sign language would be my second language."

Dr. Savage nods his head in acknowledgement.

"Also, even though I was just a baby, and may not have understood everything, I had this uncanny ability to remember and later decipher things grown-ups were saying. And then when I learned to read, nothing escaped me. I discovered the secret place where Mother kept all of the newspaper clippings, the court documents, and other mementos. But for the most part, the Voice, of course, reminded me of things."

"Doc?" Dr. Savage asks as he reaches for a pen to write something down.

I nod.

"Go on."

"Even though he was gone physically, his presence permeated every pore of my spineless sponge of a being. Anyway, Milty was four years old at the time he first laid eyes on me," I say, and then ask Dr. Savage for a smoke.

He pushes forward his case. I put the memories on hold as I light up. Shaking the match, I blow smoke into the room. And then, blinking through a tobacco haze, I can suddenly see Milty's crinkled up nose and his big indigo eyes from the inside of my cradle and beyond; I'm troubled by who else I see.

♪♫

They say people look like their dogs or vice versa, and so if Otto, her skinny wiener dog, wore a turban, he'd look like my Aunt Dodo in her black mink coat. That's not what I thought, of course, the day after they brought me home. I was a newborn, after all. Anyway, Mother's older sister and her thin-moustached husband, Arthur Weiderholz, flew in from France where Uncle Art worked as a foreign correspondent for the International News Service.

But Melody, our three-legged chocolate lab, was my first real visitor. Through the slats of my crib in the adjoining room, I could see the big waxy nose with whiskers sprouting from the top of two small cavities that expanded and contracted as she sniffed the unfamiliar venue, and then I saw one big brown eye and then another. Mel made way for my nanny, Geneva, as she lifted me from the cradle to change and then feed me. I could hear my mother's soft, lyrical voice in the other room—the sound I'd remember as I suckled on the foreign breast that would somehow be my comfort for the next few months.

As Geneva carried me into the room, Aunt Dodo spoke in her diaper-rash voice, low and rough. "It says *Congratulations.* Oh, my, this arrangement is as big as a house," she said, referring to a giant flower arrangement. "*Baby's are a blessing from God, signed George.*" She took a deep breath, looking over at Mother. "Whose grave did he steal these from? He's still sniffing around?"

"Now, Dorothy. He's been a dear friend," Mother said. "I don't know how I would have managed."

"Oh, I'm sure you would have managed," Dodo said, removing her gloves, one long, bony finger at a time.

"Sister, you've lived thirty-nine years and have survived just fine."

"Oh, yes, I've certainly survived."

1949: US Naval Hospital—
Doc

"But Phoebe hadn't wanted to just survive," Doc says, interrupting me. I stare at Dr. Savage, cock my head and hands up, I have no control over what comes out my mouth. "With me she'd done more than just survive. She'd thrived. Her life had been too good to be true. After her barren years, she knew she'd been given a gift and that you, Charley, were the gift. Her life had been all she desired and even more."

I swivel my head left and then down. "I thought it was my turn to talk here, Pops," I say, waiting. "May I continue?"

"Sure. Sorry," Doc says, and I'm secretly happy to have Doc feed me information I couldn't possibly have understood as a baby.

Looking straight into Savage's eyes, I say, "Maybe she should have been more careful what she wished for."

1930: Glendale—
Charley

Uncle Art stood in the corner of the room near a side table full of flowers. "Here's a condolence card from Charles Toberman," he said, waggling his hands above his head. "The Grand Poobah himself."

Mother turned away. "I should have been there."

"Oh, Phoebe, you were too weak after the caesarean. You needed the time to heal," Dodo said, sniffing a rose then scratching underneath her hat. "It was a lovely ceremony."

"Worthy of a Mason to the 33rd Degree," Art added.

"But he didn't want to be buried there," Mother said, swiping away a tear.

"There, there. That's just the way these things are handled," Art responded, patting her wrist. "The Brothers do take care of their own."

"Someday, I'd like to have my own ceremony for him, here at the home."

"Of course," Dodo said.

Geneva walked over and handed me to my mother where I felt content to stay in her arms forever.

"Oh, Phoebe, he looks just like Doc," Aunt Dodo said.

"You think so?" Mother exhaled as if there'd been any doubt.

"I mean . . . why, he is simply quite handsome. I am so happy for you. After all of those barren years, now you finally have a child. You were meant to be a mother." Dodo scooped up her little dog, Otto.

Mother kissed my cheek then looked into my eyes, the same way she did the moment I came into this world and back to the beginning of time. She tilted her head slightly and nodded. "He does resemble his father." She looked up. "Would you like to hold him, Dorothy?"

"Well—certainly," she said, in a voice hurting my tiny ears. "I've never been good with babies, but sure." She set Otto down, dusted her hands and scooped me out of my mother's arms.

My aunt stared into my eyes and I couldn't help but peer back into hers. She had the same familiar green eyes as my mother, but she smelled differently. I whimpered. Aunt Dodo rocked me in her arms, but I grew louder. She rocked faster and looked to Uncle Art for help. He merely shrugged his shoulders, no better with babies, but offered to take me nonetheless. By now I wailed so hard Geneva came to take me back to the nursery. I wanted my mother. I wanted to be in her arms. It would take some time to get used to this different stage of separation.

Mother could no longer hold the attorneys at bay, and since it couldn't be avoided, the next day, still too weak to descend the stairway, the nurse helped her to a chair next to a small table in her bedroom, where she received her family friend and attorney, Benjamin Bledsoe. I took the sun in from my cradle next to the window.

Bledsoe was a roundish sorta man, a beer barrel in a three-piece suit with a shiny gold chain dangling from a vest. He didn't stand very tall, but his voice boomed like a giant.

"Phoebe, I have prepared the Petition for Probate naming you Executrix of the Estate," Bledsoe said, placing a blue-backed legal document on the table before her. He pushed back his glasses with an index finger. "I'll need your signature in order to file it with the court. Is this everything?"

"As far as I know."

"And you're quite certain there was no life insurance?"

"I don't believe he ever got around to it. You might want to ask George, though. He took care of those sorts of business matters."

"My dear, life insurance isn't just a business matter. I would assume that with a baby coming along, he might have been more prepared."

Phoebe moaned. "Who is ever prepared to fall off a ladder!"

"I'm sorry," Mr. Bledsoe said, "I will confirm with George then, before filing."

And then I wailed.

Will Contest Attacks Divorce
As Fraudulent

Asserting that Dr. Wesley Charles Marnier, Glendale optometrist, married a second wife after obtaining a fraudulent divorce from his first wife, Mrs. Stella Kate Marnier, the latter filed a contest yesterday to his will which disposed of a $1,000,000 estate by giving most of it to Mrs. Phoebe Mae Marnier.

A "fantastical religious cult" was asserted to have been one of the causes of the infatuation of Dr. Marnier for his second wife.

LOS ANGELES TIMES (1886–Current File): October 18, 1930, ProQuest Historical Newspapers, *Los Angeles Times*

ESTATE BATTLE CONTINUES

———

Widow and ex-Wife of Dr. Marnier to Carry Legal Fight for Optometrist's Property to Finish

Letters in which Mrs. Stella Kate Marnier referred to her successor as the wife of Dr. Wesley Charles Marnier, Mrs. Phoebe Mae Marnier, as "the sweetest thing in the world," yesterday were read in Superior Judge Tappaan's court at a hearing on the contest of the estate of Dr. Marnier, Glendale optometrist.

Judge Tappaan late yesterday denied a motion to dismiss Stella Marnier's contest and Mrs. Phoebe Marnier, widow, proponent of the will, then presented her case.

Phoebe Marnier testified that Stella Marnier asked her to become her successor, marry Dr. Marnier, and make him happy. Stella admitted that she made Phoebe's wedding garments for her, but adds that she was under hypnotic influence, which she asserts her successor exerted. She attacks the validity of the divorce Dr. Marnier obtained in Las Vegas, Nev., in September, 1917. He and Phoebe married October 4, 1917.

The hearing is expected to conclude today.

LOS ANGELES TIMES (1886–Current File): January 28, 1931, ProQuest Historical Newspapers, *Los Angeles Times*

Dr. Marnier's Widow
Declared Heir to Estate

Sequel of a bitter court battle between wife and ex-wife over the late Dr. Wesley Charles Marnier's estate, the will offered by Mrs. Phoebe Mae Marnier, the widow, yesterday was admitted to probate by Superior Judge Tappaan. He also confirmed the widow as executor of the estate, estimated at from $500,000 to $1,000,000.

Admission of the will to probate was contested by Stella Kate Marnier, divorced wife of Dr. Marnier who was a Glendale optometrist. Joining her as contestants were her children, Mrs. Helen Marnier Carson and Karl Marnier, each of whom was left $5,000 in the will.

Sensational and unusual assertions were testified to at the hearing. Phoebe Mae testified that Stella Kate Marnier had asked that she succeed her as wife of the optometrist and make him happy Stella Kate Marnier admitted that she made her marital successor's wedding garments but contended that Phoebe exercised a hypnotic influence over her.

LOS ANGELES TIMES (1886–Current File): February 14, 1931, ProQuest Historical Newspapers, *Los Angeles Times*

EX-WIFE FAILS IN FIGHT
TO GET PART OF ESTATE

The effort of Mrs. Stella Kate Marnier, first wife of the late Dr. Wesley Charles Marnier, Glendale optometrist, to have the divorce he obtained from her fifteen years ago in Nevada declared void to enable her to share in his estate valued from $500,000 to $1,000,000, failed yesterday by decision of Superior Judge Stephens.

Mrs. Marnier No. 1 contended the Nevada divorce was invalid and therefore she was entitled to share in the estate, which was bequeathed to the optometrist's second wife, Mrs. Phoebe Mae Marnier.

"The court cannot undo what has already been done," Judge Stephens stated. "This case presents a drama of life in which I probably have no right to judge. It hardly seems proper that Mrs. Stella Kate Marnier is in a position to ask relief fifteen years after the divorce. We must take into consideration that the last communication she had with Dr. Marnier was her request that he pay her the last month's alimony."

Two years ago the first Mrs. Marnier lost the contest she entered to the probate of the optometrist's will whereupon she sought to invalidate the divorce in an effort to share in the estate.

LOS ANGELES TIMES (1886–Current File): January 30, 1932, ProQuest Historical Newspapers, *Los Angeles Times*

26
Red Cadillac

George pulled up in a brand new, red two-door Cadillac Fleetwood V-16 on a bright Sunday morning. I'd been placed in my cradle near the window downstairs, where the sunshine streamed in.

Mother's young nurse in a starched white uniform and cap wheeled her into the living room, where George, wearing a smart-looking linen suit, stood holding a large bouquet of flowers. He removed his hat and handed Phoebe the bouquet as if he'd shown up to take her to the high school dance.

"More flowers? You look quite dapper, George. New suit?" Mother asked before handing the bouquet to the nurse standing with a vase at the ready.

George blushed and nodded.

"I like your automobile," the nurse said, looking out the window as she bent over to arrange the plants.

George stared at the nurse's behind a little too long. Mother didn't seem to notice as she arched an eyebrow. "What about the car Doc lent you?"

"It's back in the garage."

Mother wheeled herself over to the window to take a look. "Oh, my. It would appear your ship finally came in. It is indeed a magnificent looking piece of machinery, George."

"Why, thank you. She's quite a beauty. I've been saving for her. When you're up to it, maybe I'll take you for a spin," he said, looping his thumbs into his pant pockets, rocking back on his heels, standing a bit taller. "But for now, I'd like to see the baby."

George came over to my cradle and peeked in. I looked up and sensed something familiar beneath those bushy eyebrows. In his eyes, little gray fish floating in water, I registered something that immediately made me feel seasick. I wanted to scream, but then, when he spread his thick, scary lips to open his mouth, I gagged. Geneva lifted me out to pat my back. I stopped coughing, but before she put me back, George reached out to hold me.

"By golly! Little Man looks just like Doc," he said, taking a second look. "The spittin' image."

The instinctual emotional reaction, like a red flag waving, warned me not to trust the arms holding me.

"So, have you had many visitors?" he asked Mother as he bounced me.

"Mostly Marie and the family."

"I saw them all at the funeral, of course," George said.

"Everyone but me," Mother said, lowering her eyes and turning away.

"You'd have been proud of your brother. He held up surprisingly well for a man who's always had trouble with his emotions," George said, bouncing me faster and harder. "Earl bawled when he got married, when Milty was born, when Milty first signed 'Papa.'"

"Yes, he is a big softy," Mother said. "Doc was like a father to him and got him back on the right track when he gave him the store to run." She paused, and then held up her hand. "You don't need to bounce him so much."

"Doc was good to him. He was good to everyone," George said, looking at me. "Saw Jack at the funeral, too."

I squirmed when I heard the name Jack. The mere mention of his name made my tiny tummy churn, and then I heard a voice in my head I couldn't understand. *The nerve. Now, that takes balls.*

I'm sure George could feel the rumbling. "There, there, Little Man," George said with a nervous chuckle, and then looked at Mother. "Jack's wife is about ready to pop herself. He should be able to keep the business going for now and provide for his family."

By ruining mine, the voice said. By now the pain in my stomach really hurt. I whimpered.

"Yes, I'm glad," Phoebe said. "George, by the way, did my attorney have a chance to talk to you?"

George rocked me desperately now. "Yes, Mr. Bledsoe. He and I spoke yesterday," he said, swinging me like a human cradle. "He said the Petition should be ready to file tomorrow."

"He kept asking me about life insurance. George, that's your line of business. I can't imagine Doc—" Mother said as she sat up straighter in her seat. "Try putting him on your shoulder and rubbing his back."

George flipped me over onto his shoulder. "Oh, Phoebe, I'm sorry. No. He was in the process," George said, swaying now from foot-to-foot, patting my back.

Not true. Like a discordant chord, something felt off key. I let out a howl, startling George, who just kept chattering. "That's one of the things he'd wanted to discuss with you. We'd been looking at different plans. He wanted to make sure you'd be well taken care of should anything ever happen to him."

Liar! I really bawled now as George patted my back. He had to speak over my noise. "He was always joking about how he was so much older and how everyone would probably outlive him."

I screamed even louder.

Mother stifled a tear. "He was younger at heart than anyone I ever knew."

"You can say that again," George said.

I wailed inconsolably.

"Geneva!" Mother called out and then turned to George. "I wonder what's bothering him. I've never heard him this way."

George shrugged his shoulders. "I don't think he likes me."

"Ridiculous, he doesn't even know you."

I quieted for a moment, gasping for air.

"Speaking of being taken care of, George, I know there are bills and other obligations which need handling. I'm sure you'll be taken care of as well. This is all just going to take time," Mother said.

I started up again.

"Phoebe, don't worry your pretty little head. Doc was my friend. I'm not worried about money. That's not why I'm here. I'm here to see if there's anything—anything at all you need. Is there anything I can do for you? For you and Charley?"

"That's sweet of you, George."

I roared. The pain of George bouncing me had become too much. I barfed up all over his new linen suit.

"God dam—"

"Oh dear, I must not have finished burping him," Geneva said as she came bounding into the room, wiping her damp hands on her apron before intercepting me from George.

Tucked back into my crib upstairs, I was alone while George sat downstairs basking in the glow of my mother. I cried big, salty tears and as I tried to catch my breath in between sobs, I saw the familiar black nose poke up over my crib. I stared into Melody's big kind, yellow eyes finally calming me to sleep.

♪♫

After winter, bound inside the house, it felt good to be outdoors in the light where the sounds of nature filled the air. Somehow, I'd missed the rush of the creek and the birds chirping, frogs croaking and even the sound of the howling coyotes in the distant hills. It had been so lonely inside sometimes I bawled just to listen to my own echo. Other times, the only sound came from the nauseating drone of adult conversation, with not even the slightest coo-cooing. George referred to me as the Little Man when he'd come around and pat me on the head. When other adults would visit, some would be polite enough to hold me while discussing the probate:

"So, I read where Stella is contesting the will by attacking the divorce as fraud?" Aunt Dodo said. And, "Phoebe, there's a hearing on Monday. You need to be there," Attorney Bledsoe said. Or, "Paper says here, case is under submission between you and Stella," Uncle Earl said. And all of these people might have been looking directly into my face or holding me, but speaking to Phoebe out of the sides of their mouth. It's a wonder I didn't learn to speak with a twisted lip. I'm sure everyone assumed I couldn't understand and as long as someone held me, I should have been fine. I should have been satisfied to get any attention at all. It's a wonder how Mother handled any of this and yet she seemed to be doing it gracefully.

She sat on a bench under a tree in the garden reading some documents, sipping the tea our cook Antonia had brewed for her.

"Good morning, Charley," she said in her lyrical voice as Geneva rolled me out into the garden to get some sun. The joy at hearing her say my name felt like sunshine warming my insides, the warmth that seedlings felt as they bloomed through the frosted earth beneath the sun. She set down her cup and headed toward me, arms outstretched. *Is she going to hold me?* I grew excited, bouncing in my seat, clapping my tiny hands.

"Oh, here you all are," George shouted as he walked up from the side of the house. "Nice day. Pedro told me I'd find you back here." Behind him I could see Pedro raking up some grass clippings. I liked Pedro and his wife, Antonia. Lately, Antonia let me taste just a few of her specialties, when Geneva wasn't looking.

As if she'd suddenly changed her mind about holding me, Mother stopped. I never even had the chance to feel her touch.

"What brings you over, George?" Mother asked.

I sat up in my pram and watched as George took Mother's hands, and then I turned away, feeling a hurt. I whimpered, but it didn't last as I stared up at the fluffy cotton candy clouds stretched out across the sky. I enjoyed the warmth of the sun on my face. Melody barked when she saw a squirrel run up the tree, where a shiny object swayed in the breeze making a musical sound like the sound of the strings I pulled underneath Mother's piano. On another branch hung a hummingbird feeder with the little creatures buzzing around it. I could smell the sweet air of the new orange blossoms coming into bloom. Being outdoors made everything right with the world.

"I worried about how you might be holding up, Phoebe," George said, "I just can't get over these proceedings." He held up the newspaper.

"George, I'm fine. I try not to read the papers. I spend enough time in the courtroom. I don't need to bring it home with me, too."

"How'd it go this morning?" George asked.

"Oh, it was awful. Stella made an appearance, hissing with the children," she said. "Helen wouldn't look at me. Stella even yelled at the judge, 'He's supposed to be with us. He was to be buried next to Leland in the family plot.' Oh, it was tiring. The judge adjourned early."

"I'm sorry," George said, and then looked at me. "Hello, Little Man. Are you ready to go fishing, yet?" With his eyes back on Mother, he patted me on the head and then held up the newspaper. "And this part about disposing of the one-and-a-half-million dollar estate—you deserve it, Phoebe. You were his true wife. She got hers. How can she think she'll get her hands on the money?"

"She can try, George," Phoebe said, hugging herself as if she might be getting cold. The sun beat down now so strongly. Under my chin, I tugged at the string attached to the scratchy knitted cap on my sweaty head. I wished someone would remove the cap and the matching sweater my Auntie Ann had knitted for me. And then if someone would just get me out of my pram, I might be a little more comfortable.

I felt so hot, I finally screamed. Phoebe and George turned to look at me as though I were about to sprout horns. Geneva finally came to my rescue and took me out of the stroller and removed my cap. She set me onto the grass where in no time I pulled up a cool handful to study even closer. I laughed before I put it into my mouth, and then looked around. No one even noticed.

"She accuses you of belonging to a fantastical religious cult, one of the causes of Doc's infatuation with you," George said. "Boy, that Stella, not only was she an alcoholic drug fiend, but he should have left her in the loony bin."

"George, please, not in front of the baby," Mother said, sounding a bit impatient.

Oh, don't mind the kid. He's just munching on grass. She rose from the bench and headed back into the cold, dark, empty house. She never even held me, but I felt quite happy being left outside chewing grass, taking in the sun with Geneva and Melody.

27
First Step First

1931: Glendale—
Charley

I was nearly one-year-old as I crab-crawled across the Oriental rug in the living room, big as the sky. I'd been eager to show off my newest talent, until I saw George striding across the room toward us. *Kill joy.* He carried the *Los Angeles Times* tucked into the crook of his arm. Snatching it out, he whacked it open on an end table and pointed to something.

Mother held up a dainty hand. "Let it wait, George. Geneva and Charley have something to show me."

"Charley, stand here. Stay," Geneva said as she walked across the carpet to the other side. Bouncing in place, smiling so big and drooling uncontrollably, I held onto the screen at the front of the hearth.

Geneva clapped, cheering me on. Mother's hands were clasped, pulled into her chest and I could see her eyes glistening.

"See here," George said, jabbing the paper as I neared Mother, whose arms were now held out to me. "It says you won."

She turned to George.

Instinctive survival skills trumped any guilt I might have felt and when I finally made it into Geneva's arms—my port in the storm—the wind seemed to be knocked out of Mother's sails. Swollen waves of pride dashed onto a shore of disappointment in only a matter of seconds.

"He's growing up without me," Mother said. "I'm missing my baby's life."

"There will be many more firsts, Phoebe, don't worry," Geneva said.

Mother took a seat, folding her hands onto her lap as George read from the paper:

"Ex-wife fails in fight to get part of estate. Attorney Joseph M. Wapner, for the first wife, attacked the widow as an interloper who took a husband away from a loving wife and children . . ."

"Loving? Maybe underneath all the booze," Phoebe said in a whiny tone I'd never heard.

"She was a drunkard and a witch," George said.

"I wouldn't go that far," Mother said.

"We all knew it. It just took Doc longer to see it," George said. "He used to tell me she wasn't like this when he first married her. She loved her booze and her pills."

"He thought it was his fault she was so unhappy. He thought everything was his fault. He only wanted to do the right thing by everyone," Phoebe said as George continued to read the article.

"Marnier obtained his divorce in Las Vegas, Nevada . . ."

And we certainly had a glorious time out there," George said with a sly grin which started fading as soon as he looked up to see the inquisitive look on Mother's face. He cleared his throat. "At least I did," he said and continued to read the paper.

". . . a fact which drew fire from the first wife's attorney. Mrs. Phoebe Marnier's attorney, Benjamin Bledsoe, argued that this is no issue in the matter of the will's validity. The trial was marked with unusual assertions. Phoebe Marnier testified that Stella Kate Marnier asked her to marry Dr. Marnier and make him happy. Mrs. Stella Marnier admitted she made the wedding garments for the marriage of her husband and her matrimonial successor."

"So much unhappiness. Stella begged me to make him happy," Mother said. "I told her only if she was sure their marriage could not be mended."

"You were the only one who could make him happy after Leland died. Poor Leland."

Phoebe shook her head.

"And that was Stella's fault," George said.

"It was no one's fault." Mother wrung her hands. "Happiness is a choice."

"You say the cutest things," George said, reaching for her hands. "You make me happy."

I saw Mother smile then lower her head, pulling back her hands. "Mr. Bledsoe even produced letters in which Stella referred to me as the wife of Dr. Wesley Marnier. In one letter, she referred to me as the *sweetest thing in the world*. Even though Stella admitted she made my wedding garments, she then said it was because she was under my hypnotic influence."

"She's the crazy one, if you ask me," George said with a laugh.

"I didn't," Mother said, smiling sourly.

As they discussed grown-up stuff, I walked back and forth across the room. I felt pretty pleased with myself as I climbed into the hearth to take a seat on top of a burned-out log. There amongst the black dust, I wondered how it might taste as I scooped a handful and put it in my mouth. Geneva appeared the moment I started to gag. She reached in to dig me out and took me into the bathroom to clean me up.

I don't think Mother ever even noticed.

"You see . . ." George said as Geneva carried me back into the room and set me down. I scrambled into the adjoining chamber room and pulled up to the piano. I reached up to feel around until I heard the sound of the piano strings. Jackpot! I plucked some more notes feeling quite pleased with myself. This felt even better than walking. Geneva swooped me up once more and brought me back into the main room.

"That's why I love you, Phoebe. This is cause for celebration," George said, taking her hands in his again, but Mother turned to look my way.

Yes, this is time to celebrate, I just walked not just one, but two couch lengths and then across the room again, for God's sake! And now I can play the piano, too.

Mother looked at me but spoke to George in that twisted way adults do. She wasn't focused on either one of us. "Believe me, Stella's not finished yet. As long as there is still money, she's coming after it. I swear if it weren't tied up in court, I'd give her the money, but now everyone seems to have their hands tied to it. And I'm tied to it and I'm missing my baby's life."

I heard the word "baby" and somehow I sensed Mother's unhappiness.

28
What Codicil?

1934: Glendale—
Charley

Coyotes howled over another kill made down by the creek, and as I lay in bed, the fear wrapped around me like a cold straight jacket. George said they're probably little deer or ducks or rabbits looking for a drink and then *kapow*. I'm four years old and scared to death, but I tried real hard to be brave as I watched the show on my ceiling where funny-looking images danced to the music. I was getting really good at entertaining myself. Mother said that if I could pretend the shadows in my room were my friends and if I could hum some tunes, I might not be so afraid. Besides, if not for the shadows, except for Melody, I'd have no friends at all. Our home was in the middle of the woods—in the middle of nowhere.

Mother and George had been married now for almost three years. It seemed almost as if the instant I first walked into Geneva's arms, Mother had accepted George's proposal.

Earlier in the evening, I'd been sent to bed for disrupting Mother's musician friends, but really, it was George who just wanted me out of everyone's hair. I'd stayed out of the way as usual by taking my spot underneath the piano, sticking my bare feet up onto the belly of the piano. The vibrations always tickled, filling me with such an ecstasy as if I were in a dreamland filled with soft, furry animals and all the NECCO candies I could possibly eat.

"Oh, look at Charley. Isn't he simply adorable?" Miss Zoula said, taking a puff from her cigarette attached to a long ivory cigarette holder. "I could just eat him up!" Miss Zoula was younger than the rest of them with maple syrup-colored hair and cocoa-colored eyes—she even treated me sweetly. As a matter of fact, all of Mother's friends thought I was adorable, except for Aunt Dodo who still stayed with us while Mother went to court.

"Charley, up to bed," Aunt Dodo barked.

"Yes, Charley, it's time," George said, eyeing Miss Zoula.

"Ah, but I'm being good. I'm not making any noise." Usually, George liked taking me around with him. Together, we always seemed to attract the pretty ladies wherever we went.

"Now," George growled under his breath, eyebrows squeezed together. He set down his drink and pulled me out from underneath the piano.

"Charley, be a good boy and go on up," Mother said, never leaving her spot on the piano bench. "I'll come tuck you in after you brush your teeth."

But, she never did.

Hugging my matted stuffed bear, I waited up in my room crammed with Tootsie toy planes, trains and automobiles. From the ceiling hung a mobile of the universe swaying gently as a gust of air snaked its way in between the window and the sill. My room was right above the music room, and through the floorboards I could hear the music, the laughter, the dancing feet shuffling, and the glasses clinking. Fortunately, my head was a radio; I could simply tune things out or change the channel. Some nights, I could hear the man with the low voice in my head telling me stuff about Mother I couldn't understand—stuff above the level of my language—like how she needed to watch herself around these people.

Staring at the glass mason jar reflecting the light of the milky moon, I noticed the movement of the caterpillars inside. I tuned out the noise and finally drifted off to sleep.

In my dream, I flew above a field with all of the pretty butterflies when the sound of coyotes howling in the nearby hills awakened me. I tried to hold my breath until they stopped and after a bit they did—probably because they'd had their fill of little animals and wouldn't be coming after me. Now, except for the sounds of clocks ticking, and electricity coursing through the walls, the inside was quiet. But then I could hear Mother crying—probably because I'd been a bad boy. Aunt Dodo always told me how bad I was and now George seemed to have joined the club, so I guessed that had to be it. I was no good.

Go to her, the voice said. I hugged my bear and pulled the pillow over my head to muffle the sounds, but the sound came from inside my head, so I hummed:

Picnic time for teddy bears,
The little teddy bears are having a lovely time today.
Watch them, catch them unawares . . .

I sang even louder.

At six o'clock their mommies and daddies
Will take them home to bed
Because they're tired little teddy bears.

After a while, the voice seemed to go away and finally I fell back to sleep.

Go to her, the voice said again the next night when I heard Mother crying. George was out for the evening on business. This time I didn't hesitate. I slid out of bed, padded down the hall in my pajamas and scooted down the stairs. I then crept across the foyer where I stared at the dark silhouette seated at the piano. Inching closer, I saw Mother's reflection through the window. The moonlight bounced off the piano keys, lighting her smile. She seemed far away again.

And then I heard the voice in my head saying: *Oh, my Darling. It disheartens me to see you looking so empty.*

I tried to ignore the voice, but then words, molded out of my shallow breathing, spilled out of my mouth in a low voice. "Oh, my Darling, what have they done?"

I slapped my hand over my mouth, hoping Mother hadn't heard. Lines squiggled across her forehead, paper crinkled creases, down from the sides of her nose all the way to the corners of her mouth. Her cheeks, little deflated balloons, were sucked in. There were smudges underneath her eyes like the ashes from the fireplace. Her hair, once thick and shiny like a copper penny, lay limp and white near the roots. She'd lost so much weight her knees and elbows were knobby, making pointy dents through the blue knit dress she'd worn to court earlier that day. Sometimes, Mother seemed too tired to change. She'd walk into the house as if each step was such an effort she might collapse. Her bubbly energy no longer filled the room.

I tiptoed a little closer but stayed hidden in the dark. I knew better than to be there out of bed and didn't want to disturb her. But then, without turning toward me, she whispered, "Doc, come closer." The words echoed off the walls of the music room.

I looked around. No one else was in the room and this wasn't the first time she'd uttered the name *Doc*. Maybe, that's my other name? I let it go. I didn't care what she called me. She smiled at me, her straight, white teeth reminding me of the piano keys. A butterfly fluttered in my stomach. I inched forward and climbed up next to her on the piano bench. She pulled me into her lap and I leaned back, tucking my head into that soft place under her chin; a place seemingly carved out just for me. I smelled heaven and roses from the garden. I placed my tiny hands over hers and entered another world where all was peaceful—full of furry animals and NECCOs. My hands floated across the keyboard above Mother's as if I were magically making music with her. She hummed while she played *Ode to Joy*, and I shivered as the vibrations came from her warm body. My tiny body trembled, but in her arms, I felt safe.

In your arms, I am connected once more. I remember the love we shared freely, purely, unencumbered. I remember the time we had all to ourselves—

George walked in and startled us, fingers snapping and bellowing from the hallway. "Charley, what are you doing up?"

He's always interrupting our joy, I heard the voice in my head say.

Phoebe stuttered as if she'd been caught doing something wrong. She apologized. "The music woke him up."

"Maybe we should have a curfew, for Charley. No piano playing after eight o'clock," George said.

"Yes, perhaps that's a good idea," Mother said.

No, it's not. We love the company of Phoebe and her music.

"Charley, to bed," George said.

"No, George," I said. I think it might have bothered him that I never called him "Father" and maybe that's why he snatched me out of my mother's arms.

"Scram!" George screamed.

Mother did nothing. I placed my hands on my behind afraid he might swat me like Aunt Dodo had a habit of doing, and scurried out of the room, crying all the way.

The ceiling in my room grew black as my drawing paper had after I spilled the bottle of ink at the kitchen table earlier trying to do my letters. Aunt Dodo had spanked me and Mother made me mad by not stepping in. I grew angrier at her again for not standing up to George. I closed my eyes and tried to sleep, but through the floor vents, I could hear George and Mother's arguing floating up like something burning on the stove.

"But what about the money from the rentals?" Mother asked George. "What about all of the business investments you had with Doc?"

I had my ear to the floor. They talked about Doc again as if he was somebody living in our house. But as far as I could tell, only Mother, Melody, George and I lived in our house. Geneva, Antonia, and Pedro lived at their own houses.

"I told you. Most is tied up in Doc's stuff for now. I'm trying other things."

"But, George, we're broke. My attorneys have liens on the properties; some of the liens even have liens on them. Everything is tied up in court or tied to the stock market; the estate probably owes money by now. I'm just shocked at how quickly I'm losing money every day. And, George, what about the house? We'll lose it."

Things quieted. I didn't understand anything about liens and stocks, but if we lost the house, I wondered if we'd ever be able to find it again?

And then, out of nowhere, Mother said, "Maybe, we can move down to San Diego—live with Dorothy for a while until we can get back on our feet."

No! I don't like Dodo, I screamed, and could still feel the sting of the slaps across my bottom. I bawled.

"Don't be ridiculous," George said.

"I'm just trying to think out of the box," Mother said. "I have to do something."

"Just leave it to me," George said. "I'll figure something out."

I'd been having a nightmare about losing the house, wandering up and down the creek bed looking for it everywhere, when the sound of the phone ringing startled me awake the next morning. I rubbed my eyes to look around my room, and saw Melody at my bedside, tail wagging and eager for me to get out of bed. I felt my warm blanket, smelled bacon, and could still hear the tone of the phone, so at least I knew all was not lost, not yet. I bolted out of bed, scrambled across the hallway, Mel's nails clicking along on the wood floor behind me, to the little table where the phone was. I waited until the ringing stopped before picking it up. Placing my hand over the mouthpiece, I listened to the rumbly voice of a man on the other line.

"Yes, Mr. Bledsoe," my mother said in a quiet, shaky voice.

"Our office was just served with an assignment from Jack Warrington's attorney who also submitted it to the court."

"But what for?"

"They're calling it a codicil to the will."

"I don't understand."

And neither did I. *What codicil?* I heard the voice in my head ask.

"The assignment was signed by Dr. Marnier and you back in September 1930."

Another lie. Hearing the name Warrington made my stomach growl. Mel stared at me with her big yellow eyes, head tilted and ears cocked.

"I don't remember signing anything. Wait a minute, September? That was when Doc died," Mother said. "Can I take a look at that document?"

"Absolutely. You should probably come by this afternoon," Bledsoe said. "I'll start preparing the response."

Before George ever offered to drive her into town, I'd already changed, grabbed Mother's purse and waited by the back door.

Widow Fights Assignment
as Codicil to Will

The assignment of J.H. Warrington of a half-interest in the Marnier Optical Company of Glendale which her husband, Wesley Charles Marnier had signed, is not a testamentary document and was not intended as a codicil to Marnier's Will. Mrs. Phoebe Armstrong Marnier asserts in a contest to the codicil on file in probate court.

Warrington, who was Marnier's business associate, had filed the document as a codicil.

Marnier died September 30, 1930, once valued at over $1,000,000.00, but recently appraised at $34,410.

LOS ANGELES TIMES (1886–Current File): September 19, 1934; ProQuest Historical Newspapers, *Los Angeles Times*

29
I've Got a Migraine

Layered slats of light filtered in through the blinds of the conference room in the law offices of Mr. Benjamin Bledsoe. Tiny motes of dust caught the light like atom-sized snowflakes floating in the air. I stuck my tongue out to try and catch some, the same as the rare day it snowed in Glendale. I'd turned my face up toward the sky, sticking out my tongue to taste them: an empty taste. I reached out to hold one and it disappeared like a frozen ghost in my warm hand. I wished I could go back to that day.

Now, the lawman's stuffy, dark-paneled room made me feel warm. There were hundreds of books with shiny gold-lettered spines lining the wooden bookshelves all the way to the ceiling. Through a window, sunlight sparked a rainbow of colors off a crystal ashtray where a cigarette smoldered. At the edge of a table stood a brassy, blindfolded statue of a lady about the size of a doll balancing some water jugs. As I stared at the figurine, a pretty secretary with yellow hair walked in and gave me a sugar cookie.

"They plan on calling a witness," Mr. Bledsoe said. "A Mr. Eric Englehardt."

"He's Jack's new associate," Mother said, tucking a napkin under my chin. I removed it to wipe the sugar from my face.

"Basically, it says here that during a hunting trip in Idlewild, California, Englehardt had mentioned to Dr. Marnier how hard Warrington was working and that he, Warrington, was having trouble maintaining the family on the salary he was getting..."

"But Doc had given him a raise," Mother said.

"...to which Dr. Marnier replied he knew he wasn't paying Jack what he was worth, but he thought of him as a son and someday the business would be his. That even if Jack worked so hard, it would only benefit him in the end since the business would someday be his, should anything happen to Dr. Marnier."

I grew dizzy from the smoke and the stuffiness and the loud voices and from staring at the overhead light fixture hanging from a ceiling fan. I looked around and when no one was looking, I reached for another cookie from a plate next to a green-shaded desk lamp on the table. The light lit up a paper with a blue cover. Mr. Bledsoe slid it right under Mother's nose.

She put on her reading glasses and peered closely. George had removed his brown wool suit jacket and had it draped over an arm to look over her shoulder. I could see the wet spots sprouting under his armpits.

Mother read the document out loud: "In consideration of my esteem and high regard as well as my appreciation of his cheerful and most faithful service, I do hereby assign to J. H. Warrington all interest in the Marnier Optometry and Optical Company located at 114 E. Broadway, Glendale, California." Mother looked up and then pointed to the document. "Why is the next part squeezed into the margins and in parenthesis? (The same to take effect at my demise.)"

Mr. Bledsoe turned his palms up. Mother read further, her eyes widening, and then she looked up over her glasses at Mr. Bledsoe and shook her head. "I don't understand. This isn't right. That's not my signature and it surely isn't Doc's either."

George lit his cigar and paced the room. With the back of his hairy hand, he wiped off the sweat beading on his forehead. "Are you sure, Phoebe?"

"Positively."

"Don't worry. We'll fight this," Bledsoe said.

"Oh, I don't want to fight. I'm sick of this. Let him have the business," she said, pushing back in her chair, getting ready to stand.

"But, Phoebe, you need to hang on," Bledsoe said. "You can't let him get away with this."

"Doc did consider him to be like a son," she said, wringing her hands. "Jack had a family to take care of." She then looked at me with a small rueful smile and cradled my chin. "A little girl just about Charley's age. I'm sure he did what he thought he needed to do to survive."

What? Kill me? I got really scared when I heard the words in my head so I covered my ears. The room clouded with the cigar smoke sucked up into the fan and twirling around like a small dust devil. I sank down deep into my chair and watched the world spinning. I closed my eyes, but suddenly I felt as if I was falling, and then behind my movie screen eyelids, I saw the ceiling fan swirling above me. Suddenly, in the doorway of my mind, I saw a man pointing a gun at me. The back of my head where it's connected to my neck felt like someone hit me with a hammer. With both hands, I reached up to hold the back of my head.

"Charley, what's wrong?" Mother asked.

"My head hurts."

"All right. We're leaving now." Mother stood to leave, looking at me. "Poor thing, it's probably because you didn't have any breakfast."

Bledsoe stood also. "Well, Phoebe, it's certainly up to you, but you're running out of money. How will you survive? Think about Charley, fight for him."

Fight? My cousin Milty had taught me some moves he learned from Uncle Earl who was a boxer in the Army. Sometimes we pretended we were in the ring. We'd dance around, punching the air. "Wanna knuckle sandwich?" Go down for the count, except I could only count to ten. I didn't want to see my mother fight. I couldn't even imagine my mother in a boxing ring. Please don't let there be a fight.

George stopped pacing and smoothed back his damp-looking hair. "He's right. We'll figure something else out. The business isn't worth the fight."

"The fact is I'm already in the middle of the ring," Mother said. "Maybe I should finish the round . . . take this to the finish."

By now I was really spinning.

"Maybe I'll go in swinging," she added.

That evening, in the chilly kitchen, I took a seat at the table to watch Mother, more delicate than snow. Soon, the metal ticked and the gas hummed on the stove as Mother struck the match to ignite a fire. Something about just the three of us getting together for a meal comforted me, even if George had to be there.

"Charley, please set the table," Mother said, but not in her usual singsong voice. "Remember Polly Plate goes in the middle. Fanny Fork goes on the left, Ned, the Knife on the right."

"And Sally Spoon goes next to Ned," I said, giggling. Mother gave names to inanimate objects and also made a game out of doing chores. Taking out the trash was always an adventure as I dodged Andres, the alligator, and skipped across tile squares that were really the heads of toothy rhinos named Tommy and Tina.

The heat from the stove warmed the kitchen and when I smelled dinner, my Tony Tiger tummy growled and Mother and I laughed. She then blew the hair out of her face and it looked like she wore a little purple apron under each eye—sorta the same as the one she wore now—the one Antonia had left behind after Mother had let her go. She couldn't afford to pay her anymore and it made me sad.

"Dinner smells good," I said, trying to lighten the mood, heavier than the aroma of whatever was cooking on the stove. It smelled the same as it did last night when we had some sorta meat stuff with celery, carrots and potatoes. Mother called it "leftovers."

"Smells worse than the horsemeat Melody eats," George said and gulped his drink.

I felt my eyes stretch and my jaw drop as I turned to George. "Melody doesn't eat horsemeat."

"George, stop it!" Mother shouted.

But George ignored her. "Sure she does," he said. "Haven't you ever read the label on the can?"

I cried. "I'm only four. I can't read that good."

"*Well*, Charley," Mother said. "You can't read that *well*."

"*Well*, let me tell you. It's horsemeat. You see, because nowadays everyone drives cars instead of riding horses, so there are too many filling the 'glue factories.' Some man in Chicago started canning horsemeat."

I was never really a crybaby, but by now I whinnied like a scared little pony. I couldn't imagine anyone hurting animals. "No, George. You're lying! When I grow up I'm never buying a car," I howled. "I'm going to save all of the horses in the world." I swiped my nose with the back of my sleeve. "I'll feed them apples and carrots. I won't even ride them. I'll ride my bike to go places."

"Charley, George is pulling your leg," Mother said, but it felt more like he'd reached down my throat with his big hand to squeeze my stomach.

I looked down at my legs and then at George who sat across from me laughing, one hand wrapped around his drink, the other slapping his own leg.

"No, I'm not. Check out the label," he said, springing up from the table and then returning with a can of dog food.

Mother refused to pay attention to him. "George, put it away."

Later, probably because she knew how upset I'd become, Mother vowed to me she would stop buying the canned dog food. Besides, it was just one more thing she couldn't afford anymore.

George set down the can and then emptied the bottle of honey-colored liquid from the cupboard as he poured himself another drink. I'd stopped crying and pretended to drink my milk as I listened and paid attention to more distressing grown-up talk.

"I'm going to fight Warrington," Mother said.

"But why?" George asked, returning to his seat.

"For Charley." Mother's sleeves were rolled up as she ladled steaming bowls of the mushy stuff from the pot.

Please don't fight for me. I felt my headache coming back and blew bubbles into my glass of milk as a distraction.

She blew some more hair out of her face. "Charley, did you wash your hands?"

"Oops. I forgot." I wouldn't be the cause of another fight, so I rushed off to the powder room just off the kitchen. As I waved my fingers through the water, I strained to listen to their conversation.

"Phoebe, I don't understand why you can't just let it go. It's not worth that much. I'm your husband now. I'll take care of you."

"And I can't understand why you wouldn't want me to fight, that's not like you. I know you to fight for tooth and nail." Then she whispered as if she knew I might be listening—never mind they'd been discussing business stuff around me my whole life. "I've got to hand it to him for forging our signatures. I must say, he did a pretty good job and except for the 'y' in Phoebe Mae, it was almost perfect."

I came back and hopped into my seat at the table.

"May?" George asked.

One of Mother's eyebrows lifted a bit. "Yes, the same way *you* spelled it when you filled out the marriage certificate."

George peered at her and guzzled back his drink.

"It's a common mistake I often simply let slide," Mother said. "But it would be nice if at least my husband were to pay more attention. It's spelled M-A-E."

George practically turned the color of my milk.

That's right, George. M-A-E. I smell a rat, I heard the voice say, but this time I kept my eyes open and gave a voice to the words in my head. "I smell a rat," I squeaked and covered my mouth, giggling nervously.

Mother and George turned, knitting their brows at me. George squirmed as if he had ants in his pants. Mother then took her seat and said, "Desperate times call for desperate measures, but resorting to forgery is pretty desperate." Mother smiled at me and then winked as if we were sharing a secret. "Don't worry, George. I'm not giving up on you just yet, but I have decided to get back to my music. I'm going to start giving piano and voice lessons. Maybe you can start helping out around here."

George sprang up and went to the cupboard. "I need to make a phone call," he said and left the room, carrying a new bottle with him.

My headache rushed back, with full force.

30

It Don't Mean a Thing

When you're not old enough to go to school yet, the days can go by at a turtle's pace, especially on rainy days. While Mother spent time in court, I spent more time at the piano trying to recapture those rare moments with her where I wasn't a scaredy cat about everything, where I wasn't worried my life would get ripped away from me.

I remembered some of the melodies I'd heard Mother playing by her favorite composer Beethoven, but not all the way through. Besides, my little fingers couldn't stretch that far. I loved picking out little tunes—some from what I'd heard on the radio and some from what I came up with on my own. The sounds were comforting, and the repetition was a meditation. I liked pounding on the keys with my hands and elbows and singing at the top of my lungs, making up simple tunes that made me giggle. I used two fingers to make the sound of the Indian drumbeat I'd heard in the new western film George had taken me to see. *Maybe he's sorry about all of that horse business and that's why he took me to the theater?*

Mother being away made me sad, but I also noticed while I kept busy concentrating on my own compositions, the voice stayed away. I don't think he was a fan of my choice in music.

One day, I sat at the piano bench and held my finger on a key a little longer as I stared out the window. I waited for the sound to disappear and then a weird sensation came over me as if I'd lived through this before. I felt as if I was a musical note floating up out of my body and then drifting along with other notes and finally connecting not just to my mother, but to a whole symphony of music where I didn't have to be so lonely. I wasn't scared. But when I opened my eyes, the moment vanished when I saw a squirrel on the windowsill. "Oh boy. I have an audience. Any requests?" I asked my new little fan.

I made up a song for the squirrel. He seemed to like it.

The next day, as I listened to the magical sound of jewels sprinkling from the sky, I noticed two brown squirrels taking shelter from the rain. I spent the morning by myself performing for my audience until Aunt Dodo came in to announce lunch. She'd been staying with us while Uncle Art worked in Europe. The idea was she'd be able to help Mother out now that Geneva, Antonia, and the maid were all gone.

I didn't want to let down my little fuzzy admirers. "I'll be right there, Aunt Dodo," I yelled, but instead I ended up outside looking for the squirrels.

By the time I made it outside, the sun had come out to burn off the rain. The kitten-shaped clouds stretched lazily across the sky before they floated away. A little hummingbird drank from the feeder as the squirrels scampered off into the woods. I followed them along the way and heard the rush of the creek and the birds chirping. I heard the leaves rustling in the wind. The bees were buzzing, the tree frogs were croaking and the crickets were chirruping, all a magical symphony of sound, and I felt connected to everything.

And then the wind seemed to lift and furl me back into the house; setting me back down on the piano bench to imitate the sounds of nature. I pecked at the keys and then slid a fist from one side of the keyboard to the other. I trilled the high notes back and forth. It took two fingers to imitate the tree frogs. *Riv it, Riv it.* I can do this all day long, I thought. Creating the sounds made me feel less lonely, as if I was part of nature.

But, it was all just the calm before the storm. "Hey Ludwig, I told you it was time for lunch." Hurricane Dodo had blown into the room turbanless. Her hair, a rusty-iron-going-gray color, stood out like one of those wiry scouring pads from the kitchen sink. She drew close enough for me to smell her mediciney breath under a sickly sweet perfume and then she yanked my ear. I stared down at my shoes so I wouldn't look at her and ignite on fire, but then, at the same time, we both noticed the mud I'd tracked in. I looked up just in time to see her drawn-on eyebrows lift up. "Well, you can forget about that now. Soup's cold anyway. Go to your room."

"But why? It isn't dark yet?"

She raised her hand, fingers clenched into a ball—a nervous, commanding hand attached to an old body smelling of the closet where Mother hung her furs kept in mothballs. "Because you've been a bad boy and I told you to."

"Mother says I'm not bad," I cried, defensively.

"You dare to talk back." Her clunky pumps sounded like gunshots as she chased me to the staircase. "Take your shoes off!"

I sat on the landing to remove my shoes, where I left them for later. Then, arms clamped in armpits, I stomped up to my room and threw myself onto my bed.

Words, too hard for my four-year-old vocabulary, seemed to blur as I absentmindedly scanned a couple of newspaper articles and more documents with blue covers like the ones at Mother's attorney's office. I'd come across them earlier in the forbidden downstairs library and had brought them to my room, but now they were pretty boring. I needed to make sure to return them before anyone found out. I'd also borrowed some sort of medical book and, as I flipped through the pages, drawings of human skeletons and eyeballs awestruck me. I stopped mid flip when I heard the footfalls outside my window. I set the book down to go and take a look.

Mother traipsed up the path looking like droopy "Daisy" from her garden. I remembered how she used to call all the flowers her children and had even given them names. "Good morning, Rosie, Gardenia and Carnation," she'd say every time she entered the back yard. And now looking so wilted, I couldn't help but think of her plants dying in the garden. It made me so sad.

She bent over now to pick up the newspaper and then opened the front door. I dashed over to stand at the edge of the catwalk and peered over as she entered the foyer.

"Oh, Sister. This is all just killing me, I can't—" Mother stopped speaking when she saw me at the top of the stairs. The railing on the catwalk wasn't very high and when I stepped onto the base, I could see and hear even better.

"Oh, Charley, back away!" Mother looked up at me with eyes wide, hands held in a teepee over her mouth. "You'll fall."

I hurried downstairs and stopped in front of her, suddenly horrified. She stood as thin as a pine tree. Her eyes seemed smudged with puffy skirts of ash.

"Charley, go back upstairs. I'll call you when dinner's ready," Aunt Dodo said in a voice so sweet my teeth hurt.

I turned to go back up as Mother reached out to hug me briefly.

"Do I have to?"

"I'll see you at dinner, son," she said in a whisper, this time handing me the entire *Los Angeles Times* newspaper, not just the comics.

I didn't want her to let go of me. She handed me my muddy shoes.

"Take them up to your bathroom and scrape off the mud over the trash can."

"Leave your mother alone. She's had a hard day."

"She's such a bitch," I heard the voice say, and I smiled as I climbed the stairs.

"What did you say?" Aunt Dodo asked.

I hurried to the top. "She's such a bitch," I repeated as I threw my shoes into the bathroom, mud splashing on the white walls. I walked into my room, picked the book back up and the page opened to the picture of a giant skull. I took a crayon and drew a turban on it like Aunt Dodo's. I busted up laughing so hard.

Aunt Dodo hadn't fed me any lunch, but squirrels weren't the only ones that knew how to store food for a rainy day. Starving, I lifted my mattress and reached for a small package of raisins and then laid back, legs crossed, and stared at the ceiling. In between the chewing, I heard the soft clicking across the hardwood floors. "I smell a rat," I said and turned to see my little friend, Peedles H. Mouse, scurrying toward me. Peedles first appeared about a week ago, eyes glowing in the dark like a tiny ghost. I'd flipped the light on my nightstand to find him still standing there, a tiny mouse in the headlights. I pinched off a piece of raisin and tossed it to Peedles. They talked grown-up stuff downstairs and didn't want me around.

I rolled onto my stomach and opened up the newspaper, but before I could get to the comic section, something on the cover of the sports section caught my eye. Bolting out of the starting gate at the Santa Anita Raceway was a row of strong, beautiful racehorses. I shuddered to think about the glue factory George had talked about the night before. And then across the page, I read: "$100,000.00 to the winner!" Wouldn't that solve all of Mother's problems?

Next to my bed, Peedles stood on his hind legs and waited until I held out another piece of raisin. More than I wanted Aunt Dodo to go away, I wanted to figure out a way to help my mother.

"This is all killing her, Peedles," I said, chewing on a raisin as if it was a kernel of an idea. "I could build a lemonade stand like the one they built on the *Little Rascals*." I'd rolled onto my side. Peedles' fat cheeks billowed in and out. Chew, chew. "I could mow lawns." I held up my scrawny arm and flexed. "But I'd have to build up some more muscles first like *Popeye, the Sailor Man*." Finally, I decided, there was only one solution.

♩♫

After dinner, I made sure Aunt Dodo was out of sight before asking Mother to come into the chamber room. "Listen, I'm teaching myself how to play piano. Maybe I can help you teach."

Mother smiled as she took my hand and accompanied me into the music room. Her hand felt so soft and I could smell her French perfume— she called it Jicky—the fragrance of all her children from the garden combined. She took a seat in the blood-colored plushy chair that looked like a throne for a princess. I bounced in it sometimes when no one looked, but now Mother, a heavy stone, sank down into the Red Sea as the chair swallowed her up. *I'd better start playing so I can keep her afloat.*

Aunt Dodo entered the room. "All he does is pound on that piano all day," she said. "It drives me crazy. It sure will be good when he starts school."

That's right, just never mind me. I'd taken my seat on the piano bench, but my feet didn't quite touch the pedals so I slid down toward the edge. At first I played slowly, just lightly brushing my fingers across the keyboard as I played one of Mother's favorites, a simple melody I heard her playing at night sometimes. She called it *Moonlight Sonata*. After a few moments, I segued into something a bit more complicated, but fun to play nonetheless.

"Oh, Charley, when did you learn to play the second movement of *Pathetique*?" she asked, as if I'd already mastered the first of three movements.

I turned to see her hands clasped over her heart. I couldn't tell whether she was blinking her glossy eyes in pleasure or pain, so I resumed my playing, quickly growing bored until I felt something in my stomach gurgling up—the music *I* wanted to play—something bubblier like what I'd been hearing on the radio lately up in my room, when Aunt Dodo was away, of course. I preferred the livelier melody of jazz. I lifted myself off the bench as I reached for the pedals, and I belted out *You know, it don't mean a thing if you ain't got a swing.*

I stretched my fingers to play the sounds now dancing in my head. I threw my head back, giggling, happy in my own world. My head was a chamber room swarming with music of nature. The birds, the squirrels, the crickets, the fish from the creek. I could hear it all including the wind rustling through the trees.

And then when I turned, the sight of seeing Mother crying, startled me. Aunt Dodo looked like a ghost or as if she'd just seen one.

"I'm sorry," I screamed, pulling my hands away from the piano as if it was on fire. "I didn't mean to—"

Mother put her hands to her mouth and moved toward me. *Now I've really done it. I just wanted to make her happy.* Mother came up to wrap her arms around me. "That was magnificent. Oh, Darling, you can play by ear." She really bawled now and I stiffened. *I play by hand.* I wasn't sure about the ear stuff.

"I'm sorry, Mother. The music plays me. I can't help it."

She took a seat next to me and cradled my face. "Sweetie, you are music." I closed my eyes to breathe in her sweet perfume.

I was in heaven, and then I heard the front door slam. I opened my eyes to see George waltzing across the marble foyer in his spiky golf shoes. Wearing plaid knickers and a bright yellow sweater, all he needed was a red rubber nose. He seemed very excited.

Fingers snapping, "What's all this?" he asked, removing his goofy flattened cap.

"Charley has got a gift," Mother said, dabbing her tears with a lacey hanky.

"Well, so do I," George said, as, once again taking center stage, he whipped out a wad of green money. "Enough to catch up on the mortgage."

"How? Where?" Phoebe asked, rising from her seat.

And then, somehow I knew, and out of nowhere, I asked, "Did you win at the horsies, George?"

George glared at me. Mother peered at him like she knew, too.

"One of my deals came through," George said, defensively, and then grinned.

So, that's what you gotta do to get attention around here? You gotta be a clown or a magician and pull out a wad of cash every once in a while. Mother's face lit up like the little night light in my room where I was headed now. So much for my efforts at trying to save the day.

"You mean we won't have to move to San Diego?" Mother asked.

"Not unless you want to."

"No!" I shouted and turned to run back to wrap my arms around George's legs.

"And that's not all. Tomorrow, we'll get up really early and drive out to Santa Monica. I have a surprise."

"We goin' fishin', George?" I asked.

"Not tomorrow."

Mother clasped her hands together and brought them to her lips. She seemed overjoyed; the mortgage was getting paid, after all. "Charley, play something for George. Show him what you've got."

But George didn't have time. "I have a meeting," he said, setting the cash down on the piano. He headed back out.

31

Life Is a Rollercoaster

A few days after George's sudden windfall, the giant Blue Streak Racer rollercoaster loomed in the distance as we pulled up to the pier in Santa Monica. My heart beat fast like when I held Sammy the first time, and my hands tingled to think George might be treating us to a day on the Pleasure Pier. He really wasn't such a bad guy after all.

We climbed out of the car and a couple of seagulls hovered above us to escort us as we walked along the wooden planks. It was around ten in the morning, but all was quiet. Still, it was summer and the shops and fun attractions should have been open. The glass house containing the carousel was locked up and as I rose up on my tiptoes to take a peek, I found myself staring into the glass eyes of one of the plastic horses.

Times before when George had brought me down, there'd been throngs of people, but now all I saw were tired-looking men—out-of-work carneys fishing off the sides of the pier.

"Why is everything closed?" I asked. "Where is everyone?"

"It's the Depression," Mother said.

There's that word again, I thought, as the morning fog, a giant gray blanket, covered us. Strangely, I found comfort in the mist, and the fact that I stood in between George and Mother, holding their hands, gave me a sense I hadn't a care in the world. *Depression? What Depression?* We continued walking out to the end of the pier where George had brought me fishing a couple of times while Mother spent time in court. One time, he even took me out on a fishing boat where the men were all drinking beers and smoking cigars and cigarettes and saying stuff like "God dam it," or "fuck it all to hell" and other stuff George said I'd better not tell Mother.

♪♫

Mother and I followed George to the end of the pier and we turned to an opening where you could see the foaming water rise and fall underneath. I could hear the echo of the water slapping on the barnacle-covered pilings. "Down here," George said.

"Oh, yippee, we're going on a boat," I squealed, skipping ahead. "I remember. This is the way, Mother."

Mother hiked up her dress, stuffing it between her legs, as if she wore pants. She climbed down the ladder where a water taxi waited for us.

"Morning, Mr. Gimble," the man driving the water taxi said. "Nice to see you again."

Mother looked back and forth between George and the driver. "Where are we going?" she asked, taking the man's hand. He helped her into the taxi.

"You'll see," George said as he picked me up and handed me over to the man.

I loved the briny smell of the air, so I sat up with the driver, hoping to get the salt water sprayed in my face. It was just a short bumpy ride over to the rocky breakwater where other yachts and fishing boats were anchored like a small fleet of empty ghost ships. The closer we came, I noticed a boat, something Popeye the Sailor Man might drive. The hull was white with three circle windows on the starboard side, but the rest of the boat was shiny wood. The little cabin house on top had a white lifesaver ring hanging from it. A blue and white awning covered the back of the boat and then, on the backside 'stern' of the hull, I made out the stenciled golden letters *Phoebe Mae.*

Watching Mother's face thrilled me as the water taxi pulled up next to the boat. Something just for her for a change. I thought she might be happy.

"What is this?" she asked.

"Surprise!" George said. "It's a cabin cruiser. Look," he said, chuckling as he pointed to the back of the boat. "I even spelled the name right. *M-A-E.*"

I jumped up from my seat ready to board the boat. Mother pulled me back. "Charley, sit down," she said. "We're not going aboard." Her face didn't look happy.

George put a hand up to shade his face as if he tried to read her reaction correctly. Mother had an angry face.

"We could barely make the mortgage, George. The country is in a depression. And you can afford to buy a boat?"

"Before you say anything else, I didn't pay for it. I was holding it as collateral. The owner couldn't keep up the payments."

"And just what will you do with it?"

"Take Charley fishing, for starters."

"Yippee!" I shouted.

"Then maybe charter it out for fishing excursions," George said. "I don't know. I haven't thought that far in advance. I thought you'd be a little more excited. I thought you'd be flattered that I named the boat after you."

"I'm sorry, George," Mother said, softening a bit. "It is a surprise. Thank you. I'm just not sure we should have such a luxury item at this time."

"Yes! I wanna go fishin.'"

Mother stared quietly out to sea and then finally, as the sun burned holes through the morning clouds, she closed her eyes to warm herself. I saw a smile spread across her face and then she stood, and we boarded the *Phoebe Mae.*

32

The Pocket Watch

Sometimes, bad news is when a bird slams into your bedroom window at night and then the bad news just doesn't stop, like the bloody nose I got again.

I'd lain awake watching the shadows of the wind, dark schools of fish swimming across my bedroom ceiling. The curtains on my window flapped like boat sails. All night, I drifted in and out of sleep. I dreamed about being out at sea on the *Phoebe Mae* just rocking back and forth, riding out a storm as everything on board got tossed about. The sound of angels bowling overhead interrupted my sleep and then at the sound of one more loud clap, I bolted upright, blinking toward the window, fearing it might have shattered.

"Peedles, are you there?" I asked, turning on the light. I was alone.

I thought I heard my mother crying again, but I stayed put. I didn't need to be told to stay away.

The first light of the day streamed in and I noticed when I looked sideways that there was blood on my pillow. I whipped back the covers and charged across the room to look in the mirror.

Not again! Mother said bloody noses were nothing to worry about and it was because the Santa Ana devil winds sucked the air dry. But sometimes my nose seemed to bleed for no reason, and I thought my brain was leaking or maybe I was turning into a white zombie like in the movie Milty and I had just snuck into down at the Alexander Theater when George wasn't paying attention. I tried to remain calm. By now the blood had crusted leaving a trail across my cheek to just below my ear. My hair, full of static electricity, stood on end like I'd just seen a ghost. But it was only the wind's phantom and Melody, who had been howling an eerie duet all night long. Melody hated the Santa Anas and so did I.

I shuddered when I heard clanging sounds outside and every time the wind picked up, the noise grew louder. Down the hall, I heard a door slam. It must be George coming home finally, I thought. Not too sneaky. Lately, he'd been coming home very late or, in this case, very early in the morning.

Slinking to my door, I thought I might be able to catch him, but behind me, something slammed into the window. I turned to look and with the dawning of the sun, I could see a streak of red dripping down the glass. I heard another thump, but it turned out to be coming from my own chest. I ran out down the hall, noticing the door to the room where George had been sleeping lately was closed. I looked toward Mother's room and her open door. I always had a curiosity about Mother's room—off limits, but half the fun of entering was breaking the rules. I stepped in to take a peek. No one was there.

Like walking into a church, I tiptoed in to take a look around, captivated by the artwork she had throughout. There were pictures of tall, skinny women with twisted hips and tilted heads with beaded headbands and fancy hats with feathers; one was of a long, scrawny lady draped in black, holding a scrawny black dog by a leash. There were paintings with sad-looking people whose eyes followed me wherever I went. In one corner stood a marble statue of a naked man and woman.

Near a window stood a tall tri-fold mirror. I laughed nervously when I saw three of me from different angles. I swiveled my head back and forth to see if I might catch up to myself. On the tabletop sat a silver tray covered with pretty perfume-filled glass bottles, lotions, silver hairbrushes and bobby pins. I noticed a drawer with a fancy golden handle. I tugged on it. It wasn't locked.

Inside the drawer, lined in paper decorated with tiny roses, I noticed a gold pocket watch; it didn't belong to George. I pulled it out. The chain dangled to the floor and as I pressed the little knob, the watch popped open. The time was stuck at two-thirty. And then on the right side, under the glass, I noticed a younger Mother standing next to a man. He appeared to be taller and older-looking than she and he wore a suit and glasses. I held the cold watch in my hand, wondering about the man. *That's me,* the voice said and I snapped the watch shut, my body seizing up and freezing solid like the naked marble statue in the corner. I looked around the room, making sure I was still alone.

After I relaxed just a bit, I noticed a tube-shaped case in the drawer. I craned my neck around the room again before opening the case to find a pair of silver wire-framed glasses; the same as the ones worn by the man in the picture, except these were cracked. My hands shook as I tried them on. Instantly, things got blurry.

Giggling, I walked around the room holding out my hands, seeing things all wavy and distorted, and then I heard the chiming coming from outside. I tiptoed across the Oriental runner, following the sound coming from just outside the open window overlooking the garden.

At the windowsill, the chiming stopped and it was at that moment I was able to put the voice to the face in the watch; or was it the face to the voice in my head? It was as if the man in the picture was now seated on the windowsill of my mind just waiting to be invited in. I'd make sure to keep the window closed and the shade pulled.

The wind whistled up through the glen and the sharp chiming began again. I closed my eyes and heard the music of a million crickets chirping. The sounds rose up from the creek, the same as the scary music Mother and her music friends played—clashing cymbals and clanging bells and shrieky violins. She called it *Beethoven's Fifth*.

The bathroom door screeched open and I turned to look, but everything was blurry.

"Doc?" Mother asked.

Quickly, I took off the glasses and hid them in the pocket of my pajamas. Mother was standing in the doorway naked. She didn't even try to cover herself up with a towel. She seemed far away in her head again, as if she were dreaming or sleepwalking. The brown parts of her sagging breasts seemed to be staring at me and I couldn't help but stare back at her loose, pink skin. Just above a patch of hair in the area between her legs, there was a scar like a frown line just below her bellybutton. I wanted to put the glasses back on to blur everything out, but she smiled at me, and it felt as if I'd caught fire. I turned to stare out the window before I might turn into a pile of ashes on the floor.

I couldn't tell whether the room or I swayed or if it was just the branches on the trees outside. The limbs, spindly arms of a witch, seemed to wave at me. I felt the floor fall away from me. Mother came up from behind to wrap her arms around me and hold me up. Her kiss on my cheek made me tense, especially when I felt she still wasn't wearing anything other than the fragrance of the bath salts and perfumed talcum, which did smell very nice. Her arms, a soft and warm snuggly blanket, wrapped around me.

"I had Pedro move the wind chimes closer to our bedroom window, Darling," she said in a purring voice. "I remember the day you bought them for me in Italy."

I stood, terrified. First of all, I didn't know what she was talking about. The only thing I knew about Italy was that's where spaghetti came from. "I, too, remember," the voice said and suddenly I felt the smooth, ancient cobblestones beneath my feet. I tried to pull the shade back down over the window in my memory. These weren't my memories!

Finally, Mother released me and I scuttled out of the room like a frightened mouse. In the hallway, spinning in circles so confused, I didn't know what I was feeling.

"Oh, Charley, I'm so sorry," she screamed after me.

33

Charley and Teresa Forever

In the back yard, the chimes in the tree clanged even louder, luring me away from the house. When the jangling stopped, I heard the distressed *caw caw* of a bird. I turned to see Melody running to the side of the house, barking excitedly. I followed her, watching as her nose twitched. She'd locked onto a scent. An injured bird had landed in a bush just beneath my bedroom window. All but his charcoal-tinted wings were snow white. His rust-colored beak was the length of a finger and as I approached, his yellow eye with a big black dot in the middle zoomed back at me, tracking and adjusting to my every move.

"Melody, no," I shouted just as she opened her jaw to chomp down on the bird. Mel backed down. "Good girl." I reached out, putting my arm around her withers to hold her back. I felt her heart thumping and noticed how her pulse seemed to be the same as the shuddering bird in the bush. I wondered if all of nature had the same beat when it was excited or near death.

In the garage, behind a shelf crawling with tools, spiders and cobwebs, I found a box and brought it out to pad it with the dried twigs and leaves scattered across the yard. I returned to the injured bird and lifted it gently into the box.

"There you go. Come on, Melody," I yelled, and we scrambled down to the creek where I knew I could find plenty of squiggly worms.

Ambling back up to the terrace, I dangled a live worm over the bird's beak. "Come on, bird, eat," I said, but no matter how much I coaxed him, he didn't seem interested or maybe he was too sick or injured. "The early bird gets the worm."

Melody tilted her head just as I thought I heard someone coming. I scooped up the box and we took off for the creek. Once we reached the water's edge, she plowed into a mound of dried autumn leaves piled up alongside. I jumped in behind her to scoop some up and scattered an armful, creating a blast of powder like the talcum Mother had dusted on her body after her bath. Mel and I were now on a mission to see what else we could find for our new pet to eat.

Underneath the giant sycamore tree where my friend Teresa Marquez, who was five like me, and I had carved our names "Charley and Teresa Forever," I found a strong branch and broke it in half, making it the length of my arm with a very sharp point at the break. Melody and I jumped into the creek puddles to splash and frolic. Butterflies and dragonflies skidded across the surface as I spotted a small fish and tried to stab it with my stick, but I missed. I didn't consider catching a fish to be killing animals, since Mother said it was okay as long as you ate what you caught. Trying to catch a fish with a stick was hard work. I gave up to take a rest and dry out under the sun on the banks of the stream. Comforted by the sound of the trickling creek, I'd drifted off into a peaceful sleep where I dreamed I was one of Mother's wind chimes with wings. I was flying over Italy with Sammy, and dining on spaghetti, with sauce the color of blood.

I didn't know how much time had passed when I heard someone singing up the stream. I knew that sweet sound. Teresa sang our favorite song about Teddy Bears at the picnic. I perked up when I realized the music headed my way. I couldn't wait as I stood at attention.

At first, I felt guilty as if I was going behind Mother's back. I would sneak out to see Teresa and when I wasn't with her, I couldn't stop thinking about her. We were one body; it seemed as if she breathed out and I breathed in. It became only natural for her to be with me in my mind at all times, but because she couldn't be with me, one night, I drew her face with my small, smudged left hand at the carved-up desk in my bedroom. With a swirl of a brown crayon, I'd shaped a pancake and then two smaller ones set in the middle for her eyes, and she would almost come to life on the dog-eared piece of paper.

And now, with watermelon-colored ribbon weaved through two long braids and cascading over her small shoulders, Teresa appeared from behind a giant oak tree. Standing next to it in her smock with flowers sewn on, she waved at me. She then approached along the fern-lined creek kicking up the dust with the *huaraches* handed down from her brother, Teddy. The dirt settled onto her already dark skin. Her face wasn't like most of the kids from this neck of the woods, but more the color of honey or sweet hot cocoa that warms and brings comfort on a chilly winter's day. And when she smiled, it warmed my heart.

"You're still in your pajamas, Charley." She giggled and I looked down in embarrassment.

"Melody and I slept outside last night," I said.

"What's that?" she asked, pointing to the box.

"My new pet. He crashed into my bedroom window. He wants to be my friend."

Teresa made coo-cooing sounds to the bird. I showed her the slimy earthworms, and without hesitation or any squeamishness, she plucked one up and offered it to my bird, who opened its beak and tugged it from her.

"He'll be okay," she said confidently, and I believed her.

"What's his name?"

"Sammy," I said without hesitation, "short for Samson." I'd just read the story of Samson and Delilah out of the book of bible stories given to me by Auntie Ann.

After a while, I heard Teresa's mother calling her. Señora Antonia Marquez had been our cook before Mother had to let her go. I didn't want to let Teresa go, she'd just gotten here.

"I have to go home for lunch. Come with me," Teresa said.

I gathered up my box with my seagull inside and followed Teresa. I liked it over at the Marquez house. There were chickens and goats and pigs and even horses that hadn't been sent to the glue factory.

We wandered up to the house, plucking grapes as we passed under the arbor, and when Señora Antonia saw me, she approached and wrapped her arms around me.

"Aye, Carlito! You are so big. Come, you're just in time for *almuerzo*!"

"What have you there?" she asked, staring at my box.

"Sammy."

"A seagull? Well, he certainly is a long way from home."

"He hurt himself when he tried to fly in through my bedroom window."

Señora Antonia peered at me and suddenly I felt self-conscious about the way I was dressed.

"He camped outside," Teresa said.

"Like an explorer," I said.

Señora Antonia simply laughed and said, "I see. So, go on now and get washed up, Magellan. And wipe that blood off your face."

"I had a bloody nose."

Antonia reached out to caress my cheek. "*Pobrecito.*"

I loved Antonia. I loved the family.

At the water pump outside, I rinsed my hands and face next to the ranchers and then came in to take a seat at the large table in between Teresa's older brother Teodoro "Teddy" and some of the other ranchers.

"Will it be all right with your *mamá*?" Señora Antonia asked.

"She won't care. I think she went to court again today, anyway," I said.

"Still in court? On a Saturday?" she asked and then paused for a moment. "And who is taking care of you?"

"Melody," I said and when she heard her name, Melody barked from out on the veranda.

Señora Antonia smiled and bowed her head. I mimicked the others and folded my hands, peeking to watch as they said grace. I then lowered my head, realizing I was starving.

When I looked up, I noticed Señora Antonia smiling at me. "*Eres muy guapo, como tu papa.*"

Teresa's legs swung back and forth under the bench when she turned to me, "She says you're handsome like your *papa.*"

I looked at her and tilted my head.

"*Papa* means father," she said.

I had never really considered George's looks, one way or the other. "Thank you," I said.

"He was a good man. He had great vision," Señora Antonia said.

"That's why Doc was an eye doctor. Get it?" Teresa's uncle said with a chuckle.

"Doc?" I wondered.

As the steaming bowls of rice and beans and cactus were passed around the table, I grew even more confused and filled with questions.

"Too bad George got hold of everything," Teddy said.

"How could she be so blind?" someone else said.

And then they all switched to Spanish.

"Anyway, now they are just carving up the land and building more houses. Soon this place will be like the rest of Los Angeles," Pedro said.

The diners stared at Señora Antonia and she peered back. "*Aye Aye Aye!*" she shouted as she brought the butt of her hand to her forehead. She jumped up and returned to the stove. "*Las tortillas! Mija,* help me!"

The workers all laughed. "*Loca,*" one of them said.

I followed Teresa and her mother into the kitchen where Señora Antonia had taken a step to the side of the stove to uncover a mound of dough on the counter. She tore off a piece and rolled it into a ball. Mesmerized, I watched as she then clapped it and patted it together, finally slapping it onto a flat counter where she began rolling it out with what looked like a short, fat wooden broomstick.

"Señora Antonia?" I asked as she threw down the doughy saucer the size of a dinner plate onto the grill.

"*Sí,* Carlito?"

I opened my mouth to respond, but just watching her flip the dough held me spellbound once, twice, then she handed it to Teresa who lobbed it *ala* hot potato to her brother. Everyone laughed. This went on until everyone at the table held a hot tortilla in his hands. I took my place back at the table as Teresa flung mine to me and I tossed it back and forth between my hands. It was hot. She sat next to me and I watched as she tore off a piece from hers and dipped it into her plate to swoop up some beans. I did the same. I'd forgotten all about what I wanted to ask Señora Antonia.

This was the first time I'd eaten a tortilla since Antonia had been let go as our cook. This was the first time I didn't have to worry about using the right utensil. And it was the first time there was no silence at the table and, probably the only time, it was all right to throw food around.

"What did you want to ask, Carlito?"

I swallowed my food, swiping my mouth with a pajama sleeve. "Can you tell me more about my papa?" I asked and pulled out the pocket watch to show her. "Is this him?"

"*Sí,* this is him. This is Señor 'Doc' Marnier, your papa."

After lunch, Teresa and I wandered back out into the woodlands. The wind had died down only slightly as we came across a clearing. We lay down in the tall grass and stared up at the passing clouds. Teresa reached over to take my hand as Melody lay beside me, licking bean and cactus juice off my face. With my best friends on either side, I was happy. I was also full from a hearty lunch and warm as the sun shone down on me. In that moment, my friends and I were the center of the world.

"I'm happy to know George isn't my father," I said to Teresa. "Sometimes, I don't really like him." I squeezed her hand. "What were they saying in there about him, anyway?"

"That he still owes Papa and some of the workers some money. He even borrowed money from Teddy. The other day George and another man came by to tell us they are selling this land."

I didn't understand what this meant, but something deep down in my stomach ached and I didn't think it had anything to do with Señora Antonia's cooking. I grabbed my stomach and focused on the clouds.

"I see clowns and circus animals, Charley. What do you see?"

I stared but didn't see anything. I'd worked myself up about this morning and couldn't let go of the image of my mother and the man in the watch, and then the image of her naked, and now I'd just learned George was not my father; Doc was. Doc Marnier. I looked across the meadow and watched as the clouds' shadows danced across the valley. I remembered the glasses in my pocket and pulled them out to put them on.

"I see my papa," I said, pretending I could see everything clearly now. "He's handsome like me." And then the giant hand of a cloud waved across the sun, darkening the sky for an instant. A strange falling feeling washed over me.

"Yes," Teresa said, "and Mamá says he was a good man, too, so he probably is up there in heaven like an angel." She rolled over and kissed me softly on the lips.

I lay on the ground having that waking-up-moment sensation right after a dream; I felt myself floating around somewhere, as if I were up in heaven. I carried the glow of her kiss with me all the way back home, fortified and yet drowsy as I staggered along carrying my box with Sammy in it. Muddled with feelings of grief and yet joy, a brilliant pain lifted me higher than a soaring seagull—my head in the clouds, my eyes full of stars, my heart swollen as big as the sky.

Teresa was my angel on earth.

34

Fly Away

My seagull got better and I worried about him flying away from me. I also worried about leaving Melody outside anywhere near Sammy, so I made sure to keep her inside most of the time. Besides, as tempting as it was for her to chase the bird, she was getting pretty old. She had trouble walking and kept bumping into things like trees and bushes. She was better off inside where I could keep an eye on her.

As the yolk-colored morning sun kissed the sky, flooding the kitchen with light, Melody and I stepped in to find Mother getting ready to fix breakfast. She hummed over the sound of the metal ticking and the hiss of the gas and then she lit a match and gasped, jumping back, hand to her heart, as the flame ignited suddenly. After a bit, she cracked the eggs and they sizzled as they hit the bacon grease in the frying pan. The smell of breakfast was in full bloom.

George already sat at the kitchen table with a cup of coffee and the newspaper.

"Charley, can you get the orange juice out of the icebox." I'd helped Mother squeeze the oranges I'd picked in the orchard yesterday. "And then go ahead and start."

"Son, elbows down," George said. "Looks like you're gonna fly off with Sammy the way your arms are flapping."

I laughed, tucking my elbows in. Mother jumped as the sound of grease popped behind her and then she looked toward the table. "Charley, why is Melody wearing—"

"Doc's glasses," I said with a smile so big my cheeks ached. "So she can have better vision. I'm going to be an eye doctor like my father, only for animals—a 'vetomotrist.'" I pulled out the orange juice.

Mother's face went white as the eggshells. She looked over at George and then marched over to remove the glasses from Melody.

George set down his paper. "Why don't I drive Charley and the bird down to the beach where he belongs?"

Mother peered at George.

"Glendale is no place for a seagull," George said and then crunched down on a slice of toast.

A trace of panic seeped into my voice. "But why not?" I thought I'd get to keep Sammy forever.

"Yes, I think that would be a good idea," Mother said, slipping the glasses into the pocket of her apron. I'd replaced the pocket watch, but hadn't been able to part with the glasses.

"Why are you both always trying to ruin my happiness?" Sniveling, I glared at George. "You're not even my real papa."

Mother pulled her lower lip over her top one. "Charley, enough." She sunk into her seat and put her hand on her forehead. "I don't think I can handle this right now."

"I'm right, aren't I? Teresa calls Pedro papa. Milty calls Uncle Earl papa. How come I don't call George papa?"

"We'll talk about it later. Now eat your breakfast," George-not-my-papa said.

Oh, sure. Nobody ever talks to me about anything. I shut my mouth and picked up my fork, staring at the two of them through the prongs like some sorta prisoner behind bars.

George watched and waited as Mother swabbed her lips with her tongue then dabbed some yolk from the side of her delicate mouth. She acted calm as always. I bet she'd act the same way even if the house were burning down.

The forks clinked on the plates. I could hear everyone chewing. Melody whimpered so I gave her a little piece of bacon. George seemed relieved to have me drop my bombshell after all of the talk last night about money and his "bookie."

As calm as she appeared, I could tell Mother was angry when she stabbed into more of her egg. I watched as the yellow part bled across her plate. I sensed a storm coming.

"Say, I've got some business over on the west side," George said, finally breaking his yoke and the silence. "Charley and I can have a little chat along the way."

Mother brought a piece of egg to her mouth, inserted it and chewed for an eternity. My head swiveled back and forth from her to George as I munched on a strip of crisp bacon, careful not to miss a beat of the unfolding drama, subtle as it had become. She then dabbed her mouth again before speaking.

"That is so kind of you, George, but really, I don't think it is necessary. The bird will find his way back eventually."

There was no more mention of Doc now, only of my bird.

"I'm not so sure," George said as he stopped to look at me, pointing his knife. "After all, Charley has done such a good job nursing him back to health, it would be such a shame to see it die—"

"What? No," I screamed, dropping the bacon onto my plate and jumping out of my chair. "Die? He can't die." I looked to my mother. "Please, let George take us down to the beach."

Mother cut a glance at me then back at George. "Very well, but please don't take all day. I think I'll call Ann to see if Milty might want to spend the night."

Smooth move, Mother. She must have thought I wouldn't be able to handle another loss. She probably hoped I'd lose interest in the subject of Doc, and the pain of letting go of my bird would somehow be eased with the anticipation of seeing my cousin again.

Off George and I drove to Santa Monica.

♪♫

The Santa Anas had picked up again, blowing razor-sharp sand along the unseasonably warm beach. George and I took off our socks and shoes to walk down to the shore. I carried the box, my arm slung over the top, with Sammy in it. The summer season was just over so there were lots of seagulls barking and scavenging the shore for leftovers. A few fishermen waded along a rippling shoreline casting their fishing lines.

"Too bad we didn't bring our fishing poles," I said. I knew what the answer would be, but I asked anyway. "George, can we go on the boat?"

"Not today."

"How about tonight?"

I knew he'd been taking guests out on our boat at night lately. Night fishing, he called it. I loved the last time George took me out fishing. I'd caught a fish and we took it home for Mother to fry up. The kitchen had smelled so fishy, but it made me feel special to be able to bring something to the table.

"We'll do it again, son," George said, taking a seat in the sand.

I did love when George called me "son." Maybe, someday I would be able to call him my papa.

"Right now, it's time to let Sammy go."

The wind blew my tears into my ears as I lifted Sammy out of the box.

"Now, Charley, it will make Sammy happy to return to his family. Look at all of them." The birds had inched closer to us. "They think we have food," George said.

"We should have brought some leftovers," I said, hugging Sammy close.

"Next time. Now let Sammy go."

I set Sammy down and he immediately shuffled into the flock of birds.

"You see, those are all his brothers and sisters," George said.

"What about his mother and father?" I asked, wiping my nose on my sleeve.

"There's his mother," George said, pointing to a larger bird with brown spots.

I giggled and then I saw a larger bird with charcoal-tinted wings like Sammy.

"And that must be his papa," I said.

"How do you know?"

"He looks just like him," I said.

"Why, yes, he does," George said. "You know, Charley, sometimes you don't have to look alike. Sometimes it doesn't matter if you're related by blood, as long as you love each other. That's all that matters." I turned to look at George just as he wiped his eyes. "Son, I do love you."

I ran up to hug George, feeling warm and understanding a little more about love.

"I'll come back to visit real soon. Be good, Sammy, I love you."

On our way home, George stopped by his office and asked me to wait in the car, but after a few minutes, I needed to go to the bathroom. When I walked inside, I caught him kissing his secretary. George smoothed back his hair, Coty smoothed down her skirt.

"Son of a bitch! What the hell are you doing?" the voice said, so low and loud it practically scraped my tonsils. I pictured the man in Mother's locket with his leg straddling the windowsill of my mind, waiting to climb in and rip George apart.

"Charley, I told you to wait for me outside," George yelled.

"You are a liar and fraud," the voice screamed out of my small mouth.

"Go," George said, pointing above my head.

"But, I need to go to the bathroom. The door is locked." I'd needed to go since we left Santa Monica. I'd also wanted to stay and splash around in the waves where I might have relieved myself, but George had pulled out his pocket watch and said he needed to get down to his office. He seemed to be in such a hurry, so I never even got the chance to pee.

George reached into his desk drawer and then tossed me a key.

At the toilet, I wondered if, like a father, husbands became bonded by blood to their wives or if it didn't matter who you kissed? I rarely ever saw George and Mother kissing the same way he and Coty kissed.

On the drive back home, I tried to keep the window in my mind squeezed shut. I was confused about what I'd seen and asked George about kissing and what it meant. "Teresa kissed me and I liked it," I said, remembering the bittersweet taste and mystery of it all.

He laughed and told me not to worry so much about Teresa and that as I grew older, there would be more girls to like and kiss. "The most important thing is to always remember to be true to the one you love," he said.

Melody approached us, wagging her tail as we arrived home. I dropped to my knees and put my arms around her withers. Mother asked about Sammy.

"I think he found his family," I said, kissing Melody on her nose. "All of his brothers and sisters and his aunts and uncles and his mother. Even his papa was there. They look alike."

Mother smiled, looking at George. "Thank you," she said. "Did you have lunch?"

"Oh, sure. We had a picnic," I said, pulling out some shells from my pocket. I set them down on the table, lining them up smallest to largest.

"Oh, how lovely," Mother said. "I'll bet it was tricky eating on the sand especially on a day like today."

"Oh, I had a picnic at George's office," I said. "Coty set me up in the kitchen while she and George did some work in his office."

Mother's smile instantly disappeared and then she left the room.

With his eyes, the color of gray pistols, George warned me to stay silent and then he turned. "She always orders sandwiches in on Thursday afternoons," he said, trailing behind my mother. "You know that."

Right then, I heard the doorbell ring. "It's Milty!" I shouted and dashed off through the living room. Melody followed me. Sharing with Mother what I'd witnessed at George's office would have to wait. Then again, I wasn't sure I wanted to upset her.

35

Repatriation

Teresa and I were so happy to be in the same kindergarten class. We'd become inseparable, innocently holding hands in the schoolyard to the dismay of the academia. Inside the classroom, we were immediately separated by our teacher. Classmates made fun of us. The parents were up in arms. Mother tried to explain that our "behavior wasn't appropriate." I didn't see why nor did I care.

It was my turn to swing when another, older boy came up to Teresa to talk to her. I jumped out and scrambled to her side. Teresa belonged to me.

"Dumb Mexican lover," he said, pushing me away. "My father says Mexicans have *duseases* and that's why we have the *dapression*."

Chest out, I approached the boy again and he pushed me down. We broke into a fight. Teresa threw sand in the boy's face and pulled him off me, clawing his arms in the process.

I came home pretty scuffed up also and missing a tooth that was loose anyway. After school, my mother had to come and pick me up. Pedro and Señora Antonia came too. I headed upstairs when I heard Mother telling George what had happened in the schoolyard. I took a seat on the middle landing.

Mother said, "Antonia hadn't wanted to bring this up. As a matter of fact, she was quite embarrassed."

"About what?" George asked.

"She says you still owe them wages. And you borrowed money and you haven't paid it back?"

"That's bullshit."

"You and another man came by? You're selling the land? You can't do that. My attorney is holding the title as collateral. No one can do anything without my permission, without my signature. This probate is none of your business, George."

"Of course not. Calm down, Phoebe, I'm just looking out for you and the boy. I was only accompanying Taylor. He was simply appraising the property that, by the way, isn't worth as much anymore since it's no longer producing anything. Anyway, Mrs. Marquez must have misunderstood. Stupid Mexicans."

Mother parted her lips to speak. One of the rules of our home was you weren't allowed to use the word "stupid." When George lumped the two words together, I thought for sure he was in for it. I waited but she didn't say anything.

In the evening, Mother received a call from my school principal. I was to stay home for a few days until things settled over, until the school board could figure out what to do with us.

I missed Teresa terribly and couldn't wait to see her. The following week I was able to go back to school. I'd learned my lesson and wouldn't be holding her hand, at least not at school. But, she wasn't at the bus stop. She wasn't in the classroom. She was gone. Something felt terribly wrong. I ran home and then sprinted through the orchard in a panic to her house. The adobe, unusually quiet, had never been empty like this. I spun around in the middle of the room. The Marquez's were gone. I walked back out to the porch, slumped down on the step and shed a waterwell full of tears.

Later, at home after dark, I heard my mother talking to George. I heard him talking about something else I couldn't understand: "Mexican Repatriation."

"But Antonia is an American citizen; part of the Verdugo family that once owned this land," my mother said.

"Apparently, Pedro isn't," George said.

"And Teresa is fluent in English," Mother added, still pleading the case.

When I heard the name Teresa, I walked out into the hall to stand outside Mother's bedroom. I had a glimmer of hope that Teresa might be coming back.

"It doesn't matter," George said.

"I hated letting Antonia go," Mother said, "and now I'm really going to miss Pedro. I'll never be able to replace him."

Replace? Even though I couldn't exactly understand the word, I wondered how I could ever replace Teresa. Was it like switching socks? Or trading cards? I ran my tongue over my lips, trying to remember the flavor of her chocolate kiss, and I would try to hold onto her sweet image forever.

"They'd been with Doc and me since we built this house," Mother said. "Pedro helped Doc plant the orchard, plant that tree in the back yard. I can't believe you withheld wages from them. I am appalled. What have you been doing with the money from the estate?"

"What do you think I've been doing? You know nothing about finances, Phoebe. Do you have any idea how much it takes to run this household?"

"Yes, as a matter of fact I do. And the estate was set up to handle just that. There should be enough, George."

George brushed past me as he came through the bedroom door. He stopped when Mother called after him.

"Your bookie called."

George turned and saw me standing there. I never noticed George read anything other than the newspaper and I wondered why the librarian called about a bookie.

"What are you talking about? You're just fishing, Phoebe. You don't know what you're talking about?" he said, continuing toward the stairs.

"Mr. Dragna wanted me to give you a message," she said, and George stopped like he'd hit some sort of invisible wall.

I, too, stood glued to the floor, hands on hips. "Still running with Dragna?" the deep voice asked.

George peered at me as he stood on the landing. He opened his mouth to say something, but before he could say anything, Mother said, "He wants the money by the end of the week, or the stores are his."

"It doesn't mean anything."

"Oh, I think it means something pretty serious," the voice said.

"Have you leveraged the stores?" Mother asked. "Why would he stoop so low as to phone my home and involve me?"

"You're right. It's your home. Everything is always yours and Doc's and Charley's. It's all yours. I have nothing. Charley can't even call me father. Who am I, Phoebe? Who do you want me to be?"

"You're my husband, George, you know that. You are part of all of this. I've never denied you anything."

"Except your love," he said and walked out.

George always managed to get the last word. I heard him speed down the drive.

36
Norma Jeane and Hollygrove

It was Thursday afternoon. I could feel my six-year-old smile spreading wider than the grill on our Buick when I saw Mother pulling up to my school. She was beaming, too.

"Where's George?" I asked, climbing onto the front seat.

She didn't answer my question. "How was school today?"

"Too long. I can't wait to get home and play with Laurel and Hardy."

On Monday, George had brought home new puppies, chocolate labs. He'd said the owners had moved away and left them behind and the pups needed a new home. Mother saw how happy I was and I'm sure she didn't have the heart to make George take them back. I also had a feeling George was making up for stuff, plus he wanted to make sure I never said anything to Mother about him kissing Coty.

"You can play with your puppies later," Mother said. "Right now, I'd like you to come with me over to Hollygrove."

"But, I wanted to play with them," I whined.

Mother put the car into gear and we rolled away from the school. "There's no one at home to watch you," she said. "Laurel and Hardy will still be there waiting for you when we get home later."

♪♫

It was love at first sight, the moment I walked through the doors of the Hollygrove Orphanage on El Centro in Hollywood. Around the orphanage, where every Thursday afternoon Mother gave music lessons, we also owned a couple of rental cottages. I quickly forgot all about my chocolate labs. Norma Jeane Baker's hair was like butter-cream frosting and her eyes were the color of the sea. A bit older than me, there was something inviting about Norma, but even as fascinating as she seemed, I promised myself

I'd never forget Teresa. But come the next Thursday, I couldn't conjure up Teresa's face. I begged my mother to pick me up from school again to let me tag along.

One time, Norma and I sat quietly on a couple of metal chairs while Mother gave some redhead kid with a bowl-shaped haircut a piano lesson. "Is that a he or a she?" I asked, pointing to the kid.

Norma shrugged her shoulders. "I don't know, but I'm going to be the next Shirley Temple," she said, and with the bright pink ribbon in her hair, I believed her. "My aunt is making the arrangements. Someday I'll be a star."

I had no doubt.

When funny haircut finished his lesson, I reached up to whisper something to my mother. She scooted over and I sat down. I searched my memory and soon the music came to me. I played the familiar tune and even remembered the words as I sang along. Norma seemed ecstatic, clapping her hands and joining in as Mother took over on the piano playing in harmony with me:

Where bon-bons play
On the sunny beach of Peppermint Bay.

When we finished, Norma skipped up to my mother and hugged her. "I'll miss you, Mrs. Marnier." My heart sank to the bottom of Peppermint Bay. I didn't understand and then she walked up to kiss me on the cheek. "Oh, Charley, you're so much fun. You're a sweet little bon-bon!" My insides got all gooey.

In the car, I asked Mother if Norma Jeane was going to live with her aunt. "Is that what she meant by saying she would miss you?"

"I'll explain everything later," Mother said as she pulled away, but she never did and I wouldn't see Norma Jeane again until many years later.

After the lessons, usually we'd go and collect the rent money from the rest of the bungalows on El Centro and Selma. Mother had been doing this for several months since the night she and George argued about his "bookie." She would then deliver the money to attorney, Mr. Taylor. I couldn't understand why she had to do that, especially since we seemed to need the money to pay bills. But it's the reason she also gave piano and voice lessons to some of the kids over at the orphanage, she'd told me, and I certainly hadn't minded tagging along, especially once I'd met the most beautiful yellow-haired creature I'd ever laid eyes on, except for maybe Shirley Temple, but she wasn't real.

There'd been a change in plans and we drove away without stopping. "Aren't we collecting rent today?" I asked.

I didn't understand, but before I could try to figure anything out, we'd pulled onto the street in front of George's office. "We're stopping to see George?"

"Just a little surprise visit," Mother said.

Anxiety washed over me. It was Thursday—sandwich day. What if Mother caught him kissing Coty? I suppose I wouldn't have to squeal on him after all. But the fact that I hadn't said anything ate me up worse. Where did my loyalty lie?

"So, we're just popping in to surprise George?" I asked, anxious to get this part of the day over with, but at the same time wanting to share with George about Norma Jeane. I touched the cheek where Norma had kissed me. I'd been torn when I finally had to leave her. I couldn't understand my feelings. Nothing could ever change what I felt for Teresa and yet I remained conflicted. After Teresa had gone away, I'd missed her so much it hurt. I'd walk along the creek and pine for her as if I'd been holding my breath underwater and needed air. I'd lay awake at night trying to remember her but, after a time, I couldn't see her face anymore. And once I'd met Norma Jeane, I suppose I felt guilty.

I knew George to be good with the ladies so maybe he'd have some advice when we got to his office.

"Yes," Mother said, looking at her watch. "It's Thursday just around 'picnic' time. Let's see what Coty has on the menu for today."

I reached for my door handle.

Mother said, "No, Charley, wait here. This shouldn't take long."

Part of me wanted to go catch him in the act, but the other side of me sort of felt bad for George, because I thought I understood what it felt like to love more than just one woman. Geneva, Teresa, Norma and my mother, but I hadn't known who to be true to until a few minutes later when Mother returned and handed me a sandwich.

There'd been food on the table at home; George seemed to be doing a better job lately of providing, but at that moment I knew on which side my bread was buttered.

♪♩

In the kitchen, I munched on a snack. George never even set down the newspaper when Mother walked in—a sign he didn't want to be bothered. She'd been in court all day. Her whole body seemed to be shaking like an alarm clock. She looked at me. "Charley, I want you to pack an overnight bag. You're going with Aunt Dodo and Uncle Art."

"But why?" Was I being punished? I hadn't said anything wrong for a long time.

"George and I have some things we need to work out."

George set down the paper.

"Please, I'll stay in my room. I won't listen. I promise. I'll be good."

"What's up?" George asked.

"It's over. The probate is finally over," Mother said.

I thought I might see them jumping for joy, but instead the mood seemed sort of glum.

"Charley, I told you to go upstairs," Mother said, then turned to George. "I'm just happy it's over."

George didn't look very happy.

"We're better off than most, especially during this depression."

I took my time about leaving, but George quickly stood and stormed out the back door. I knew I'd best scram so I hurried out of the kitchen and ran upstairs.

Aunt Dodo arrived later in the evening, something highly unusual. I smelled trouble and knew better than to hang around with Aunt Dodo here. I tried to stay out of her sight, and so I stayed upstairs where I crouched down quiet as a little mouse at the top of the landing. Through the slats of the stair rails, I could still see and hear the goings-on in the living room where Mother and Aunt Dodo sat. My aunt then stood and shuffled to the cabinet to pour drinks.

"So, the probate is over. This calls for a celebration."

Mother took a sip. "Oh, Dorothy," she said. "Stella got nothing more. Warrington was ordered to turn back the business, but everything is gone."

"What do you mean? Gone?"

"Warrington is bankrupt. There's nothing left of Marnier Optometry."

"That greedy scoundrel," Aunt Dodo said. "What about the other businesses over on Central?"

Mother quieted. I could see her shaking her head. "He also had oil rigs pumping up in Ventura."

"What?" Aunt Dodo asked.

"And now I've come to know Taylor also sold the plot of land containing the nine rental units over in Hollywood."

"But how was he able to do that?"

"We all know I didn't have the money for attorney's fees. I'd given him the deeds to hold the rental units as collateral. Apparently, he arranged for the property to be sold to a third-party named Gaston, but I never signed anything. I swear. I can never go back to the orphanage and give lessons."

What? I wanted to scream, but I realized my noggin was stuck in between the stair rails. I calmed down enough to pull my head out. *But, does that mean I'll never see Norma Jeane again?* I stood to go downstairs.

"You need to get the property back from Gaston," Aunt Dodo said.

"Yes, let's go now!" I shouted, running into the living room.

"Charley, go back upstairs," Aunt Dodo yelled.

"Darling, why don't you go into the kitchen and get a snack," Mother said.

I didn't want another snack, but I didn't want another smack from Aunt Dodo, either. As I headed toward the kitchen, my chin leaning on my chest, I heard Mother say, "George says there's nothing that can be done. He said he already confronted the attorneys. The third-party person is innocent in all of this."

"George. What's he good for anyway?" Aunt Dodo said.

"Ostensibly, nothing," Mother said, wiping a fresh tear from her eye. "I've hired a private investigator."

I stopped in my tracks and tiptoed back to a corner where they couldn't see me.

"It's about time," Aunt Dodo said.

"George hasn't been faithful. He's been wining and dining women like he's Rockefeller."

"Where's he getting the money?"

"That's what's being investigated."

"I never liked George," Aunt Dodo said.

There she went, badmouthing George again. It scared me. I'd learned to feel some kind of love for George, and when Dodo would go off, I'd step in to defend him. "Don't talk about my George like that!" But lately he'd changed. Learning he wasn't my papa did nothing to help the matter. I'd also sensed his sadness, too.

"I thought he'd be good for Charley." Mother blew her nose into a hanky. "I never knew Doc owned property up on Valley View above Brand Avenue."

"Well, that certainly must be worth something."

"It was . . . before George sold it to Taylor."

I heard Aunt Dodo gasp and then get up to pour herself another drink.

"Dorothy, I need more time, but in the meanwhile, I must hold things together. I need to confront George and get some answers. Would you please take Charley?"

My stomach lurched. *No!* I didn't want to go to Dumb Dodo's.

"Of course, but let me send Arthur over. I don't think it's safe to leave you here alone with George. Art's just over at the hotel working on a news story, he can take a break."

"No," Mother said. "George is capable of many despicable things, but he would never hurt me."

"Maybe not physically, but I'd say he's certainly already done some horrible damage."

I kicked and I screamed and I wailed until Aunt Dodo shoved me into her car, threatening to give me something to cry about. She twisted around in the front seat, her eyes sliding over me without regard, giving me a shiver. "That drama won't work with me," she said, in a voice so cold an icy feeling spread across my chest until I froze. "Now, dry the tears and quit acting like a child."

37
Ashes to Ashes

The day before my seventh birthday, a package bigger than a breadbox was delivered to our house. I ignored Mother when she told me she'd get it, and I beat her to the door like we're in a race for our lives.

Mother and George seemed to have reached an uncomfortable impasse, lately. The house had grown even quieter and lonelier as I waited for the next shoe to drop, but I was just happy to pretend everything was normal.

"Oh, boy! For me?" I shouted, opening the door to a deliveryman. Mother scooted me away and anxiously signed for the package. I followed her as she carried the box into the living room. She looked around and then proceeded toward the fireplace and set the box in front of the hearth. She smoothed her hand across the top of the box and then she took a deep breath. I couldn't wait for her to open it, but instead she walked away and took a seat on the couch.

I noticed her trembling lips and as she pulled up her hands to cover her mouth, they too were shaking. My stomach did a little somersault.

"What is it?"

"I'll tell you later." I hadn't seen her this shaky since the last day of trial when the probate had finally ended.

She simply sat there staring at the box and I figured that if I, too, stared long enough at it, maybe something would jump out.

"Can I open it?" I asked, a little nervous she might say "yes."

She ignored me and then rose and inched toward the box. Wiping her hands on her thighs, she then slowly removed the contents. She lifted out what looked like a vase.

"The urn containing your father's ashes," she said, as if a seven-year-old should be able to comprehend.

"His . . . his what?" I did a double-take.

I gazed into the hearth full of ashes as she set the vase on the mantel above the logs. I didn't understand. *My father's ashes?*

She walked away. "Come, Charley."

♪♩

Later, I followed Mother, carrying the vase, into the garden. I carried a shovel. We buried Father under the lemon tree as if he were Melody's dog bones. On her knees, Mother wept silently. I hated to see her cry, and as I knelt down to take her blistered hand, she pulled me into her. "Now you can rest in peace," she said, looking into the fresh dirt, sobbing now in a way I'd never seen her do before. It all terrified me.

There would be seven candles on my birthday cake later. In the meanwhile, Mother was getting ready for a concert, her first in seven years, and Milty and I were housebound and bored.

"Why don't I take the boys downtown?" George suggested as he grabbed Milty and me by the scruffs of our shirts. "Get them out of your hair."

"Oh, that is very thoughtful," Mother said, looking quite relieved. "Don't forget your umbrellas. We may be getting some rain, finally."

The Alexander Theater on Brand Avenue played a double feature and a cartoon that day. We pulled up to the theater and George walked us in, handing me some money.

"Aren't you staying with us?" I asked.

"Not this time," he said. "I have to take care of some business. I'll be back to pick you up after the picture show. Wait for me at the curb."

I nodded, suspecting George might be up to funny business again and that's the only reason he volunteered to bring us into town. I had to believe Mother knew this also, but when she focused on her music, everything else seemed unimportant. But that was their business and today I was the beneficiary.

"There should be enough there for some jujubes," George said and drove off.

We took our seats in the dark theater. Up on the screen according to the newsreel, apparently, we were in the middle of tough times. I watched as thousands of people lined up for food somewhere. But, thanks to George, obviously we had enough money for us to go to the picture shows and buy popcorn, candy and soda.

After the newsreel, *Popeye the Sailor Meets Sinbad the Sailor* played. I rolled up my sleeve and flexed my muscle imitating Popeye. Milty pelted me with popcorn and we settled in to watch the next feature. The Three Stooges in *Disorder in the Court*. By the time it was over, my sides ached from laughing so much.

Milty sat wide-eyed as we watched another flick I didn't think Mother would have given her stamp of approval. I closed my eyes for most of the film, sure to have nightmares at night.

The movies had ended at least half an hour before George finally pulled up to the curb where we waited, splashing us with a bucket-load of water with his big old Cadillac.

"Sorry, kids." I noticed the red lipstick on his right earlobe when I got into the car. I didn't say anything and worried Mother might also notice.

When we walked in through the back door, Mother gasped when she saw us. "Oh, my! Did you boys swim home?"

I could hear the musicians practicing in the background as Milty and I took off our rain jackets and hung them on a couple of hooks.

"How was the movie?"

"Just swell," I said as a violinist screeched in the background. I pulled my hands up to cover my ears. "The Stooges were funny, but the *Devil Doll* was about this mad scientist who shrunk humans to the size of a doll." I brought my hands together two inches apart.

"Sounds scary." She glanced over at George.

"Yeah, but we liked it," I said, signing so Milty could see. "Sometimes, it's fun having the bejesus scared out of you."

Milty smiled.

"Charley, watch your language," Mother said and then turned to George. "Thank you again. I hope it wasn't too painful sitting through something so fiendish."

George glared at me with those gray pistol eyes, warning me not to say anything.

"Oh, he didn't mind," I said, wishing I had the courage to throw him under a streetcar, but I didn't want to hurt my mother. Instead, I couldn't resist saying, "George, is that blood on your ear?" I then left the room, hands shoved into my pockets.

♪♫

Sometimes, we'd head into the orchards to play hide 'n seek or to have orange fights, but today it still drizzled outside, so Milty and I dodged raindrops, hurrying out toward the back of the property into the old storage area. Melody, Laurel and Hardy followed us in, wagging their tails. I woke up the moths when I pulled a chain attached to a dusty naked bulb hanging from a beam. Some bats flew out of the rafters and Milty and I both jumped back.

"Damn bats, nearly scared the bejesus out of me," I signed.

He made like he was laughing out loud without the sound. "Yeah, me too."

Inside were stacks of orange crates and an old grimy tractor. Making my way through some spider webs, I climbed aboard.

I never imagined the engine would start. The ground rumbled and Milty looked up and burst into laughter. I felt the powerful pulsating up from my bottom through my belly and into my hands. And then Milty signed, "Turn that off and get down!"

We were good at building stuff like forts or mazes, but today the *Three Stooges* had given me another idea. Milty helped me set up some of the old orange crates.

"Milty, you'll play the judge," I said, handing him a hammer from an old rusty tool box. "You sit behind that crate."

"Mel, Laurel, Hardy, sit." I pointed to three other crates. They would be the jury. Since I was the only one who could talk, I would get to speak most of the parts, including witnesses and jury.

I motioned for Milty to hammer down and bring order in the court.

Melody waited patiently in her orange crate. "Now, Mel," I said, lifting her right paw. "Do you solemnly swear to tell the truth, the whole truth and nothing but the truth?"

She barked. "What's that you say?" I cupped my hand to my ear, turning to the drooling jury. "Why soytenly, what have I got to lose. Nyuk, nyuk."

"You're dismissed. Next witness!"

I then ran outside, dodging raindrops, to pluck a flower from Mother's garden. As I ran back in, I stuck the white flower behind my ear and approached the orange crate, shaking my tush along the way just like the actress did in the movie. I stopped and raised my hand to Judge Milty, who laughed so hard he had tears running down his cheeks. His hands sliced through the air as he signed, "Do you solemnly swear to tell the truth, the whole truth and nothing but the truth?"

"Truth is always a good thing," I answered, remembering the lines the actress had spoken earlier in the film.

"Were you in the Black Bottom Café on the night of February thirteenth?"

"Soytenly," I said.

Milty signed, "Were you under the desk in the foyer when you saw my uncle fall from the ladder?"

"What?" I turned to Milty, acting all serious now—out of character.

"Did you see the man smash his head with a gun?" he asked.

This wasn't part of the script. "Your honor," I said, noticing his quick mood change. "My honor, you're out of order! Why, I'll squeeze the cider out of your Adam's apple. Milty, what are you talking about? That's not how the movie went."

Milty looked straight into my eyes. His eyebrows formed into a small teepee as his mouth opened. And suddenly I felt real dizzy and couldn't stand anymore. I had a haunting vision and I fell flat onto the ground, face up. The rafters spun like bicycle spokes.

It seemed as if I'd stepped through a filmy white curtain into an office somewhere. I found myself lying on a linoleum floor staring into a younger Milty's eyes as he tried to comfort me. His small hand rested on my cheek. I smelled chocolate on his breath.

Far away I heard Auntie Ann calling us for supper. I opened my eyes to see Milty, Laurel and Hardy all staring at me.

♪♫

The house overflowed with people for Mother's concert. I shared my cake with some of the musicians and Milty, who still seemed upset. I tried talking to him last night about what he'd said about a man being pushed from a ladder, but he seemed lost, so I ended up mostly trying to remember on my own. I couldn't erase the image of me on the floor bleeding and Milty leaning over me wide-eyed, scared to death.

Milty walked into the living room now with my Auntie Ann, but the sight of a man in the foyer distracted me. His hair looked sorta brown with some white at the sides near his ears and, as he stepped into the living room, he held the hand of a little blonde girl in a pink satiny dress. I recognized her from my class. Her name was Barbara Warrington. Left-handed like me, she used the same hand to swipe back a loose piece of hair when she noticed me.

"What's he doing here?" George asked Mother as he stormed in. I could tell George was mad, but he just kept smiling. "You still sweet on him?"

She smiled back, but I could tell by her eyes, she wasn't very happy. "I shouldn't even dignify that with a response, George. What's done is done. I miss the family and just want to move forward."

Fuming now, George took Mother by the arm and led her away. I couldn't hear what he told her.

Milty tugged at my coat sleeve. I turned. "What is it?" He then pointed to Barbara's father and signed, "He was there that day. I recognize the ring."

"What day?" I asked, noticing a ring, the same as George's. "So, it's a Mason's ring." We followed the crowd into the chamber room and sat behind Barbara in the third row. "He was there what day?"

"The day Uncle Doc died," Milty signed.

I felt like a bowl of jelly stung by a jellyfish. I slithered out of my seat and stood to face Milty, who wouldn't look at me. He seemed more scared than I'd ever seen him.

"Uncle Doc? My daddy?" I laughed nervously. Parts of the missing puzzle I'd tried all night to put together were slowly filling in. I knew the man but didn't know why. My heart raced and I looked at Milty to help me with more clues but he still wouldn't face me. "Look at me, Milty," I pleaded, pushing his arm. I wanted to know more. Milty stared at the man, who slowly turned to look our way.

"He pushed Uncle Doc off the ladder. He hit him with a gun," Milty signed, his hands whipping around just above his lap.

I never doubted my cousin, and I, with the ability to speak, had been Milty's mouthpiece, but I couldn't figure out how or who or whether to tell. My cousin never lied.

I'd just turned seven—there'd been a cake for me at breakfast—on the day I learned my father had been pushed to his death, for goodness sake. At once I felt a part of something, something bigger than anything in this room. It thrilled me to hear such grown-up news. In a world where I'd been surrounded by grown-up chatter, I couldn't wait to share my new-found knowledge the way one might talk about the probate or the state of the economy or the food lines and the recession. But how could I explain that my cousin suddenly remembered seeing that man, seated over there next to the cute left-handed little girl, at the office the day my father died? And who could I tell?

Suddenly, Mother spoke up. I'd never heard her address more than one person at a time. She was a princess in her long shimmering gown, her soft fairytale voice echoing throughout the castle. "Ladies and gentlemen, at this time I wish to take a moment to remember my late husband." She pointed outside. "I had his ashes brought home. Charley and I buried him under that lemon tree."

There was a collective gasp from the crowd as they gazed out the window. "That tree he planted when we first moved into this magnificent home he built for me to play my music—for occasions such as today's. He would be so pleased, so proud."

We were in the middle of a very solemn occasion. Many of the guests had shed tears as she spoke about the man who was my father. I looked over at George, who checked his nails. I recognized some of the ladies with whom Mother socialized.

"A little birdie told me it was your birthday," pretty Miss Neva said, ruffling my hair, and I blushed to the roots.

I even recognized Mother's attorney Benjamin Bledsoe. Next to him sat his curly-haired wife, dabbing her eyes with a hanky. But I'd only heard the names of the others, or maybe I'd met them before. I didn't know.

George chewed at the edge of his thumb. My mother placed the empty urn on the piano as if my father would be able to listen to the music. Her eyes looked wet as she took her seat at the piano. Milty's eyes bristled with fear—the same fear he must have experienced long ago. I grew excited. I'd never seen nor met the man Milty pointed to, but suddenly I sensed his significance.

There were many times before when I couldn't explain what I felt; maybe it's what Milty had experienced before learning to sign. But there were more times when I didn't keep things to myself and embarrassed my poor mother, like the time I told her music friends I'd seen her boobies. I looked around the room now and saw Mrs. Hotchener. Maybe I could tell her? No, she'd been after Mother to get me to go with her to some of their strange meetings. Or George? No, not George. He would just tell me to behave and then send me to my room. I contemplated the different hypothetical scenarios floating across the stage of my brain when all of a sudden, Mrs. Hotchener headed to the stage. She was going to sing—her gift to the crowd.

I couldn't wait. On this special day where they honored my father, I felt compelled to add—as if this was my gift—my contribution to the ceremony, and, at the risk of being punished once more for yet another childish outburst, this time it didn't matter how it came out for it was as simple as walking up to the stage, where I took my place next to Marie Hotchener and pointed to the man in the third row.

There I stood and in a very grown-up voice, I said, "That man killed my father! Milty was there. He saw everything!"

Milty's eyes lit up like an explosion of dynamite. The crowd hushed and all eyes riveted on me, Milty and Jack Warrington. Before I knew it, I'd been swooped up by George who clamped his hand over my mouth. As he marched me out of the room, I couldn't help but see the hurt look in my mother's eyes. Soon, I could hear the first notes of *Beethoven's Ninth*.

My bedroom was right above the chamber room and I could hear the music clearly. A hurricane had built up inside me. Sometimes, it's safer to stay in the eye of the storm, but I wanted to break out. I tore upstairs to my room. "Why won't they believe me?" Why am I always the one who gets in trouble? What about George? What about Mr. Warrington? I didn't do anything. As the music played downstairs, I stomped a Sousa march back and forth across the floor, hoping my protesting would be disruptive. Sure enough, George blasted into my room like a French horn.

Some sort of tempest had also swirled up in George's belly. Removing his belt, he told me not to make another sound.

"Get out!"

George had never hit me before and as he raised his arm, I sensed this would be my end. I tried to take cover, and for the first time in my life, he swatted me. I screeched as he threw me face down onto my bed, holding my pillow over my head. I felt his knee in my back as he held me down and then his belt smacked me on my butt. I thundered as loud as I could into the mattress. Let them all hear me.

In between sobs, I thought I could hear George crying and finally he left the room. I felt purged.

♪♫

Later, I heard a knock at the door before Milty walked in holding a glass. He handed it to me and then signed, "I took it when no one was looking. It seems to calm my father down when he's upset."

I brought it to my lips. The fumes tickled my nose and made me cough. I tentatively took a sip and as it slid down my throat, it burned. But then my insides warmed and it was a nice feeling. I emptied the glass and Milty pulled a near empty bottle of whiskey out from underneath his coat.

"Milty, you need to tell someone what you saw," I said and took a sip straight from the bottle. "Mr. Warrington shouldn't be able to get away with killing my father."

"I can't. Before he left tonight, he warned me, 'You'll be next.'"

"We've gotta tell Mother," I said.

"No!" Milty shook his head, waving his hands like a windmill.

I tried to figure something out, but anything I knew about revenge, I'd learned from movies, comic books and my own sense of justice; the bad guys get it in the end with a stick of dynamite or they go to jail, dragging a ball and chain behind them. "Milty, you need to tell a grown-up what you saw." I made my way toward the door. "We need to go to the police."

Milty barred the door. "No, please, he knows where I live!"

"Okay, I'll try to figure something else out." I took another swallow but by now the booze had relaxed me until I lost all motivation. "Tomorrow."

I noticed the music had stopped and I could hear chairs scraping and dishes clinking as the clean-up took place downstairs.

I dropped the bottle and it rolled under my bed. I laughed and dropped to my knees to chase after my new friend. "Can you get me some more?" I asked just as I noticed a woman's pointy satin slippers. By the time I stood, wobbling and woozy, Milty had disappeared.

"Charley, what was that scene downstairs all about?" Mother asked.

The room spun around as I plopped onto my bed, both feet planted on the ground to steady myself.

"That scene? You mean the concert?"

"You know what I'm talking about, young man. Your childish outburst."

"Milty was there the day Doc fell," I burped. "But he didn't just fall; he was hit in the head with a gun! And Milty saw everything but didn't know how to talk, and now he recognizes Mr. Warrington, but he's too afraid to tell grown-ups."

I felt a grumble in the pit of my stomach and panicked when a deeper voice not my own rose up from my core. I looked into the mirror and saw a frightened little boy whose eyes were so much like the man in the pocket watch. I saw Doc's eyes.

"Jack murdered me," the voice said in a low voice out loud. Mother's eyes widened and she backed away. "Milty saw Jack smash in my skull. The greedy son-of-a-bitch couldn't wait. He didn't have my vision. And now since you know, something must be done."

"Oh, my God! Doc?" she whispered, looking at me hard and then she cried. She came and sat next to me on the bed. In the mirror, I could see my frightened, tear-stained face. Mother put her arms around shoulders too tiny to bear such a heavy voice. I felt the comfort and warmth as all sorts of memories, not my own, returned to me. I leaned my curly head onto my mother's arm and wrapped my skinny arms around her.

"What will we do?" she asked.

In her arms, I felt at home. I rested my head against her body, feeling a weight lifted. I anticipated I would be free from now on and that Mother and the voice she called Doc would figure things out and leave me out of it; that they would at last notice my pain, too.

On this day, my seventh birthday, my childhood changed forever.

Mother looked at my image in the mirror and asked, "Charley, have you been drinking?" She then turned to face me.

But before I could answer, I felt the rumble in my stomach. I spewed all over her sequined lap and her pointy, satiny shoes. I just wanted to die.

38
An Exorcism

1949: US Naval Hospital—
Charley

"Charley, that must have been rough." Dr. Savage is staring at me.

I shrug my shoulders and turn to look at the picture frame on his desk. For days now, I've been curious about it and I'm tired of just looking at the backside of Potemkin's Village. I wonder if Savage is even real; does he have a family? Would he flinch if I reached out and poked him in the belly? "Who's in the picture?"

He smiles, turning the picture frame to face me. *He trusts me now? Can I trust him?* I reach out to pick the picture up. In the photo, Dr. Savage is in full dress naval uniform. Next to him stands a pretty woman, a boy and a girl. "My wife and my children," he says.

I gaze at the picture until I can see my reflection in the glass—as if I'm part of a bigger family.

"So, what happened to Warrington?" he asks.

1937: Glendale—
Charley

The morning after the concert, Mother gave me another aspirin and we headed over to Milty's house to talk to my Uncle Earl. Milty walked into the living room holding Auntie Ann's hand.

"Sweetie," Mother said in her fairy tale voice. "Can you tell us what you told Charley? What you might have seen that day?"

Milty shrugged his shoulders.

"Come on, Milty. Tell them what you told me," I said, signing as well just to make sure.

"Please, Phoebe, that was so long ago," Auntie Ann said. "Perhaps, the boys were imagining things. It might have been easy to imagine what with all of the discussion about the probate throughout the years."

"They're not imagining anything, Ann. Jack killed Doc out of greed," Mother said.

"Well, I don't know how you'll prove it, but we certainly don't want to traumatize Milty by bringing up the past," Uncle Earl said. "It was tough enough on him just watching his uncle die."

"Well, then, I want you to confront Jack," Mother said to Uncle Earl. "See what he has to say about it. Ask where he was that day. Tell him you know things . . . things Milty told you . . ."

"Stop, Phoebe. I told you I didn't want to involve Milty. It will set him back," Uncle Earl said.

"But what about Charley and what it's doing to him?" Mother screamed. "What about what it's done to me?" She calmed down and then stared at my uncle. "Earl, I'm so ashamed of you. After all we did for you and Ann," she said and then she looked at my cousin, "and Milty."

As Mother headed for the front door, Uncle Earl said, "The police won't do anything. You have no proof. This is a closed case."

Mother turned around. "There is no statute on murder."

1949: US Naval Hospital— Charley

"And so, Jack got away with it?" Savage asks.

"For the time being. Later, Mother had actually gone to confront Jack and Mrs. Warrington, all to no avail, she'd told me. Had I known, at the time, I would have hated her even more for letting them all get away with it."

Savage shakes his head.

"While something within strongly urged me to do something, I was only seven with a limited comprehension of retaliation. Jack Warrington would continue to get away with what he'd done—at least for the time being. In the meanwhile, I'd come to know Jack wasn't the only one involved in ruining my family."

"Sounds like he did get away with murder," Savage says.

"Oh, he'd get his all right," I say, "but not until I was a little older. Nothing could be proven just yet."

1938: Glendale—
Charley

I was sitting at the piano when Mother walked in one day before the floods began.

"Doc?" I pounded the keys even louder. "Charley, please stop," she said, reaching out to lower the piano lid.

I turned to face her.

"I need to talk to you."

"Did I do something wrong?"

"Don't be silly," she said in a tired, faraway voice. "Can we talk about the voice?"

I looked at her and felt the tears sting my cheeks.

She took my small hands in hers and looked deep into my eyes. I felt dizzy as if I were swirling down a toilet. "Doc, you know I'll always love you. You know how much I miss you," Mother said as if I wasn't in the room. Her calling me Doc always confused me. "You always wanted to have control, but you see how hard this is for all of us. Please leave our son alone. Please, let it go."

I felt the voice wanting to say something and sensed it would be impossible to undo what had been done, but I clamped my mouth shut, too scared to hear what that meant.

Mother seemed frustrated when I didn't respond. She let go of my hands, probably feeling a little like she might be crazy talking to me that way, and then, still with my mouth sealed, I heard the voice push through. "To let go would be the death of Charley."

Scared to death now, I reached out to hug my mother. She put her arms around me. I didn't want her to let go of me.

"Oh, what are we going to do? We mustn't lose hope."

"Mother, I don't want to die."

The next morning, as sunlight hemmed the roll-up shades on my window—Mother had purchased the new window treatments to help me sleep, but it would take more than blacking out the windows to make Doc go away—I jumped when I heard a knock at my bedroom door and then looked at the little clock on my nightstand. Was I late for school?

"It's me, Charley, Mrs. Hotchener. Can I come in?"

She didn't wait for my answer and proceeded to walk in and take a seat at my desk chair. She wore all black and, against the morning light, her silvery hair glowed like a ball of white fire. I sat up in bed, rubbing my eyes. The details of her face weren't in focus yet. "Charley," she said. "Can I ask you about this voice that talks to you?"

"I don't know what you're talking about."

"Your mother says there's a voice."

"Well, then, maybe you should ask her about it?" I said dismissively. "I need to get ready for school." We weren't getting anywhere and never would as long as Doc could help it.

After breakfast, Mother called me back downstairs, and as I reached the bottom stair, I could hear Mrs. Hotchener speaking from the room that had always been off limits to me.

In the middle of the library sat a massive mahogany desk. In the corner stood a skeleton wearing glasses. It cracked me up. Needless to say, I'd snuck in a few times before, engrossed by all of the medical books with pictures of the human body, but most especially the ones about eyeballs. I loved the musty smell of all of the books mixed with the faint odor of sweet tobacco, the same kind George put in his pipe—Mother had asked him kindly not to go into that room. My favorite part about the room was when I took a seat in the high-backed leather chair to stare up at the ferocious-looking stuffed bear with pointy teeth and the sad-looking moose head hanging on the opposite wall. But what turned my head the most was the glass case filled with two rifles and a shotgun. Every time I entered the library, I placed my hand on the glass to peer in, leaving smudge marks. I actually found some comfort in the room and only felt nervous to think I could get shot for trespassing.

On the desk, I opened a small wooden box trimmed in leather. Inside were lots of round glass pieces to fascinate me. Each had a different view out of them. Some made me see things smaller or bigger, but mostly things appeared very blurry. They were also good for starting small fires down by the creek.

"I should use his desk," I heard Mrs. Hotchener say. "It's full of his energy."

"I hope this works," Mother said. "It's killing poor Charley."

I had no idea what they were up to, but whatever it might be, I also hoped it worked because I didn't want to die.

"Oh, son, good you're here," Mother said as I walked in, hesitantly, a little sideways so I could break into a run should I need to. Her voice sounded weak and shaky. Was I in trouble again? Maybe I hadn't put a book back in its proper place. Then I saw the space where a book should have been; the one about the human eyeballs; the one still up in my room. Dead give-away.

"Hello, Charley," Mrs. Hotchener said. Dressed in dark clothing, she looked like some sorta scary witch. "Please close the door and then take a seat over there." She pointed to one of three chairs surrounding a small round end table. I was really scared now. Mother had always let everyone else do her dirty work when it came to my punishment. She'd allowed George and Aunt Dodo to whip me, and now would she allow Mrs. Hotchener to discipline me? Marie walked over to the table and set down three silver candlestick holders with white candles. Next, she set down a glass of red wine and a roll from last night's dinner. She took a seat across from me. "Charley, we're going to hold a séance. Do you know what that is?"

I shook my head. I stared at the gun case and wondered where I might find a key.

"Well, please don't be scared."

When they tell a kid not to be scared, you know you're in for something terrifying.

"A séance is when you call forth the spirit of a dead person," Mrs. Hotchener said, folding liver-spotted hands on top of the table. "I want to talk to the voice which we believe is your father."

"But why?" I asked, my voice cracked; my feet kicked back and forth under the chair.

"We need to make him go away. We want to ask him to leave you, once and for all."

"Okay," I said, intending to fully cooperate if it meant having peace at last. "But won't I be late for school?"

"You won't be going today," Mother said. "I've called in."

"Phoebe, close the drapery tight," Marie said.

Outside, the wind howled. A storm was coming. Mother walked over and pulled the curtains closed, then came to take the seat next to mine. The room was dark until a single flame shot up to the ceiling. Soon two more little flames flickered. Marie had taken off her glasses and the shadows on her face seemed to melt her into a monster. I looked over at Mother who looked even more beautiful in the candlelight.

Marie reached across the table to take our hands. "Close your eyes." Mother squeezed her eyes shut as well. Too scared, I needed to keep at least one eye open, just in case of something. Mother held my clammy hand.

With her eyes closed, Marie then spoke up in a flat voice. "Beloved Wesley, we bring you gifts of life into death. Commune with us and move among us."

The candles seemed to answer in a flicker and then settle down. "Be guided by the light of this world and visit upon us."

Suddenly, as if a wind had blown in, the candles went out.

"Damn it!" Marie said and proceeded to relight the candles as Mother squeezed my hand.

Marie looked into the candles. "Doc, can you hear me? Knock twice if you do and once if you don't."

I giggled and rocked in my seat.

"I mean just twice," Marie said, calmly and flatly.

Nothing happened and then, with her eyes still closed, Mother lifted her head. "Darling?"

They called on him for a while, eyes closed, turning their heads every which way as if he might be hovering behind them, and yet nothing happened. They opened their eyes to look at each other over the candles. "Maybe he just needs more time," Marie said, closing her eyes again. Mother did the same.

After a while, I couldn't stand the quiet or the waiting. Finally, I said, "Doc, I need to talk to you." But for once, the voice stayed quiet when I called upon him. As long as there was a stranger in the room, someone other than Mother or me, Doc seemed to be speechless.

And then I heard his voice in my head. *Charley, I don't want to bring you any more harm. I promise to try and remain silent from now on, but I cannot leave.*

"Charley, what is it?" Mother asked.

"He says he's not gonna talk anymore, but he's not going to leave either," I said, crushed. I was stuck.

"Why not?" Marie asked.

Mother cried, as if she already knew the answer. "It would be the death of Charley."

I stood, scared to die.

But Marie wouldn't give up. "Doc, make yourself known!"

Of course, Doc would not be making an appearance from the dead. He wasn't dead, after all. His ashes were buried under the lemon tree, but the rest of him merely occupied the space in my tiny body. His purgatory had become my hell.

Marie finally gave up and blew out the candles. Mother opened the drapery and I charged out like a horse out of a starting gate.

The whole ordeal horrified me. As much as you tell a kid not to think about or look at something, he'll think about it; he'll look. The day after the botched séance, I returned to the scene of the crime and sat at my father's desk, the place where Mrs. Hotchener said she could feel his energy. Rubbing the surface of the desk, I closed my eyes, willing my father to appear. After a while, I pulled on the top right drawer. This time it wasn't locked. As I rummaged through, my small hand brushed across something taped to the bottom. A key. I stood and walked over to the rifle case. It fit.

I wandered down to the dry creek bed, where I lay down along the dusty bank with the rifle in one hand and the Bible Auntie Ann had given me in the other. In the weeks following the silly séance, I'd read the Good Book to pass the time, which was going by as slowly as creation in the book of Genesis. Mother had made me go to church with Milty and my Auntie, where I was that leper Pastor Elwood talked about at the First United Methodist Church. Auntie Ann had bookmarked a prayer for me to read whenever I felt troubled, which was pretty much all the time. She told me the prayer had something to do with God, my Father; a father for which I had no concept. I picked up the Good Book and read.

The Lord is my Shepherd; I shall not want. He maketh me to lie down in green pastures: He leadeth me beside the still waters.

He restoreth my soul. He leadeth me in the paths of righteousness for His name's sake.

I couldn't understand. Whose namesake?

Yea, though I walk through the valley of the shadow of death, I will fear no evil: for Thou art with me.

But, I do fear evil for Thou art with me, Doc, my father.

As I sat, leaning on a tree, I found no comfort in the book, it only frightened me more. So lonely and scared, I just wanted to die. I thought I might have been better off dead except that I'd learned in church how people who killed themselves ended up burning forever in hell. I'd burned myself plenty of times playing with fire—had even burned down part of the orchard last year with a glass lens and singed off my eyebrows when a branch fell from a burning bush. That hurt like, well, like hell. So, I couldn't imagine burning there forever.

I picked up the gun to examine it closer; it felt warm and I could smell rotten eggs. And then something fell out of the barrel. Rolled up tighter than a cigarette was a piece of paper that seemed to relax once out of the tube. I unrolled it the rest of the way and noticed there were words typed on it. I read out loud: "California Certificate of Death—Gunshot wound through the brain inflicted accidentally by himself."

My body tingled and shook, and it seemed as if the fog had rolled in, and yet it had been a warm day with a blue, cloudless sky. I closed my eyes to stop the world from spinning and when I opened them, I saw a young boy in striped pajamas leaning on a lemon tree across from me. Blood seeped from a hole through his head, but I hadn't fired the gun. He appeared to be dead, but he still held onto the Winchester '86. *Is that me?* I felt terrified. *Is that going to be me?* I wondered, but then I noticed he'd been wearing eyeglasses. It felt like my heart had exploded into millions of tiny shards in my chest. I squeezed my eyes shut.

The Lord is my Shepherd; I shall not want . . .

I felt raindrops. The boy disappeared when I opened my eyes. I shot up to take a look all around me and then I went back and slumped down where I'd been leaning on the tree. I looked over at the creek, hoping it would fill with enough rainwater to float me all the way down to the ocean, where the birds and fishies might make a meal of me. Maybe, I wouldn't die, and Sammy would be there and teach me how to fly away.

The rain was really coming down now. Mother, in a polka-dotted, pink apron, stood waiting at the back door when I returned. She couldn't help but notice the gun I carried. She gasped, clutching the fringe of her apron.

"Charley, oh, my lord. What are you doing? Where did you get that?" she screamed, snatching the gun from me.

"I don't remember. I guess I got it from the library," I answered calmly. "I saw a boy, Mother. He was as dead as the bear in the library."

Mother's hands shook as she held the weapon. "What boy?"

"He shot himself in the head," I said, "right here," pointing to my temple.

Mother set the gun down and then ran for the kitchen phone.

"No, he's gone," I yelled, running behind her. "It was only in my imagination again."

Mother stopped and turned toward me. My hand trembled as I handed her the paper that dropped out of the gun barrel. Her eyes widened as she looked at it and then she knelt down to take me in her arms; hugging me as if she'd never let me go; like she'd never let anything happen to me. I could feel her body shaking as she sobbed. "Oh, Leland," she whispered, and then finally, she pulled away; her face blotchy and stained with tears, her hair falling from a bun.

"Mother, I don't want to go back to Milty's church."

"Why not?"

"Because they talk about burning in hell, and I don't want to die."

"Oh, Charley, you're not going to die," she said, hugging me even tighter. "Besides, hell doesn't exist. When we die, we just keep coming back until we learn our lessons."

This time I pulled away from her. "So, then, why were you trying to call Doc back from the dead?"

"It's complicated."

My mind was a swamp of confusion. Confusion is hell if you ask me! And yes, I feared dying especially if it meant I'd end up like Doc. But at that time, to be honest, living frightened me more.

"Mother, in Milty's church, I did learn something about prayer and God the Father. I've been praying for Father to let me go. 'Please go away,' I say.

'And when I do die, don't resurrect me like Milty's Jesus, but if I do come back, let me be a fish or a bird or even the sacred cow in India Marie talks about.'"

Mother pulled up her apron to wipe her tears and then smiled. "Oh, Charley, not a cow."

I laughed, smelling the leftovers simmering on the stovetop, and felt a little better.

After that day, I never saw the guns in the house again.

39

What Insurance?

December, 1941: Glendale—
Charley

I heard a knock at the front door. I got up to race George to answer it. On the stoop, stood a tall skinny man in a stripey blue suit.

"Is Mrs. Marnier home?" he asked, the apple bobbing in his throat. "My name is Mr. Beaufort. I'm from the Newport Development Company. May I please speak to her."

"Mrs. Gimble isn't home," George said, which I knew to be a fib. "I'm her husband. Perhaps, I can help you. What is this all about?"

I knew how important this had to be so I ran off to find Mother.

George was getting ready to close the door on the man when we walked up.

"Here she is," I said, galloping in, slightly out of breath.

"Oh, Mrs. Mar—Mrs. Gimble," the man said when he saw us step into the foyer.

"Charley tells me you're from Newport Development?"

"Yes, my name is Mr. Beaufort," he said, extending his hand. "Several of the buildings on Broadway are scheduled for demolition. We were clearing out the office when we came across some of the old books on the shelves and some medical journals we believe belonged to your late husband. There are some interesting medical instruments and other things which we thought might be of interest to you."

"Absolutely," Mother said. "Thank you." She then turned to George. "You know, after Doc died, I never even had the chance to go in there. I assumed Warrington had turned everything over. I assumed you had brought everything home."

She turned back to Mr. Beaufort. "I didn't imagine there was anything left."

"Just a few odds and ends. Apparently, the office has been sitting vacant for some time now," the man in blue said. "Perhaps, you might know something about the vault?"

"The vault?" Mother asked.

I felt tingly and then I heard the voice in my head say, "Of course I do."

"Yes, it seems to have been hidden behind some of the books on the top shelf," Mr. Beaufort said. "Anyway, should you be interested, I can meet you at the office sometime within the next couple of days."

"I'll follow you right over," George said.

Mother looked at George with a cool smile. "That won't be necessary." She then turned back to the man in blue. "Mr. Beaufort, would it be possible for my son and me to meet you there in about an hour? I'm sure Charley would love to take a look around."

I already stood there holding her coat, her purse, and the car keys.

I hung my newsboy cap on the coat rack just inside the small dark foyer of the office on Broadway. Mr. Beaufort had lit a lantern and handed it to Mother. He also had a flashlight with him and went to wait in the reception area. "Take your time," he said and I'd already marched into the office with all of the bookshelves.

"Charley," Mother said, stepping into the dark, windowless office. "Where'd you go?"

"I'm up here."

From the top of the ladder, I could see her face light up by the lantern she held. She gasped. "Oh, come down, now." She set the lamp down on a desk and walked over to hold the ladder.

"In a minute," I said, proceeding to move some books. The vault was there like the man said—like I already knew.

I worked the combination, turning the dial on the vault.

"Charley, is it open?"

"No, but I know the combination," I said, narrowing my eyes to see better. The lock clicked open softly. I reached into the vault and pulled out some important-looking papers and lots of dollar bills. I climbed back down and handed the papers over to Mother.

She spread everything on the desk and then picked up the papers with the blue backing.

"What is it?" I asked when I saw her face twist into a pretzel.

"It's a copy of the most recent will where your father had made provisions for you, 'the unborn child.'"

She set the document down and I saw her eyes widen as she picked up the next document. She gasped.

"Mother, what is it?"

"It seems to be a copy of death benefits offered by the Masons, and a life insurance policy issued by Western Masons Mutual Life Insurance Company." She paused. "George Gimble, Agent." She looked up, mouth open, and didn't seem to be breathing. Finally, she shook her head and continued to look at the other documents.

She looked closer at another document and used her index finger to help her read it out loud, "Deed of Trust showing the transfer of property—it has my attorney's name on it. Taylor O. Taylor representing, Dr. Wesley Marnier and George Gimble, September 1930." She looked at me. "That's when Doc died."

I wanted to throw up. Doc could no longer remain silent, shaping his silver-tongued words out of my breath, like a weapon sent into the room to search and destroy. His voice was a cannon booming through my mouth.

"Deception, betrayal. My best friend George." My heart raced now as I stomped around the room. "The attorneys and George. Him too. Oh, he must be stopped. I will stop him." My throat hurt.

Mr. Beaufort, who had been waiting in the reception area, walked in and looked around. "Is everything all right in here? I thought I heard a man's voice."

"Everything is fine, Mr. Beaufort. We'll only be a few more minutes."

I closed the door behind him.

"Doc—Charley," Mother said. "Let me think." She put her head in her hands. "I can't believe this was all happening right under my nose. I was so caught up in the estate battle—how stupid of me not to see what was going on—how stupid to trust George—and how could Taylor, my own attorney who owes me a fiduciary duty—how could he swindle me this way?"

"They must be punished," Doc shouted just as the door opened and George came sauntering in.

"How could you do this to us?" Mother asked.

"What are you talking about?" George's forehead pleated.

She held up the evidence. "The money, the property, the insurance. You helped yourself to all of it."

George walked toward Mother, but I blocked his way. Hands-on-hips, I opened my mouth to speak. "How could you leave me here to die?" Doc said in his low voice.

George scrunched his eyes. "What are you talking about, kid?"

"You killed Doc to cash in on the insurance money," Mother said. "The money that was intended for me and the baby."

"Now wait a second. I did not kill Doc." He let some air out of his nose like a bull, turned and then paced a couple of steps away from the desk before turning back to face Mother. "Phoebe, please hear me out."

"We're listening," Doc said.

George looked at me all scaredy-like and then looked at Mother. "You wouldn't have known how to handle the business affairs. I made sure you and Charley benefitted from the insurance proceeds. I took care of both of you. You wouldn't have known how to handle the money."

"You killed Doc for the insurance."

"No!" George yelled, running a hand through his hair. "It's what the papers said. It was an accident. He fell."

Accident? Confusion, contradictions and lies swirled through my head like the spinning gears of a broken clock; nothing engaged. I suddenly felt betrayed by George. I reached for the back of my neck to massage it and then Doc spoke through me again. "And then Jack hit me in the back of the head with the gun just to make sure and you watched him do it. I saw you there, George. I saw you walk away to let me die."

"Is that so?" Mother said, eyes brimming with tears.

"I ought to turn you in to Western Mutual Life. Let them know what kind of an agent they have working for them."

"The insurance company won't do anything since we were married at the time it was cashed."

"So, that's why you married me?"

"You know you wouldn't marry me unless I had money."

"That's not true." She cupped her hands over her face and really sobbed. Her whole body shook.

George's face crumpled up like a piece of wadded paper. He tried to leave the room, but I blocked him. "Get out of my way, Charley," he said.

"What else have you been lying about?" Mother asked, reaching for the phone, but George grabbed it away. "No one will believe you."

"Why does this deed have your name on it?" Mother asked, stabbing the paper with her index finger.

"Phoebe, you know you never cared about his business. The day he fell, Doc was gathering everything to show you. He wanted to show you how everything was set up so that you and the baby," he looked over at me, "would be set for life should something—should something ever happen to him."

"That's the only honest thing to come out of your mouth," Doc said.

With nothing left to discuss, we finally walked out of the office where Mr. Beaufort asked, "Find anything interesting?"

The time had come for Mother to take the bull by the horns. First, she put George out to pasture. She told him she'd send his things to his office and for him not to bother coming back to the house.

We drove back downtown the next morning. Mother had let me stay home from school. I didn't ask any questions. I trusted she'd finally take control of our lives.

I recognized the tall brick building on Brand Avenue jutting out like an index finger. We parked the car out on the street and walked into the foyer. And then, as if I wasn't having enough fun, Mother let me press the elevator button to the floor where Taylor O. Taylor had their law offices.

"Mr. Taylor is at a construction site for the new development," the young secretary said.

"I see. Is that the one over on Verdugo?" Mother asked.

"Not exactly. It's the Valley View Development, you know, just above Brand."

"Yes, I know."

Mother drove to the highest point in Glendale. We climbed out of the car and walked toward some men wearing hard hats.

Under his hard hat, Mr. Taylor's eyes compressed into slits when he saw us. He rushed over to greet us.

"The view is certainly breathtaking from up here," Mother called out, waving to Mr. Taylor. "I can certainly understand now why Doc bought it in the first place. Up here, you can see everything so clearly."

"Yeah, you can practically see Hawaii," I added, noticing the tractor glistening like a shiny penny held up to the sun. It was much newer than the one we kept in our storage garage, and more fascinating with all its sparkly gears and levers just gleaming now. I walked over to take a closer gander at the gigantic machine, tall as the law office building we'd just left. I heard it idling, but no one was near. Looking around to make sure I was alone, I climbed up.

I loved the powerful feeling as it rose up from my bottom through my stomach, into my fingers and onto the wheel.

"Hey, Mr. Taylor," Doc boomed, so loud it scuffed my throat. "Take a look over here."

Mother screamed when she saw me on the tractor.

Mr. Taylor ran toward me. "Hey, kid, that's not a toy," he yelled. "That's an expensive truck!"

The tractor lurched forward toward the edge where the view of the city below looked out of this world. Mr. Taylor stood now in front of the tractor as if he could stop it; as if I could stop it. I saw where it was headed and so I jumped off.

The last thing I saw before the tractor leaped off the cliff, taking Mr. Taylor with it, was the look of horror on his face—like the wide-eyed man in *The Devil Doll* when he first recognized the shrunken human.

All the workers came running to the edge and stood staring as a plume of smoke rose up from the canyon below. The tractor exploded, sending flames and rocket-sized debris into the sky. Mother clung to me so tight that later there were grape-sized bruises and nail marks on my forearms.

The workers surrounded me to see if I was all right. I was shaken up slightly, but otherwise I felt fine. Mother released her grip, looking down at me.

"Charley, what were you thinking?"

"I wanted to see the tractor and then the voice called Mr. Taylor over—"

"The voice?" Mother asked calmly and then asked, "What else did Doc say?"

"Something about karma and that Taylor shouldn't steal from helpless widows."

In the afternoon, Mother let me take Melody down to sit by the creek. I tossed some pebbles into the water, fascinated by how the ripples appeared and then slowly disappeared, like my thoughts did sometimes. I watched as bygone days floated through my eyes. I couldn't think straight and tried to go over what had just happened—what I'd caused to happen. I kept this up so I wouldn't cry and to get the image of my upset mother out of my mind. I tossed in another pebble and thought about how I loved my mother more than anything and hated seeing her cry. Mr. Taylor was dead now because of something I'd done. I'd have to carry this small pebble of anxiety in my stomach for the rest of my life.

I chucked the stones, sometimes underhanded, sometimes skipping them over the water. Each stone represented all of the emotions I experienced—love and hate, sadness and fear, confusion about the voice inside. I wondered about what had happened and whether I was truly to blame.

"Doc, why?" I asked out loud. "Why did this happen? What is happening?"

"Karma," Doc said. "It's a consequence of his action. It wasn't your fault, Charley."

"Was it yours?" I asked, feeling a bit better knowing I wouldn't have to take full responsibility.

"I merely wanted to confront him," he said.

It turned dark outside, and when I realized no one had come looking for me as I sat by the creek with just my dog and the moon sneering down at me, I cried. In part, I grieved for Mr. Taylor, though I'd never really known him, but mostly I cried for Mother, and for us, Doc and me, because we belonged to two different worlds, and because I realized she could not love me the way I needed to be loved, nor the way *he* wanted.

Mother sat in the living room with her ear to the radio when I finally walked in. She had the radio turned up loud and looked as if she'd been crying. The reporter on the radio sounded familiar.

"Is that Uncle Art?"

"They've bombed Pearl Harbor," Mother said, pulling me into her arms. "Oh, Charley, we're going to war."

I didn't understand. *Bombed? War?* And then Mother rose to close the curtains and turn out all of the lights. I huddled into a little ball in the corner armchair. Hugging my knees tight, I buried my head as deep as I could into my body, hoping to disappear into myself like the sun slipping away into the night.

Out of a dead sleep, ringing woke me up the next morning. I nearly fell out of bed before running down the hall to get the phone.

"Don't pick it up," Mother said. "I can't handle any more questions right now." She then picked up the receiver and hung it up again.

Moments later, I heard a car pull up and pulled back the drapery from the front window. I saw the old red car. "George is coming up."

Mother sat in the chair opposite me and gasped. My heart pounded as I watched George get out of his car and march up the path. I sat frozen in my seat, but Mother stood and rushed toward the foyer as I heard his key at the door.

I sprinted into the foyer just as George made his way through the front door. His eyes grew big when he saw us standing there.

"Phoebe, I was so worried. I read the paper. What a bizarre accident," he said.

"Accident? This is war, George," Mother said.

"I'm talking about Taylor. Are you all right?"

I squirmed just a little, feeling my blood had drained to my feet.

"Why wouldn't you answer the phone?"

"What are you doing here?" Mother said, wiping her hands on her dress.

"You haven't sent all of my things."

"I've been just a little preoccupied," she said, smoothing back her hair.

"Phoebe, please. You need to hear me out."

"What other labyrinth of lies do you have for me?" She turned away from him.

"I'm not lying. I was only trying to protect you," he said. "Even your bootlegging brother. Who do you think bailed him out the last time?"

Mother turned back around. "My brother. Sure, I'll bet you helped him, but with Doc's money. With Charley's and my money." She looked up and slowly shook her head. "I'm filing for divorce."

"You have no cause."

"Oh, I have plenty," she said and looked at me, pointing upstairs. "Charley, please—"

"No. I won't go to my room or into the kitchen for a snack," I said, stomping a foot as my voice squeaked. Suddenly embarrassed, I grabbed my throat and looked away. I'd noticed the difference in my voice lately; more unusual than the Doc voice; more creaky.

George had called the change "puberty." After I'd screeched once before, he reached out for my neck, examined it and said, "Soon you'll have an Adam's apple the size of a man, pimples, and a moustache like Groucho Marx—and that ain't all."

I'd been perplexed, not wanting to believe George, not wanting to believe my lying eyes. Now, as I cleared my throat, I peered at him, crossing my arms in front of me. "I know the stuff you've been up to. Believe me, I know," Doc said this time.

George turned white as the paint on the walls.

"I've hired an investigator who's been tailing you for quite some time now," Mother said.

"I'd think hiring a gumshoe would be stooping too low—too degrading," George said as he lit a cigarette. "Especially for a lady like you." He blew the match out.

"First of all, and it's no secret. It's quite obvious you've been cheating on me."

"But, I told you that was over."

Mother narrowed her eyes at him. "Secondly, you and—" her voice cracked, "you and my brother bootlegged for years." Her voice grew stronger. George opened his mouth to respond, but she put up a hand. "Thirdly, you have a huge gambling problem. You've been using the boat to carry passengers over to a gambling ship off Santa Monica."

I peered at George. *Our boat?* That part I didn't know nor did I really understand the rest.

"You've been forging my signature for years now. Who knows how long you forged Doc's signature and who knows how many others. And finally, you and Warrington had something going on. I don't know what, but rest assured, I'll get to the bottom of it."

"Phoebe, you're crazy," he said. "You don't know what you're talking about. Who's this investigator anyway?"

O'Shaughnessy. I remembered from the phone call I'd eavesdropped on months ago.

"None of your business," Mother said.

"And my business is none of yours," George said, climbing the stairs to his room across the hall from Mother's.

♪♫

The little boy in me felt sad to see him go. I watched as George packed his stuff. On the way out, he stopped to look me in the eyes. I made like my nose was itching and I scratched it. "I was only looking out for you and Phoebe," George said. "The two of you would never have survived without me around."

I wanted to cry when I felt the voice coming through. "You always wanted my life, Pal."

George had just pulled a shirt from a hanger and stopped to stare at me.

"Trouble was, you could never be half the man I was," the voice said. "You couldn't stand that she chose me. Here's a little something the investigators couldn't dig up—I'm quite sure you never told her about all the little bastards you ditched in Vegas?"

George hightailed it out of the room so fast, he left his suitcase.

I came down the stairs carrying his valise to see Aunt Dodo standing in the foyer. Uncle Art had flown immediately over to Hawaii to cover the news. I walked up to hand George his case and then he rushed past Aunt Dodo without saying a word.

"I thought we told you to scram!" she yelled, making like she was booting him in the butt.

December 8, 1941, my world turned upside down. I was alone.

40
School of Hard Knocks

Only fifteen and I'd spent the night in jail again. By then, it was getting to be pretty damned routine, but this time it was a little more serious than the previous drunk and disorderly incarcerations where I ended up in juvie. An untethered small planet, I'd been drifting through the galaxy bouncing off the stars. No one could keep me in line.

After a weekend bender, the police had found me at the top of the Colorado Street Bridge, on the other side of the guard railing, staring into the trickling stream of the Arroyo Seco below. I was just about to end it all, but I got dizzy and, for some stupid reason, I thought I needed to be clear-headed before I jumped, and then Doc spoke out.

"Charley, stop!"

"Why, so you can continue to manipulate me?" I screamed into the dark night. "Go to hell!"

Melody had died earlier in the day and, except for the time when I found out I'd never see Teresa again, I never bawled so much. I wanted to die, but first I buried Melody in the back yard next to Doc's ashes. Funny, ashes normally meant the person was dead, but Doc had gone on living, continuing to make my life pure hell. And once George had left, we were able to have Phoebe all to ourselves, but lately, she'd been having trouble looking at me.

George had been gone a couple of years by then, and if it hadn't been for Laurel and Hardy—and later the booze—I don't know how I would have made it. Mother had her music, but somehow that didn't seem like enough for her. I hated seeing her so sad, but feeling her pain peeved me even more, as if her feelings were my responsibility.

After burying Melody, I came back into the house and, from the shadows of the living room, I watched as Mother quietly took her place at the piano; so quiet, I heard myself breathing, my torn heart thumping and the blood coursing through my veins. Her lips were moving and I thought she might be singing, so I inched a little closer. The music could barely patch the hole in my aching heart. *Go to her,* I heard Doc say.

"Oh, Doc," she said, turning to me. "Come sit with me."

I couldn't take it anymore. I stood rigid, hands balled into fists. "Go to hell! I'm Charley," I said. I was in charge. Since George had left years ago, I'd become the man of the house. I tramped into the kitchen to open the cabinet where George used to keep his booze. This time, I didn't use a glass.

Later in the evening, on the bridge, I sobered up as I found myself staring into the spinning blue lights on the top of the black and white. I got popped for stealing a vehicle. If you ask me, it was an accident. I was so soused, I thought I recognized Mother's white Buick parked outside the market, but I was wrong. Never mind that I'd been about to jump to my death. My sentence this time would be sixty days in juvenile hall where I'd have plenty of time to think about stuff; stuff like how much I missed my dog.

1949: US Naval Hospital—
Charley

Dr. Savage removes his glasses and rubs his eyes.

"Leland was also fifteen when he killed himself," he says, replacing his glasses. "Don't you find that interesting?"

"Yeah, well, I'm here, aren't I? I didn't kill myself," I say, my voice cracking and dropping an octave.

"The California Certificate of Death described the cause of death as a 'Gunshot wound through the brain inflicted accidentally by himself,'" Doc says, defensively. "It was an accident."

"Just like I was," I add.

1945: Glendale—
Charley

I suppose I wasn't the easiest kid to raise after the most recent arrest. By then, I'd already been in and out of jail, juvenile hall, hospitals, and I'd dropped out of school. I'd been warned that the next time I messed up, it would be the big house for a long time.

My mind was the Pleasure Pier's amusement park, with a rollercoaster full of fear zipping up and down and a carousel full of worry spinning out of control. As broke as we were, I'd made matters worse by making Mother have to come up with bail money. The hospital bills mounted and I'd gotten way out of control. But the straw that broke the camel's back, I guess, came after my release from juvie.

During my stint there, I'd met seventeen-year-old Ralph, a pale and thin kid, not very clean, with a head covered in orange hair, spiking out like a rusty porcupine. His pink-rimmed blue eyes were set in a face the color of cookie dough with a splash of freckles as big as chocolate chips. I imagined he might've been an adorably sweet baby. Ralph told me he was an orphan from birth, in and out of foster homes ever since. He sort of reminded me of the kid Mother taught piano lessons to years ago back at Hollygrove.

Back at the juvie group home doing some homework, my hands were clasped behind my head, pencil bobbing from my lips as I balanced myself against the wall on the two legs of my chair. Ralph loved to flap his lips. "I shot a man and watched him die," he said. "I didn't even flinch."

I didn't flinch either and I didn't know whether to believe him or not, but it didn't matter. Those were the kinds of big stories hotshots told in places like juvie. It was one way to put the fear of God in the other kids and to ensure they wouldn't mess with you, especially if you looked like Ralph. It didn't strike me as odd, him telling me he killed someone. It didn't affect me either way. I kept the pencil in my mouth but looked askance at him. He didn't seem so different from the other delinquents I'd met, then again I hadn't really studied them, but now I wondered if his could be the face of a killer—so different from Jack Warrington's face.

What was odd was my apathy about what Ralph told me. I knew he'd just fed me a load of crap. But I froze in place when he told me, "The man deserved to die. I took justice into my own hands. There are those who do evil and then there's me," he said. "In the law of nature, there's gotta be a balance." I stopped my balancing act and set my feet on the ground. When I turned to look at him, the first thing I noticed were his callused hands with dirty nails chewed to the nub. I sat up a little straighter in my chair. "I'm here to set the world's scale. Call me the Equalizer. You see, we're all just a bunch of ants marching along; some make it to the ant hill by working hard and minding their own business, some carry another ant's load, and there are those who don't stay in line and wander—those will be squashed, but I tell you, those who climb over the others, they need to get squashed. And that's a job for the Equalizer."

Ralph told me he'd been paid to kill the first time and the second time he did it for his own justice. On a Tuesday, he'd staked out Harry Jones, his third foster parent. Ralph knew Mrs. Jones usually did the grocery shopping on Tuesdays when the older foster kids were at school. She'd leave Mr. Jones at home with the younger ones so they could nap.

"You gotta make sure the coast is clear. You gotta be clear in the head, patient, and when the time is right—when you see that he's finally put the last toddler down and he goes into the kitchen for a beer—Bam!" Ralph said, holding up two fingers and pretending to fire a gun at me. My stomach lurched and I fell out of my chair. He laughed and told me he'd never been caught. Not yet, at least. I knew for sure I'd never want to run into Ralph in some dark alley.

"You kinda toss the furniture around and raid the missus's jewelry box before you slip out the back door," he said.

"Say," I said to Ralph, "By any chance, don't I know you from Hollygrove?"

"Hollygrove, Maryvale, Stepping Stones—you name it. They're all the same."

I nodded. It didn't matter really. And to think, he'd had such a sweet voice. Hell, compared to Ralph's life, my life so far had been a cakewalk, a sugar-coated path attracting crazy ants. I would sleep with one eye open around Ralph and would always remember his story, but only because he made it clear what kind of ant I needed to be, going forward in this world. I needed to march in line under the radar or my next stint would land me in the big house.

During my detention, I had plenty of time to think about what I'd done, even though I'd had no recollection of stealing a car. I used the time to really think about where I was going in my life and, just to make sure I kept my head screwed on straight, I'd been ordered to get a job as soon as I got out of juvie, part of the condition of my being released to Mother.

I had to prove myself. This time I was gonna fly straight. I landed a job working as a busboy at the Bob's Big Boy Restaurant up on Glenoaks Boulevard. I liked the routine. Get up, have breakfast, brush my teeth, pedal my bike to work. Bus the table, set the table, wash the dishes, sweep the floor, smile moronically at the customers. Be a good, busy little ant.

One day, I'd dropped underneath a table trying to sweep out a bunch of errant French fries from the small crumb catchers. When I stood, I found myself staring straight into a man's face as he came walking into the restaurant. It was Jack Warrington. He didn't seem to recognize me. Since the blood in my head had drained, I felt dizzy. The place started spinning. I grabbed the edge of the table to steady myself and watched as the hostess seated him at a booth in the corner near a window overlooking the busy street.

It had been eight years, even longer for Doc, but I would never forget that face—a kind face, really—on the kind of man that should be sincerely sorry to see his neighbor's children devoured by wolves.

"Charley, can you get table five a cup of coffee? I think I just slammed Tina," the hostess asked as she hurried by holding a stack of menus.

Finally, here's our chance, Doc said. *Simply run back the utility closet and grab some rat poison—just dessert for a rat like him.*

I set the cup down in front of Warrington and he thanked me without putting down the newspaper.

Confront him, Charley.

My body tensed as I tried to keep Doc at bay, all the while watching as Warrington ordered. I swept around his table, continuing to stare as he ate. At one point he asked me for a refill on his coffee. I just about had a heart attack. Finally, finished with breakfast, he set down his utensils, left money to settle his bill and then he proceeded to walk out.

Don't let him get away!

I found the manager and told him I felt a little queasy and I needed to step outside to grab some fresh air. I then followed Warrington out to the parking lot and watched as he drove away in a brand new automobile.

Dammit! He got away. Again! I flipped out. I couldn't stand it. I couldn't get him out of my head. *Don't let him get away!* It started again. But what could I do? I couldn't chase him. I couldn't call the cops. What would I tell them? We'd already been down that road and, without proof, there's nothing I could do. I noticed a phone booth at the corner and ran over, grabbed the phone book and ripped out the page with Jack Warrington's name and address on it and stuffed it into my pocket. The rest of the day, I squeezed my pocket willing an answer to come.

By the time I arrived home, I'd become good and frosted. Mother sat in the music room giving a piano lesson. The kid played a song from my child-hood. I remembered the days at the piano, under the piano. But the music took me back to another time. I looked at Mother and felt something ten-der, the way her head tilted, the nape of her neck, her hands. I remembered the smell of her Jicky perfume. I remembered a time before the fall, before Warrington killed me. Why had he done it? Was it just greed?

Climbing the stairs, I pulled out the page from the phone book and used the phone in the hallway to dial his house. It turned out he lived nearby, and to think that all of these years, I hadn't run into him sooner. I needed answers.

A woman answered, "Hello, Warrington residence. Hello?" I hadn't anticipated a dame's voice and I quickly hung up. I tried again later and this time a male answered. "Hello. Warrington residence."

My hands were sweating and I gripped the phone tighter. The only thing I could come up with was, "Is this Jack—the Killer?"

"Who is this?"

I hung up.

I phoned routinely at four p.m. every day for the next week. I'd hang up and then wash up for dinner. There I'd sit across from my mother and she'd ask about my day. I'd tell her it was fine and then we had nothing more to say to each other.

41
Right Out of *Good Housekeeping*

The Warringtons lived on a street lined with Spanish bungalows surrounded by white walls and covered in red tile roofs. They had an avocado, lemon, and mimosa tree in their nicely manicured front yard; and a boy and a girl. Perfect little family. President Hoover promised a car in every garage, and a pot of chicken on the stove, but after Doc's death, and in spite of the Great Depression, Warrington had obviously been able to afford two cars. I'd know soon enough what they had cooking on their stove.

One day after work, I took a shortcut home through their neighborhood. I parked my bike in some bushes across from their place and sat on the curb eyeballing the ants march in and out of the nice house. The neighborhood seemed too nice for anything bad to ever happen. One of their neighbors, a smallish man in a straw hat, mowed his lawn, up one row and back down another; a cigarette dangled from his lips, but somehow he still managed to whistle. I noticed an Ivy Leaguer pull up in a hot rod with a bunch of cats sporting college varsity sweaters. One hotshot jumped out and waved as the chariot burned rubber down the street. He must've been the son home from college. Just a couple years older than I, Junior'd probably come home for one of mom's home cooked chicken dinners, complete with mashed potatoes and gravy and an all-American apple pie. I heard the whirring of the blades on the lawnmower as the neighbor man cut his lawn. I'd seen enough and hopped back onto my bicycle.

The next day I noticed a hotsy-totsy come bouncing out of the house. Barbara Warrington wasn't beautiful like Norma or Teresa, but okay. She'd been in my grade in school back when I used to go, but I had never really paid attention to her. She used to be a plain girl like the bun of the burger at Bob's Big Boy—a bun without all of the toppings. But now, she looked pretty dolled up in her tight red cheerleader sweater with the black GH letters stitched to the front. I'd never paid attention to her peepers, the color of blue silk stockings. She had a high, arching chest and moved with an erect arrogant haughtiness, a real stuck-up. She wore her blonde hair pulled into a ponytail with black and red ribbons, the school colors for Glendale High. She turned to wave at her mother in pearls standing at the door and then, after walking a short distance down the street, she pulled out a cigarette.

As the days went by, I watched the dynamics of what appeared to be a normal family. Some days, I'd arrive before the milkman or the morning paper. If there'd been an agenda for spying on Warrington, I'd forgotten as I watched Barbara now with more of a curiosity about the female species than anything else, and as a distraction it turned out. It had been a long time since I'd seen the inside of my own mother's bedroom; she'd kept it locked up since I was seven. Pretty shy, I was considered quite handsome, already standing a lean six-foot-one inch, with broad shoulders, wavy blond hair and blue eyes. Even though girls had always been interested in me, sending me notes or calling the house, I really hadn't taken the time to figure them out. So, by spying, I killed two birds with one stone.

One day the coast was clear. I watched as the family had marched off in different directions. The milkman had just made his delivery on the back porch, taking away with him two empties. The back kitchen door wasn't locked and I came in carrying the two fresh bottles of milk. I opened the fridge and placed the bottles in front of a carton of eggs. The lingering smell of bacon hung in the air; the breakfast dishes, freshly washed, were draining at the sink. I walked into what seemed to be a regular living room, I suppose; the kind I'd seen in department store advertisements suitable for this type of place. Certainly, nothing compared to Mother's chateau. The Warrington home boasted with family pride. Hundreds of family pictures were framed and wallpapered in every nook and cranny of the place. There were a series of bucolic paintings with cows. On a table in the corner sat a Bakelite radio. Next to it sat an ashtray and a pipe that I brought to my nose. I smelled the sweet tobacco and it took me back, reminding me of the place from which I'd come.

Everything seemed to match. It all seemed so normal—straight out of Good Housekeeping. *So, this is how a murderer lives?*

The first door on the left of the hallway opened to a boy's room. I smelled body odor, dirty socks, and underwear. Bookshelves were stuffed with trophies from basketball, football, and baseball. On the floor were free weights and barbells, golf clubs and a tennis racket. Gold-plated plaques and awards hung on the walls like artwork in a museum. I slipped into the next bedroom, pink and frilly and smelling of carnations. More first and second place satin blue and red ribbons hung from a white-lacquered four-poster bed that looked as if it was made for a princess.

Barbara was keen on pink Bazooka bubblegum. She kept a pack underneath a crocheted doily on a highboy near the window. Occasionally, on my visits, I'd bum a piece of gum, but I'd make sure to replace it with a new piece the next time I paid a call. She also kept a couple of cigarettes tucked into the pack of gum. A string of pearls spilled out of a little ivory ceramic jar. I picked it up and ran it through my fingers before putting it back. I pulled a couple of strands of yellow hair from the silver brush and stuffed them into my pocket. I then removed the cap from a lipstick to smell it. It smelled sweet. There was also another little tin container labeled "Kiss and Belle" with a picture of a fox on it. I opened it and swiped an index finger over the smooth balm, then spread it across my dry lips. In her top drawer, she kept her underwear that felt soft and lacy. I pulled out a pair of silky gloves and then ran a satin slip across my nose. It felt cool and had a lilac detergent smell. This was all just a game to me. A real kick. How much could I get away with?

Meanwhile, back at the ranch one evening, I'd pedaled home to find Mother waiting for me at the back door. Her eyes looked wet and the line parting the sea of her brow ran deep. She struggled to keep her lips from trembling.

"What's up, Phebes?" I asked.

"Your work called. You weren't there today."

"Nothing to get your knickers all twisted up about."

Charley, have some respect, Doc said for my ears only. *Can't you see she's worried sick?*

"I got a call from Jack Warrington. Charley, have you been phoning his home?"

"No. Did he say I was?"

"Well, he says he's seen you loitering in his neighborhood."

"For Chrissakes it's a free country. Besides, it's a shortcut to work."

"I suggest you take another route."

"Fine. Nothing to flip your wig over."

She looked into my eyes. "Doc, please leave him alone."

"This has nothing to do with Doc, anymore," I said, truly believing my words. This was one time I couldn't pass the buck. Watching the War-ringtons had become my obsession, like watching a movie over and over and studying it to find those little details you missed the last time. While the family seemed pretty boring, it was all quite entertaining. All I needed was a box of popcorn and a soda pop.

The next day I took the regular route up Cañada Boulevard. When I showed up to work I found out I'd been written up and nearly fired for not showing up. I apologized profusely and told the manager I'd been too sick to make it to the toilet much less the telephone.

"You should have had your mother call," he said.

"Sorry, but it's not really up to her. I must take full responsibility."

The manager told me not to let it happen again and I promised I wouldn't.

Now that Mother was on to me, I tried to reel in my fixation and ease up on my peeping. For a couple of days, I took another route and really tried not to go down that road. But one day, it rained and Mother let me use her car. She'd built up some trust in me. I discovered sitting in the car made it so much easier to watch the comings and the goings of the Warrington family in comfort. I had it made in the shade. I could even take a nap if things got too boring.

I continued my surveillance of the home before and after work; not every day at first, but then it became more of a routine, an obsession. I did this for weeks.

There were times I'd find myself reclined on top of Barbara's nubby, pink chenille bedspread blowing circles of cigarette smoke to the ceiling while the three bears were away, but mostly I would sit in the car and wonder how my life might have been different had I been born into this family.

But now, I also had to wonder, as I'm sure Mother must've given it some thought at the time, how her life would have been had I not been born. It's obvious to me she never wanted ankle-biters or why else would she have waited twelve years? Had I been a mistake or had Pop insisted there be someone to carry on his legacy? I hadn't known yet about Leland, the first born, heir to the throne, but I had to wonder about poor Karl and Helen, my half siblings. They must've felt like chopped liver.

I remembered last year when I rode the streetcar across Los Feliz to their house in Hollywood. All sweaty, I finally knocked on the front door. Karl, living with his mother Stella who still survived even with a bad liver, came to the door. Rather than invite me in, he stepped quietly out onto the porch and shook my hand and then he wrapped his arms around me, seeming happy to see me. He asked about my mother and had nothing but nice things to say about her. He'd remembered visiting her and Doc, but that was before everything had blown up during probate. It warmed my insides to hear him talk about more normal times. Stella came to the door and Karl introduced me. She yelled at me, "Get out! You son of a bitch! You call yourself Charles Marnier. You're not Charles Marnier. There was only one and you're not him! You bastard!"

Sure, it hurt, but it hurt me more to look at Karl who seemed mortified and embarrassed. I remembered the conversations during probate about how horrible Stella was. I knew how it was growing up in my own home during that time; I couldn't imagine how it must've been for Karl growing up in a home swarming with such bitterness and hatred.

After my earlier visit, the bitch called Mother and warned her to keep me away.

I wondered how their lives would have turned out if Doc hadn't fallen in love with Mother, if he hadn't left. I felt bad for Karl and Helen; they were, after all, my half siblings. I suppose I wanted a family, brothers and sisters, a family like the Warringtons.

Every time I started that fantasy, I heard the voice remind me of the truth. *I was deprived of witnessing the birth of my son—of holding him. If Jack was capable of murder, then what else? He must be stopped.*

The destiny of my life would have been different only if Warrington hadn't gone and murdered my father, if he hadn't stolen from Mother— from Doc. This man ruined, or as my mother so pragmatically might have said, changed our lives forever.

Mother had hidden the keys from me again. Apparently, she'd been snooping around, a skill she was good at. I had to hand it to her, but really it wasn't so hard, all she had to do was phone over Bob's Big Boy to discover I'd been fired and hadn't worked there for several weeks.

"You're right, Mother. I cannot tell a lie. I haven't been there all week."

"Charley, this isn't good. What will you tell your probation officer?"

"Don't worry, I already got another gig lined up." I chuckled through the lie.

"And what have you been doing in the meanwhile, what have you been up to?"

"Ah, Mother, what is this? The Spanish Inquisition, for Chrissake!"

"Charley, please don't talk that way."

"Well, then, cut me a break. Anyway, I have an interview. I need to borrow the car."

"I want to believe you, Charley, but I'm still not giving you the keys. You haven't told me where you've been."

"What if I told you I've been at the library doing some research on the human brain? I'm thinking about going into medicine. Yeah, I think I might have a knack for it. It's in my genes, after all. Or, maybe psychology." It wasn't a lie.

I'd also made a couple of visits to the Glendale Library. I really took my study seriously. I'd been reading up on Freud. Warrington was the lab rat under my microscope. "Did you know that the structure of the consciousness receives its final form during childhood, specifically at the time of the Oedipus complex? You know Oedipus, Mother?"

"Of course I do, from Shakespeare."

"Anyway, Freud doesn't talk too much about family—more about individuality. But if you ask me, a family consists of multiple individuals interacting on a daily basis. I want to figure out what makes the brain tick, what makes the family gel."

I saw the muscles in her jaw constrict several times as if she clenched to ten. "That would be a wonderful career," she said. "And if you're serious, I'd recommend Maslow's *Theory of Human Motivation* while you're at it. He gives excellent insight on how a person can find social satisfaction by establishing meaningful relationships with other people and the larger world. In other words, he establishes meaningful connections to an external reality—an essential component of self-actualization."

Mother was on a roll. "In contrast, to the extent vital needs find selfish and competitive fulfillment, a person acquires hostile emotions and limited external relationships—his awareness remains internal and limited."

"Maslow, huh? I just might take you up on that," I said.

"Good," she answered with a smile, "but you're still not getting the car."

"That's so stupid!"

She narrowed her eyes at me.

"That is so . . . injudicious!" I tried.

She didn't change her look.

Fine, that didn't stop me from hot-wiring Mother's car one last time while she attended a breakfast meeting in town. Marie had picked her up the next morning for one of her Womens' Club meetings. I had a meeting of my own to get to.

There I sat in front of the Warrington home. A couple of autos passed, ants in their cars on the way to work and school, and then one stopped further down the street in front of the neighbor's house where the man in the straw hat raked twigs and dead branches into a pile. He looked up when the car honked. Barbara soon bounced out the front door, blowing a bubble with her gum. I could see Warrington yelling at her as she crossed the front lawn. Without turning to look at him, she waved her arm above her head then spit her gum out onto the sidewalk. She walked a small distance and then pulled a cigarette out from her pack. Barbara was an ant marching off the trail. I knew, given the chance, we could be friends.

Shortly after, I watched as Warrington, in a gray, double-breasted suit, emerged from the home carrying his briefcase. He climbed into his car and drove off. It wasn't too long after that Mrs. Warrington pulled out of the garage in another car and sped down the street. I'd noticed her habit of sneaking out every day after the family had gone.

I'd been sitting on the fence for too long, the time had come to do something and yet I didn't know what. I was too far gone to drop everything. I'd case the joint one last time; maybe steal something of value; something to get Warrington back for what he'd done. The coast was clear. I came in through the kitchen again, this time carrying the morning paper and setting it on the counter—nothing cooking on the stove. I had a strong urge to visit Barbara's room one last time before stopping this nonsense.

I passed the Bakelite radio in the living room and turned the dial. What do you know? They appreciated the classics; I recognized Beethoven's Pastoral as I waltzed down the hall and entered Barbara's room.

As I rummaged through her pretty things, I heard a car pull up. In two steps, I was at the window peeking out behind ruffled curtains. The milkman came walking along the hedges to the back of the house. And then I watched as his big white truck, "Adohr Farms" stenciled in black on the side, pulled away down the street. I returned to the bureau to borrow a cigarette. Pretty soon, I heard a car door slam. This time I waited to exhale before moving toward the window. In giant hedge clipper strides, Warrington crossed the front lawn toward the house. He'd probably forgotten something. I crouched down in a corner beside the bureau, figuring I could hide out quietly until he left again, but then I knocked over a perfume bottle.

The doorknob turned once and Warrington burst into the room like a bomb going off, just as I dove headfirst through the window. I stumbled across the front lawn and then broke into a run. Jack was on my tail. Exhilarated, still hearing the music blaring in my head, I ran across the street toward Mother's car.

I didn't see the milk truck coming. It could have killed me. Who knew a milk truck could go so fast? The milkman had completed his deliveries on this street, obviously in a hurry to get to the next block to finish his rounds. I made it to Mother's car just in time to turn and see the big, white "Adohr Farms" truck plow into Warrington. His body went flying through the air, landing about a hundred yards away. The driver's hat flew off as he screeched to a stop, his head hitting the wheel. He threw a hand up to cover his face as he slowly inched forward. I hadn't noticed the picture of the dairy cow on the side panel. The milkman and I hurried over to where Jack had landed, face up, bloodied and flattened—crumpled like a pile of dirty laundry.

♫♪

A crowd gathered as he lay dying in the street. The neighbor in the straw hat threw down his hissing garden hose, and ran to the edge of the sidewalk.

No one came any closer as I stood above Warrington, watching his chest swell, a wheezy accordion expanding and contracting. He coughed, and the blood percolating up his throat rippled out all over his gray double-breasted suit. Every breath he took seemed like the suction of a carpet sweeper; every exhale, the percussive strike of a cymbal. His big, frightened cow eyes looked into mine, blood welling in his mouth. He wanted to say something. I leaned in, but the words were only a gurgle down his chin. I stared at him and opened my mouth to say something. In a voice so low, I hardly recognized when Doc spoke. "I am so sorry, Jack, but now you know how I felt. Now you can look into the eyes of the person who caused your death."

Jack's leg twisted up near his ear like a broken tree branch. Had he lived, it would have been impossible for any doctor to be able to set that thing. I noticed the pink Bazooka bubblegum on the bottom of Jack's shoe. I remembered I still had a stick of my own. I pulled it out from my pocket as I heard the sirens in the distance. I popped the piece of Bazooka bubblegum into my mouth and walked away as a gust of wind whipped up the leaves from the neighbor's yard, sending them swirling high above the rooftops.

♩♪

I came downstairs for breakfast as Mother brought in the morning newspaper. She gasped. I didn't need to ask.

"Jack Warrington is dead." Her eyes glided across me as if she was afraid to see me, and then she slowly slumped into her chair at the table. "It says he was chasing a Peeping Tom." She set down the paper and the tears slipped down her cheeks. I put my arm around her shoulders to try to comfort her and me as well.

"Ah, mother. I'd think you might be happy. He got his just dessert, after all." I rubbed her shoulder the way she liked.

She pulled away and looked up at me with wet, wide eyes. "Oh, but Charley, what have you done?"

It felt like a slap in the face. Sure, I felt guilty for how things had turned out, but that had not been my intention. "It wasn't my fault," I said. "It was his own bad karma, the consequence of his actions."

Her nose ran as she grabbed a napkin from the holder near the sugar and cream in the middle of the table. "But Doc—"

"And I told you to quit calling me that!" I pounded down so hard on the table the creamer fell over. I picked up the sugar and threw it against the wall leaving a dent in the plaster. I then yanked the newspaper out of her hand and ripped it in two as the milk dribbled over the side of the table.

"What the hell do you people want from me!" I stormed out the back door.

"You're not the man I married," she yelled after me.

"You've got that right!" I yelled back.

The next day, Milty came home for the summer from college to visit his parents. They stopped in after church like old times for Mother's Sunday chicken dinner.

We sat at the dining room table, on the blue mohair seats with goat-hoofed legs. Flanking a crystal vase, now holding the flowers Auntie Ann brought, were two small Spanish statues of gilded angels. I was mesmerized by the chubby, cherry cheeked cherubs with black-lacquered eyes staring vacantly at the ceiling. So innocent-like and holy. Why won't they look at me?

"Milty, did you hear the news?" I said, without looking up. "Jack Warrington is dead." I heard the collective gasps and turned to see all eyes now on me. Slowly, Milty broke into a smile, but then looked at me curiously. "Pass the salt," I said.

42

Bullseye

After Warrington's death, I tried to get by the best I could but I kept having nightmares, the ones where I saw his eyes and the way he looked at me in recognizable terror—that shoe with the bubblegum stuck to it. None of this had been my plan. Was it just his bad karma, and if so why did I need to be involved? It depressed me to think about who I might hurt next.

I'd gone back to school in the fall, but within the first two weeks, I ran into Barbara Warrington who seemed to shy away from me. I could feel her pain. The time I'd spent surveilling her home had given me an insight into the family unit.

It became impossible to get the vision of Jack heaving his last breath out of my mind. I couldn't get Doc's voice out of my head. "I am so sorry, Jack, but now you know how I felt. Now you can look into the eyes of the person who caused your death." Those eyes belonged to me.

How could I tell her I felt sorry for her loss? I felt guilty for what had happened, but honest to God, I didn't mean for anything to happen. It wasn't my fault. The bounce in her step had gone and I felt responsible for that, but it hadn't been part of the plan to ruin the family. I was living proof that growing up without a father was hard and I wouldn't wish that on anyone. I wasn't red-headed Ralph from juvie. An eye-for-an-eye. He may have called himself the Equalizer, but I wasn't his equivalent. I could never compare to him. I had known love. I was conceived in it. After that, Phoebe did the best she could and I knew it, but I would never let her know.

After everything, I wasn't able to make it to any of my classes. I walked off the campus instead and never returned.

If you go out in the woods today,
You'd better not go alone.

It's lovely out in the woods today,
But safer to stay at home . . .

I'd brought the Winchester '86 with me. Mother had hidden it in a small opening in a wall behind a workbench in the garage with the other rifles. I'd discovered the hole when I looked for a place to hide my booze.

Slumped against a tree down by the creek on the north side of the property, I noticed the sycamore across from me where Teresa and I had carved a heart shape with our names inside: *Charley and Teresa Forever.* Memories of that time had kept me going for years. Boy, how I ached for those days. I mooned around for Teresa knowing she was gone forever. Even as full of turmoil as my life had been, it had all been worth reliving those moments if only for an afternoon. I pulled out the bottle of whiskey I'd stolen earlier from the Chinese market up on Verdugo, as a rattler came slinking by out of the sun. I froze in place until it slithered on to burrow somewhere beneath a rock. My life had snaked behind me; so many boulders to hide under. What had been the purpose of it all?

I stood to trace the grooves on the tree where we'd carved our names; trying to feel connected to her. I missed her terribly and wished I could talk to her—just lie on the creek shore like we used to as kids and hold hands. She'd been there for me during a time when I thought no one cared. I found myself humming a familiar tune as I traced her image with a stick in the dirt. *Ode to Joy* had always been what I associated with happiness. Mother would play it when I was little, and for brief periods I was glad to know she was in her element as she played the song.

I used to think it was normal to have your mother absent in court everyday and then, when she'd come home, I'd become invisible as everyone would gather around her to discuss the favorite topic of conversation—Doc and the probate. The scene was familiar, normal. Crazy, but I even missed George. I missed those times as a very young boy, naïve and still innocent, when I didn't quite understand the evil ways of man. I missed the peace I felt sitting in Mother's lap. I wanted the peace I knew, before the voice imposed his will on me.

It hadn't been my intent to steal anything this morning. I hadn't eaten anything nor any of the other mornings before school. I'd been too nervous to eat. So, as I'd wandered the aisles of the Chinese market, picked out a loaf of white bread and some peanut butter, I figured I'd find a nice quiet place down by the creek and enjoy a meal. I saw the bottle of whiskey and slipped it into my backpack. I left the bread and peanut butter, but paid the cashier fifteen cents for a pack of cigarettes, instead.

Now, at the base of the sycamore, with a swirl of the stick, I shaped a pancake in the dirt and then two smaller ones set in the middle for her eyes. An upturned slash forms her smile and she seems to come to life. And now in braids falling over the front of her delicate, but sturdy shoulders, Teresa appears from behind a big, strong live oak that dwarfs her tiny frame. Wearing the embroidered muslin smock, she waves a lithe limb as she approaches along the fern-lined stream. Her *huaraches* kick up dust that she fans from a face framed in the glossy tresses woven in ribbon the color of watermelon. Her skin is the color of honey or sweet hot cocoa and it warms my insides.

I wiped my mouth with the back of my dirty hand. I was drunk by now and Teresa was only in my imagination. She'd been gone for many years, deported long ago, and George had done nothing to save her family. Oh, George, crazy, but I even missed him. George the coward, looking out only for himself and his best interests. No different than the rest, really—Warrington, Taylor and the others. Difference between him and all the others was that George was still out there somewhere alive and living a life he stole. *No different than you, Doc, wouldn't you say?*

I picked up the rifle, weighing it in my hands. Ah, most of mankind was selfish and greedy, I'd discovered. I took aim. Bullseye. Right through the heart of *Forever*.

I walked up to the old adobe house, boarded up for some time now, ready for demolition. This was all part of the property that had been sold to the crooked real estate developers who now developed a new housing tract. Dormant, twisted grape vines dangled like snakeskin from the grape arbor leading to the old place. I cleared the cobwebs criss-crossing across the two posts on either side of the steps to the veranda, and then planted myself on the porch in an old dusty rocker made out of tree branches. I looked across the way and noticed the giant land movers parked, ready to go. I sat down and took another swig, remembering the day Mother and I had gone to confront Taylor at the site on Valley View. I remembered how he'd jumped in front of the tractor; the look of terror on his face; and then the impact before he disappeared and went sailing off over the cliff.

I took another swallow as I listened to a songbird calling through the trees, blending now with Antonia's voice. "You remind me of him, Charley," I could hear her say. "Your father was a kind man, always with a sense of justice."

♪♫

I cried buckets of tears, blind as I walked back along the creek. I looked into the rippling water at my blurry reflection. My eyes were red and my cheeks streaked with tears. I looked much older than I was; after all, I was an 'old soul.' I knew more and had seen more than any sixteen-year-old should have to. And then slowly all of their faces bubbled to the surface, one by one—George, Taylor, Jack, Barbara, Teresa—all the people whose lives were changed because of me. Trying to stop thinking about them was no different than trying to stop thinking about a migraine.

"A kind man? Where's the justice in what you've done, Doc? I'd say revenge isn't what it's cracked up to be."

The guilt was a house demolition, falling in and crushing me. What I failed to see was how their lives had also affected me.

I lifted the rifle, weighing it in my hands, and before I could think it through, Doc shouted, "Charley, don't!"

"And why not? Maybe I can find a nice head to invade," I said. "Oh, but you'd sure miss your darling Phoebe if I was dead, wouldn't you?"

I placed my finger on the trigger and tried to move the barrel toward me. Impossible, how had Leland done it? I then set the rifle down and reached for the whiskey instead. I polished it off. "God damn it! Doc, go away. Please leave me alone. Let me live my own life," I said, tossing the bottle into the creek and watching enviously as it bobbed all the way down toward the ocean.

43
Welcome Back

1947: Glendale—
Charley

My days were numbered. I'd spent a week in the hospital after crashing Mother's car. I couldn't remember a thing. Even though I was free to go home after three days as long as someone watched over me, I stayed a couple more deliriously, drowsy days in the hospital. I'd discovered, besides heavy drinking, a stay in the hospital was one way to get the voice to leave me alone, to be separated from Mother, but it didn't stop the memories.

At first, I drifted in and out of sleep where the fringes of my dreams bordered my reality, hazy and full of shadows. I kept thinking about Jack Warrington. *I have to warn him,* I thought, pulling back the covers to get out of bed, but then I'd be falling and I'd wake up before I hit the concrete floor. My head killed me. Other times, I'd see Jack standing in the doorway holding a gun and I'd wake up before the bullet hit me. My heart would be racing inside my bruised ribs like a frazzled little bird stuck inside a collapsed cage; and I couldn't tell if I was awake or still dreaming. Time was Mother's Buick, speeding away until I crashed and was flung onto the present's highway.

Mother was holding my hand when I first opened my eyes. "Oh, Charley, you're awake," she'd said. Poor thing, she probably hoped I'd finally reached my low point, rock bottom; the point where I wake up from the concussion and turn my life around.

"Mother?" I lifted my heavy head, eyelids feeling even heavier—I had two black eyes—to look around the room. I dropped my head back onto the pillow. Obviously, I was in the hospital. I reached up and felt the gauze wrapped around my head and then slid my hand across my right temple. It stung.

"Twenty-four stitches. You're lucky to be alive," Mother said.

I traced along the ridges. "What happened?"

"You were in an accident."

"Did I hurt anybody?" I asked, holding my breath. There had been too many moments by now where I'd blacked out and couldn't remember things.

"Nobody but yourself—"

"Well, that's good news."

"You did, however, wreck my car."

"Shit. I'm sorry." It was hard to breathe. "I'll get you a new one. I promise."

"With what? You don't even have a job."

"I'll get one of those, too."

"That's good because you have a court hearing set for next week. You'll need to pay for the damages, not to mention attorney's fees."

"I thought you said I didn't hurt anyone."

"You smashed into the *Welcome to Glendale* sign."

"It was ugly anyway." I chuckled and it hurt my chest.

"Charley, this is not a joke. Your drinking, your behavior, it must stop. This isn't the life I wanted for you."

"Oh, yeah, tell me about it," I strained to yell as I tried to sit up. "Like I wanted this life. Let's hear your goddamn fairytale, Mother. Get real. This is real. No, this isn't the life you wanted for me. Let's be honest and back up. You never wanted me in the first place. I'm a mistake. I'm sure you rue the day I was born."

She looked at me, jaw dropped as a tear escaped. "You were not a mistake. You were a blessing."

I snorted out loud, chest and head killing me.

"The mistake was Doc wanting to continue on," she said sadly, turning away. "What was he thinking?" She peered at me closely. "What were you thinking, Doc?"

"Oh, please don't put me in the middle again. You know Maslow says that's not good for a kid." I laughed as I pulled back the covers and swung out my legs. "Hand me my clothes so I can bust outta here. I gotta go find a job." I fell back onto my side.

"Yes, you've got to, but not until the doctor says you're ready."

At dusk, I wandered down into the park. It'd been about a month after my release from the hospital. I needed to get out of the house; to stay away from Phoebe. The shadows of the Verdugo Hills loomed eerily across the valley. Night had fallen, yet it was alive with the sounds of crickets chirping, owls hooting and other creatures I was too afraid to imagine. The noise stopped as if all of nature strained to hear each other.

I must have fallen asleep for only a short time until I awoke to the sound of growling—my own stomach. I crawled around on my hands and knees disoriented by my surroundings, and then I heard the roar of a mountain lion echo through the park. I pulled my knees into my stomach to silence my hunger and I covered my ears to muffle the sounds. The air had cooled my skin and I rubbed my upper arms. I stared up through the invisible wind and the stars seemed to vibrate as if they might be whispering something to me. I strained to listen, but after a while I was too hungry, too cold, and too frightened to wait around for answers. I found a bush in which to curl up and take shelter.

I woke up staring at the sky through the canopy of sycamore trees. Dew had formed on the grass. So damp and freezing, I felt like a skinny, dirty icicle.

Since Mother had either flushed the booze all down the toilet or thrown every bottle away, there'd been nothing to snatch on the way out. I had the shakes so bad and now I was really hungry.

Earlier in the evening, Mother had come to my bedroom and set a tray of food on my nightstand. I couldn't eat. I wasn't hungry. I hadn't found a job; hadn't looked. Hungover again and still weak from the hospital, what I needed was a beer.

"Darling, you must eat something. You're skin and bones." She smoothed the hair back from my forehead, the stitches having been removed a week ago. For a moment, I was a two-year-old again. "You need help. What can I do?"

There was nothing she could do. Nothing anyone could do.

"Just leave me alone."

It killed me to see the hurt, helpless look in her eyes.

"How do you think it makes me feel to see my son in those jail clothes, those hospital gowns?" she said.

"And how do you think it makes me feel to see you act so trusting, so perfect," I shot back. "How do you think it makes me feel to watch you be used by men?"

"Charley, what are you talking about?"

"Warrington, Taylor. Father wasn't even cold before you let George serenade his way into our lives. Couldn't wait for the next musician to come and tickle your ivories and then *wham,* the piano lid gets slammed down. You just keep gettin' played. What a dope."

"Oh, Charley, please," she said, dabbing her eyes with her ever-ready hanky. "I did it for you. I thought you'd need a man in your life—a father figure." She sounded so pathetic.

She reached down to put her hand on my shoulder. It felt as if the blood boiled in my veins. And then for a brief scary second, I felt as if I might grab her by the throat and put her out of her misery, but then I saw my reflection in her tear-filled eyes. My love for her was greater than for any other person in my life, but I couldn't tell her that. Somehow I thought it might come out all wrong. All I knew at that moment was I needed her more than ever, but my feelings were scrambled and I knew the reason and it wasn't because I was hungover. Sadly, I knew why part of me wanted to hold her, to kiss her, make love to her, and I had to restrain Doc. Suddenly she pulled me into her arms.

"Please, Charley, they'll take you away from me," she wept softly onto my shoulder. "I couldn't bear it."

I pushed away. "Mother, it's too late, I'm already gone." There was a part of me prepared to be removed, and another part terrified of being separated from her.

"No, don't say that, Darling."

So weak, my spirit had left me. I felt Doc rising up and I was too feeble to fight him.

"Darling, why don't you play us something," Doc said as I slid out of bed. "You know it always made you feel better."

I gave her my hand and she helped me downstairs, where I took a seat in the plush crimson-colored chair near the piano. She took her place at the piano and looked at me, waiting.

"Perhaps, something from Beethoven's Ninth," Doc suggested. "I was always partial to the Second, so cheerful."

I recognized the first stanza from the second movement of the Ninth; the music playing in my head the day I trespassed into the Warringtons' home, the day Jack chased me into the street; the day I saw the deep red blood spewing from his mouth, the pink bubblegum on his shoe.

"What are you trying to do to me?" I said, burying my head in my hands.

The music had taken her away, but she stopped herself and pushed away from the piano. I opened my eyes to see her feet in front of me as she lifted my head. "Look at me," she said, holding my chin. "Doc, please. Get out. You must leave us alone."

"I can't stand it anymore," Doc said as I pulled her into my arms and kissed her hard on the lips, her scent bringing back memories of all those kisses from long ago.

1949: US Naval Hospital— Charley

Savage has stopped writing and stares at me, mouth gaping. He clears his throat before speaking. "And how did you feel after that kiss?"

Are you fucking kidding? I stare back at Savage.

"The thought of it makes me want to puke."

"Interesting. As we've already discussed, Freud theorized that all young boys subconsciously wish to usurp their fathers and become their mother's lover—"

"And the thought of *that* makes me want to kill someone." Fuming, I stand, nails digging into the palms of my hands. "If we've already discussed it, why are you bringing it up again? I'm not a child." I head toward the door.

"Charley, sit back down," Savage says, sitting straighter in his chair.

This time I take a seat on the fake leather sofa further away from his desk, so I won't be close enough to reach out and strangle him should the temptation take over.

"These are just normal things people don't talk about, but it's important—"

"So, it's normal for a young boy to want to kill someone?"

I detect a smirk on Savage's face before he shakes his head. "It makes you that angry?" he asks, jotting down in his notes. After a spell, he sets down his pen, looks up and adjusts his glasses. "You know, I'm curious. Charley, if she believed all of this, why wouldn't your mother do something more about Doc?"

"Like what? Like hold another séance? Remember, the last one didn't go so swimmingly, just another big shit storm. Anyway, I was out of there. The kiss was the last straw and I wasn't going to stick around to find myself in bed with my mother."

1947: Glendale—
Charley

Somehow, I'd made it through the day out of the house, and by nightfall, the moon had made an appearance, lighting up the creek. I noticed a couple of kindred lost souls coming down from the scorched hills like coyotes and deer in search of water. The evening's twilight was their dawning. As I watched the hobos washing in the brook that ran through the park, a straggler spotted me and approached.

"You must be new," he said. "Got anything to eat?"

I shook my head and he tore off a piece of bread to give me. I followed him to a small campfire where others had gathered. By the end of the evening, they'd passed their reefers and shared their booze with me. Getting blotto was the only way to erase what had happened to me.

♪♫

For the next few weeks, I made my home in the hills, coming down to the park at twilight with the others. After a while, I was unshaven with long greasy hair. At least no one would recognize me and I wouldn't be an embarrassment to Mother should someone happen to come into the park someday. She was free to tell them I'd gone off to college, to France, to the moon for all it really mattered. She could act as if I'd never been born. What she told her friends was her own business.

I'd remembered that on Tuesdays, Mother had her women's club. That's when I'd sneak home to raid the refrigerator. After a while, she left me really good stuff, whole chickens and pies, and then I'd go back out and share everything with my new family. I was learning how to interact with others. Mother would be proud.

I'd found social fulfillment by establishing meaningful relationships with these other people in the larger world, an essential component of self-actualization. Isn't that what she talked about? Isn't that what she wanted for me?

Sometimes, she'd leave me little notes I'd eventually tear up and use for kindling. Sometimes, I'd steal her precious things, silver, jewelry—anything she didn't have locked away or tied down, but only enough to get by until the next time. It hadn't been my plan, but I was a survivor, after all. Some punk would drop by every once in a while and we'd make a deal—one silver candlestick for a bottle of booze or a joint.

As I leaned on a tree one evening, taking a drag of my cigarette, I reached into my pocket and felt my father's cold gold pocket watch I'd just pinched. It had been too easy, just lying there where it'd always been. One thing Mother taught me was not to place too much value on things. I'd have to think about it before I actually pawned it. I opened the watch and looked at the picture. The guilt of not being able to be the person she wanted me to be, the person Doc wanted me to be, the probation officers, and all of society, for that matter, weighed heavily on me. "Talk about bad karma and consequences. I hope you're satisfied, Doc. Was this your plan? To have me living in the fucking park. I gotta admit, it's a pretty simple life. Isn't that what you were searching for, Doc? It's ironic, it doesn't take much effort. All you gotta do is let go. Isn't that what Phoebe says? 'Let it go.'"

I waited for Doc to respond, but I had a feeling he didn't dig hanging in the park.

"You wanted to give her the world. You wanted a different life for me, one with a mother and a father. Well, I had neither. You gave her everything, except for the time to enjoy it. She was gone for the first part of my life fighting your battles in court. I hope you're happy." I exhaled and snapped the watch shut.

I blew smoke rings. The trouble was no one had left me alone, really. People don't wanna let you be. Not the law, not society, not the church, not your mother and especially not your father. They all want you to be who they want you to be. Some days, I'd be catching a few *zzz's* in the park, out in nature under a beautiful tree, when some nosy asshole would come by and offer to help me, feed me, give me a few coins, a cup a Joe. I didn't ask for anything. I only wanted peace. I wrapped myself tightly in a blanket I'd stolen from home. The air grew damp and chilly. It would be another long night.

♪♫

That night the police made a clean sweep of the park rounding up several of us. There'd been reports of burglaries in the nearby neighborhood. It was a surprise attack and now my gig was up.

Hours later I sat in a jail cell thinking I'd finally hit my bottom. I needed a cigarette and reached into my pocket; instead I found a heart-shaped stone I'd picked up down by the creek. I remembered thinking it was a sign when I found it. I had a heart as cold as stone. My veins ran ice water.

I checked my other pocket and pulled out a folded up piece of paper— one of Mother's notes that had escaped the campfire. I couldn't bring myself to read it.

They released me to my mother and gave me my personal belongings, which included nothing more than my father's pocket watch. I hadn't the courage to pawn it with the other stuff. I reached into my pocket for the note and folded it tightly into the watch to read on another day.

44
You're in the Navy Now

1947: US Navy, San Diego—
Charley

At midnight, several days after my jail time, I turned seventeen. I hadn't changed my ways and so it had come to this.

The next morning everything felt the same except for the rough sheets in the bed I found myself in on the naval barracks in San Diego.

Weeks prior, the judge presiding over my arraignment had given me an option. "Mr. Marnier, this is getting to be like old home week. I don't want to see you in my courtroom again," he said. "Next time, it's the big house."

I heard my mother weeping behind me. It killed me.

"At this stage you don't have too many options, but I'm going to make a recommendation for what I think might be in the best interest of you and your family," he said, looking past me at my mother.

Aunt Dodo had accompanied Mother to the naval base for support.

"Be safe, I'll miss you," Mother said, her eyes tearing up as she stared intently into mine.

"Both of us?" I asked, chuckling. Part of me grew excited about this chance. The other side of me was petrified and was going to miss Phoebe terribly.

Aunt Dodo screwed her face up tighter than a mason jar as Mother pouted.

"You'll be all right, Mother. I'll miss you, too." I hugged her and then pulled away. "You still have your music. That's all you ever cared about anyway."

It was a parting shot, not really intended to sting. I shouldn't have said it, but as long as we were there in that moment, I suppose it needed to be said.

"Oh, Charley, that's not true," Mother said, dabbing her eyes with a hanky.

Aunt Dodo put her arms around Mother. "Charley, you're a rotten kid, nothing but trouble. Hopefully, the Navy can make a man out of you, someone to make your mother proud."

I knew I was a punk with a smart mouth and I wouldn't mind emerging from all of this with some sort of discipline, some goals, and some purpose. But no matter how much I changed, nothing would change the way I felt about Dumb Dodo.

"And someone to finally stand up to you, you old battle axe." This time I got the last word in.

1949: US Naval Hospital— 19-Year-Old Charley

It's late afternoon when I stub out my cigarette. In the three months I've been here, I've ingested God-knows-what and have smoked a million cigarettes. I've gone through a whole pack just today finishing up my saga. Dr. Savage is busy filling out some paperwork.

"I tried real hard to sail smoothly, but soon I was getting into trouble. As a matter of fact, now it was easier and more tempting. And just like the judge, my commanding officer had taken a liking to me and had given me only one option.

"So, that's it in a nutshell, Dr. Savage. That's how I ended up here in the Oakland Naval Hospital," I say during what is to be my last meeting with Dr. Savage. "Now, how much longer 'til I get outta this joint?" *Just keep it cool, Daddio, and you can walk out the doors.*

Savage turns off the recorder and reaches for his clipboard.

"I'll just finish up this paperwork, Charley," he says, looking up at me with a smile. "I'm sorry to see you go."

"What?"

"Charley—or, do you still think you're Doc?"

Trick question. "There's only one Doc." I smile that killer smile I use when I'm joking around. The smile I practice in the small mirror in the latrine. Only thing is, I'm not joking; besides, it's the answer he wants to hear.

"Well, as long as you're no one else." He chuckles.

"Oh, but I'm Jesus Christ," I say, giving him the serious face which I've also spent time practicing. Dr. Savage has asked me time and again to be serious; saying I wouldn't get any better unless I did.

"Jesus Christ?" he asks.

"The Father, the Son and the Holy Ghost."

We both laugh. Savage doesn't break his smile as he hands me some papers. "Charley, you are quite a character, indeed, highly intelligent with a wild imagination, but my conclusion will not change."

My hands tingle as I hold onto the document. "So, just like that you're discharging me. I'm confused."

"During these past few months, you've told me about your uncanny ability to remember and later decipher things grown-ups were saying and that when you were first able to read, nothing escaped you."

I nod.

"You discovered the secret place where your mother kept all of the newspaper clippings, the court documents, and other mementos. Your father's safe, the death certificate stuffed in the barrel of the rifle. It's clear that with your *false beliefs,* your *unclear and confused thinking,* the fact that you're hearing voices . . ."

"Only Doc's voice," I say, interrupting him.

". . . you've created this alternate personality you call 'Doc.'" He folds his hands on his desk. "It's not a classic case, but I've diagnosed you as a schizophrenic."

I feel my jaw drop. I know better, but what can I do? I walk to the window.

"Bullshit. How the hell am I supposed to survive, especially with this sorta bogus diagnosis? How? Where am I supposed to get a job?"

"Charley, calm down. No need to worry," Dr. Savage says. "Employers won't ask."

I look at my walking papers, thinking about it for a moment. If this means I can leave this shithole, then so be it.

"Fine. I can live with the diagnosis. At least, I now understand who I am and why I've been having these crazy thoughts all my life. Doc is the crazy one—not that trying to unscramble some of this shit hasn't fucked me up. But that's what the medicine is supposed to be for, right?"

"I don't find you to be a threat. You'll be fine as long as you don't forget to take your meds," Savage says.

I look at the prescription in my hand: five milligrams of Depakote twice a day and twenty milligrams of Lithium once a day. "Well, it's sure been swell," I say, reaching out to shake his hand.

"Get out of here, Charley," Dr. Savage says, walking me to the door.

Savage has done his job. I must admit the cat helped me sort out some of the crazy shit I grew up with. My stay has been therapeutic, to say the least. The 'therapy' seemed to help me look deep inside and not be so afraid. I have my diagnosis. I've been labeled. I'm no longer a danger to society. I'm just a little schizo. I'm not going to argue or resist anymore. And maybe the reason I no longer resist is because of the treatment—the meds. And because I'm discharged with a disability, like I'm some sort of mentally retarded person, because I'm military, I also get these benefits. I get all the medication they say I need; all the stuff to make you "normal," to make you fit into society. So, then, if I don't fit in, the VA always has a room for me. You see, there's always someone wanting to take care of me.

I'm given my belongings, including a deck knife I'd been given after boot camp, and then I'm ceremoniously booted out of Camp Project Chatter. Trouble is, I've lost twenty pounds and am being labeled and released out into the world to start a new life; medically discharged with no skills other than to push vets around in wheelchairs. I may not have had anything to prove, but in the end, all Savage can do is discharge me with a lifetime prescription of medication.

Forget that shit.

Now we can go home, Doc says the day I'm released.

"Never," I respond.

And now, a couple of days since flying the coop, I notice the longer I'm away, the longer the intervals are in between hearing his voice. Some days are better than others, but unfortunately, no amount of medicine is going to make Doc go away, especially while he still has an agenda. At least I know I'm not schizophrenic, I just happen to be two people. If that ain't a paradox? Pretty soon, we'll have a little sit down, the real crazy one and me—arm wrestle or a duel at dawn or a showdown at high noon at the OK corral, and he's going to lose.

It will be bittersweet finally saying goodbye to Papa Doc. After all, he's been a part of my life since before I was born. But it's time to figure out another way to make him leave me alone. Even though I'm afraid of what my life might be without him, I'm petrified of how my life will end up if I let him stay. I figure if I just keep driving north I can outrun him.

45
Cousin Milty

A brisk wind blasts my face and I suck in the taste of freedom as I travel north along the coast. Doc's been laying low from the moment I'm discharged and my head feels much clearer now that I'm off the meds. Unfortunately, I'm still acting like a spaz, finding trouble all around me.

And because I've quit checking in at the VA, that also means I won't be getting my monthly benefit. So, with only three dollars in my pocket, I take a job as a deckhand on a fishing boat up near Ventura. On payday, the other deckhands and I go out to celebrate. I figure I deserve to live it up a little and so I get drunk. One of the mates accuses me of stealing his cheap-ass watch. Oscar forgot he'd pawned the watch for two dollars at the beginning of the week.

"You son-of-a-bitch!" Oscar says and it's lights out. The police show up and arrest me.

I wake up in the can. It takes my whole paycheck to make bail. Maybe if I'd stayed on the meds I wouldn't have gotten into trouble in the first place, but no one gets away with calling me a son-of-a-bitch without getting beat up. She's still my mother.

Next, I land a job in a service station, but by my second day, I'm ogling this young platinum blonde Beverly Hills' doll-type as she's telling me she's headed up to San Francisco to hang with all the other beatniks. I end up getting axed for failing to remove the gas nozzle before the chassis takes off.

By the time I hit Pacific Coast Highway again, I've decided it's time for me to visit Milty. A couple of weeks before my release, he'd come to visit me at the hospital and offered me a place to transition once I was discharged.

Springtime, time for renewal. I've left my old life in the dust. Bursts of orange poppies like hotspots line the road as well as mustard seed plants, giant eucalyptus, pink and white oleanders, and pepper trees. The umber-colored rolling hills looked like dormant camels.

Along the highway, blackbirds are perched on the barbed wiring between wooden fences. They remind me of music notes on staves between brackets; notes Mother tried to teach me to read, but I'd refused. I can hear piano music now as the fragrant wild flowers bloom into memories I can't put my finger on. Splashes of Queen Anne Lace sprout all around, reminding me of the plant Mother grew on the property. She used it as filler in floral arrangements she placed throughout the house. The place reeked of death. I remember her telling me how the white flower was named after Queen Anne of England, an expert lace maker.

Mother had a story for everything and everybody, except when it came to Doc. I couldn't care less about flowers. Mother should've had a girl. "And that little red flower in the middle is from the drop of blood that fell onto the lace when she pricked her finger," she said. "Oh, cool. I bet there was lots of blood when Doc died," I'd said. "Oh, Charley, why do you have to go and talk like so?"

I try to push the thoughts of her out of my head. I rev up the engine and keep my eyes on the pavement.

Nearing the giant Magu Rock on the bluff, I'm excited to see what answers might be lurking around the point. And then, I nearly skid off the road when I hear his voice boom over the roar of the engine.

"Find George!" Doc is back. "George always had the answers," Doc yells. "I need answers now!" I gun the engine and head north.

I spend a sleepless night arguing with Doc under a starry sky on a cliff in Big Sur. I tuck in my head and zip up my sleeping bag, but his voice will not leave me. "Find George!"

"Go away!"

The next morning, a cold damp wind keeps me alert as I cut across through Salinas and onto the highway north. Late afternoon, I roll up to a Victorian-style home in Marysville.

In the front is a nicely manicured little yard dotted with olive and citrus trees. Birds of Paradise border a white-fenced veranda where potted red geraniums flank two cane-backed rockers. The sound of my motorcycle coming up the dirt road brings my cousin Milty out onto the porch, hand shading his eyes.

"Charley," he signals, arms waving, as he strides up to greet me. "You made it."

We stand looking at each other, tear-welled, eye-to-eye, and then, as he hugs me, I look past his shoulder to see two small children, a boy and a girl around five and six. His wife, Susan, is a tiny woman in a flowered apron standing on the porch. Her hair is short and curly, shiny and blonde. She has large blue baby doll eyes, kind and full of wonder. She wipes her hands on her apron, and I notice the round belly. I extend my hand and she reaches up to kiss me on the cheek, instead.

"Welcome, Charley. You must be hungry," she says sweetly. She's been expecting me, although I hadn't told her where I was calling from when I used my one call from the jail. "Come inside. You're just in time for supper."

I hand Susan the dozen daisies I'd picked along the way and she uses a white milk bottle as a vase. She sets the flowers in the center of a blue and white gingham tablecloth where the family takes their seats. I can't remember the last time I had a home-cooked meal.

I close my eyes and chew. Heavenly.

"The chicken is from your mother's recipe; like the one she cooks on Sundays," Susan says. "One of these days she'll tell me what she puts in the—"

I look over at Milty. He signs, "We still go to visit her, especially on holidays."

I set down my fork and pick up my glass of milk. It doesn't take long for me to feel I'm home. Milty, Susan and their children make me feel like family. After dinner, Milty joins me out on the porch, where I'm smoking.

"Charley, you're looking good," he signs. He has no idea where I've spent my nights.

"Thanks, cousin. I'm really happy for you. You always seem to have your shit together."

Milty opens his mouth to laugh but no sound comes out. "It's not so hard," he signs. "Susan is a godsend, the children are a blessing, and I have a terrific job in town with the phone company."

My look of confusion is undoubtedly obvious to Milty.

"Sort of ironic for a mute to be working in telecommunication, wouldn't you say?"

"Boy, you're not kidding. What kind of job could you possibly have?"

"Charley, remember I can still hear."

Milty has done well for himself at the Yuba-Sutter phone company. He'd started out as a field technician connecting and installing cable phone services. He knew the technology inside and out. "I can troubleshoot, repair phones. I've prepared all of the how-to manuals for both the technician and the customers."

I laugh. "You're right. Who needs to talk, anyway? You were always one smart cat."

"I'm in accounting now," Milty signs. "But, you know, recently I did read something about augmentative and alternative communication. Someday, there will be a phone for people like me and I'll be the first in line to sign up."

"And I'll be right behind you," I say. "Can you imagine us being able to talk to each other on the phone? Almost as if talking to the dead or—"

Milty's smile suddenly disappears.

"I'm sorry. I just mean . . . shit, there I go again."

It's no secret to Milty I'd been admitted to the hospital for many reasons but primarily because I talked to that voice I called Doc, and whether Milty believed me or not, I never knew.

"Not to worry," Milty signs, smiling. "If you can talk to Doc, I see no reason why you and I won't be able to talk on the phone someday."

Milty is the most kind, sensitive, empathetic human being I've ever known. He has a heart of gold and would give me the shirt off his back.

"Say, do you think you might put in a good word for me over at the phone company?"

"I'd be happy to," Milty says.

"Then all I need to do is find a good woman like Susan to love me and I'll be all set."

"It's a good thing you're so easy on the eyes, Charley."

"Yeah, I've got a face only a mother could love." I chuckle. "Hell, I'm really not so loveable. Even she couldn't stand having me around. I was a mistake, after all. They never wanted children."

"Stop." Milty holds up a hand. "Not true. I remember Uncle Doc talking about the way things were going to change once you were born. I'd never seen him as happy as that last day."

"You mean the day Warrington killed him?"

"Charley, can we not go there right now?" he says, looking inside the house toward Susan. "Can't you just let it go?"

"Now you're sounding like Phoebe."

Milty stands and walks over to lean on the railing. He turns to look at me, lifting his hands to speak.

"I loved my uncle. He was a good man, kind and yet so set in his ways. I remember the morning before. I was lying underneath the piano with my feet stretched up to feel the vibrations."

"My favorite spot in the whole world," I say with a smile.

"Uncle Doc bent down to take my hand. 'Come, Milty,' he said. 'Pretty soon you'll have a little playmate.' I'd never been more excited.

"On our way outside, we'd bumped into someone carrying an oboe, who, in turn, bumped into a short man carrying a cello. Aunt Phoebe put on quite an affair. There were eight musicians that night to entertain eighty-five guests.

"We'd walked about one hundred feet toward the perimeter of the back yard property to a lone citrus tree. Uncle Doc said, 'We planted that tree when we first broke ground on this property, Milty,' and then he climbed up a ladder leaning on the tree. He pulled down a branch so that he might have a closer look. He showed me a lemon, which to me wasn't very impressive, it was just a lemon; but there out on a branch next to it hung a small, waxy orange.

"'Well, what do you know?' Uncle Doc had said. 'The grafting took and soon this tree will be growing not only oranges, but lemons as well. This fruit is a lot like you, Milty. It will grow up strong and good and sweet. And my new baby will be like this little lemon, a little tart, but full of zest—a survivor like his father.'"

Milty is staring at me now intently and I feel the tears burning tracks down my cheeks.

"Uncle Doc was right, Charley. You're a survivor."

I clear my throat, wiping my face with the back of my hand. "Just full of piss and vinegar."

Milty smiles. "I remember when Uncle Doc turned to look out toward the orchard and I could barely hear him when he said, 'At the rate it's growing, I'll be dead before I taste the fruits of my labor.' I didn't understand. After a moment, he scooped me up and said, 'Ah, but Milty, this is a good sign, indeed. Oranges for health, California for wealth!'"

I grow quiet. "And that's where Mother and I buried his ashes," I say. "Under that tree."

I grow quiet. Milty gets me a job outside as a lineman. But working as a pole climber isn't easy for me. It's only a matter of time before I lose concentration.

I'm up on the pole one day when Doc makes an appearance. *Charley, we need to go home.* I clutch the post before I might slip to my death.

"This is my home. Leave me alone," I say, proceeding to finish up some wiring.

The next day, he starts up again, but this time he has a different command. *Find George.*

"Forget about it." I'm about to scale another telephone pole. "And what would you have me do to him when I find him?"

George will have the answer. Doc is insistent.

"Nice try. What's the question?" I ask, turning to see my foreman staring up at me.

"Who you talking to?" the foreman asks.

This goes on for about a week. Doc's as persistent as a virus. *Find George,* he says.

"Fuck off," I yell one day from the basket fifty feet in the air. The wrench I'm holding slips out of my hand, just missing a co-worker standing underneath. I've been warned and I'm sure, as hard as I try not to, seeing me argue with myself doesn't help matters. I'm let go. Fired.

"It's not that I'm ungrateful, Milty, but I just don't know what I'm cut out for," I say to Milty who tries to console me when I get home after being axed again. "Maybe, I'll go work the land somewhere."

"We know a family that does pretty well in Salinas," Milty says. "They have a farm."

Before I say 'goodbye' to my cousin, we walk around to his neatly landscaped back yard. With all of the Rosies, Gardenias and Carnations sending off their fragrance, Susan's garden reminds me of Mother's children back home. I try to block her memory, but Doc is anxious.

Charley, let's go home.

"No," I whisper under my breath.

Find George.

I close my eyes and shake my head. When I open them, Milty is looking at me, head tilted slightly. He smiles.

"Milty, that day—" I say, but then see his jaw clench and his hands coil into fists. I put my hands on his shoulders. "Please, it's important," I say, dropping my hands. "Listen to me. That day—was George there?"

Milty takes a deep breath and then exhales. "Just Jack. I remember running out to find help. I never saw George."

"What about lately? Have you seen him?"

Milty shakes his head and signs. "He's in Soledad."

46
I'm Legal Now

Sitting at a juke joint in Salinas about twenty-five miles south of Soledad Prison, I'm just buying time, gathering some courage before paying George a visit. Now, I'm really curious. Besides, I only see two choices—three really—it's either pay George a visit, return to Phoebe, or drive myself off a cliff. Warrington and Taylor both died because of me, not because I'd planned it that way, not because I had any control. I was only a child. It was all Doc's manipulation. Oh, God, I don't want the same for George. If Doc wants to exact revenge, I'm not sure I can control him or restrain myself. But, if I don't get some answers soon, I'll be the one who ends up dead.

I can see my reflection on the large smudged mercury glass mirror on the back wall. My forehead is furrowed with stress, lined like music paper. My eyes are as red as a Shirley Temple soda. I order a beer.

Taped off to the side of the mirror is a picture of a large Mexican family, probably the owner's, celebrating either a wedding or someone's *quinceañera*; it's hard to tell, but they all seem happy. I stare down into my sad, sweaty glass. It's the cocktail hour—just past noon. Dusty bottles of tequila, rum, bourbon and scotch line the glass shelves behind the counter, but I'm drinking cheap beer in honor of my twenty-first birthday. I'm legal now. What a joke.

Happy Birthday, Son, Doc says and I nearly fall out of my seat.

I remember the day you were born. I'm sorry I couldn't be there for Phoebe . . . and you.

I'm one giant clenched fist, not open to listening at that moment.

She needs us now. It's time to go home.

I reach for my glass and speak into it so no one at the bar can see what's up. "She's got her music. Go away."

We need to go home, Doc says.

"Get the hell outta here," I whisper, willing myself to ignore him. I feel the blood bubbling at my temples. I close my eyes and hum *Ode to Joy* like it was part of my DNA.

Ah, from Beethoven's Ninth. Phoebe's favorite . . . my favorite, Doc says.

I stop. It's been a long time since I hummed that tune. Damn, it makes me nostalgic and today, of all days, I don't want to go back. I lift my head to take a drink, but catch a glimpse of myself in the smudged mirror the first time I took a drink—on my seventh birthday, as a matter of fact. It was also the first time I'd ever gotten drunk.

Through the mirror, I can see myself the morning before Mother's concert of the Ninth Symphony. There'd been a chocolate cake, but no school friends gathered around the kitchen table. Mother's musician friends took a break and came in from the chamber room to sing to me. Mother handed me a colorfully-wrapped gift, but honestly, I can't remember what it was. Besides the chocolate cake, the next best part about the day had been having cousin Milty there. But I missed my best friend in the whole world. Teresa had gone away, repatriated to Mexico, George said. And it was he who'd had something to do with it. After he'd chased off the Marquez's, he bought me a new bike—an early birthday present.

Typical George, always trying to buy you off, Doc says.

"And so why should I go home now, where I'm only the afterthought?" I say.

Phoebe's concert had gone off without a hitch except when you strode up and stood next to the grand piano, Doc says. *You looked out into the audience, and locked eyes with Warrington. "That man killed my daddy," you shouted. Boy, the look on Jack's face, eyes contracting to the size of atoms—the same look of recognition he had just before he died in the street in front of his own home.*

"Doc, that was wrong," I say.

His home where nightly you'd watch his teenage daughter having the life you should have had, if her greedy father hadn't killed me.

"That wasn't right either." I pause. I'll never forget the look on Barbara's face when we bumped into each other at school—a look saying she knew I had something to do with her daddy's death. Afterward, I could never go back to Glendale High.

I peer into my glass. "I'm so sorry, Barbara."

It wasn't your fault, Son.

I grip my glass so hard, I'm afraid I'll bust it. I think about smashing it against my skull. "He got his. Doc, isn't that what you wanted? Thy will be done. Now, just leave me the fuck alone. Let me enjoy my birthday in peace."

That seems to shut him up, at least for now.

Except for Doc, I'm all alone on my twenty-first birthday. There will be no special dinner, no devil's food cake with enough candles to set off a fire alarm. I'm used to it. I'm really feeling sorry for myself as I throw back remnants of liquid gold. I'm just draining the last drop of beer when a couple of sweaty *braceros* with a week's worth of stubble pull up beside me.

"This seat taken?" The taller one asks. With thick, straight black hair slicked back, it looks like he's wearing a helmet. He has an easy smile and you can drive a beer truck through the gap in his front teeth. I shake my head. The shorter one is still standing. He wears a ten-gallon cowboy hat, bringing him up to a lofty five-foot six inches with his shit-kickers on.

"*Hola, amigo,* I'm Cesar Chavez," Smiley says, and hooks a thumb at his side-kick. "This is Chapo, short for *chaparro*—shorty."

Blessed with a noggin topped with wavy blond hair and blue eyes, I don't exactly look like I'm from around these parts. "*Mucho gusto, soy Carlos.*" I always get a kick out of watching the Mexicans' faces when they see I can speak Spanish.

My arm is outstretched, still clutching onto my ghost of an empty beer mug.

"I like your tattoo." Cesar stares at the *Viva Mejico* scrawled out on my right forearm.

I twist around and point to my upper left with the typical anchor all the swabbies get once they go out on their first drunken shore leave. "I got 'em in Tijuana," I say in Spanish, "while stationed down in San Diego."

He smiles the size of a Navy ship and rolls up his shirtsleeve to show me his anchor. "Me, too," Cesar says. "So, it is your birthday?"

He must've overheard me telling the bartender. I nod and make an effort to smile.

"Let me buy you a drink."

"Thank you, and only because it's my birthday—and because I'm broke—I'll let you buy me a beer."

"Who were you talking to?" he asks, pointing at the empty mug.

I figure there's nothing to lose; I'll never see this *gato* again. Let them think I'm drunk. What the hell. "My old man," I say. "My father."

"I didn't take his seat, did I?" Cesar asks, lifting his butt from the seat, grinning. "I talk to my papa all the time."

Over the sound of the Mariachi music blasting from the jukebox, the sound of clinking glasses and laughter fills the room. The climate has changed; things suddenly look brighter.

"What about work around here?" I shout. I'd decided I needed more time before I confront George; besides, I have a good feeling about this place and these people.

"There's plenty for anyone who wants to work out of doors," Chapo says.

"But what about for a gringo like me?"

"The growers are happy to use anyone willing to work for low wages, even a gringo like you," Cesar says.

"Low wages are better than no wages," I say. "I ain't afraid of hard work."

"Chapo here happens to be the foreman," Cesar says.

"It's near the end of harvest, but you can come check it out on Monday. See if you like it." Chapo's gold-framed front teeth remind me of the gilded abstract paintings lined up across Mother's walls back home.

"I'll be there," I shout and the beer sloshes over as we clink glasses. "*Salud!*"

I lose count of how many beers just as I've lost count of how many lonely birthdays I've spent in my lifetime. But it doesn't matter now. On my twenty-first birthday, like candles on a cake, I've added some new friends to my life, *amigos* who make me feel as if I've come home. On this birthday, I have the gift of hope that I might be able to have a normal life in a place where I can make a living outdoors and where it isn't so strange to talk to your papa.

Hope will forever smell like strawberries.

On the day my life turns around, the red berries glisten with morning dew as the sun rises beyond the eastern mountains. There are already hundreds of migrant workers hunched over the sea of crimson. The air buzzes with the sound of bees and the sweet smell of fruit sprouting from rows upon rows stretched out across the horizon. Overhead, large fluffy clouds like herds of lost sheep skitter across an indigo sky as their shadows drift over the field. I'm ecstatic being outdoors, sweating alongside these *braceros,* singing soulful tunes that seem to be keeping Doc at bay. I was born to work the land. I love these people, the salt of the earth. After a couple of hours, I can feel the blisters forming. My hands will get tougher.

I'm happy getting to work early in the morning and continuing until the day is done when the sun sets over the coast range. We only get a few minutes to eat, and today in my eagerness to catch the sunrise, I've grabbed an apple for breakfast but hadn't thought about packing anything for lunch. A cigarette will have to do. I bend down to cup my hand to light it and notice a larger shadow has spread across my path. I look up to see a young woman standing over me. She's blocking the sun. When my eyes finally adjust, I notice the watermelon-colored ribbons weaved into two long braids dangling over her chest. She offers me a tortilla.

"Thank you."

"You're new," she says in perfect English and I sense something familiar in the tone of her voice.

I rise to make her acquaintance. Standing eye-to-eye, she's a tall Mayan princess. Underneath her straw sombrero, there's something even more familiar in the soulful, dark eyes—eyes like the rich, fertile soil. I extend my hand. "My name is Charley. *Como te llamas?*"

She purses her lips together, looks down and away. "Teresa. Teresa Marquez."

My whole body tingles. I just might melt into the earth. I drop the tortilla. My heart floods with all of the old love and pain and memories, and my eyes well with tears.

I wipe my eyes. "Teresa?" My childhood love Teresa and I stand staring at each other until the whistle blows signaling it's time to get back to work.

"We'll get fired," she says, and quickly disappears back underneath the vines to the other side of the row of berries. I call out to her but, like the images we used to make out in the clouds when we were little, she's gone.

I've been beside myself after the encounter. Teresa has completely disappeared. Was that all simply an apparition? After all of these years, how could I let her get away again? Had she gone to another camp?

Saturday night, my fellow *braceros* invite me to a *baile* where there are plenty of girls who like to dance. At the dance, I ask everyone about the tall beauty named Teresa.

"Sure, I know Teresa," my bunkmate Freddy says. "She's married to Guillermo Lopez."

I'm crushed to learn she's hitched, but then my heart does a jig when I see her floating into the hall with some of the other girls from the camp. I'm surprised to see her without her husband. I know I'll just be pouring salt into an old wound, but I slide up next to her anyway. "*Hola,* Teresa."

She stretches her full lips over her teeth, trying not to smile. "Hello."

"Where's your *esposo*?" I ask.

She giggles and it's obvious now why she won't smile. Her teeth are slightly buck, but her dark eyes do all the smiling necessary for me to know I'm in love with her and have always been. Teresa has grown up to be a pretty thing; more reserved than back when we were children wandering aimlessly like puppies around the Glendale property—back when my affections were only considered puppy love. "I am not married," she says.

Of the three options I thought I had, falling in love had not been one of them. If I'd been a praying man, I'd say Teresa is the answer to my prayers. She's my destiny, my fate. A month later, I'm baptized a Catholic and on a Saturday afternoon, we are married in *La Mision de la Parroquia del Sagrado Corazon:* Sacred Heart Church. I haven't invited anyone, not even Milty. Señora Antonia Marquez is seated in the front pew holding a hanky to her nose as her husband, Pedro Marquez, walks his beautiful daughter down the aisle to give me her hand.

Sunday, the day of rest, we spend the remainder of our honeymoon in a cabin for married couples—in our case, newlyweds. In the light of the dappled morning sun streaming through frayed calico curtains, I wake up to see the flecks, yellow nuggets, in Teresa's eyes. I've struck gold. I now have someone to love, to understand me, and someone willing to spend the rest of her life with me. She'd been watching me while I slept. "You talk in your sleep."

"Oh, yeah? What did I say?" I ask, afraid to hear the answer.

She angles her head slightly and smiles, her long brown hair splayed all around her pillow like a bronzed halo. "I couldn't make anything out. Just ramblings," she says. "You did mention your mother's name, Phoebe."

Shit, I strain to remember what I might have been dreaming about, but then just as I see something growing on the fringe of my memory, I have to let it go. Teresa has rolled onto me. "Charley, it's like you've unlocked something in me, as if I've been a caged animal for all of these years."

We make love again for what seems like the hundredth time. "You're a real natural, a mama bear, a lioness, a jaguar." I chuckle. "It was time for you to come out of your cage."

She laughs. I kiss her. "But to me you're also my Mayan princess, my Aztec goddess."

"You make me feel special," she says, cupping my face.

"I know you're special," I say.

"Oh, yeah? How?" she asks, sitting up to plump her pillow.

"I just know things," I say, sitting up to light a cigarette.

"Like what?" she asks, waiting for me to exhale.

"Like we're going to have a dozen children and be happy for the rest of our lives." I get out of bed.

"You'll be the best papa," she says.

I nod and walk to the window to look out across the field. For some reason George pops into my mind. I remember sharing with him about my first kiss. Sick, but I miss him, and I know if I'm finally going to be able to move on and have the life I deserve, I need to take care of George. It's time to go and pay him a visit.

47
Papa George

It takes a lot of courage for me to walk into Soledad Prison. It's the last place I ever want to visit, but at least I'm on the other side. I'm afraid for what I might cause to happen. Warrington and Taylor had died because of me. I don't want George to die, but unless I get some answers, I'm afraid I'll be the one who ends up dead. I feel the deck knife rubbing against my ankle inside my boot. The guards haven't done a good job patting me down.

I feel a stabbing in my heart when I see George shuffle into the waiting room in heavy-looking, black boots that could sink a man in the ocean—should he decide to end it all, and should he be near an ocean. He removes his billed cap and what hair he has left on his head is white as sea foam. In a faded blue denim shirt, tucked into belted baggy dungarees, he's as thin as a prison bar. Above his eyes, it looks like a fuzzy dark caterpillar is crawling across a ruddy road. His pistol-gray eyes, as lively as ever, fire up when he sees me.

"So good to see you, Charley," he says, reaching out to me. I stiffen. "Thank you for coming."

I can't tell whether it's good or not to see him; either way I won't betray my feelings, happy or sad. I light a cigarette and remain silent, doing my best to keep Doc from speaking up.

The guard escorts more visitors into the room; the first, a shabby-looking woman in her late twenties, pulls along two little tow-headed kids.

"How've you been?" George asks. "How's your mother?"

I blow smoke, not in his face, but over his head.

"Can I bum a smoke?" he asks.

"What are you in for?" I ask, instead. I won't let him control the conversation. I push my pack and matches across the table. He pulls out a cigarette and lights it.

"You know, a little forgery," he says, shaking out the match, "insurance fraud and identity theft; other stuff like that."

"Other stuff that landed you in a lousy state prison," I say.

"It ain't so bad. Three hots and a cot." He grins.

I know he's lying. News around the country shows prisoners rioting from overcrowding and neglect. They live in horrible conditions and mismanagement. It had taken months of persistence on my part to even be able to visit George. And then one day, a new guy answers the phone and arranges this little social call—he must've just gotten laid or something. One of the reasons I've been trying to fly straight is to stay out of this sort of joint.

"So, the law finally caught up with you, huh?"

George takes a deep breath. "I forgot to leave my gun at home when I went to the bank to make a withdrawal," he says with a snort. "Tried to go straight, but the goons wouldn't let me."

Behind George's shoulder, I notice another inmate being escorted into the room. The children squeal. "Daddy!" The woman gets up to hug him and the guard gives the couple a few moments before he pulls them apart.

George chuckles, running a hand through his sparse hair. "It's been so long since I've had a woman's arms around me."

"I feel for you," I say. "Must be tough for a man like you."

"I loved your mother. She just wouldn't let me in." He smiles weakly then sets his cigarette down in the ashtray and pushes back in his chair, crossing his legs in front of him. "I had a pretty good run for a while, but you know sometimes you just get so tired. That's when you mess up," he says, raising his arms as if in surrender and then lacing his hands behind his neck. "You've done some time yourself, I hear, Charley."

"What's it to you?" I say.

"Listen, kid, I know you've had it tough. I give you credit for managing to stay on that side of the bars." George leans forward, clasping his hands in front of him.

"Last time was for assaulting a shipmate," I say, conceding.

George slaps the table then bursts out laughing. "I'll be damned."

"What's so funny?" I ask.

"Takes me back to '09, when I myself was dishonorably discharged for assaulting the company cook."

"Yeah? So?"

"So, I simply forged a new certificate of honorable discharge. That happened right before I met your father who ended up hiring me to work for him." George looks off into space. "I did right by him for a couple of years." He nods sadly. I look away.

"So, why'd you attack your shipmate?" he asks.

"He called me a sonofabitch."

George becomes somber. "Phoebe was a lady. She was music. You did the right thing. Me," he says, tapping his thumb onto his chest, "I've never done a right thing in my life. Just a fake good at faking. There's nothing I couldn't forge. I became Doc's fixer. Even used to doctor up prescriptions for his first wife, Stella. I'm ashamed to admit it, but she would beg me. Morphine and other shit. He knew about it, too, but looked the other way. Again, desperation will make you do crazy things." George laughs. "That Stella, she was one crazy dame. It was also no secret Doc had me sign documents for him, like when he was out of town."

George looks at me sheepishly. "Phoebe though, your mother, she was the symphony everyone wanted to be a part of," he says, and then smiles as if remembering. "Doc used to say I was so full of it and that if bullshit were music, I'd be a symphony."

I don't laugh. The knife inside my boot is irritating me.

"You were there," I say, reaching down to adjust my boot.

"What do you mean?"

"As Dad lay dying, Milty saw you there. He saw the blood on your hands."

I'm lying. Milty hadn't seen him that day, but I have nothing to lose by tricking George now. The guard is standing near the doorway behind George. I set the knife on the table where George can see it.

His eyes widen and then the tears stream down his face. "I had nothing to do with that. You've gotta believe me. I knew Doc was meeting Jack that day. I'd stumbled in to see Jack holding a gun dripping with blood and Doc bleeding on the floor. As Jack ran off, I dropped to my knees to see if Doc was still alive. I held his head. I talked to him. I wanted to help, but time was running out. I told him to hang in there, that I didn't know what I'd do without him. I needed him. He could always fix things. He'd always rescued me. We all needed him. I told him he had a baby on the way. He had the life I always wanted. I loved your father, Charley. I loved Doc."

George is bawling by now. He buries his head in his hands. After a few moments, he lifts his head. His nose is running so he uses his sleeve. I call for the guard. Through a small window in the door, I can see the guard standing just outside before he walks in.

"He needs something to blow his nose," I call out to the guard, sliding the knife back onto my lap.

The guard comes in and whips out some sort of rag into which George blows his nose. The guard goes back out to his station.

"It's been so long holding this stuff in. I wanna go straight with you, Charley. I wanna get this shit off my chest. I'm not proud of myself, but I'm a survivor. You gotta hand me that, at least." He peers into my eyes. "You gonna kill me?"

I simply sit and glare at him.

"Can I at least make my amends first?"

I get up, unable to look at his weakness—his humanness. He is, after all, the only human father I've ever known. I shrug my shoulders and then nod, turning to see him smiling at me, ruefully. I let him spew his guts as I slip the knife up my sleeve.

"At that moment, I had a thought," George says. "I realized that if he were to die, I could have his life or at least one like it. I was the one who knew about his business and his life insurance. I signed on his bank accounts. I was also a terrible gambler and at that time, my life was in danger. I'd really gone into debt and if Doc were to die, I could take care of a lot of things. I could start a new life with his money.

"It was no secret to Doc that I used to sign for him, but what I'd arranged with Jack was not part of the understanding. Jack was originally to get twenty-five percent of the business should anything ever happen to Doc. The other seventy-five would go to Phoebe. I remember hearing the sirens in the distance and decided not to stick around. I did feel guilty about what I'd been thinking and I didn't want to explain the blood on my hands."

"So, you left me there?" Doc's voice blasts out of my mouth. I'm surprised he's stayed silent this long.

George peers into my eyes, tilting his head. "You still talk to Doc?"

"I try not to," I answer. "But, he's a persistent bugger." I take a seat.

"You know I loved him, loved you, but I did what I had to do. And then, Doc—" George says, examining me closely, "he died and afterward, Jack came to me to ask about the shares of stock. I had to tell them they were phony; that I'd been in trouble again and it was just something I used as collateral. Jack threatened to turn me in. He was going to frame me for Doc's death. So, I came up with a plan to satisfy Jack and keep him quiet. I doctored up the assignment document arranging for Jack to get a bigger percentage."

"And then you went and cashed in the life insurance," Doc says, "and finally ended up with my wife, never even letting her know such a policy existed. I should have gotten rid of you a long time ago."

"Doc, that hadn't been the plan," George says, obviously forgetting about me. "You knew how much I always cared for Phoebe even after you'd stolen her from me." He sniggers like an anxious schoolboy.

I take a deep drag of my cigarette, waiting for the rest of the story to unfold.

George gazes at me, pointing with his cigarette. "Well, he did steal her from me." He inhales and holds the smoke in for a moment.

"You were seeing another starlet at the time," Doc says. "I literally caught you with your pants down."

George coughs as he exhales. "You don't steal another man's girl until he's finished trying to win her heart. Anyway, things just worked out that way. Phoebe needed someone and, by then, I'd fallen in love with her little baby boy—with you, Charley. I wanted to show her I could take care of a family."

"With my money," Doc says. "George, you lived a lie."

"I tell you, I was good at being a fake. You knew that. Besides, the ball was already rolling. I did the best I could. If only you could've been around to straighten me out—to bail me out," he adds with a nervous chuckle.

The woman and children gasp as I raise the knife just above my left ear. George doesn't even blink as the knife whooshes down just inches from his balding head. The knife ends up buried an inch into the tabletop. The guard peeks in, but his view is obstructed by George's frame. The other prisoner quiets the frightened woman and the children as if admonishing them to keep quiet and mind their own business. I feel rotten.

"All right, I've heard enough," I say, snatching the knife and then pushing back in my chair. I know if I don't cut out now, I might not be able to hold Doc back.

"I don't blame you for wanting to kill me, too," George says.

"I never wanted to kill anybody," I say.

The round clock on the wall reads eleven-fifty-six and I know the guard will be stepping in to take the prisoners back for lunch. I want to exit first.

"So, how much longer?" I ask, before heading toward the door.

"Another ten years." George stands and reaches out to me. I step back. "Please, promise me it won't be as long before we see each other again."

"I'm not good at keeping promises," I say.

"I hope you're happy, Charley."

I decide not to share with him about Teresa. Besides, I don't have the energy to ask him about what part he had in having her family deported.

"You know I never stopped loving you, son."

As I reach the door, I turn to say, "I loved you, too, George."

48
End of the Harvest

Love is painful. Even though I'm married to the most wonderful gal in the world, I can't be completely happy. When you're in love, you're supposed to feel like shouting out your newfound joy from the rooftops; you want to share everything with those in your life who are supposed to matter the most. I hadn't shared the news with George and I can't share any of this with my mother.

Through the years, I've become numb when it comes to Phoebe. Keeping my distance has helped, and beer simply dulls the pain. Beer also seems to frighten Doc away most of the time because he knows better than to engage with me when I'm blotto.

Charley, when are you going to stop? Doc asks. *You promised Teresa. You promised your mother. Are you trying to kill yourself?*

"Killing myself would certainly be your end as well, wouldn't it?"

Son, what's wrong with you?

"I'm sorry, but I'm not a doctor," I say, raising my hand to get the bartender's attention. "I don't have a diagnosis for this."

I'm hung over again. It's just about the end of harvest time and I'm stooped one row over from Teresa picking the last of the grapes. I notice the dress Teresa has worn all season is now as withered and tattered as the leaves on the dried brown grapevines; twisted vines, the new barrier between us. We've been at each other lately. She accuses me of being closed off. I accuse her of nagging too much. We need a change. She must sense I'm looking. She turns to smile, then giggles and blows me a kiss that just about kills me.

I stand to arch my back for a moment and clear my head. Thankfully, the weather has cooled, making my hangover a little more bearable. I blow a kiss back.

And then, I can feel a roughness rising up my throat. *We need to go home,* Doc says.

I clench a stained fist and the juice from a cluster of grapes drips through my fingers. "Leave me alone."

"What's wrong, Charley?" Teresa strains to peer over the tops of the vines.

"A damn bee," I say, fanning myself.

She holds the chinstrap to keep her hat from flying off. I look into soulful, penetrating eyes to see the same worried look I'd noticed in her lately; the same one that drove me away from Phoebe.

I return to grape plucking, hoping Teresa will do the same.

Phoebe needs me, Doc says louder this time.

I pause, take in a deep breath, and squeeze my eyes shut. "Phoebe doesn't need anyone." I snatch another cluster of grapes. "She has her music," I say, trying to ignore Doc by whistling something—not *Ode to Joy.*

"Charley, who are you talking to?" Teresa asks.

I shake my head, continuing to whistle even louder; this time I don't turn to face her.

"Phoebe is dying," Doc shouts through me loud enough so that Teresa can hear.

Low blow, Daddio. I cover my ears, a futile act, but the words are like a sledgehammer to my heart. I throw up my hands then stagger off the field. I won't get paid today.

After dinner, Teresa clears my place at the table, and then takes a seat next to me. "*Mi amor,* talk to me." She wraps her hair behind her ears. "Why did you say Phoebe was dying?"

I push back from the table and then notice a dewdrop of a tear at the corner of her eye. I reach out to swipe it with a calloused thumb. She places a gentle hand over mine as her large eyes widen. "How? Why do you think that?"

I can no longer hold it in. "Doc told me."

"Who? Doc?"

"He lives here." I point to my head. "He's part of me. It's like reincarnation or something. I have his thoughts, his consciousness."

Teresa scrunches her face, pulling her chin back. "I don't understand."

"No one does. The doctors diagnosed me as schizophrenic, gave me some pills and sent me on my merry way."

She inhales and straightens a bit. "What will you do?"

"There's nothing I can do."

"But, you say you have his thoughts. What about your heart? Does he live in your heart, too?"

I don't know how to answer. She asks questions like the answers are so simple.

"You have to go home and see Phoebe," she says. "I want to go with you. She's always been so good to my family."

"You mean she used to before George got you kicked out of the country."

"But she also helped us come back."

I push my hair back and squeeze my scalp. "What are you talking about?"

"She contacted the proper authorities. Of course, we could never go back to the property, so we ended up working up here."

I shake my head. Everything is fuzzy. "You mean . . . does she know about us?" Somehow, I feel betrayed—hoodwinked.

"We haven't talked in years. Oh, please *mi amor,* take me with you."

"No. I can't," I say. "Whenever Mother sees me, she sees Doc." Teresa jerks her head like a little bird. "Through the years, he's used me to stay close to her. Telling me she's dying now could all be part of his manipulation. You see, he's used me to carry out what he couldn't finish and still it's not enough. Now, he just wants to spend the last days with her."

I stare into Teresa's tear-filled eyes. "It's not how I want to spend my life. I don't deserve this. You're the one I want to spend my life with," I say, "my whole life and I don't want to share you with anyone else. I can't stand that Doc's been a part of this—or Phoebe."

Teresa cinches her tattered sweater a little tighter around a thickening waist and looks around the room. "He's here now?" she asks.

"Always, and it takes all of my strength to ignore him—to block him out. Sometimes, he just lays low. It's exhausting. I don't know how much longer I can do this," I say and bury my head in my hands. I let out a gasp and then bawl like a baby. "I'm so ashamed," I say, lifting my head to wipe my runny nose with the back of my sleeve.

I spill an ocean of tears and when I finish, it feels as though I've just returned from a voyage after years at sea and have opened up a steamer trunk full of soggy, mildewed memories. "It's not my fault. I tried, but I can't stop the bad stuff from happening. I have no control."

Teresa takes my hands and wraps them around her waist. "*Te amo, mi amor.* I love you." She kisses me on the lips. "We'll get through this together."

The farm season is an ocean tide. It comes and it goes, and after the grape harvest, it will be a couple of months before there'll be more work picking lettuce in Arizona. Doc, in the meanwhile, is driving me Looney Tunes. He wants to go home.

"I need to cut out for a while," I tell Teresa one morning. "I gotta go to the ocean."

"But why?" She's been supportive ever since I told her about Doc. In her culture, they talk to the dead all the time, but she doesn't quite understand the complexities of my situation. She doesn't understand my need to outrun Doc, my need to get rid of him once and for all.

"Why the ocean?"

Why, indeed? I scramble to come up with a reason making any sense. "You see, if I hold my breath under water, maybe he'll go away."

"Hold your breath?" she says, narrowing her eyes. "But what if you drown?"

I stare at her and wonder. *So what if I drown.* "I need some peace," I say. "I need time to clear my head. I can't think straight around here."

Teresa brings her hand to her lips. "For how long?"

"I'll meet up with you and the others in Yuma—in January."

49
Ghosts of Christmas Past

A week after Christmas and except for the red, green and blue lights still strung along the eaves—every other one broken—Mother's house is dark. I've made it home just as a crack of lightning lights up the inky blue sky and it starts to rain. The wind has already blown off some of the shingles from the roof, strewing them across a dormant lawn that hasn't seen a mower in months. The place looks haunted; the paint on the house and the windowsills is curled and peeling. The pine tree I planted with George when I was just six years old stretches taller than the chimney now puffing a gray smoke into a dreary sky. I crunch up along a pea-gravel walkway and notice a hunched-over silhouette of a figure walking across the front window like the ghost of Christmas past. A holly wreath with red velvet ribbon hangs on the door.

I light a cigarette and then ring the bell as I peek through the half-moon-shaped etched glass. Soon I can see the top of her head beneath some withered old mistletoe hanging on a string of green ribbon. Aunt Dodo opens the door and gasps, eyes wide as snow globes beneath her bifocals.

"Hi-de-ho, Aunt Dodo." I hold up my hand and waggle my fingers.

Slowly, the door creaks open and a fat, black cat escapes to curl itself around my ankles. I'm in leather, unshaven and not sporting the signature crew cut Dodo last saw me in. She looks past my shoulder and sees the Indian motorcycle, my trusty side-kick.

"It's me," I say, brushing off some of the raindrops beaded up on my shoulder.

"Charley?" she asks.

Dodo takes a stance, as if she can bar the entrance. She's the same old fuddy-duddy, smelling of mothballs, only this time she isn't sporting a turban. Her hair falls loose and I'm tall enough to see the streak of white parting the middle of her scalp. I'd learn later how tough times had been for her and Uncle Art after he'd been blacklisted and unable to find work.

I reach down to pick up the cat and then step across the threshold into an air of nostalgic decay. I hand her the little fur ball as her eyes blink in confusion. She stares out at my motorcycle. "Is that your mode of transportation nowadays? What are you doing here?"

"I do believe this is still my home," I say, brushing past her.

"Where do you think you're going?"

"What, are you writing a god-damned book? I thought Art was the writer. Where's Phoebe?" I ask, patting my upper arms. It's freezing in the foyer. "It's like a goddam morgue in here. Why's it so cold? Somebody forget to pay the gas bill?"

"Now, look who's full of questions." Dodo crosses her bony arms over her chest.

"Where's Mother?" I ask and take a puff.

"Your mother is unwell," Dodo says, tugging her shawl tightly around her neck.

"Unwell?" I chuckle and choke. My family loves sugarcoating things. "For chrissake, just give it to me straight," I say, looking up the mahogany staircase to see an older-looking nurse in white tiptoeing ethereally across the catwalk. I gasp.

"She has leukemia. She's dying."

My heart stops. I stub my cigarette into Shirley Schefflera in the foyer and take the stairs two steps at a time.

"Charley, you can't just barge in there," Aunt Dodo yells after me.

I pause at the first landing to catch my breath. "Just watch me." I look up to see colorful teardrop shadows splashing across the wall as the rain slams onto the stain-glassed window. I turn and climb the rest of the way, passing gilded mirrors before I reach the top of the stairs where I slip, nearly tripping over another gray cat. It hisses at me. The house spins and I have the eerie sensation I'm falling; like I'm in some sort of house of mirrors at the circus. My heart races and I'm dizzy as I stare down into the foyer, white knuckling the railing on the catwalk. Composing myself, I turn to find a bucket that's been set up to catch the rainwater dripping from a giant hole in the ceiling where I can see the murky sky. Water stains from the cavity spill over like tributaries out of a lake, or blood from a gaping wound.

Bracing myself, I walk into a sepia-colored room highlighted by splashes of bruised, red poinsettias and other festive, fragrant holiday arrangements that sugarcoat the smell of mold, antiseptic, cat piss, and disease.

The first thing I hear is the rattling as if an ocean tide is swirling seashells in her lungs. Her bloated face swallows the eyes that used to see into the depths of my soul; those once sparkling emerald ocean eyes now dull and covered with a lifetime's worth of flotsam. My mother is unrecognizable. This isn't what I expected. I thought I'd come home to the same proud, confident woman I'd always known and give her a little start; kind of swagger around and let her get a good look at her little boy; let her see what a good job she'd done bringing him up—a real pillar of society. I thought I'd come in and finally tell her how pissed off I've been about Doc and with her for allowing the men in her life to take advantage of her. I thought I'd tell her how she'd ruined my life. But now a furry cat jumps up onto her bed. Laurel and Hardy had gone to doggy heaven years ago and so now the cats have obviously taken over the house. The old nurse quickly scoops up Fluffy and sets her outside the bedroom door.

Mother's sparse auburn-tipped hair is white at the roots and lusterless. Seaweed thin and pallid as oyster meat, she cranes toward me. "Oh, Darling, I'm so happy to see you," she says in a faraway, raspy voice. "God has answered my prayers and brought you home to me at last."

But then, before I can utter anything, Doc interrupts me. "I'm here, my Darling. I've missed you so."

"Doc, please, haven't you caused enough trouble?" Mother says. "Go away. Just let me have this time with our son."

I listen and wait, lips clamped. I hear my heart pounding. I hear Teresa. *Does he live in your heart, too?*

I scan the room to see a museum dedicated to me. Throughout are knick-knacks and dozens of silver-framed pictures of a curly-golden-haired me; some I can't remember posing for. On a wall next to Mother's bed is the clay handprint I stamped in kindergarten. Framed next to that is a Crayola drawing of circle-headed stick figures, a mother, a father, a son and their pets; a juvenile's idea of a perfect family. Ceramic figurines of dogs and birds and reptiles rest on dusty bookshelves. I pick up the ceramic turtle I'd made in Miss Cappell's class and look closely, it's missing a leg. I turn it carefully over in my hands. *Charley Gimble* is carved into the turtle's belly. I used

George's last name? I set it back down and blink away. And then, over the fireplace, I see a childhood picture of Teresa and me holding hands like we used to do when we were only five years old. I get up to take a closer look.

"Charley, I've looked . . . everywhere for you," Mother says, breathing staccato-like in between every couple of words. "I worried so. I didn't want to . . . die without getting . . . chance to tell . . . you sorry . . . for everything. I wanted to make sure you knew how much . . ." She's really coughing now and I'm having a hard time processing all of this.

Driving down, my intention had been to punish her; shock her even, by telling her I'd married a Mexican. *How would that look in the Blue Book Society pages? Wasn't it always about appearances with you and Doc? And hadn't George done a good job getting the Marquez family deported?*

"I love you, my son. All I've ever wanted . . . for you to be happy."

As hard as I try to hold on, the vise around my heart is loosening its grip. I listen, vulnerable now to Doc, and then I speak up, rushing as if this might be my only chance before Doc can take over forever.

"I got married," I say, now holding the picture of Teresa and me.

I see a glimmer in her lifeless eyes as she looks at the picture.

"I'm so glad you found her," she says in a drowsy whisper.

"We found each other," I say. "She's the best thing that's ever happened to me. You remember Teresa?"

As if it's too much of a strain to comprehend, she furrows her brow and flutters her heavy eyelids until she can no longer hold them open. She nods and then opens her mouth to speak, but the words are lost. And then a single tearful memory slides down her gaunt cheek. "Marquez. I had no idea. George . . . I am so sorry. I loved the family. Teresa was such a little angel."

"And now you're probably thinking she's a saint for putting up with me."

"Oh, Charley, you were always trying to put words in my mouth," she says, lifting her blue-veined papery eyelids. "I only say what I mean. You don't give me enough credit, or yourself."

"Well, I happen to love what I do," I say, defensively. "I'm a farm worker now."

Mother smiles weakly. "You know, your father wanted to be a farmer. He loved working in the fields as a boy—came here. Used to say: 'Citrus for your health, California for your wealth.'"

She's hacking her lungs out and I think about smothering her with the pillow to make it stop. *After all of these years and now you think you're going to share something nostalgic with me about my father. I had to learn about Doc from the neighbors, for God's sake.*

The nurse comes to pat her bony back. She then hands her a glass of water.

"I'd love to see Teresa again," Mother says after swallowing. "The Marquez's were the salt of the earth. You must bring her by for Sunday dinner."

"I'll think about it," I say, and suddenly panic when I realize Mother could just be dead by Sunday. "I'll give her a call."

"Wonderful," she says and closes her eyes.

After a fearful moment, I turn to the nurse and ask quietly, "Is she—"

"Charley," Mother says, and I go to sit next to her. "It's been so long. Would you play something for me on the piano? Your choice, my Darling."

I catch myself smiling my jokey, juvenile smirk as I glance at the mirrors on my way downstairs. I cross through the foyer, and at the entrance to the empty living room, I turn on the only lamp in the room, the one with gold tassels and a crystal—the only crystal left in the house—at the end of the pull chain, and stare at the bleached white shadows on the walls where paintings of faraway places are now missing. The room seems to have been closed off for ages, smelling mildewy, yet dusty like dead leaves. All but one Oriental rug and most of the gaudy furniture are gone from the floors. Through the years, Mother always sold things off in order for us to get by. "I'm not attached to material things," she'd said, time and again. I panic and charge into the chamber room, footsteps echoing as if I were running through a cave. Oh, God, not the piano!

There stands Cleopatra, looking dusty and forlorn, but still as beautiful and grand as ever; the nine-foot Steinway survived the fire sale. I take a seat on the piano bench and turn to look out the french glass doors overlooking the creek. There's a reflection in the window, the image of the man I'd become, unkempt, unshaven, ungrateful—undone. Since I've come home, I've been acting like a child. I look up at the spot where the goddamn crystal chandelier used to hang. Shit. It doesn't matter. Since I never learned to read music, I don't need the light to play.

My choice, huh? I let out a belly laugh and pull back the lid.

I'm busting up as I pound out "Roll Out the Barrel." *What a riot! It ain't Beethoven—not what you taught me, but what the hell. This is my choice, what makes me happy.* Again, I look at my reflection. I'm still grinning ear-to-ear, really hammering out the notes, when suddenly a warmth envelops me, and my body tingles. A little hummingbird flutters around, bouncing off the insides of my gut. In the window I see a ghostly vision of Mother seated next to me. Her face is radiant, her eyes twinkle livelier than stars and her cinnamon-colored hair glows brighter than a summer sunset. She stretches her hands out over mine. Her laughter, like wind chimes, echoes throughout the chamber room and then she surprises me when she sings: *Roll out the barrel . . . the gang's all here!*

I lift my head up to prevent the tears from dripping onto the keys; instead they slither into my ears. *I deserve this pain. I've been such a bad kid. You never deserved any of this. Mother, you loved me; Phoebe, you loved me and you loved your music.* I finish the silly song, sorry for being so childish.

"Don't be sorry, son," she murmurs. "That was the most beautiful song I've ever heard. Music to my ears."

My tear-dampened ears tickle and as I rub them, I turn to find the space next to me vacant. I look through the window and her image is gone. The little hummingbird inside me has stopped beating its wings. I close the piano lid, push back on the bench and run through the cold wind tunnel of a living room. I take the stairs, two-at-a-time, careful not to slip.

I know before I enter her room Mother has died.

Aunt Dodo is crying as she sits on the edge of the bed holding Mother's hand.

"You put a smile on her face, Charley," the nurse says to me as I look down to see the peaceful, happy-looking shell of my mother.

Deep in my heart, I feel a phantom pain for the bond that should have been there.

I don't know whether it's the man in me or the boy. In the little chapel of Grandview Memorial Park, I want to jump into the coffin with her. In the black suit Mother has kept in the closet for me, I walk up the aisle past the cedar box, feeling the eyes of the congregation, like quiet moths boring holes through me. I take a seat at the upright walnut piano.

I can hear them whisper. *What will Charley say? What will he play?* Poor Mother, I'd always given people something to talk to her about besides music, and I'm sure she handled it with grace.

I honor her by playing *Ode to Joy.*

There isn't a dry eye in the place. My mother was loved by many. She never knew a stranger, and yet she was always a stranger to me.

I finish and walk down the aisle and out the door.

50
The Call of the Wild

I don't stay to watch them put my mother in the ground. That's not where she's going to end up anyway.

I need to get to Tucson. I need to get to Teresa. I've thrown my brown leather jacket on over my black suit but can still feel the icy wind piercing through to my core as I zip west across Los Feliz Boulevard *but this isn't the way to Arizona.* My face and hands tingle like tiny needles jabbing at me. The heavy, dark clouds threaten to dump on my bare head. All the while, Doc just won't shut the fuck up.

Charley, we must go to her.

I roar into the wind so as to fight back his noise and keep my emotions at bay, but soon my anger and my tears fog the lenses of my goggles. "Shut up. Leave me alone."

But, does he live in your heart, too? My heart hangs on for dear life; one wrong move and it'll be splattered all over the highway—one way to end it all and finally get rid of the old man.

I need something to alleviate the pain. Maybe it's time to go back to the hospital; go back on the meds. No! I've handled things so far without anything. *Yeah, and look how you're handling things now.*

The tears well inside my goggles; it's as if I'm drowning. I'm so tired of treading water, but as long as I can still put a pedal to the metal, I have to keep on. "You're not going to win, Doc," I scream, knowing I'll always be looking over my shoulder. I have no idea how long I'll be able to keep this up. My vision is blurry as I try to focus on the hazy lines of the highway.

Pay attention, Charley. Stay in between the lines. And then out of the corner of my eye and above to my right, I notice a ray of sunlight piercing through a cloud reflecting off the copper dome of the Griffith Observatory. The sun will be setting soon. I turn south onto Highland. My eyes sting as

I turn west onto Hollywood Boulevard. I notice a neon billboard advertising a new movie introducing the best Young Box Office Star from the Hollywood Foreign Press Association, Marilyn Monroe. Miss Norma Jeane seems to have done okay for herself, I think, wondering if I might have been better off growing up at Hollygrove Orphanage. And then, out of nowhere, I think about Teresa and how guilty I'd felt when Norma Jeane kissed me long ago. I remember how George had said there would be more girls to like and kiss and that the most important thing was to always remember to be true to the one you love. The cars come to a stop, giving me an opportunity to remove my goggles. I wipe my eyes and see a crowd gathering out in front of Grauman's Chinese Theater. The marquee reads *Sunset Boulevard, a Hollywood Story*. Hell, who in Hollywood ain't got one of those? Across from the theater looms the Hollywood Masonic Temple with its massive columns framing the entrance.

Ah, those were the days, Doc says. *At the piano, up on stage. Her music transformed me. Oh, Phoebe. Charley, we must go to her!*

"Shut up. She's gone. Your story's over, Doc," I scream over his voice, gunning the Indian through a new opening in between a couple of vehicles. I travel a few more blocks and turn south on Fairfax.

The clouds spit down on me as I speed along Sunset Boulevard. On either side are swanky mansions with their leftover holiday decorations displayed across sprawling manicured lawns. The tinseled palm trees lining the streets seem to whip into some sort of headless tunnel as I race toward the setting sun. I need to make it before the sunset. I can't understand, but somehow I believe if only I can make it to the shore, I might survive. I might calm down, think more clearly; find balance. I'll be able to get into the rhythm of the ocean. For aren't we all just children of the sea—part of the tides to return again and again. Where had I heard that?

The shore is cold and windy. The sand welcomes me with a brisk slap across the face as I make my way down to the water. I smell the briny salt and sand, bird shit and everything left of the earth after it's been washed clean. Dozens of sandpipers skitter back and forth in a synchronized choreography as if they're dancing with the tide. A seagull squawks and I watch as he scavenges the shore, taking what he wants and leaving the rest. That's all I want. I don't need much. I don't ask for much. All I want is to be left alone.

Near the water, I take off my shoes and socks. As I strip out of the suit thoughtfully preserved by Mother, the pocket watch falls out. I pick it up and think about tossing it into the ocean, but instead I drop to my knees onto the sand and open it. Mother's note pops out. Slowly, I open it. "Son, know I love you. Don't ever give up hope. Please come home." She'd written it years ago and left it with the chicken pot pie I'd taken with me into the park.

Can't you hear her calling? Doc says. *Listen to her.*

I cover my ears. "I won't listen. I'm tired of standing, jumping and sitting for you. I won't do it anymore. You and Phoebe have made me your dog, a pet that you bring into your home to feed and to keep by your side or on your lap or at your feet. Let me out! Let me go! I am not man's best friend. No one asked you to bring me home. Just let me be. I am a lone wolf."

Barefoot, I follow the imprints of the seagull's webbed feet to the water's edge where they disappear. I'm standing knee-deep in the frigid water. In my life everyone has tried to domesticate me, but I'm an animal, I'm nature. I want to live with nature, in nature. I'm a prehistoric songbird, a monkey beating on a hollow log, a coyote stealing down from the hills at twilight to quench itself in the stream. I'm the black crow visiting every day under the tree in the park. I am the snake slithering across the desert in search of a rock to take shelter.

You do hear the call, Doc says seductively.

And it's hard not to hear the call of the wild—the music of the untamed.

Listen to the orchestra of the ocean, he shouts.

I hear the sonar whistle of a dolphin, and the low-groan clicking of a whale. The crash of waves, like kettledrums smashing over my head, and soon I can hear the fish humming on the ocean floor.

I bob to the surface and above the sounds of waves crashing, I can hear what Doc is hearing, but this time, the memories of my own music flood me: jazz and blues, a German Polka, Mexican Mariachis, Taps and a child's lullaby. Mother sings to me. I struggle to hang onto my own thoughts, to separate myself from Doc, but my memories are poisoned arrows, piercing my heart and killing me over and over again.

And then in the midst, I hear her at the piano. The music is accompanied by flutes and oboes; horns and trumpets; timpani and cymbals. Cellos and sounds of violins fill my ears with a fortissimo in D minor.

Lightning cracks on the horizon and I can see my seagull friend has returned to my side, wings flapping and ready to take flight.

I'm coming home, my darling, Doc says, pulling me out of my trance. *Let's go home, Charley.*

"For God's sake, aren't you finished using me? She's gone." I scream past the breakers, but can only hear the answer of the waves. *He won't give up. He'll never stop.* I drop onto my knees in the water and with the butt of my hands, I punch at my head until I see stars. I realize I feel no pain and bury my battered head into my bruised hands as the water churns all around me.

"I'm not you! Father, what more do you want?" I scream. "Everyone's either been jailed, killed, or died of old age. You've used me to exact your revenge. Can't I have some peace? Some happiness? Can't I just have a simple life?"

"I only want what is best," Doc says.

"Bullshit! You said you wanted a simple life, but you haven't let go even in death. You're nothing but a narcissistic rat who doesn't give a shit— doesn't care that he's been a squatter taking up space in my body in order to carry out his unfinished deeds. You've hijacked my life and have held me hostage for way too long."

"I had no choice."

"No choice! We all have choices. What about just letting go like any normal dying person? I've been used by you."

"It was the only way. I'm sorry, son."

"That's all you got? 'I'm sorry.' I'm not your son!" I shout. "This is all your fault. I've been everyone's child, unable to escape. I can run, but I can't hide. My body's not my own. It's not my temple."

But, does he live in your heart, too? I hear Teresa's voice, like a silver thread running through my mind to my heart.

My heart? I tilt my head and then stare into the horizon as lightning strikes again. A few seconds later, thunder rips and the palette of the Beethoven's Ninth Symphony, a brilliance of color, engulfs me. The seagull lifts its wings and for a short time skids across the surface of the ocean, finally to take flight into the west, to my destiny. I witness a most dazzling sunset;

sun kissed like the fruit that lured me over. And then, a green flash, the color of Mother's eyes.

"Doc, you win. I'm drained. I don't have any answers. There are no other solutions, even if it means I, too, must die. You will be free. I will be free at last."

A dark glorious wave, the size of a mountain, rises up in front of me and I hear Teresa's voice again, *But, does he live in your heart, too?* "No," I scream. "You do, *mi amor.* You live in my heart!"

I have no choice but to dive through to the other side. I come up after a few moments just as a second wave slams down on me. "Oh, Teresa, I want to live. I want to come home to you!"

"No, son, it's time to go," Doc says and another wave hits me; water shoves up my nose and into my ears. I'm slammed head first onto the ocean floor. I'm flipped over and, from the bottom, I can see darkness as if I'm stuck underneath a grand piano. And her music grows louder, as the vocals from the discordant chorale finale fill my ears. *No! I won't listen! I won't get sucked in anymore!* I push off from the sandy bottom and break the surface, gulping for air. But I'm caught in a riptide. Like the wreckage of my life, the water churns flotsam all around me. *Just swim with the current, Charley. Don't panic,* I tell myself. My arms flail about, feeling light and detached as if I'm slapping seaweed through the water unable to get any traction. My legs are heavy anchors chained to a little boat, sinking to the bottom of the ocean. I'm taking on water; trying, one thimble at a time, to scoop the ocean out. I'm exhausted. My tears mix with the saltwater until they are one. I look up from the bottom of the ocean floor through a spiraling vortex toward a shimmering light. I can hear the music. *Adagio,* the finale.

I hear the pounding of the ivory keys. I hear the crash of cymbals and then the peal of thunder so ferocious. I can no longer fight back. Another clap of lightning jolts me out of my skin and I hear the violins beginning in the key of G. Gradually more notes and chords and flutes and trumpets sound until at last I give up. I let go. I've been sucked in and sucked down.

My head feels light, as if a great weight has been lifted. The vise grip that was Doc is gone.

"Darling, I'm home," I hear Doc say, but this time it comes from a distance outside my head. "I'm free. Thank you, Charley."

Doc floats away through a tall portico. Through white noise like swirling foam, I hear the music, but these are notes I've never heard before. I don't follow just yet and look around. Is this heaven? The music grows louder. There are no doors or windows here, so I can see everything and everywhere since the beginning of time. Beyond the archway on a downy cloud is the grandest ivory piano I could ever imagine. There are more than just the eighty-eight keys and the music is the most heavenly; so pure, it's indescribable in my language. I close my eyes and let it swallow me like the ocean did, what seems like only an instant ago. "Isn't it lovely, Charley?" Doc calls out from the other side.

At this moment, I'm not filled with sadness, anger, remorse or guilt. I understand now that everything is as it must be. I'm happy and serene as I listen to the music keeping me in the present. But there is another song tugging on my heart strings, like a piano key reverberating through the silver wire connected to the hammer pounding on my still-beating heart; my heart where Teresa still lives. We're still connected.

I hear her calling me now. I smell strawberries. I close my eyes and strain to listen.

"Please come home." Through my mind's eye, I can see her wandering through a field of sweet ripe red strawberries and orange poppies; her hands cradling a swollen belly. Teresa looks up. "You will always live in my heart, *mi amor. Te amo.* I love you. Charley, please come home to us."

I'm cursed.

"You were my destiny. I never meant to leave you, my angel," I say.

I open my eyes and beyond, seated on the piano bench, is a boy around fifteen years of age. He turns to me and in the reflection of his orange-tinted glasses, I see the clouds of his short life pass swiftly by. I know he is Leland, Doc's first son, his favorite. Seated next to him is my mother, Phoebe, the love of their lives. They'd learned to feel because of her; they'd written poetry and music because of her and about her; they'd wanted to be part of her symphony of life. I, too, had loved her in spite of myself.

Mother turns to me, simply smiling with those sparkling eyes, seeing to the very depths of my soul. She then returns to play *Ode to Joy,* their cursed song from Beethoven's Ninth.

"I think I'll stay here for a while," Doc says, squeezing in with the others. They are reunited at last.

There is no room for me on that piano bench. Still, I am plagued by the shadows of their limelight.

"Go home. You are free," Mother says. "Good bye, Charley. I will always love you, my Darling."

I don't understand. *How?* My head feels light but my heart hurts. Like an anchor chain pulling me down, the tug at my heart is so strong it aches.

But are you supposed to hurt when you get to heaven? This can't be heaven.

The sun has gone down, stealing away all of the color with it and leaving behind a dark, cold surface. I'm a seagull hovering above, watching as the ocean spits me up and then dashes me onto the shore, where I upchuck a belly full of ocean water. A sandy-haired surfer rolls me over onto my stomach, pushes on my back and then rotates me face-up to breathe life back into me.

I open my eyes to see the surfer standing over me, a silhouette against a now tangerine sky. In the distance, the moon rises above the mountains, white and immaculate, delicate as the tip of one of Mother's pearly white nails. I have another chance.

A small gathering of other surfers are clapping. I'm wrapped in a towel. I'm coming home.

A New Dawning

Teresa and I want lots of children, and now Woodside Manor is complete with the joyful sounds of happy feet. The whole place smells fresh—fresh paint, fresh wood, fresh new-furniture smell—since we've stuffed the mansion with new modern fixtures. We are financially able to do so, thanks to Mother. She'd been able to put away a little inheritance for me since Doc's death and all of that legal mumbo jumbo. She'd also paid a little visit to George in prison and somehow persuaded him to fess up about having committed insurance fraud. Mother consequently sued him, naming also Western Masons Mutual Life Insurance Company in the lawsuit. George was also convinced to deed over and quitclaim some of the property he'd invested with her money and hidden (he wouldn't want to deal with Doc and Phoebe in the afterlife). In her Last Will and Testament, she'd left a little something for the Marquez family. I also learned that after the Marquez family had been deported, Mother had arranged to have them come back. With nothing but a little money my mother would send, they'd settled up north to work the land. I can't begin to understand how our paths crossed again all those years later.

In addition to all of that, Mother also had a life insurance policy naming me and Teresa as beneficiaries.

We will be able to send our children off to college and yes, we can afford to buy new furniture. I don't need any more reminders of the past save for a couple of heirlooms including the grand piano, an Oriental rug and Doc's pocket watch which I still plan to pawn someday.

"Mommy and Daddy, come sit down. We're going to do a show for you," our caramel-haired five-year-old daughter announces. She has a red bow in her hair like some sort of Christmas present.

Teresa and I enter the living room and take a seat on a sofa, smelling of new leather. The music begins and our three- and four-year-old daughters, also in bows, pirouette in front of us, hopping and leaping from one large flower on the rug to the next; the three-year-old clutching her doll by the hair.

A child prodigy, I think as I watch our little piano player, whose tiny fingers barely cover an octave. It will take some time to see whether our other two little ballerinas have a future in dance.

"At least one of the girls has inherited your mother's ear for music," Teresa says, smiling proudly, as I rub her stomach, bulging with a new life. I'm hoping it's a boy this time, but as long as she's healthy, I don't mind.

"Yes, music was the marrow in her bones. Mother would have been proud to see her music living on," I say.

"You know she does have her eyes," Teresa says.

The music stops and five-year-old Phoebe Anne turns to stare at us with those soulful, green eyes. *Are you talking about me, Darlings?*

Acknowledgments

First, to the ancestors who have transferred over and encouraged me to search for truth, thank you.

For their inspiration, motivation and superb guidance, I'm indebted to Lynn Hightower, Jessica Barksdale Inclan, Liz Gonzales, and Francesca Lia Block. I'd also like to acknowledge the staffs at the Glendale Library, the Los Angeles Archives, CSUN, UCLA, and the *Los Angeles Times*. Paul Zollo's "Hollywood Remembered: An Oral History of its Golden Age" helped set the stage as did so many other resources I fail to remember.

A million thanks to E. L. Marker, WiDo Publishing, and their supportive, enthusiastic team. Especially for their editorial insights and support, a big thank you to Forrest Gowen, Karen Gowen, and Summer Ross, my new friend.

To my husband, T. Jeff Gunn, USCG Retired, I love you more today than yesterday.

Finally, I'm grateful to my daughters whose exceptional talents and generosity I've leaned on heavily: Joy Hepp and Alexandra Dawson.

About the Author

Ruthie Marlenée is a California native and lives in Los Angeles with her husband. She is blessed to have her children and grandchildren nearby.

A James Kirkwood Literary Award nominee, she also earned her Writer's Certificate "With Distinction" from UCLA. She is the author of several novels: *Isabela's Island, Agave Blues,* and is currently working on "The Granddaughter," the sequel to *Curse of the Ninth.* Marlenée is a ghostwriter, screenwriter, novelist and a poet whose work can be found in several literary publications.

CPSIA information can be obtained
at www.ICGtesting.com
Printed in the USA
BVHW032150130220
572381BV00001B/1

9 781947 966239